THE
Viscount's Vices

THE
Viscount's Vices

The Love Story of Brook and William

Debbie Zello

authorHOUSE®

AuthorHouse™ LLC
1663 Liberty Drive
Bloomington, IN 47403
www.authorhouse.com
Phone: 1-800-839-8640

Published by AuthorHouse   05/15/2014

ISBN: 978-1-4969-1360-9 (sc)
ISBN: 978-1-4969-1359-3 (hc)
ISBN: 978-1-4969-1361-6 (e)

To my good friends that continue to support me and give me the feedback that I need to improve, thank you sincerely. Angela, Stacie, Stephanie, Nicole and Brenda, thank you for asking for more.

Alisa, my rock, without your guidance and help I would still be thinking what to do instead of actually doing it. You are a miracle worker and deserve so much credit. Thank you for everything!

To Josh Groban~Thanks again for the music.

CONTENTS

Don't build your
Castle walls so
high that your
loved ones can't
get in.

Debbie Zello

For

William's Love

CHAPTER 1

I FLY. WELL, NOT EXACTLY fly. I'm a flight attendant. I travel around the world. However, New York City is my home. I have a great little apartment. 2025 Broadway at 70th Street, Chelsea-716 square feet of heaven. My roommate Sandy and I have opposite flight schedules. I fly out on Sunday and she flies in. I am back Wednesday night and she leaves.

We have one rule. Every piece of bedding gets changed before you leave. I don't want to know what went on there, just change it! It has worked for us for three years. Neither one of us could afford to live here separately. Sandy and I chose this building first because of it's location and second, it is so quiet. We spent the better part of two weeks looking for a place to call ours. Many of the buildings had a number of children living there or loud tenants. The two times we came to see the apartment, you could hear a pin drop. That is until March 1, 2012, when the neighborhood stud moved in next door.

I was cleaning and finishing the laundry when I heard him. I expect noise when someone moves and that was fine. It was after the movers left and the welcoming party started to arrive. The first one knocked on my door looking for "Link Decker." She looked like a model-perfect body, beautiful hair and a face to match. Let's just say she was a screamer. I know for sure that Link lives next door because his name comes through the walls perfectly.

Link, day two. This one had a high-pitched, whiney voice. The kind that makes you want to drown the person speaking.

3

Link was hitting all of the right spots with Maddy. I know this because that is what Maddy kept saying, over and over again.

It is now Link, day three. As I pack to leave for the airport, I can hear yet another voice calling out in ecstasy, "Oh my god, Link, right there, that's it." I love a woman who gives good directions. I leave a note for Sandy explaining the play list from next door. As I am leaving, Link's door opens to allow the direction girl to leave. I can't see Link but the woman is tall with auburn hair. Stunning describes her best. It seems that he has very good taste in women, even though there are a few too many.

At check in, I meet up with my flight crew and we board our plane. Bill is our pilot and Steven is co-pilot. Wendy, Regina, Christina and I are the cabin crew. I will work the first-class cabin and the other three will work the rest. Our route this week is JFK to Miami, Miami to Fort Worth, Fort Worth to Los Angeles, then LA back to JFK. I will have this route for the next six weeks and then it will change again.

We start to board the passengers and ready ourselves for takeoff. I close and lock the door once everyone is aboard. We begin our safety talk as we taxi to the runway. As I walk the aisle asking the passengers to put their seats in an upright position, I see him again. "Good afternoon, William. How are you?" I ask.

"I am just fine, thanks, Brook. I didn't realize you were on this route now."

"I start today and I'll be on this route for the next six weeks."

"Good to know. I have a shoot tomorrow in Miami. Next week I am in LA, so I will probably see you there. My flight back is Wednesday."

"That will be me."

I get to my seat and Regina sits next to me. She leans in to talk to me as we take off. "I see your favorite photographer is on board," she whispers in my ear.

"You saw that? We talked for a few minutes."

"I can't believe he never asks you out for a drink."

"I guess I'm not his type. He might be married or have a steady girl. He isn't interested in me. I see him all the time around the city. We talk, say hi. He has never asked to see me."

"Maybe he's blind."

"He's a photographer, Regina. I guarantee he is not blind."

"Stupid then. You are a knockout. Maybe he thinks you aren't interested. Have you ever asked *him* out for a drink?"

"Company policy, Regina. We are not here to find husbands. We are here to do our job."

"There's no reason why you can't run into him at the airport bar and have a drink. Just tell him you will be at a certain bar in LA at a certain time and see if he shows up. If he doesn't, you will know he's not interested."

We land in Miami ten minutes early. As William exits the plane, I quietly speak to him. "I will be in the bar closest to the American Airlines gates in LA two hours before boarding if you would like to have a drink."

He smiles and nods to me. "Have a good week, Brook," he says.

I finish my route and get home. I walk in my door and throw myself at the couch. The flight crew has maximum hours that they can fly, but the cabin crew does not. I go through so many time zones back and forth I should wear four watches. I drag myself to the bedroom and change to go to bed. All is quiet next door and I fall asleep in seconds.

In the morning, I start the laundry as I read the note left by Sandy. "No noise at all from Romeo next door. I was all ready with my Diving Dolphin and my Cricket if he got me wound up. Alas, no big 'O' for me," she writes. Sandy and her toys. She went to a "naughty party" and came home with male substitutes. I'm glad we have two dressers so I don't have to see them.

I call my two friends Millie and Carol to make sure we are still on for dinner Friday night. Carol has made reservations at a place in Little Italy for us. I can't wait to see them. I finish my chores for the day and turn in around 10:00 to read in bed. I must have dozed off because at 11:30 I wake up to the sounds of Link and the screamer.

Twenty-five minutes of how good it feels is quite enough for me. Just as he is bringing it home, I wonder where Sandy's cricket is and how to use it. Screamer finds her last hurrah, and for the love of all that is holy, so does Link. I almost sit up and applaud the performance. I have to call our super to find out about soundproofing the wall. I wonder how long Link's lease is.

Friday night, I meet my girls at the restaurant. We order a bottle of wine and I look over the menu. Currently, my girls and I are single. A fact that Millie tries to rectify continuously. "I think I am going with a Caesar salad with grilled chicken," I advise.

"Why do you always have to be good? I want you to order a fattening dinner for once," Millie responds.

"She can't. She has to fit in between aisles all day," Carol adds.

"If I eat something bad, it is an extra five miles I run. I am not sleeping as it is, so I don't have the extra energy for that."

"Why aren't you sleeping?" Carol inquires.

"My new neighbor. Let's just say he has nocturnal habits with loud partners."

"Partners? As in plural? At the same time?" Millie delights in asking.

"Plural, but as of yet, one at a time. Every night that I am home. Evidently Sandy hasn't had the pleasure yet."

"Now I have to know, how loud?" Again, curiosity gets the better of Millie.

"He has an all out screamer, one that gives precise directions, and one with a voice like a cat dying."

"Does he have a name?" Carol is listening with rapt attention.

"Oh, yes he does. 'LINK, LINK, OH GOD, LINK'."

"Have you met him?" Carol asks.

"Not yet. One of his ladies knocked on my door, though, and I saw one in the hall after their passionate evening."

"I would knock on his door and talk to him. Tell him that he is bothering you and you need your sleep," Millie advises.

"And then he will say that he doesn't hear anything coming from my apartment and I will be mortified."

"Why? Because you aren't a man-whore like he is. Why is it a double standard? If I were sleeping with three men at the same time, it would be a scandal but a man can do it and it means he is virile?" Carol asks.

"Another question without an answer," Millie adds.

Our meals come and our conversation moves on to other subjects. After a few more bottles of wine, I decide to call it a night. We make plans for three weeks later and I go outside to find a cab.

I get home and all is quiet. I walk into my bedroom and put on some music. I take a shower and get into bed to read for a few minutes. I must have dozed off again, and my wake up call this time is the stunning direction girl. Thank God, Link got it right, according to her, and the directions come to a glorious crescendo. Perhaps I need to invest in a good pair of earplugs.

Saturday I wake to a beautiful day. A great day for a long walk or a run. I suit up and get outside to stretch. The air smells so fresh and the birds' singing warms me. I start out with a brisk walk and as soon as I feel the urge, I break into a run. I love the park. It was made for people to enjoy in the middle of chaos. I pass by all kinds of humanity. Mothers walking their children in strollers, men playing chess, other runners and walkers.

As I near the end of my run, I see the screamer girl. She is on a bench facing me and with her is a man. I can only see his back, as he is facing away from me. His left arm is across her body at her hip pulling her to him. He leans over and kisses her. It is a very warm scene and I feel he does have feelings for her. Maybe he isn't as bad as I imagine. Then again, maybe it isn't Link after all.

At home, I shower and start to pack for work. I answer e-mails, have a light dinner and settle in to watch a movie. About halfway through the movie, I hear voices from next door. Link is having a spirited discussion with a woman. I don't know why, but I turn down the television so I can hear better. My god, I am turning into some kind of voyeur. After several minutes, all goes quiet. Then I hear the door slam. I can't help myself I go to my peephole to look out.

There is screamer girl obviously crying, walking past my door to the elevator. Now my imagination runs wild . . . did she find out about the other girls? . . . did she give him an ultimatum and he said no? . . . did he find out something about her? This is all just too good. I have my very own soap opera right next door. Maybe it won't be so bad living next to Link after all.

I sleep later on Sunday. Changing the bed linens, I hear Link and I think he is singing. He's no Josh Groban, but his voice is pleasant. Can't hit the high notes, but passable. Then the duet starts. My guess is that Link doesn't like to be alone even for a day. I have been alone for so long I don't even remember what it is like to live with someone.

I finish my chores and leave for the airport. Meeting up with everyone, I stow my gear and start to make the plane ready for our passengers. I put on my happy face just as the passengers board. We go through our preflight instructions and I walk to my jump seat. "Did you have a good weekend?" I ask Regina.

"I didn't do much but it was nice to sit around," she answers.

"I went out with Millie and Carol for dinner. I was good to see them."

"What is new with the neighbor?"

"Well, he entertained his usual bedmates. Then I think I saw him with one of them in the park but I couldn't see his face. And this morning, I was treated to a duet of sorts."

"A duet as in singing?"

"You bet! He is not half bad either. Now I wonder if Sandy will have the pleasure of hearing him."

"Sandy hasn't heard him yet?"

"Not yet. I don't know what he does, but she hasn't heard a peep from him."

"That's odd. Wouldn't it be funny if he were a flight attendant, pilot or something? Moreover, he has the same schedule as you."

"What if he turns out to be Bill or Steve with an alias? Now *that* would be funny."

"Funny for whom? Bill is married and Steve has a fiancée."

"You're right. Not so funny," I admit.

We take care of the passengers and before too long land in Miami. The next day in Fort Worth and finally LA.

CHAPTER 2

WEDNESDAY, TWO HOURS BEFORE BOARDING, I am in the bar closest to the gates waiting with my glass of wine to see if William shows up.

I am staring at the entry and I see him come in. He looks around. I wave my hand towards him. He smiles and starts to head my way. I study him the entire time it takes for him to walk to me. He is tall, over six feet. Curly medium-brown hair and hazel eyes. He has broad shoulders and a slim waist. He is wearing a short sleeve white button-down shirt and I can see his muscular arms with corded veins running the length of them. His khaki-colored Dockers hang on his hips suggestively. He is Adonis in the flesh. I have a sip of wine to stop the drool from running out of my mouth.

"I almost didn't recognize you, Brook without your uniform. The dress is a nice change," he says smiling.

"The passengers frown on cabin crews in bars before a flight. Not to mention the airline. I felt the dress would be less conspicuous."

"I can see how that would be a dilemma. But surely one glass of wine two hours before the flight won't be a predicament, will it?"

"No. How did your shoot go this week?" I ask wanting to learn more about him.

"Good. I did some work for the San Diego Zoo on Monday and for a vacation time-share all day yesterday. I met a friend for breakfast and now I am here with another friend."

Wow, he called me his friend. I guess that is progress. "How long have you been a photographer, William?"

"My Aunt gave me a camera for my fifth birthday. I shot all six rolls of film that came with it on that first day. The pictures were good, in focus and framed well. I was a photographer. In high school, I joined the photography club and the rest is, as they say, history. Now, what about you and flying?" he asks putting the spotlight back on me.

"Don't laugh, but it was all a mistake. I went to the job interview with my best friend in college. Christy was a hospitality major and thought she would open her own travel agency one day. The interview was for flight attendants. Christy decided she didn't want it. When she came out of the interview, the man motioned me in. He thought I was there to interview, as well. After he explained it all to me, I took the job. I can fly for free anywhere I want. Who wouldn't want a job like that?"

"Wow, that is quite a story. Where is your friend now?"

"Married with a daughter, living in Connecticut with her accountant husband, happy and content."

"And you?"

"Living in New York City. Happy, but not content. I love my job. I have great friends and a nice apartment, but it is hard to find someone to share this life with. I'm gone four days a week in many different cities and sometimes countries. I'm tired when I get back. It is not easy for a man to put up with my schedule."

"I have the same problem. I have female friends who provide companionship and even exercise," he says with a wink, "but a long-term relationship is difficult with me flying all over the world, too."

"So, what is our answer, William? New job or single life?"

"I will always have to take pictures. Maybe I can change to portraits and settle down. Maybe work at Wal-Mart or some photo chain saying goo-goo to babies to get them to laugh."

"Somehow I can't see that. How about something like that woman Ann Geddes? Her work is beautiful. You just need a concept to start with."

"That is a good idea. Now, how do we fix you?"

"There is no way to fix me. I am an enigma and can't be helped. I was a business major. There is no business now, so I fly. I have no interests or hobbies besides reading and running. I don't think either of those are payable occupations."

"I think you sell yourself short. You are beautiful, and you have fantastic legs. Not that your uniform shows anything off, but what you have on now is quite an imagination starter. You could model, do commercials or print ads."

I blush to my core with his words. I don't think I am ugly, but model-beautiful has never crossed my mind. "You are blushing. You don't think that you are a looker. I have news for you, Brook. I have seen and worked with many beautiful women. You are right up there with them in the body and face departments. Why don't you let me take some pictures of you and send them in to a friend of mine and see what happens?" he offered.

"How much have you had to drink before you came here? I know I'm not ugly, but I am not a model. I have seen them. Actually several lately, coming in and out of my neighbor's apartment."

"I have only had this one glass of wine and I don't have a pair of rose-colored glasses either. Let me do this for you. Please, Brook."

"Fine, if you want to waste your time and take the risk of ruining your camera, you can take my picture. When and where?"

"I live near Central Park, so lets say Friday afternoon on the east side of the turtle pond. Wear something flirty, with soft color that shows some leg. After, I will take you to dinner."

"I would like that, William. We have been talking for over an hour. I have to get changed and ready to work. I will see you on board. I'm very glad you joined me for the wine."

William takes my hand and kisses it. "I am glad too. I will see you in a few minutes," he says.

I get up to leave and he gets up too. I feel him watching me as I leave and my heart skips a beat. I am acting like a teenage girl with my first crush. The problem is that I really do like him. I change in the ladies' room and get to my gate just in time to board before the passengers.

"So nice of you to join us," Wendy teases me. "I saw you in the bar with the dreamboat photographer."

"You did? I just happened to run into him there. I was so early and thought I would have a glass of wine before takeoff."

"Mmmhhhmm, I see. Just by chance you ran into him?"

"Purely by chance. You know how that is, same place, and same time."

"Happens to me all the time," Regina comes to my aid.

"Me too," Christina adds. "I am always running into people I know at the strangest places."

We get to work and load the passengers, give our speech and take off. In flight, I tell Regina all about my talk with William. "You're going to meet him to take pictures?" she asks.

"Yes, and then dinner. He might be the only man who would understand my schedule and vice versa."

All through the flight, William smiles and winks at me. I do hope none of the other passengers sees this. I don't want to be called in to a meeting for an explanation.

Friday at noon, I sit on a bench at the east side of the turtle pond eating a sandwich. He said afternoon, but not an exact time. I do enjoy people watching, so I can pass the time doing that. I finish my sandwich and turn slightly to rest my left arm on the back of the park bench. From here, I can watch the people as they approach me.

"Have you been waiting long, Brook?" William asks.

"Not long. I have indulged in my favorite pastime."

"And what might that be?"

"I watch people and try to imagine what their lives are. See that man on the bike? He is a professor of literature at NYU. He is out today for exercise away from his stuffy office. The woman crossing the path is a writer looking to do research for her next book-a scandalous romance novel set in the city."

"You got all of that by watching them walk? What do you make of me?"

"You are a photographer attempting to make a purse out of a sow's ear. That is one of my gram's favorite sayings. Thank you for giving me a chance to use it." I laugh.

"I am not a very good sewer and I know nothing about sows, but I can take pictures and I appreciate beautiful women. You are one of them Brook and I intend to prove that to you. I already took thirty shots of you on your bench, so walk with me and we will find a spot for the rest."

I take his offered arm and we start to walk around the pond. I continue to watch people as he looks for his perfect spot. He stops every now and then to study a place and then we move on. After twenty minutes or so, he stops.

"This is it. Good light and fair background." He takes off his backpack and opens it. He pulls out a tripod and two more cameras. One camera he mounts on the tripod and the other joins the one already on his neck. "I am going to place you, but I don't want you to stand still. Move around in a six-foot area. I will direct you to do things. Smile, look sexy, sultry, childlike, stuff like that. Any questions?" he asks.

"I don't think so. Just say when."

He moves me to the spot he wants and starts to take pictures. I move, smile and pout just as he asks me to. From time to time, people stop to watch us. Several even take a picture of him taking my picture. As I said, people, watching is fascinating.

After over a thousand pictures are taken, he finally stops. I see him open up his backpack and put a camera in. "Happy William?" I ask. "I am exhausted and you must be, too. Let's have a late lunch or early dinner," I suggest.

"I would like a drink and a kiss. It doesn't have to be in that order," he says.

"I rise up on my tiptoe to offer a kiss on his cheek, but he turns his head, capturing my lips with his. He wraps me in his arms and pulls me close. The kiss lasts forever and feels fantastic. My body molds to him for a perfect fit and I am lost in the sensation of being in his strong arms. He pulls back to look at me. "Sorry, I got a little carried away. I've wanted to do that all day. You are quite intoxicating, Brook."

"Don't apologize. I didn't try to stop you, if you noticed. I rather liked you kissing me."

"Good, because it just might happen again, and soon."

We leave the park and grab a cab. William has a favorite restaurant in Chinatown he wants to go to for dinner. Once we are seated, our conversation can pick up again.

"Tell me about your childhood, Brook. Where did you grow up?"

"How long will it take to eat because it is a long story? My mom raised me and my brother alone. My dad had problems and my mom left him when I was a baby. I saw him once, when I was two and that was it. He died when I was nine. We moved around a lot. I even lived in California for a year, but we came back to Connecticut. My mom died a year ago of cancer. I see my brother several times a year and we talk on the phone every week."

"That sounds rough. Did you have a good childhood?"

"The best. My mom was a free spirit. She was fearless and strong. She was great until I was in high school and then she started to drink. I became *her* mother, putting her to bed at night. She got help, though and things straightened out for her. What about your family?"

"I have my mom and dad, an older sister, Emily, and a younger brother, Jonathan. I grew up in a Philadelphia suburb by the name of Upper Darby. I had a great childhood with plenty of aunts, uncles and cousins around. I got into so much trouble, but I survived. I came to New York after college to make my name and fortune."

"How is that going? I know you fly all over for work. Are you happy with that?"

"I do love the work. I have been everywhere and had the opportunity to see so much. I am thirty-two, Brook, but I don't have a home life, kids, the things my sister and brother have. I am starting to think I miss that and want it. Like you though, who will put up with a part-time husband and father? This is all that I know how to do and it requires me to travel to do it."

"Teach me how to take your picture and maybe you can model, too!"

"Now you are being funny. This mug isn't worth breaking a camera over, trust me."

"That is a matter of opinion. I kind of like your mug."

He takes my hand, brings it to his lips, and kisses my palm. I feel something shoot up my arm and my breath hitches. "You have lovely small hands, Brook. Pleasant to kiss and hold," he murmurs sweetly.

I don't know what to say so I am staring at him. Thankfully, our food arrives and breaks the silence. We eat in relative quiet. Every time I look up, he is looking at me and smiling. I feel that I am falling under the spell of William Barry, photographer.

We finish eating and start to discuss what to do next when William's phone rings. "Please excuse me. I have to take this," he says looking at the number calling. He gets up from the table to move away. I can see him at the door talking in a very animated way, waving his arms in the air. He finishes and walks back to me. "I am so sorry, Brook. A close friend is in some trouble and needs my help. I am going to have to cut our evening short. I'll pay the check and put you in a cab home."

"Don't worry, William, I'll be fine. You go to your friend. We will talk later. Thank you so much for today and for a lovely dinner. I had such a great time."

"Me too, Brook. Thank you and I'll see you." He throws some money on the table and practically runs out of the door. I use the restroom and leave to catch a cab home.

CHAPTER 3

OVER THE NEXT SEVERAL WEEKS, William and I meet for coffee, walk in the park, and talk on the phone. He is very attentive and sweet, apologizing several times for his abrupt departure from dinner. Our conversations run the gamut of socially accepted topics.

William invites me to another dinner. Once again, the phone rings just as we are finishing our delicious meal. "Hello." he answers. I watch as he listens to the caller. He continues, "Okay, Jonathan. I'll be there as soon as I can. Good-bye." Turning to me he says, "I'm sorry, but once again I have to cut our evening short. Please accept my apology. I'll see you home."

I haven't seen nor heard from William in two weeks. He has not flown on my route, and from what I have found out from friends on other schedules, they haven't seen him either. I don't want to call him because I don't feel like I have that kind of relationship with him. I start my last week in this rotation and finally William is on the flight manifest. I help to ready the plane for boarding and wait to see him.

"Christina, I am going to see if I can find William in the waiting area."

"Okay, Brook, I can hold down the fort for now."

I walk up the gangway and find him in the first class lounge. He smiles as soon as he spots me. Standing, he walks over to me. "Hi, Brook. You look gorgeous." He says taking my hand.

"I was worried about you William. You just disappeared after our dinner."

"I am sorry about that. I can explain. How much time do you have between your flights?"

"I have a layover in Miami. My flight is 3:30 tomorrow."

"Spend the night with me?" His question takes me by surprise.

"Define *the night* for me, please," I say nervously.

"It can be whatever you want it to be. I know what I want it to be, but you're the one to decide that, Brook."

"I'll think about it, but right now we have a plane to catch." I turn and walk back to the gate and board the plane. I smile and welcome the passengers aboard. William takes his seat and we get underway.

I take care of my passengers, including William, with the same care that I always use. I see him staring at me every time I enter the cabin. I can feel the sexual tension radiate from him with every look. I have entered, unconstrained, into his thralldom.

When the plane lands, we taxi to our gate and the passengers vacate quickly. William is the last to leave. Standing before me, he touches my cheek with his fingers. "I have a car waiting for us outside the main entrance of the terminal. We will be dining at The Villa in South Beach. My clothes are at the Ritz-Carlton South Beach. We have to stop there for me to change. Do you have something to wear?"

"I have a black dress and a shawl. Will that do?"

"With you in it, I am sure it is lovely. I'll see you outside." He leans to me and kisses my cheek where his fingers just left. I turn and my audience of five pretend to swoon in front of me.

"Very funny! I am glad that I can provide you with entertainment."

"Don't be mad," Bill teases. "We live to witness dramatic moments like that!"

"I may have to dry my eyes." It's Steve's turn to torment me.

"Fine, get it all out now. Remember, payback is a bitch. I am a patient woman, but there will be a reckoning," I warn them.

"Don't pay any attention to them, Brook. They are just jealous because they aren't getting any!" Wendy defends me.

"Good to know, but I'm not getting any yet either," I muse.

"You at least have the prospect of it. Those two have a smut magazine and their hands, right guys?" Wendy continues.

"There is nothing wrong with smut, and my hand needs to stay active for my job." Steve defends himself.

"I am done with this conversation, and besides, I have a date. I have a car with a handsome man in it, dinner at Gianni Versace's house and a suite at the Ritz that I might stay in."

"You lost me. What do you mean, *You might stay in?*" Regina asks.

"I haven't decided if I am going to sleep with him or not."

"I *have* decided. Where is the car?" Christina exclaims.

I shake my head, grab my bag and head up the aisle. Once in the terminal I head for the door. Leaning against a long, sleek limo is my date for the evening, a sly smile on his lips. The driver walks to me and takes my bag. I walk to William, lean into him and kiss him. He wraps his arms around me and pulls me close. "I think this will be a most interesting evening, Brook. I have you all to myself in a fabulous city."

We drive to the Ritz. The driver lets us out at the door. The sun is just about to set. It is an exquisite sight. I stand there looking at the flowers for a few minutes. William breaks my absorption by whispering in my ear, "Their lovely flowers but nothing is more stunning than you."

William walks me into the lobby with his arm around me and his hand on my hip. I am still in my uniform, so I feel very out of place with the clientele. He confidently speaks to the desk clerk, who greets him by name. "Welcome back, Mr. Barry. We are so glad that you are joining us this evening."

"Thank you, Paul. This is my date, Miss Kennedy. Is my suite ready and my bags delivered?"

"Everything is in order, Mr. Barry. It is a pleasure to meet you, Miss Kennedy."

"Thank you," I answer.

"If there is anything that you need, please call for me. I am on all night," Paul continues.

"Thank you, Paul. We have dinner reservations, so we won't need your help right now," William answers him.

William takes the key card and leads me to the elevator. I watch as he presses the button for the top floor. The elevator sweeps us up and the door opens. William guides me out left to a door. Using the card, he unlocks it and swings the door wide to let me walk in first.

This is no ordinary room. There is a bedroom with a king-size bed to the left. A living room and dining room with floor-to-ceiling windows. A wrap-around balcony with a view that leaves you breathless. I walk out onto the balcony. As I am looking star-struck at the view, William closes in behind me. He pushes my hair aside and kisses my neck. "A penny for your thoughts," he murmurs.

"I am thinking that I have no idea exactly who you are, do I?"

"You know more about me than most people ever will. So, what else do you want to know?"

"I want to know how a photographer travels first class, has a limo, and stays in a room like this?"

"Let's change and go to dinner. All will be revealed in good time, Brook. I am not an outlaw, nor am I in a gang. You are safe with me."

I change in the bathroom, fix my hair and make-up. When I come out, he is sitting on the couch in a black suit, white shirt and tie. I stop to look at him-he is so relaxed, gazing out the windows to the ocean. When he hears me, he stands. "You look ravishing in that dress, Brook. Let me help you with your shawl." He places my shawl on my shoulders, lifting my hair and kissing my neck again. I hear him breathe deeply, lifting his nose to my ear. He nips my earlobe with his teeth and lips. "You smell and taste heavenly, Brook. What are you wearing?"

"It's just vanilla shampoo, William, plus soap and water."

"If that is all, it is still wonderful. I'm starving. Lets have our dinner, and we can talk there."

The limo and our driver meet us outside. It is not far to the restaurant and we ride holding hands. He massages the top of my hand with his thumb. I find myself staring at the movement.

"You are deep in thought and so quiet, Brook. What is going on in that mind of yours?" he asks.

"I am trying to puzzle you out William. I know that you are not all that you have told me. There is much more. You're wearing a handmade Italian suit."

"Well done, Brook! You know men's fashion. How did you come by that?"

"You forget that I travel for a living. I have been to Italy countless times. I usually have a layover there of a day or two. I have a friend in Rome, Vincenzo. He works for a tailor. Your suit is probably the finest that I have seen."

"Tell me, what else do you see?"

"It is not so much what I see as what I hear."

"What exactly do you hear, sweet Brook?"

"You lapse into a decidedly British way of speaking. I think your American accent is not real. It's an act. I think you are much more comfortable with a British accent."

The next time he speaks to me, it is with a full British accent. "Again, well done, Brook. Perhaps I am not as cunning as I thought I was. I think we may have a spot for you in the Yard." I pull my hand away from him.

"Now I have to tell you, William that I am not as comfortable as I thought I was with you. Actually, now I'm slightly frightened. So before I do anything else, I want to know exactly who you are."

"You are due an explanation, Brook. My name is William Barry, but there are a few more in between and after. It's William Warren George Mitchell Barry, Viscount Barry. My father is the Duke of Wessex. I am to inherit his title upon his death."

"Why the photographer story?"

"I *am* a photographer. I love it, actually. I am a gentleman to be sure, but I still have to earn a living. The family business is shipping and commerce. All that, I find boorish. I leave that to my younger brother to manage. I enjoy travel, meeting people and taking pictures."

"Why the story, though? You are who you are. Why make this up?"

"I am treated differently once people know. They want to impress me, even use me. I like being just William the photographer."

We arrive at our destination. The driver stops and opens my door. I look at William and he says, "Will you still dine with me, Brook, even though you now know what a blighter I am?" he asks with a wicked grin.

"Only because I don't know what a blighter is. However, I will be on my guard with you, William. I now know that you did not grow up in Philly."

"Alas, that is true. But the aunts, uncles and cousins were all there."

We enter the restaurant to the delight of the owner. He walks immediately over to us. "Welcome, Mr. Barry. It is so good to see you again. We have your table ready. Please follow me," he says. We follow him to the back of the restaurant to a lovely table next to a window. "I hope this is to your and your lovely lady's liking."

"Yes, very much, Alfonse. My complements," William answers him in his American accent.

"How do you do that, William?" I inquire.

"Do what, Brook?"

"Go back and forth with your accents."

"Practice," he answers me with a grin. He seats me and I am handed a menu. I put it down so I can watch my date. "Are you going to order Brook?" William asks.

"I would like you to order for me, please. I have passed by this restaurant but I have never eaten here. You have obviously been here several times. I leave the ordering to you."

"Is there anything you don't like?"

"Liars and con-artists come to mind," I quip.

"Touché, Brook. I hope that I can change your opinion of me. In fact, I need to."

"Why is that, William?"

"I have a proposition for you to consider. However, I get ahead of myself. That discussion is for later."

The waiter takes the order from William and comes back with our wine. He opens it with a flourish and has William taste it. Without taking his eyes off me even for a second, William tells him it is fine. After the waiter leaves, William moves his chair so that we are very near each other. He leans in towards me and again kisses my neck. He lifts my chin with his fingers and kisses me.

"What are you doing, William? Everyone will stare at us."

"If you have to ask, then I am not doing it right. What kind of foreplay do you enjoy, my lovely Brook?"

"If that is what this is, William, unfortunately you have missed your mark."

"I want to build your desire for me, Brook, and seduce you."

"You are very sure of yourself, Mr. Barry. I won't deny that I am attracted to you. I won't deny that I would probably love to, I think your expression is *shag*."

Our meal comes and it is delicious. The chef outdid himself with our feast. William continues in the same vein of discussion-how and what he would like to do with me. He has my rapt attention, but not my submission.

The check paid, he stands to move my chair to leave. Taking my arm, we walk to the door and out into the evening air.

"Would you like to go for a walk on the beach?" he asks holding my hand.

"Yes, I would love to."

His driver comes over to us and they converse. We cross the street to the beach with the driver following behind. I look at William with a raised brow and he says, "Bodyguard, just in case you can't keep your hands off me."

William guides me to a bench and I sit down. He kneels in the sand and lifts my foot to his pants to remove my sandals. He smoothes his hand up my calf to behind my knee, then leans forward and kisses it. "You have the most beautiful legs, Brook."

"Thank you, William."

He gives me his hand to pull me up to him. Wrapping me in his arms again, he kisses me, open and passionate. I have to concentrate to keep my head from swimming. "And what if *I* need your bodyguard to protect *me* from danger?" I ask smiling.

"You are in no danger, Brook, not from me," he says sincerely.

After removing his shoes and socks, we start to walk down the deserted beach with our driver a discrete distance behind us.

"Exactly how do you envision this seduction going, William? Will you simply abduct me or entice me?"

"I would rather have you want me much the same as I want you."

"The thing is, William, I don't want one-night stands. I'm not interested in momentary conquests. I have had two men in my life, both long term. The first ended when we went to college far away from each other. The second when I took the job that kept me on this crazy schedule. I am twenty-six years old and sex is more to me than just pleasure. I need to feel important to you . . . valued, safe and wanted."

"Brook, do you remember the first time I flew with you?" he says, taking me back.

"Yes, we were on a flight to England and you didn't sleep at all the entire night. You had me bring you so much coffee, tea, and orange juice, we all thought you would explode," I say smiling at the memory.

"Right. I had to keep you near me. I wanted to see your face, brush my fingers against you. What did I say to you just before we landed?" he asks earnestly.

"Something about a museum wing opening the next day?"

"Yes. I was dedicating the wing to my uncle. I was hoping you might come and I would see you away from the airport. The next time it was the gardens of Versailles. I told you were the most beautiful at 2:00 in the afternoon. Again, I was there but not you. Finally, I was going to a movie premier in LA, but again you didn't come," he says quietly.

"I didn't catch what you were saying. It never occurred to me that you were looking for me."

"When you asked me to meet you at the bar before the flight, I almost thought I was dreaming. All this time I wanted you, needed you and thought you weren't attracted to me. I got to the airport a full hour before you did, but I hid behind a newspaper so I could watch you walk into the bar and sit down. I watched you stare at the door waiting for me. Then I knew you were interested at least. You gave me hope. Then you agreed to let me photograph you. You let me kiss you and then feed you. If my damn brother hadn't called with a family problem . . . . well, I don't know what might have happened between us. Brook, I don't want you for tonight or for this week or even for this year. I want a relationship with you. I want you to know all of me, and I all of you. I want to take you to meet my family and I would like to meet your brother."

I turn to face him and he stops walking. I put my hands on his waist and move them up his chest and around his neck. "Kiss me, William."

"With pleasure, Brook, with the greatest pleasure." He leans down and pulls me against him. Kissing me, his hand moves down to cup my butt. I moan into his mouth. He whispers against my lips, "So what is it to be, Brook? A walk on the beach . . . a dip in the ocean . . . or a drive back to that wonderful room at the Ritz?"

"Surprise me," I answer, feeling that I am safe with him.

William bends down and throws me over his shoulder, heading back to the car at a fast pace. "William, put me down. I can walk, for God's sake."

He yells to his driver, "Luke, please bring the car around." He bends down to set me on my feet. I continue to walk to the bench to sit and put my shoes back on. William sits next to me and dusts off his feet to get into his socks and shoes. I hear the car come to a stop behind us. William pulls me to my feet and we walk to the car smiling. Once inside, he moves me so that I am cradled in his arms facing him. William presses a button and a dark window separates us from the driver. He pulls me further onto his lap. He starts to kiss me, mouth and neck, back and forth.

He softens my moans with a kiss. Looking down at me in his arms, he is smiling. "You are so beautiful, Brook. I've waited so long to have you and finally you're here."

"Has anyone ever told you that you have such a silver tongue, Viscount Barry?"

"You can drop the title, Brook. I am just William, with any luck your soon-to-be lover. And pleased as punch to be that. Thank you for trusting me. I intend to worship you to distraction."

"You will have to stop speaking British because I don't know what that means. What is 'worshiping me to distraction'?"

"I will let you know while I am doing it. We can have a translator in the room with us if you would prefer."

"No thanks, one Englishman is enough for me. Why do you want me, William? I am sure that with your looks you could have any titled woman in England. Why the American with no family or money?"

"I don't need your money or family. I have enough of both. What I want you have in abundance. Kindness, wonder, peace, beauty and the most alluring . . . reticence."

"Don't alluring and reticence mean the same thing?"

"Yes, I am quite stuck on a theme with you."

We arrive at the hotel and William whisks me inside. Passing by the desk, the attendant stops us. "Mr. Barry, I have three messages for you." He is waving papers at William.

"Will you please pass them on to my man Luke when he comes in? I am not to be disturbed this evening unless the building is on fire or a missile is landing on it. Do you understand?"

"Yes, Mr. Barry, I will leave complete instructions sir."

As I turn in the elevator, I see the desk clerk's grin. I'll bet he knows what worshiping a body to distraction means.

CHAPTER 4

AS THE ELEVATOR DOOR CLOSES, I find myself staring at William. "You have to stop looking at me that way, Brook," he says seductively.

"Why? Nevertheless, before you answer that, am I looking at you the same way you are looking at me right now, Wolf?"

"Hungry eyes, my darling. Elevators and hallways in good hotels have surveillance cameras. If I touch you, I won't be able to stop. I will take you right here. Then some desk clerk, bellhop or night watchman will have the pleasure of seeing you as well. I can't have that-you are for my eyes only. We also run the risk that they will upload our lovemaking to the social networks. Someone will recognize me and then we will cease to be William and Brook. I don't relish being followed around by the paparazzi. I want to keep us, and what we will have between us, just for us as long as possible."

The elevator glides to a stop. The door opens and we step out. William retrieves the key card from his pocket as we approach the door. The door unlocked, he swings it wide open for me to walk through. Placing the "Do Not Disturb" sign on the door, he closes and locks it securely. Turning to me, he shrugs off his jacket and loosens his tie. Capturing me against the wall, he moves my hands, fingers clasped with his, above my head. He holds me to the wall with his hips. Kissing down my neck and across my breasts he whispers, "Now, my lovely Brook, now we touch."

I whisper in between kisses, "There is a problem, William, I can't touch you. You have my hands." He immediately brings my hand down to place it on his chest.

He whispers, "Better?"

I smile and say, "At least now I know what you feel like under that shirt."

"I promise you the rest of the evening will be enjoyable. How many times would you like to climax, Brook? I do take requests" he says shocking me.

"Sorry, William, but I have never been asked that particular question. In fact, I don't remember anyone ever caring about my climaxing or not. But I will take what I can get since you are offering."

"I need a number, Brook. I have been known to overdo things. I don't want to scare or hurt you in any way. I want you to think every time we do this that it is the best you have ever had. What is your number, Brook?"

"I am not being deliberately obtuse, William. I literally don't know. Is three enough or six too many?"

"You may not be a virgin, but you do lack experience. Six is a decent starting place. Pick a word, Brook, that will tell me you have had enough. Not *stop* or *please* . . . something that has nothing to do with what we are doing."

"Now you are scaring me. I've read about safe words. I don't do that."

"Neither do I. I am not going to tie you up or whip you. I just need to know when you have had enough."

"I choose *gardenia*," I answer.

"Well done. Favorite flower?"

"Yes."

He picks me up and heads towards the bedroom, kicking off his shoes in the process. He gets to the bedroom door, kicks it shut and locks it. "Just in case some bloody fool ignores the door sign and comes in," he says absentmindedly.

I am enjoying the back and forth American~British thing he does. He sets me on my feet by the bed. Unbuttons his shirt, shrugs it off and throws it on the floor.

"Now that fetching dress, Brook. My shirt is lonely on the floor. Should we give it company?" I reach around my back to lower the zipper when he says, "Allow me, please." He unzips it and I slide the dress off my shoulders. It floats down my body to the floor, puddling at my feet. He holds my hand to step out of it. His eyes inspect my stockings, garter, panties, and finally my bra. "You are a vision. Aphrodite, Helen of Troy and Venus pale in comparison to you, my darling."

"Let's get these pants off and see if Jupiter, Zeus or perhaps David will ravish me tonight."

"Sorry, Love, it will be me doing the ravishing. The other men you mention will have to wait."

He helps me to remove his belt and unbutton his pants. I slide the zipper down keeping my eyes on his. In one move, his pants and boxers hit the floor. He bends down to remove them as well as his socks and then stands before me naked. I bring my hands to his chest and slowly drop them to his waist, hips and then his butt, smiling through the whole process.

"I think chiseled in granite is an accurate description. You have a most gorgeous body," I say.

"All the better to worship you with, my dear. Now I need to see what is under that tantalizing bra and panties."

I slip off my panties and remove my bra. The carnal, appreciative look he gives me makes me blush. He moves his hands to cup my breasts. "You have beautiful breasts Brook, and this . . ." He moves one hand down to my curls, "this is salient." I have a sudden urge to make you climax until you scream my name and grab the sheets. I am going to kiss you, pet you, and then I am going to make love to you."

He moves me to lay me down and lies next to me. When he asked me earlier what I like in foreplay, I didn't answer him. The truth be told, I love it when a man takes charge and talks dirty to me. I love hearing what he is going to do to me almost as much as what he actually does.

He is touching me everywhere and my hands move over his body. "Careful there Darling, let's not be too vigorous. We have a lot of work to do before we get to that. I don't want to be embarrassed prematurely," he says.

His mouth teases me, his hands move over me. I moan in pleasure. "Tell me if you like this, Brook. I take my cues from what you say."

"It feels so good, William. What can I do for you?"

"Nothing, my pet. My pleasure is giving you pleasure."

Before I have any sense of what is happening, I find myself screaming, "GARDENIA, ROSES, CARNATIONS! Stop, William, please!"

William is chuckling at me. He crawls up my body to cradle my face. Looking directly into my eyes he says, "You are very easily pleased, my love. So few orgasms . . . we will have to work on that."

He sinks into me with an easy grace. We move together and I again tell him how good he feels to me. He speaks the words that I long to hear. How soft I feel, how good I smell. "Darling, that tightening you do is exquisite. I am lost in the sensation. You are going to be my undoing. I am afraid I will never have enough of you."

A few more minutes and William calls out my name and shudders his release. He flips over, still inside me, so that I rest on him. I kiss the sprinkling of hair on his chest. When our breathing begins to return to normal William says, "You are going to be a like a drug for me, Brook. I am going to need more and more of you, I can tell already. You are addictive."

"And the problem with that is . . . ?" I ask.

"Your schedule and mine. Impossible and yet I have to have you. How hard is it to have sex in the bathroom of an airplane?"

"If it is sex like what we just had . . . impossible!"

I wake to William feeling my body. His hand cups and massages my butt, then moves to my hip. With me on my side, he manages to tease both breasts with one hand. "My god Brook, I have barely touched you. Or, on the other hand, have you been dreaming?" He asks, smirking at me.

"It's all you, William. Dreams or reality, it's you."

"If you are dreaming about me already, I will take that as a compliment. How are you feeling?"

"Relaxed and rested, thank you," I answer with a smile.

"Are you sore at all after my rough treatment of you last night?"

"You were not so rough. I feel great."

He repositions my leg forward and slides into me from behind. Kissing my neck and shoulder, he pulls me close, holding me against him. His hand skims down my body to give me pleasure. "You are a goddess. I am so lost in you," he whispers in my ear.

We move together in the early morning light until we both find our grand release. We lie together still kissing until I break our spell. "I'm sorry," I say. "I have to shower and get ready. I have a plane to catch in a few hours."

"Rightly so, and I have work to do as well . . . You shower and I will order room service."

I shower, pack and walk to join him in the living room. Just as I enter, there is a knock at the door. William answers it to find our breakfast. Coffee, thank god for coffee.

"Please set this up on the balcony," William says motioning to for the waiter.

William takes my hand to follow the waiter through the door to the balcony. He seats me and then takes his chair. "How is this, Darling?" he asks.

"Brilliant, thank you," I answer with a smirk.

The waiter finishes. William tips him and he leaves. William takes my hand.

"Now, about the proposal that I spoke of last night at dinner," he says, his demeanor changing from blissful to serious.

"Yes, I am intrigued, Mr. Barry. Do go on," I say teasing him.

"As I have already told you, I want you, desperately. With that, I have certain expectations, one being exclusivity. I don't share well, never have. While we work on this relationship, I will only use two items for my sexual gratification."

"Two items? Which two items?" I ask intrigued.

"Your cunny and my hand." I swallow my coffee loudly as he continues. "And you can use the same on my person with the exception that I have a dick."

"I thought you Brits were refined. Your use of language does not bear that out," I say, admonishing him for his vulgarity.

"My apologies, Miss Kennedy. Your vagina and my penis, I believe are the correct terminology."

"I agree to the exclusive use of said items, Mr. Barry. Anything else?"

"When we are in the same city, we reside together. Your place or mine in the city and I will obtain a hotel for anywhere else."

"Agreed, but now I need one assurance from you."

"Give it."

"That from now on you tell me the complete truth. I am not spending time with someone who keeps his life from me. I share the real me with you and I expect the same in return. You don't hide from me, ever."

"Done. Do you need specifics such as bathroom usage or will a simple overview suffice?" he teases me with a huge grin on his face.

"I think an overview will be sufficient. I mean it, William. You being who you are was an important omission. I understand your reticence in sharing your identity with the public, but not with me anymore."

Our merger discussion over, we eat our breakfast with a view of the ocean at our feet. As I watch him, my curiosity gets the better of me and I find myself asking, "Where did you learn how to make love like you do?"

He bursts out laughing. "That is a question that I have never been asked. You constantly surprise me, Brook. This relationship is certainly going to be entertaining. How shall I start? After prep school, I attended Cambridge University. At University I met several women who . . . how should I put this? . . . schooled, tutored, or coached me in the art of pleasuring a woman. It was my favorite class and I excelled in it."

"Yes, I can see that. I benefited from their instruction. How do you . . . ?"

"Stop struggling, Brook, and just ask me."

"I have never had multiple orgasms with anyone else. How do you do that?"

"Simple anatomy, Brook. A woman can have several in one encounter. Unfortunately, men can accomplish two, maybe. We are rather like a gas tank. Once empty, you must stop to refill it. A woman is all nerve endings, with the majority in the clitoris. Your vagina has a few and there are more at your anus. By stimulating these at different times and with different combinations and pressures, you can achieve several orgasms."

"And this is what they taught you?"

"Yes, and now you want to know what is the top number that I have witnessed."

"And how did you know that?"

"I can see your eyes, Brook. They give you away. Eleven is the most that I have seen. The intensity lessens with each one. I am told the first few are always the best," he says, dropping his voice conspiratorially.

"I can attest to that, but with you William, they were all worth the effort."

"Thank you. To change the subject, you said this was your last week in this rotation?"

"Next week, I start with a six-week rotation of Chicago to San Francisco and back to New York. Same days, Sunday to Wednesday night. The last rotation is the worst. New York to London, then I shuttle to Paris for three weeks, then Rome for three weeks, then home. I am usually a zombie after those six weeks."

"Can you make the time to meet my family in England?" he asks.

"I can see who is available for the shuttle and try to skip one. I'll have to work on that."

We finish our breakfast and get ready to leave. William calls Luke to take me to the airport. We stand at the door holding each other. "I will be back on Friday afternoon. Will you come to my apartment or do you want me to come to yours?" William asks.

"Would you mind terribly to come to mine? I have a rather prolific neighbor. I would like to give him a taste of his own medicine."

"Sounds like fun. We get to be loud and rambunctious?" he asks, grinning.

"Carte blanche, Your Grace."

CHAPTER 5

AT CHECK IN, I MEET my fellow crewmembers. Within three minutes, the Regina/Christina/Wendy inquest begins. "We want details. Don't leave anything out," Wendy says.

"I am not going to give you details. I will just say I had a most pleasant evening and morning. Interesting and full of surprises," I reply.

"You slept with him! Was he any good?" Regina inquires.

"He is not what I expected, not even close. He is a gentleman and very attentive."

"Sounds boring and I guess you will never see him again, right?" Christina asks.

"Actually, we are going to date exclusively for a while and see where this takes us."

We ready the plane for takeoff, welcome the passengers and leave our gate. When we arrive in Fort Worth, it is so hot and muggy that none of us wants to leave the coolness of the airport. I venture out and get us a cab. The girls and I get in, giving the driver the address to the jump house. We have apartments in several cities~we split the rent with about twenty-five other people. We jump in and jump out. This one is a one-bedroom that has four sets of bunk beds in it. There are two pull-out couches and a TV in the living room and a small kitchen that rarely gets used.

When we arrive, we all throw our bags on the bunk that we will sleep in. I go into the bathroom to change out of my polyester pantsuit for a most comfortable sweat suit.

"Are Bill and Steve staying here too?" Wendy asks.

"I think they are. I told them we would be here," I answer.

"Is there anything good on TV tonight or should we get a movie?" Christina asks.

"I am turning in early, so count me out," I answer.

I walk back in the bedroom to find my bedding in the closet. I make the bed and lie down to read for a while. It is only 7:00, but I didn't get a lot of sleep last night so I fall asleep fast. Around 9:00 my cell rings, waking me. I see that it is William. I answer sleepily, "Hi, William."

"Did I wake you, Brook?" he asks.

"I might have fallen asleep. I had quite a workout last night and I need to recover."

"A workout? Get some rest because I plan on another vigorous workout this Friday night."

"Looking forward to it. Where are you?"

"I am in bed thinking about you."

"At the Ritz?"

"Yes. I asked them to make the bed but not change the sheets this morning. I can still smell you and me."

"Lucky you. I am at our jump house and I don't have anything here to remind me of us."

"What's a jump house?" he asks.

"We rent apartments in different cities so we have a place to stay. We split the rents between twenty-five to thirty of us. It is much less expensive than hotels."

"Sounds lovely."

"Obviously you have never been in one! I miss you."

"You too, more than you will ever know, Brook. I called to keep my promise to you."

"What promise is that?"

"You have forgotten since this morning? I will refresh your memory. I told you I would only use your vagina or my hand for sexual gratification."

"I remember now."

"I can smell you in this bed. I just need your voice to complete the picture for me. Can you go somewhere private for our discussion?" he asks.

"I can go into the bathroom. That's the best I can do for privacy."

"Good, go in there and turn on the shower. You might need the sound to muffle your voice."

I walk to the bathroom close and lock the door. Turning on the shower, I go back to talk to William. "The shower is on, William."

"Good. Are you naked?" he asks, with a sexy whisper.

"No. Are you?"

"Absolutely. Get naked for me, Brook," he says, but I sit on the lid of the toilet fully clothed.

"Naked and waiting, William," I say, lying.

"Now close your eyes and picture me naked and stroking myself. I want you to touch your breasts for me. Pull your nipples, tease them. Does it feel good, Brook?"

"Yes, William. I wish it was you doing this."

"I am, Brook. My hands are on you right now. My tongue and my lips are on your breasts. Feel me, Brook." I moan loudly. "Move your hands down to your warmth, where you want me to be."

"Yes, William. I feel you with me." I hear him groan and the air rushes through his mouth.

"Oh dear god!" William shouts. "You don't play fair, Brook."

"I am, William," I say in my defense.

"Oh god, Brook!" William yells and I know that he has finished. I smile and chuckle to myself.

"Will the sheets need to be changed tomorrow?" I ask.

"Bugger me, no way! I did a good job of this. I don't want the sheets changed until I can't smell us anymore. I need to feel that you are still here with me, Brook. I have gone and gotten myself pussy whipped. Won't my mates be happy to know this~and all over a visit with Rosie Palm and her five sisters."

"You've lost me, William. Who is Rosie Palm?"

"Think about it. I miss, you Brook, and I wish I were with you. Get some sleep. Thank you for the phone sex. It was extraordinary."

I wake early because of my nap yesterday. I yawn and stretch, walking to the living room. Every bunk is full in the bedroom and there are bodies all over the living room. I guess we had a full house last night. I see Ned on the floor and I step over Jace to get to him. Ned is a pilot and needs his sleep. I tap him on his back.

"Ned, go in and get in my bed. You shouldn't be sleeping on the floor."

"So, you are inviting me into your bed, Brook?" He questions.

"Not exactly. I have vacated it and it is only 5:30. You can sleep for a few more hours in relative comfort."

"Wait, is Brook inviting you to sleep with her? You lucky bastard! Brook is the one woman I would risk pissing off my wife for," Jace wakes up to say.

"I am going out for a run. You two can circle jerk all you want. I was just offering my empty bed," I say, not wishing to engage in their fun.

"I'll take it. I have a flight to Tokyo at 11:00. Thanks, Brook," Ned says.

"My pleasure, Ned."

My running shoes on, I leave the apartment for the street. It is still very hot and humid, but it's tolerable. I do this for exercise and to sweat out the calories consumed at dinner with William. So maybe some heat will help the process. I stretch for ten minutes and then hit the pavement.

Passing by people walking their dogs and other runners and walkers, I hit my stride after twenty minutes or so. I love the Dallas-Fort Worth area. Bustling city and yet quiet country areas to raise your family. I run through a park that is just starting to come awake with the birds singing. I turn up my iPod shuffle so that Josh Groban is singing loudly in my head.

I slow for a water break, just jogging for a few minutes. I jog in place at a red light waiting to cross the street. I turn to see a man behind me, also jogging and waiting to cross the street. I remember seeing him shortly after I left the apartment. I have run a few miles away from there now. I am familiar with where I am because of running here for three years, but I am now aware of this man. I turn off the music and pop out my ear buds.

The crossing man appears on the pole and I jog across the street. So does he. I turn to head back to the apartment and he follows. The little hairs on the back of my neck start to prickle on me. I get back to the park but instead of entering, I stay on the main road where more people are. My legs are burning because I am no longer having a relaxing run. I cross the street several times and he follows me.

At a corner grocery store, I see a parked police car park. I head for it. As I near the car, the police officer comes out of the store and I run right up to him.

"Officer, I think I need your help."

"What's wrong, miss?" he asks.

"There is a man behind me with black shorts on who's been following me for several miles. I cross the street and so does he," I explain.

"Wait right here. I will have a conversation with him."

I watch as the officer talks to him. He pulls out a wallet and hands the officer something. The officer speaks into the mic on his shoulder. The man puts his hands up as the officer pulls the man's sock down, revealing a small gun. I almost faint, he has a gun. The officer continues to talk into the mic.

After several minutes, the officer gives him back his gun and he walks over to me. He calmly says, "Miss Kennedy, it seems your boyfriend has hired this man's agency to keep an eye on you. If you leave your apartment to run, they are to follow you and keep you safe. He has a license to carry and he has a private protection license. You are safer with him than you would be alone." He smiles at me.

"I see. I have a boyfriend who evidently has separation anxiety. Can I make him go away, stop following me?" I ask.

"I would speak to your boyfriend first. There may be a reason that you aren't familiar with," he responds.

"Thank you for your help. I was scared, and I'm from New York City. We don't scare easily."

He laughs, "Enjoy your stay in our city and please come back to visit."

I walk over to the man. "Why does William feel it is necessary for you to follow me around?" I ask him.

"Perhaps you should ask him yourself, Miss Kennedy. My job is to make sure no one bothers you and to keep you from being hurt. That's all. I don't do relationship counseling," he counters.

I run the rest of the way to try to relieve my growing concern that William is more than he says. I have a part-time relationship with him at best. We will see each other two days a week. I don't live with him. Whom do I need protection from?

A few blocks away, I start to walk to cool down. My shadow walks behind me. When I open the outer door to go into the building, I turn to him. "I won't be leaving again until I go to the airport with my flight crew of five other people. You can go hound someone else now."

"Sorry, Miss Kennedy, but you don't sign my paycheck. Mr. Barry does. If he says to stay with you until you leave the terminal on the plane, I'll be with you," he says.

"Ggrrr! Wait until I see him." I am already planning my revenge.

We leave the apartment to enter our waiting cab, and sure enough, my shadow is in a car behind us. I feel bad now because it's not his fault, he's just doing his job. I don't even know his name.

"Is that the guy you were telling us about?" Wendy asks me as she looks behind us.

"That would be him," I answer. I wave at said shadow and he smiles back.

"Just who is this man that you are seeing, Brook? Is he a gazillionaire or something? Who can afford to have someone followed just to take care of them?" Bill asks me.

"He is a photographer, Bill. Evidently a rich one. I am flattered that he cares, but at the same time concerned that he didn't mention it to me."

"I am in the wrong business if a photographer has that kind of money and I have the responsibility of two hundred people or more on every flight. Some things just ain't right," Steve agrees.

On the way to the airport, I get a text from Sandy. *Kennedy, WTF? You have a huge, messenger-delivered package here. Six letters* *that I had to sign for from modeling agencies. And Link is f#$%ing someone's brains out. I want a do-over!*

I text her back, *No do-over. New boyfriend, thinks I'm pretty, crazy huh? Link has big appetite, maybe little wanker? Try to ignore.*

She texts back, *Can't ignore. Pictures bouncing off walls. Going to talk to him. Wish me luck.*

I answer, *Careful. Don't succumb to his charms. Don't want him banging you!*

As I walk through the terminal to my gate, my phone rings. I see it is William. "Hello, William," I say, intentionally sounding grumpy.

"At least you are still speaking to me. Is that a good sign?" he asks.

"For now. What is this all about, William?"

"Security, my peace of mind, protection . . . pick one," he answers.

"And what would *you* think if *I* hired someone to watch you?" I question.

"You forget, darling, I have Luke to watch me. I have had someone my whole life. You get used to it, eventually," he says, sounding defeated.

"I don't know if I want to get used to it, ever."

"I am afraid it goes with the territory, luv. I can't have you hurt accidentally *or* because of me. You are too dear to me. Please allow me this."

"I will see you on Friday. We can discuss it then. Will I have a Peeping Tom in LA, too?"

"Indulge me at least until I can fully explain on Friday. Please, Brook."

"I miss you, William. I will indulge you only for that reason. Friday."

"I miss you, need you and want you, Brook. Friday." He hangs up.

As the plane taxis to the runway, I sit with Christina. I am deep in thought when she asks me, "Will you have company in LA?"

"Yes. William says I should indulge him. He worries about my safety away from him. I wonder if I lived with him, would he cage me?"

"Probably. One question . . . do you love him?" she asks.

"Not yet, but I teeter on the brink of the abyss. He is so unlike anyone else that I have ever known. He knows so much about . . . women and the world."

"If you don't want him, don't get sucked in by the sex, "she advises. "It is three quarters of the relationship in the beginning but fades to one quarter later. You still have to want him." Who says Christina doesn't know about relationships.

We land in LA and I venture out into the terminal. A man and a woman walk over to me. The man asks, "Miss Kennedy? I'm Robert and this is Kim. I was told you are expecting us."

"Yes, I guess that I am, Robert."

"We will not interfere in your plans, Miss Kennedy. One of us will be with you at all times. When you are at your apartment we will be outside all night should you need us." He hands me a card. "Our numbers should you need us in the apartment."

"Are you armed, Robert?" I ask.

"Yes, we are."

"Even in here?"

"Yes, Miss Kennedy. Everywhere." He studies me.

"And if someone was to, shall we say, grab me. What would you do?"

"Whatever is needed to secure your release."

"Would you shoot someone dead?" I ask, afraid of the answer.

"If that is needed, yes, we would," he answers matter-of-factly.

"You know that I am a flight attendant, not a president or even a celebrity, right?"

"Yes, we know what you do."

"You realize how screwed up this is. You would kill someone that needed it over a flight attendant."

"I am aware how this might look to someone."

"Okay then. I am going to grab a cab with my cabin mates and head to our bat cave. Good to know that you and Cat Woman are on the job, Robin. Should I need you, I will shine the signal in the night sky. Do be watching, please." I at least get a half-smile from Cat Woman.

We grab a cab. Our apartment in LA is on West 91st Street and Loyola Boulevard. It is minutes from the airport. LA is special,~75 degrees with a 1% chance of rain or wind 356 days a year. Unfortunately, you pay dearly for that kind of weather. This apartment is by far the most expensive one that we rent.

The four of us are the only occupants at the apartment. We grab the bunks that we like and settle in for the evening. "Do you want to get a pizza delivered for dinner?" Regina asks.

"I'm not hungry. I'm too mad to eat," I tell her.

"I want to go out. I love LA. Who wants to hit a dance party with me?" Wendy asks, moving her hips and dancing around. Christina and Regina raise their hands.

"You won't come with us?" Regina asks.

"If I go, Mutt and Jeff will come with me. I am going to veg and get to sleep early. I want to run very early in the morning."

"Suit yourself," Wendy answers.

My girls glam up and head out with a wave good-bye. They are gone about ten minutes when there is a knock on the door. I look through the peephole to see Kim and Robert standing there. I open the door. "Can I help you?"

"I'm sorry, Miss Kennedy, to bother you, but we saw your roommates leave without you and we are checking on your well-being," Robert says.

"Thank you, but as you can see, I am fine."

"Yes, have a good night," he says as they turn and leave.

I slump on the couch and my phone rings. It's Sandy, so I answer. "Hey, girl, how is our neighbor?" I ask, laughing.

"You didn't tell me how gorgeous he is."

"That is because I have never seen him. So, he's a stud for real."

"He has jet black, slightly curly hair, "she says, "and the most amazing deep blue eyes. He answered the door wearing a towel around his hips. For at least thirty seconds, I couldn't speak."

"And then?"

"My brain engaged and I asked him if he wanted to come over for dinner some night next week."

"And he said?" I ask with growing concern.

"'That would be great. Which night?'"

"And then?"

"'Which ever night you are free. I thought you could knock the pictures off the wall on this side.'"

"You did not say that."

"I did and he smiled. Then he told me he would be more than happy to knock anything I wanted or needed knocked. And I quote, "'I can put you up against the wall and knock it.'" She is giggling.

"So, is this going to happen?" I ask slightly worried.

"That's why I'm calling. It did, last night. He's right here. Would you like to talk to him?"

"If this happened last night, why is he still there now? Isn't it almost midnight there?"

"Well, last night, tonight... I won't see him until Wednesday, so I had to get in what I could."

"Goodnight, Sandy. Don't forget to change the bed." I roll my eyes. Uncomplicated sex. My special gift is complicating sex.

CHAPTER 6

OUR PLANE LEAVES AT 10:00 AM. I am up by 4:30 so I can get my run and a shower in before we have to leave for the airport. I get to the street to see Kim and Robert in a car in front of the apartment. I decide my warm up this morning will be a fun one. I place my palms against the building and back up to stretch, bending and straightening my legs alternately so my ass wiggles at them. I turn to face them and do jumping jacks to increase my heart rate.

They get out of the car in their running gear just as I put on my iPod and put in my ear buds. I warm up with the first mile or so and then I hit my stride. I know it's childish, but I would love to smoke my shadows. I can full-out run a mile in five and a half minutes. No world record, but I am no slouch either. I think about it for a few minutes and then go for it. I won't look back because they would know what I am doing. I just run my finest race like I did in college. Me against the clock, personal best. I check my watch for the time and the distance that I have run. Five miles~I have to head back. I turn around to see my armed guards and I am alone! I lost them. I do my Rocky impersonation with my arms in the air. I am dancing around just as their car pulls up to the curb. Robert and Kim fly out from the backseat. I stare at them. There are two other people in the front seat.

"Miss Kennedy, that was a dangerous stunt you just pulled. You could have been seriously injured or killed. I will jog alongside you or you will get into the car for the ride back."

"Robert, you are not my parent nor my husband nor my keeper. I will run back as I do every day. You are welcome to follow me in your car or run with me, if you can. Those are *your* options. If you persist in bothering me, I will wrestle your gun away from you and hit you with it. Have I made *myself* clear?" I say with my hands on my hips.

"Crystal," he says, and motions to the driver to follow us.

I start to run back with him by my side. This time I run full-out but I do not try to outrun him. We make it back to the apartment in record time. As I open the door to go in, I turn to him and smile. He is bent over with his hands on his knees breathing in huge gasps. "You need to get in better shape, Robert, if you are going to be my Tonto. I took it easy on you today."

Trying to slow his heart to speak, he says, "I appreciate that, Miss Kennedy. I may look into hiring you for our more difficult clients, like yourself."

"Difficult . . . me? I'll see you in thirteen weeks when I pass back through town. Let's see what you can accomplish between now and then."

The flight to New York is mercifully uneventful. I have had enough for one day. We land and I say good-bye to the girls. I walk out to catch a cab, but a man holding a sign with my name on it stops me. "Miss Kennedy? I am here to drive you home."

"I don't need a ride, sir. I can grab a cab."

"I can't have you do that, please. I have a limo waiting," he advises me.

"A limo, really. This is over the top." It is after 7:00 PM and I am tired, so I can't argue for long. I follow him out to the limo and get in.

"Would you like some music for the ride, Miss Kennedy?" he asks.

"Do you have Josh Groban?"

"Oh yes, miss. Mr. Barry informed us of your music preferences. Any particular CD that you want to hear?"

"Yes, the new one please, *All That Echoes.*" I sit back as the music fills the car. I relax and start to feel much better. The limo pulls up to the door of my apartment and I get out. "Thank you for the ride. Will you be stalking me or does someone else have that privilege?" I ask.

"I just drive the limo, Miss Kennedy. Your personal safety is in the hands of Luke," he answers me.

"So, you don't have a gun?"

"I am sorry. Yes, I am armed. We can't be too careful when it comes to you and Mr. Barry," he replies.

"And exactly why is that, please? What do we have to be careful of or whom do we have to be careful of?"

"I can't answer that," he says, and I know our discussion is over.

I walk wearily into my apartment. I see on the table the package and envelopes that Sandy texted me about. I don't open the letters, but the box peaks my curiosity.

I cut the strings and then untie the ribbon. I remove the top and tear through tissue paper. What comes into view stops my breath. A dress that looks like spun silver. I gingerly remove it from the box, holding it up to me. It has a sweetheart neckline, skimming down my body to the floor. Also in the box are a pair of silver Jimmy Choo shoes with a five-inch heel and a pair of silver elbow-length gloves. Past that, I find a matching clutch and, finally, a black velvet box. With shaking fingers, I open the box to find a card. Under the card is a diamond and emerald necklace with matching earrings set in platinum.

I set everything back down on the table and open the card.

To my lovely Brook,
The enclosed is for you to wear on Friday night.
We have tickets to the Metropolitan Opera House
Our dinner reservation is for 6:00. I will pick you up at 5:15.
Until then, I am yours,
William

I can't even form a coherent thought. I read the note a few times more and then sink back on the couch. I am way out of my league here. We had the photo date, then dinner, coffee, and then Miami. Yes, we spent a night and morning in each other's arms, but we have been dating for four days. This has to be some kind of land speed record.

I find my phone in my pocket and call him. He answers on the second ring. "Brook, darling. I hear that you got home safely."

"Yes, I did, William. Then I found a box in my kitchen and I opened it. What I found inside is frankly stunning. I am calling to tell you that I can't accept it. It is too much."

"You can and you *will* accept it. I picked these items out for you myself. If you were not to accept them it would crush me and I might never recover."

"I doubt that you are so fragile, William. I mean it, this is too much."

"It is enough to know that I want you to have them. They cannot be returned. Let me see you in them Friday night, please, Brook."

"I will think about it. We have a lot to discuss on Friday. What are you doing now?"

"I am pining away for my beloved. Wishing that she were here or I were there," he says poetically.

"What did you do today, you sap of a man?"

"Do not cast disparaging names upon me. I shot all day in the Everglades. I have been bitten by every fowl creature in Florida. I have bites on top of bites. You will think I have the pox when you see me," he says with a small chuckle.

"No one gets *the pox* anymore, William. You are positively medieval. I admit that I have missed you, too. I have had so much company for the last few days, however that I haven't had much time to myself."

"Rest tonight, Brook, because when I get there you will have very little rest. I plan on spending as much time in you as I can."

I begin by doing my laundry Thursday morning. Cleaning and some grocery shopping soon follow. Around 3:00, I decide to go for a run. I warm up in the apartment so I can hit the pavement running. As soon as I run a few blocks, I spot Samwise Gamgee, my sidekick for today. I call him that because of his overly large feet. He should be able to keep up with me, covering twice as much asphalt as I can with my small feet.

I enter Central Park and go all out. With Josh singing to me and the sun shining, I clear my head and focus on my breathing and heart rate. I am almost to my halfway point where I turn to start back when a guy on a bike moves right into my path, hits me, knocking me down. I skid along the ground and onto the grass. He jumps off his bike and runs to me, saying, "I am so sorry. I just got this bike and I am not used to riding it yet. I zigged when I should have zagged."

He barely finishes his thought when Samwise is on him. I watch in mock horror as he pushes the cyclist to the ground and puts a gun put to his head. Sam is yelling, "Stay still and I won't shoot you. Who are you?" He takes handcuffs out and puts them on his wrists. While the bike man is trying to figure out what is happening to him, Sam comes over to me to assess my injuries.

"I am fine, jerk." I say. "This is an accident. He crossed my path, that is all. He didn't do it on purpose, for Gods sake," I yell at him. "Talk about overreacting." I walk over to the man to apologize.

"What the hell?" the man says. "I said I was sorry. Are you a celebrity or something?"

"I am the girlfriend of a nut job with more money than sense," I say.

Sam puts his gun away and moves to remove the handcuffs. Sam tells him, "You need to be more careful. The next time you could get hurt."

"I am going to get rid of the bike and join a gym." Then he looks at me, "You don't belong to a gym do you?" I shake my head no. He gets on his bike and turns to me again. "I am sorry, and I hope I didn't hurt you."

"You didn't. And I'm sorry about the overreaction." I watch him ride off and then I turn to Sam. "Are you crazy or something? You put a gun to a man's head for bumping into me?"

"I have my orders, Miss Kennedy. To protect you with my life if necessary."

I am so having a discussion with a certain English twit on Friday. I jog back to my apartment, watching every movement lest I cause some poor unfortunate soul to be pummeled by Samwise.

After I shower, I open one of the letters that came for me. A modeling agency has received the pictures that William took and is interested in working with me. The other five have the same basic information in them. *Please call to set up an appointment.* I said before that I like when a man takes charge . . . I am beginning to doubt the wisdom in that. William has taken charge of every aspect of my life so far. I put the letters aside to think about it later.

I am on the phone talking with Millie when my doorbell rings. I look through the peephole and I think I'm looking at Link. Opening the door I say, "Hi, are you Link?"

"That would be me. And you are Brook for sure," he says.

"Why 'for sure'?"

"Sandy described you as tall, with long, beautiful, sandy blond hair and emerald green eyes. She left out drop-dead gorgeous, though."

"Thank you. Nice to finally meet you, Link. Come in."

"Thanks. Sandy told me I was disturbing you with my friends with benefits. I want to apologize for that. I had no idea how thin the walls are here. I never heard anything from you. I didn't think it was because you were so quiet," he confides.

"Don't worry about it. I had fun talking about your conquests. I got you back."

"I know Sandy told you about us. We really hit it off. I like her a lot. I wanted to let you know that if you need anything, I am right next door. I work for an ad agency and I do some work from home."

"Thanks. It was nice to meet you. Take care of Sandy for me. She is a great person."

"I know that already. See you around."

I start out Friday morning at the salon for a manicure and pedicure. As I tell my clinician about my uberdate, she comes up with a fantastic way to do my hair and make-up. I decide to splurge and go all out. When I leave the salon, I look like I stepped out of Vogue *Paris*, just with sweats on. So, the illusion is only neck deep. I will fix that later.

At home, I shave, wax, and moisturize. William tells me how soft I am~this is why. At 5:00, I am dressed and waiting for my William. The doorbell rings and I open the door. There is William in a tuxedo and a wide smile. "Brook, you look extraordinarily beautiful. I am a fortunate man to be escorting you this evening. I will be the envy of every man in New York." He walks in and takes me into his arms.

"And you are devastatingly handsome tonight. I, no doubt, will have to fight off some female admirers."

"No need. I can't see anyone but you." He bends down and kisses me. "I know I risk messing up your make-up, but I had to kiss you."

"Kiss all you want. This lipstick doesn't come off. It is William-proof."

"Clever girl. I have missed you. Now you are mine until Sunday afternoon. I know we have some things to iron out, but I am starving. Shall we?"

He helps me with my shawl. I get my clutch and off we go. I see Luke waiting for us by the limo. "Good evening, Luke," I say. "How are you?"

"Fine, Miss Kennedy. How are you this fine day?"

"Very good, thank you." I step into the car and William gets in next to me. "Where are we going for dinner?" I ask.

"The Russian Tea Room. Have you ever been there?"

"Never. And what is at the Met?"

"A ballet about you . . . *Sleeping Beauty*."

We make our way to the restaurant through light traffic. It is a beautiful balmy evening with a slight breeze. The kind of night made for lovers. Think of lovers, I remember Link. "I forgot to tell you, I met my neighbor last night. He and Sandy have become an item. He came over to introduce himself."

"I know all about him, Brook. He works for a prestigious ad agency here. He has a good reputation in the field and has never been arrested. He does not have a gun permit. His family lives in Iowa and he visits them regularly."

"Stupid me, I should have known you would know everything about him. What size does he wear, William?"

"I will have to look at the report and get back to you with that," he says with a smirk.

"What is going on, William? Why the surveillance and the bodyguards? Are you checking up on me?"

"No, I trust you absolutely. I trust no one else except my people with your safety."

"Who am I in danger of getting hurt by, William? Yesterday, Samwise Gamgee pulled a gun on a guy who bumped into me when I was running."

"You named a highly-paid professional bodyguard after a fictional hobbit. And isn't it Robin and Catwoman in LA? Are you hung up on sidekicks or something?"

"I don't need babysitters, William. Surely you know I am a grown woman, as you have already demonstrated." I hear a loud growl.

"Don't remind me, or you will make me hard and I have dinner and the ballet to get through." He closes his eyes as if to concentrate. He is so handsome sitting there, I can't even be mad at him.

I lean over and kiss him. "Do not think that this conversation is over, mister. I will have answers or you will have blue balls. Do they have those in England?"

"Unfortunately, yes, and I have acquired them on many an occasion."

"Good. Then we are on the same page, darling," I say with a tip of my head and a big smile.

CHAPTER 7

WE ENTER THE RESTAURANT AND I feel as if we have entered a set from *The Godfather*. We are seated at a table against the wall. The maitre d' pulls the table out for us and we snuggle in behind it. William sits next to me, immediately puts his hand on my leg and squeezes it. I am completely charmed by the place. "William, this is lovely. Thank you for bringing me here."

"As ever, darling, you are easily pleased. You amaze me, Brook. You find such wonder in the common. I love looking through your eyes."

We are given a menu but I don't open mine. I can't stop looking all around me. I am sure that some of the people here are stars or directors and the like. I imagine them discussing their next projects. William brings me back to him by asking, "What do you want to eat, darling?"

"You order for me, please."

William orders Chicken Kiev and Kulebiaka. This is a salmon dish. I take William's hand and put it behind my shoulder. I burrow into him. "Now it is just the two of us, William. It is time to spill," I say, coyly.

"How much do you know about being in the Royal Family, Brook?"

"They smile a lot, attend ribbon cuttings and wave funny. I almost forgot, cheat on their wives."

"Yes, we are all that. We are loved and hated. Some want to keep us and some not. I am part of the Royal Family and I have business dealings in the private sector. A few years ago, our family business had a problem. I won't bore you with all of the details, but suffices it to say, we pissed off some people with some tough decisions that we made. One of those decisions caused a man to lose his grip on reality~killed his wife and three children. His wife's family wants what they think is justice, not only from him but also from my family. They have threatened to take from us what we hold dear."

"You think that means me?"

He cups my face with his hand. Looking into my eyes, he says, "If they really want to hurt me, yes. That is what *I* would do, because you are the dearest thing I have."

His statement almost makes me cry. I pull his head to me and kiss him. "Okay, I won't give you or my sidekicks a hard time again. If you think this is necessary, I will play along. Do you carry a gun, William?"

"Yes, I do. This is serious, Brook. They have made attempts with my sister and my mother."

"I am so sorry, William. They must have been so frightened."

"It was last year and it shook all of us up. Revenge clouds your mind and you are willing to do anything, hurt anyone, for it. My sister was with her children, two of her friends and their children. They all would have been killed if not for a tip."

"Unbelievable. I can't imagine that much hate. Why can't the police do anything to help?"

"Quite. They are very smart and cover their tracks thoroughly," he says. "But tonight is for us. No more of this talk for now. I want to enjoy being next to you."

Our meal comes and we share it. I feed him some salmon and I get chicken in return. This feels very intimate to me and I enjoy the experience. The food is divine, the wine delicious. I pass on desert, as I am too full with dinner. As we leave we are stopped by the manager. "Mr. Barry, good evening. I hope you enjoyed your dinner."

"Very much so, thank you."

"May I be so bold as to say that you and your lovely lady look stunning together. I hope you have a most pleasant evening."

"Thank you. Goodnight." William responds.

It is a few-minutes drive to the Met. I sit close to William in the car and hold his hand. "I am having a wonderful time, William. Thank you."

"You are welcome, my beauty. You have collected another heart it seems."

"Sorry? What heart?"

"The manager of the restaurant. He is in love with you."

"Really! I seriously doubt that."

"No doubt, darling. I have seen it before. Lust in a man's eyes. If you look, *I* have it around you all the time."

Luke pulls up to the entrance and opens the door for William and me to get out. I take his arm to walk in. As we walk, William says, "I am glad you wore this tonight. I worried that you wouldn't."

"I followed your request, William. I wore everything that was in the box. The problem is I was missing two articles."

"I don't follow you. What was missing? I see the dress, shoes, gloves, purse, and jewelry. What is missing?"

"Under things, William. No bra or panties. There weren't any, so I don't have any on."

I watch his face darken and his breathing alters. He leans toward me and whispers in my ear, "*You* are not wearing any underwear?"

"None."

"And you tell me this *now*. Knowing that I have to sit through a ballet next to you."

"Anticipation is part of desire. Desire part of seduction. Seduction part of my grand plan," I say with a smile and a wink.

He groans. "I didn't think you were so literal, Brook, or I would have included the said items. I can see that life with you will not be dull."

We are shown to our box. We have a fabulous view of the stage. This is a magical place. The performance starts and I am transported to a fairytale. The music and the dancing are striking. I have never been to a ballet before. There is very little scenery and it seems to be all about the music and the dancers.

Even though I don't want it to end, there is the final curtain call. I look at William, smile and tell him, "That was so amazing,

William. Thank you for taking me. I have never seen anything like this."

"I watched you through the whole performance. Your childlike wonder was spectacular, Brook. I am completely under your spell. You own me. Tell me what you want and it is yours."

"That's simple . . . you. Not your title or your money. I loved this whole night, but I would have been just as happy watching a movie in your arms. I am a simple girl with singular desires. I just want you and to be happy."

Walking out to the car, William asks me if we are going to my place or his for the weekend. I answer," I think I would like to go to yours. I feel funny now that I have met Link, knowing that he would hear us making love. I have never done that in the apartment and I don't know how much noise we would make."

"Luke, we will be going home tonight. Miss Kennedy has a nosey neighbor."

"Very good, Mr. Barry. Miss Kennedy." Luke nods to me, smiling.

The ride to Williams home is punctuated with kisses. When he lets me look out the window, I can see that we are on Fifth Avenue. Luke pulls over to a gate and it swings open allowing us to enter. The sign outside reads 800 5th Avenue. William lives just a few blocks away from me, but in a completely different world. Luke parks and opens the door to let us out. William escorts me to the elevator and it opens for us. I watch as he presses the button for the top floor (of course). In seconds, the door opens and William takes my hand. We walk to his door and he opens it, swinging it wide so I can walk in first.

I step onto a white marble floor, surrounded by stunning paintings and three marble busts~Eros, Shakespeare, and a nude woman. "Who is she, William?" I ask.

"Venus. The most beautiful female form until I met you."

"Flatterer. The busts and the paintings are dramatic."

"Thank you. The kitchen is to your right. Through the kitchen is the dining room and next to that is my office. Next to that is a second bedroom. The living room is here on the left.

I walk into it and the view of Central Park in the floor-to-ceiling windows is breathtaking. There are very dark hardwood floors. I ask William, "What kind of wood is this? I have never seen anything like it before."

"It is Macassar Ebony, also known as Calamander wood. It grows in Southeast Asia. I had it brought here and installed. I like the gold streaks in the wood. It adds character."

"It is so different and beautiful," I answer. The furniture is covered in a deep burgundy fabric with geometric pillows in gold. Bookcases line one side and the room still has a huge appearance.

"Our bedroom is next on the left." he says smiling. I hone in on the word 'our'.

I enter the bedroom. It has the same floor as the living room and the same view of the park. A massive bed is facing the windows, with cream-colored coverings and at least twenty pillows of varying sizes and shapes. A two-person chaise lounge covered in a gold fabric is on one side.

"Your closet is over there," he says pointing. "This one is mine. The bathroom is through this door." He walks over to turn on the light. I follow him to the bathroom. It is done in beige marble with flecks of gold. There is a large jetted tub and a separate two-person shower.

"You are very quiet. What are you thinking?" William asks.

"I think that you are very rich. Even more so than I originally thought. I think you must be crazy. What is your family going to say when you tell them that you have chosen to start a relationship with a poor airline attendant? You will be disowned." I say frowning.

He walks over to me, takes me by my upper arms, and says, "I don't give a fuck what my family or anyone else thinks. I have done what they asked of me. I have to be happy with my choices too. You don't know how amazing you are. How much you have to offer me. I may have the money but you have a soul, a spirit, which I lack. We balance each other, Brook. Can you see that?"

I look into his eyes and he is serious. I reach up, undo his bow tie and unbutton his shirt. Neither of us speaks. I pull his shirt out of his pants and take off his jacket, placing it on the counter. Then I slide off his shirt and put it on his jacket. Smiling, I feel his chest with my hands. "Right now, my spirit is hoping that your body would like to make love with my body. What say you, Mr. Barry?"

He turns me around and unzips my dress allowing it to float to the floor. As promised, I have nothing on underneath. I hear him groan in his chest. He helps me step over the dress and into his arms. He picks me up, walks over to the bed and sets me down on the edge. He removes my shoes, cups my face with his two hands and kisses me. "My body would like very much to make love to you, Brook. Help me off with my pants and you will see just how much my body wants this."

I unbutton his pants and let down the zipper. He slides out of his pants and boxers. Kicking off his shoes and yanking his socks off, he stands before me gloriously nude as I am. Looking at him I raise my eyebrow at him and ask," Magnetized?"

"Engorged and waiting to please you," he answers me.

CHAPTER 8

"YOU FIBBED TO ME, WILLIAM."

"Did I? How did I fib?" he inquires.

"You told me you were like a gas tank that once emptied needed time to fill. You emptied four times last night with very little time for refueling."

"It must be your sexual influence, darling. Or perhaps pent-up energy. I am not complaining, are you?"

"Absolutely not. You can four-me anytime."

He runs his fingers through my hair and down my back. "Your hair is so soft and it smells so divine." Turning to face me, he asks, "What would you like to do today?"

"I'm good right here. Very comfortable."

"Would you like to go for a run? We could do some shopping. Take in a movie?" he asks.

"You can always talk me into a run, but what do *you* want to do?"

"After breakfast, we will go for a walk and if we happen to run, so be it."

"I am going to take a shower and then I'll make us something to eat."

"My housekeeper, Angela, is here. She loves to take care of me. She is my American mum. Breakfast is probably made as we speak."

"Do you want to shower with me?"

"I thought you would never ask," he says with a grin.

Clean is such a relative term because if you are to become clean, first you have to get dirty. William and I accomplish this in the shower.

While I dry my hair, I ask William, "Do you know where Luke put my bag last night?"

"It is probably in the gallery. I'll go look. You should check out your closet." he says, pointing.

I walk back into the bedroom to the closet door and open it. Lights automatically come on and I walk in. The closet is bigger than my whole apartment. There is an entire wardrobe hanging inside it. To my left, blouses and tanks over skirts and pants. Ahead, dresses from cocktail to formal and on the right, suits. Down the center of the room is what looks like dressers back to back with a marble top the whole length. I open a drawer and inside are bras. The next is panties. I find nightgowns, running clothes, bathing suits . . . nothing is left out.

"William, what is all of this?"

"I want you to feel that this is your home too, Brook. I don't want you to pack to come here." He comes behind me and wraps me in his arms, "I want you happy here and comfortable."

"This makes me *un*comfortable. I don't need all of this, William. It is too much. I will never even wear all of this."

"Yes you will. Put something on and meet me in the kitchen. I want to introduce you to Angela. I can't wait to see her face."

"Her face? Why?"

"I have never had an overnight guest before," he says as he waltzes out of the door.

Just like that, my objections are dealt with, William-style. Everything is so matter-of-fact with him. *You'll wear everything and that is it.* I can't keep up with him. I put on a pair of running shorts and a tee shirt. I put my hair in a ponytail and go out to meet Angela.

"And here she is," William says, coming over and kissing my forehead. "Brook, this is Angela. Angela, my girlfriend Brook. The two ladies that I cannot live without."

"So nice to meet you, Miss Kennedy. I trust that you slept well," Angela says.

"Yes, thank you. It is so nice to meet you. William tells me that you are his American mum."

"I guess I am. It is my pleasure to take care of him. Will you have breakfast out on the terrace, sir?" she asks William.

"Yes, please, Angela." he answers her. "Brook, I'll show you the rest of the house."

We walk through the typical New York City kitchen. Compared to the rest of the house, it is small. The restaurants are fabulous here so we do tend to eat out often. His dining room is decidedly masculine, with heavy dark wooden chairs that I doubt I can move. A credenza with beautiful cut glass decanters full of various colored liquids and matching glasses. Floor-to-ceiling windows with a glass door in the center. Through the door, I can see the terrace.

Williams's office walls are lined with framed photographs. I stand in front of them to study them. "William, these are remarkable. Did you take them?" I ask.

"Yes, they are mine. I am glad that you like them. I only frame the ones that I love."

I walk the wall, looking at each of the pictures. I recognize many of the shots and he has been everywhere. I see all of Europe, South America, Asia, Africa and the Far East. Mixed in with all of the wonders of the world is a picture of me sitting on the bench in Central Park. I am smiling and feeding what is left of my sandwich to a pigeon perched on the back of the bench. *He only frames the ones he loves.*

"Come on, let's have breakfast. I'm starved," he says.

"I'm not surprised. You are getting extra exercise lately. Using up calories faster," I tease him.

We walk back to the dining room and out on to the terrace. Angela has set a table for us. I grab a cup of coffee and one for William. Breakfast is an assortment of muffins and pastries, eggs and bacon. I don't eat much because we are going out to run. I can't run on a full stomach.

"Does Luke live here in your house?" I ask, curious.

"No, his apartment is next door. It is slightly smaller than this one."

"Is it his or yours?" I probe further.

"I provide it for him. I have already told you that I have money, Brook. This is not a surprise to you, right?" he says looking at my reaction to his information.

"Everything that you do is a surprise to me, William. The first time you kissed me, I entered paradise and I guess I will reside there as long as I know you. I don't mean the money . . . I mean you.

"That, Brook, is probably the most wonderful thing anyone has ever said to me. You take my breath away on a regular basis."

From where I sit I can see a glassed-in staircase that seems to go to the roof. Curiosity gets the better of me and I ask William, "Do the repair people have to come through your home to fix something on the roof?"

"Not exactly. Follow me and I will show you."

We walk over and climb the stairs to the roof. As I get near the top, I can't believe what is in front of me. It is a rooftop Garden of Eden. Trees and flowers, a pond with a waterfall, seating areas and an outdoor kitchen. I turn my shocked face to William and say, "You did this? I can't believe how beautiful this is. Who else has access to this?"

"Just us, Brook. This is my personal piece of heaven. I come up here to escape from the world. At night, it is a wonderland of stars, but you can still hear the sounds of the city. It is magical."

"Have you ever made love to anyone here?"

"Not yet. Are you offering?"

I grin at him and giggle. "I might be talked into it. Maybe after a few glasses of wine and in the dark."

"Come on. Daylight is burning. We can walk and plan our evening."

We walk together through the park, holding hands and talking. Anyone looking at us would guess that we are comfortable with each other, as lovers should be. As we walk, he periodically lifts my hand and kisses it. We stop walking and he pulls me to him and kisses me. The way he kisses me is almost embarrassing because it is so intimate. I want to tell us to get a room.

As we head back, William says, "I want to take you dancing tonight. We could go to the Copacabana. I have been there several times. The music is always great and the drinks flow. Does that sound like fun?"

"I would love to dance with you. The Copa is fine with me. Would you mind if I called my friends Millie and Carol to see if they want to grab a date and join us?"

"I would like very much to meet your friends. Tell them we will meet them at the door around 9:00."

I call my girls. Millie has plans for the evening, but Carol will meet us with her date, Luca. I have not met Luca so this will be interesting. Carol tends to go for the real urban male. I can't wait to see who she shows up with.

BACK INTO THE CAVERN OF a closet. Fingering through the clothes, I stop on a deep red cocktail dress, very short and low-cut. Thinking about the colors in Williams's living room I figure this must be a color he likes. I smile at the thought of going panty-less again. This dress is too short for that. Bending over would be a photographic moment. I try on a pair of black five-inch heels and I like the way my legs look. Dating a tall man gives me more options in footwear.

I step out of the closet dressed and ready to go. William turns to look at me. I see him close his eyes and when he opens them, there is a fire there. He walks over to me and takes me into his arms. "If I had known how stunning you would look, I would have not suggested going out. Every man who sees you is going to have a wooden problem tonight."

"I doubt that, except maybe for you. If we weren't meeting people I would say forget it and stay home. I can't do that to Carol."

We get to the car and Luke opens the door for me. He smile, "You look especially happy this evening, Miss Kennedy."

"I am, Luke, thank you."

"Go ahead, Luke, you can tell her she looks like a million bucks," William jokes.

"Yes, sir, that too!"

When we arrive at the Copa, there is a long line outside. My face falls, showing my disappointment. "I don't think we will get in, William," I say.

He laughs at me. "First, that dress will get us in, but not to worry. We will have no problem. Do you see your friend?"

"She is in the line, at the back."

Luke pulls over and lets us out. I walk over to Carol, with William beside me. "Hi, Carol. I want you to meet my William. William, this is my dear friend Carol."

Carol stares at William a few seconds before she awkwardly says, "So good to meet you, William. This is my date, Luca."

William and Luca shake hands. William says, "Step out of the line, please, and come with us."

The people in line seem to protest our advancing to the front. William has his arm around me protectively. When we get to the door, William greets the doorman, "Hi, Joe, how is the family?"

"Good, Mr. Barry, growing like weeds. Here for the evening?"

"My beautiful lady and her friends want to dance."

"You came to the right place. Enjoy yourselves." He opens the barrier and lets us in.

"Is there anyone that you *don't* know?" I ask him.

"There are a lot of people that I don't know. Luckily for us, they aren't doormen."

Once inside, a woman walks over to William and says, "Mr. Barry, welcome back. How many are in your party?"

"Four, Bri. Not too near the celebs, please."

We follow Bri to a roped-off section. She opens it and shows us to a booth. We sit down and Bri says, "Your server will be right over. Have a nice evening."

I see Luke at the door with his arms crossed over his chest. His eyes sweep over the crowd, stopping from time to time to stare at someone as if he is assessing them. I lean close to William and whisper, "Luke doesn't look happy. Is everything okay?"

"Luke doesn't like crowds. Doesn't like us in them."

"Are you worried?"

"Somewhat, but I have the most beautiful woman next to me and all I want to see is her."

Our server greets us and takes our drink order. The music is electric and the whole space is pulsing. You can feel it in the table and the seats. William looks at me and says, "We came to dance . . . shall we?" He holds out his hand to me. I take it with pleasure and he leads me to the dance floor. He pulls me to him with one hand on my upper back and the other flat on my ass. He swivels his hips into me and we move around the floor. We are dancing so close you could not put a sheet of paper between us.

"What are you doing, William?"

"Dancing. Staking my claim. I don't want to have to kill some guy for touching you. If they know you are mine, they will stay away."

I contemplate the words *if they know you are mine* and I smile. I know I'm his. Of this, there is no doubt in my mind. I hold him in my arms and tell him, "I am yours, William, and you, my sweet man, are mine."

"Is this a declaration, Brook, or just a statement of fact?"

I know if he is asking me if I love him, but I feign ignorance. "I am telling you that you don't have to piss on me to mark me yours. I wouldn't entertain any other man."

I can see in his eyes that was not the exact answer he was looking for, but, mercifully, he drops it. I know that I love him, but I am not comfortable enough yet to give him that information.

Carol and I catch up on the girl gossip. William and Luca hit it off, talking guy stuff. By midnight, I am very tired. William sees me and asks, "Are you ready to go, Darling?"

"Yes."

I say goodnight to Carol and Luca. William waves to Luke and we make our way to the door. We get outside and a few minutes later Luke pulls up. Joe opens the limo door for us and I get in. I see William pass Joe a very generous tip. William slides in next to me and pulls me close. "Did you have fun with your friends?" he asks.

"I had fun with them and especially with you."

I fall asleep on the way back to William's house. Luke opens the door and that wakes me. "Can you walk, darling, or would you like me to carry you?" William asks.

"I can walk, thank you. I am not drunk, just tired."

William opens the door to his home and I walk in. He guides me to the bedroom and starts to undress me. I look at him because he does this without the usual feeling and kissing. "Is something wrong, William?" I ask, concerned.

"No, darling." He continues to get me ready for bed.

"You don't want to make love?"

"You are exhausted and I am as well. Usually, that makes for a disaster. I want a rain check for the morning," he says, smiling.

He puts me in bed, strips off his clothes and gets in next to me. He pulls me close, kisses my head and tells me goodnight.

I wake curled up next to a familiar chiseled chest. William is on his back with his left arm over his head. I lift myself up and kiss his chest, moving my hand down to feel him. I look at his face and he is smiling. He says, "This new alarm clock I found has a great way to wake me up. I wish I had it in college~I might have made it to a few classes on time."

"No, you still would have been late," I answer, crawling over him to kiss him. He flips over, pinning me under him. And so my day begins . . . .

"I am going to go for a run this morning. I will be cooped up on a plane walking ten steps this way and ten steps back for six hours," I inform William.

"I have some calls to make and correspondence to answer. Lois Lane will run with you."

"Lois Lane? Is she my New York sidekick?"

"Yes, she is. Her name is Joyce, if you prefer. She is a former long distance runner. You might even grow to like her, "he says with a grin.

Taking my shuffle, I hit the street to the park. Joyce falls in behind me with a nod of her head towards me. I hit my stride, and, I have to say, she keeps up with me easily. With Josh singing to me, I cover the park. I slow down to jog back to William.

He greets me at the door with a kiss and a glass of orange juice. "I am all sweaty," I say. "Let me take a shower."

"I like you all sweaty. It is better when I make you all sweaty, but this will do."

I shake my head, drink the juice and head for the shower.

I finish dressing and look for William to say good-bye. I find him in his study looking over proofs. "Here you are. I have to get going. I have a 4:00 flight and I have things to do at home first. What does your week look like?"

"Slow this week. I have things to catch up on, but no work this week."

"We never talked about the modeling thing. I have six letters at home to deal with."

"I told you the camera loves you. The pictures are exceptional. You need to at least consider it, Brook."

"I'll take them with me. It will give me something to do at night. I'll call you. Maybe we can have phone sex again," I say with a smile.

"I don't want to let you go. Waking up next to you like this morning makes it more difficult to let you leave me."

"I confess, William, that I would stay and make love with you all day if I lived in my perfect world. Sadly for us, my world flies over the planet, bringing me with it. I will be back Wednesday night," I say, walking to him. I sit on his lap and kiss him.

Luke drives me home. I change the sheets and pack my bag. I write a note for Sandy about meeting Link. I leave for the airport early because I want to put in for some vacation time. I haven't taken a vacation in two years, so I have a few weeks. I want to go with William to England and spend two weeks.

I meet up with my girls at check in. "How was your weekend with William?" Regina asks me.

"Wonderful. We went to dinner and the ballet. Saturday, we went dancing at the Copa. It was perfect," I answer.

"You should see your face, girl. You have it very bad. Does he know?"

"I haven't told him and he hasn't told me. I guess we're waiting to see who jumps first."

We ready the plane and call the passengers to board. I am in the far back of the plane, doing our inventory count as they board. I work my way forward, helping passengers stow their bags. I finally make it to first class. Sitting there is Mr. Barry. I am in shock, but I walk to him. "Mr. Barry, how nice to see you again. I didn't know you were on this flight today."

"I have a few days off, so I thought I would spend a few days in Chicago and San Francisco with a friend of mine."

"Lucky for your friend." I say grinning.

CHAPTER 10

WE LAND IN CHICAGO. MY favorite passenger is waiting outside, standing next to a sleek red Corvette. I walk up to him and say, "Howdy, sailor, want to have a good time?"

He folds me in his arms and says, "Seven."

"Sorry, what did you say?"

"Seven. No *gardenias* until we make it to seven," he says with a huge grin.

I am in big trouble. I hope I can walk tomorrow.

William drives through the streets of Chicago. I decide to tease him. "You know, we can stay at the jump house with my cabin mates."

"If we stay there, Brook, when you come everyone will know it. If that's, what *you* want, what's the address?"

"I guess it *is* a bad idea. Where are we going?"

"The Four Seasons."

"Where is Luke? I thought you always traveled with him."

"I left him home to handle some things for me. I am here to protect you and I have help should we need it."

William pulls into the entrance of the hotel and a very happy attendant runs out to help us, saying, "Welcome to the Four Seasons, sir. May I take your bags and park your car?"

"We can get our bags," William answers. You can park the car if you promise not to break it."

"I will be very careful, sir," he says with a grin.

William tips him and we walk in to the hotel. The lobby is packed with people. I am looking around at the earth tones that make up the lobby area, when I hear the desk clerk say," Welcome back to the Four Seasons, Mr. Barry."

I bring my gaze to William. He looks at me and says, "What?"

"Do you know every desk clerk in every five-star hotel in the US?"

"I am well-traveled, as are you, Miss Kennedy. You stay in jump houses and I stay in hotels."

"Would you and Mrs. Barry like to have champagne and strawberries sent up, sir?"

"Yes, Mrs. Barry and I would love that. Thank you." He says with a huge grin. I stare at him. He smirks at me. "Come, Mrs., Barry, our room awaits."

We walk to the elevator and are whisked to our room. I say nothing, as the room attendant is with us. He opens the door and ushers us into the room. "Is everything to your liking, Mr. Barry?"

"Everything is fine, thank you." William tips him and he leaves.

I say, "Mr. Barry, you let them think that we are married."

"Yes, I did, and someday if I have my way, we will be."

"You shouldn't say that, William. We don't even know each other that well yet. You haven't seen me when I have a cold and I'm miserable. Or when I'm hormonal and difficult to get along with. The worst nightmare though, is Brook when the Packers or the Cubs lose. You don't *ever* want to see her."

"I hadn't figured you for a sports fan."

"Think about it, William. I live in New York, but I'm a fan of a Midwestern team. Do you really think I would talk about that around the rabid Yankee' fans? They would eat me alive!"

"Speaking of that Brook, we have a deal."

"What deal?"

"When you got into the car, I told you I wanted seven."

Mercifully, there is a knock at the door. William answers it and our champagne is brought in. He thanks the waiter and he opens the bottle for us with a grand flourish. The champagne is sweet and the strawberries bring that out even more. I take my glass and walk over to the window to look out at the city.

I feel William's warmth behind me. He wraps his arms around me and says, "I can't make any promises to you about the future right now. I have to untangle myself from some difficulties. Once I accomplish that, I will be able to ask you a certain question. I need some time and patience."

I turn to him and say, "William, I am not pressuring you in any way. If you asked a certain question now, I would say no. So you see, I need time and patience too." I kiss him passionately. "I'm having fun right now. I enjoy dating you. The sex is stupendous. Let's leave it at that," I continue.

"The sex is phenomenal. Unparalleled dates and the anticipation of more is killing me slowly," he adds.

"What do you want to do for dinner?" I ask as we watch the sun set. "I'm not very hungry."

"I was thinking of room service and eating in bathrobes, after a shower together, of course."

"Sounds lovely. I'll meet you in there."

William answers the door in his bathrobe. The waiter brings in our food and sets it up for us. I sit in the chair, wearing my robe, and chuckle.

"What is so funny?" William asks.

"That counts as two," I answer.

"No, it doesn't. Seven is seven, my rules."

William tips the waiter while I formulate my plan. I learned in college that attack is the best form of defense. I believe Mr. Barry won't know what hit him.

We eat our dinner, eyeing each other warily. "Something is going on in that beautiful head of yours. You don't think that I know you very well, but I can see your wheels turning," he teases me.

"My wheels are spinning around this delicious shrimp and Caesar salad that I am eating. Other than that, I don't know what you are talking about."

"I bet. Would you like to watch a movie after dinner? If not, I am taking you to bed."

"Why don't we see what movie is on in the bedroom."

He looks at me quizzically. "You want to watch porn?" he asks.

"A no. Do you?"

"I did a long time ago, in college. I hadn't figured you for a porn enthusiast~you sort of threw me there for a minute."

"I am into participation, not watching."

"That is good for me."

"I just thought we could watch something in bed. Cuddle and neck."

A short time later, with my head on his chest, we watch TV naked in bed. I slowly move my hand under the covers to feel him. "Easy, tiger," he says softly. "I have a lucky number to achieve before we get to that."

"Why is it always me first, William? I want to do something nice for you."

"I took several courses at university in human sexuality. I read studies done with hundreds of women. The overriding complaint from them was the lack of orgasm and the lack of caring on their partner's part as to whether or not they had one. You said yourself that you didn't remember your partners caring about your pleasure.

I want you to come to my bed willingly, happily, knowing you are going to orgasm with me every time. I don't want you to ever have to pretend you are asleep or have a headache to avoid sex with me. It will always be you first and then I will take my pleasure from your body, gladly."

With this said, he lays me back and then demonstrates his theory of female submission through multiple orgasms. He is right, of course. If you know in advance that your partner is going to take care of your needs and wants, it makes the submission so much more pleasant. With his theory tested and completed, he crawls up my body to look in my eyes. "Seven. My new favorite number, darling."

With my body covered in a sheen of sweat and my breathing ragged at best, I answer, "Me too! But I can't think right now, because you have wiped my mind clean of any coherent thought."

He chuckles saying, "My pleasure, Brook, purely my pleasure." He flips me over so that I am on top and says, "I want to see you, Brook. Your beautiful breasts, your body, for me to enjoy."

Smiling, I say, "My pleasure, Your Grace." I move on him and when I can see that he is close, I squeeze him as hard as I can. He throws his head back and yells my name and the most amazing look comes over his face. As he comes down from his climax he says to me, "Runners, with their lower-body strength, give what is undeniably the best orgasms ever. That was stellar, Brook. Thank you."

We sleep satisfied in each other's arms.

When I get to check-in on Monday, there is a message waiting for me. My vacation has been approved. I have two weeks with William in England. I fold the paper and put it in my pocket to show William when he boards. We ready the plane for our passengers.

"What did you guys do last night?" I ask Wendy.

"Christina got tickets to the Cubs game. It was great and they won, so all the better! In the bottom of the fifth inning, Josh Vitters hit a foul ball right to Regina. There was a kid behind her and she let him catch the ball and keep it," she answers me. "What did you do?"

"We had dinner and watched some TV. A very relaxing night."

"Mmmhhmm. Relaxing . . . I bet," she says with a smirk. "Where did you stay?"

"The Four Seasons. It's beautiful, Wendy. You wouldn't believe."

The passengers board and I hand William the paper. I see him read it in his seat. He looks up at me with a huge grin on his face. It looks like the second and third weeks of September, William can show me his England.

CHAPTER 11

WE LAND IN SAN FRANCISCO in the early afternoon. As I exit the terminal, William waits for me with yet another man toy. This one is a Jaguar XJL Ultimate in black. He opens the door for me to get in. The seats are like sitting on a marshmallow covered in butter.

"Do you like this car?" William asks me.

"It's magnificent, William."

"I think I might have to get one. I don't know if I want it for here or England."

"Get two," I tease him. "Where are we staying?"

"At the Ritz-Carlton. It's near Union Square, so you can go shopping."

"I don't need anything, so no shopping." I hear his loud sigh.

We pull up to the Ritz, and this time the valet is pulsing when he sees the car. William has some fun with him, and again tells this guy not to break it. William ushers me inside with his hand on my back. As we approach the desk the woman behind it says, "Welcome back, Mr. Barry. Your room is ready for you."

"Thank you, Greta. It is good to be back. How have you been?"

"Good, thank you. Will you need any reservations or tickets for your stay?"

"We haven't thought about that yet. If we do, I will call down to the concierge desk." He turns to me to see the *who-are-you?* on my face.

"What?" he says to me and then turns to Greta. "Greta, my lovely lady thinks I know every front desk clerk in every hotel in America. Will you please explain it to her for me?"

"Certainly, Mr. Barry. Miss Kennedy, Mr. Barry makes a concerted effort to learn everyone's name and even a little about him or her. I don't know if he writes it down or if he just has a great memory, but he always knows us. We, therefore, know him."

"See," he says to me quirking his eyebrow up.

I smile and shake my head. We walk to the elevator and ride up to our room. He opens the door and swings it wide for me to enter. I walk in and right over to the windows. The city view is striking. William folds me in his arms and kisses my head. "Change into something comfortable," he says. "I want to take you to Telegraph Hill to see the sunset. I'd like to take some pictures of you there."

I change and freshen up. We are back downstairs in half an hour. William hands his valet ticket to the attendant and he grins. The guy gets to drive the car again.

We head to Telegraph Hill so that William can take his pictures. We have an hour and a half until sunset and I am told he needs every minute to set this up. I watch William work with precision.

"I want a series of shots of the two of us. We start out holding each other. We get closer and closer, and finally, we kiss. With the sun setting behind us, it will look magical."

"What are you going to do with pictures like that?" I ask.

"Some will go into your portfolio and some on the walls of my home."

William positions me. When the sun is at the exact angle he wants, he steps over to me and holds me. He snaps the pictures with his remote. We move closer until only a breath separates our lips. Then he kisses me and I can hear the camera snapping away.

William walks over to his camera and takes it off the tripod to view the pictures. He motions for me to come and see them. "Look at the curve of your neck. The light on your hair and face." Then he finds the last picture before we kiss. "This is the million-dollar shot right here. This one is the prize winner."

The picture is striking. The sun is right between our lips, like a beam. "It's beautiful, William. Just like you are."

"Besides taking the pictures, I wanted to bring you here because it is on my top ten list of favorite places. I love the peace and the sunset." He takes me in his arms. "I want you to know that I am in love with you, Brook. Hopelessly, helplessly, and fully in love with you. I am over the moon and not likely to come back." He kisses me, winding his fingers through my hair, and then says, "I can only hope that you will love me at some point."

"You asked me the other day if I was declaring. I didn't really answer your question. Today I do declare that I love you too. I can't imagine ever being with anyone else. I want to wake up with you and go to sleep in your arms every night."

"Well, then, it is settled. We can't live without each other, so let's live together. When we get back to the city, will you move in with me?" he asks.

"I'd love to, but I have to keep the apartment. Sandy couldn't afford the rent without me. I won't leave her like that."

"I understand. I love you, Brook. Whatever you need to do, do."

I help him pack his equipment and we stow it in the car. "What do you want to do tonight?" I ask him.

"I thought we might have dinner at a jazz club and listen to the music. Les Joulins Jazz Bistro is near the hotel. The food is great and the music is the best in the city."

"Sounds French. I'm sure I'll love it."

William parks at the restaurant and we walk inside. The musicians have started to perform and I am drawn in by the sound. We enjoy our dinner and just being together. After a couple of hours, I ask William to take me back to the hotel. "With pleasure," he responds.

The tub at the hotel is so inviting that I decide I have to have a bubble bath. William has some e-mails and appointments to set up that will take him some time. I relax in my cherry-vanilla scented water thinking about the man in the next room. He loves me and I feel cherished by him. I decide while I prune that I am going to pursue the modeling. I have to find a way to tailor my schedule closer to his. I hate to give up flying, but William is very important to me.

I get out and dry off to talk to William about my decision. I open the bathroom door to see William in bed, his laptop next to him. He is sitting up naked with the sheet around his waist, sleeping. I wish I had his camera to have this shot to look at whenever I want. I step to his side of the bed and kiss him. His eyes pop open slowly as he kisses me back.

"You smell like a milk shake, Brook," he says.

"Cherry-vanilla. Do you like it?"

"Very much." He pushes the laptop away to make room for me. Shutting off the light, he takes me into his arms.

"When we took a shower together last week it was the first time a man has seen me naked with the lights on," I tell him.

"Really? Were you shy?" he asks.

"My first time I was seventeen. Justin didn't have much experience. I didn't even take off my shirt with him. The whole process took less than three minutes. The two years or so that we were together was pretty much the same. He was a fast finisher. In college, I met Craig. I never let him put the lights on. I look back on it now and it is silly, but then, I guess I was self-conscious about my body."

"You have nothing to be self-conscious about, darling. You have an amazing body, in and out of clothes. In fact, most of the time you stun me into silence."

"I never had an orgasm with Justin. I had some with Craig, but they were few and far between. *You* seem to have woken up the little powerhouse between my legs so much so that it could light up the entire city."

"That is quite a compliment, my love. Thank you. It's been my pleasure to do so."

"I can have this kind of discussion with you and not feel awkward at all. I have never felt that before. I am so comfortable with you."

"That is the way it should be with lovers. You can say what you want without embarrassment or shame."

William kisses me and runs his hands down my body. "Your body recognizes me, my scent and touch. It knows that I will take care of it and pleasure will result. Without as much as a minute of foreplay, you are ready for me. I find that remarkable."

I wake early in the morning. William is still asleep. I get dressed and go out for a run. I cannot go more than two days without it. Running releases endorphins, which acts like a drug that makes you feel marvelous. I run my five miles or so and head back to William.

When I see him, I know he is not happy with me. "Please don't go running without someone, Brook. I thought you understood the danger in this," he says glowering at me.

"I do, but you were asleep and I didn't want to wake you. At this time in the morning, there are very few people around. I was completely safe."

"Exactly my point, Brook. Few people around means less than likely someone will hear you if something happens. Please don't do it again or I won't be able to sleep, worrying you will sneak out without me."

"Fine, I won't go by myself again," I say with a childish tone.

He comes over to me and kisses me. "I can't bear the thought of something happening to you," he says squeezing me tightly.

"I am going to take a quick shower. What do you want to do today?" I ask attempting to change his mood.

"I thought we might go to Chinatown and Fisherman's Wharf."

"Sounds great. I'll be right out."

CHAPTER 12

WALKING AROUND CHINATOWN IS ALWAYS an adventure. There are dead, featherless chickens hanging in shop windows. The wonderful smell of food cooking in the air. The color red everywhere. We stop to watch a man making fortune cookies. This is really something to see. I thought they were machine made.

I see an herb shop and go inside to find some tea. The aroma of the herbs is overpowering. A tiny man shows me an ancient herb plant and points out potions that he has for me. He hands me a list with common ailments such as diarrhea, stomach cramps, gout, and even dry skin that he can cure with special teas. I look over the list to see if I suffer from any of them, and thankfully, I don't. I buy some green tea, thank him and leave.

I find William taking pictures of shops. I wrap my arms around him from behind and rest my cheek against his back. He asks me, "If I wern't here today, what would you be doing?"

"They would offer us shuttles for the day if we wanted them or we could sightsee."

"Where would you shuttle to?"

"LA, Portland, Seattle, even San Bernardino. We shuttle there and back today."

"Do you usually take it?"

"Not always, but half and half. I was going to talk to you last night about modeling but, I was sidetracked and bedded by a passing photographer."

"And did you enjoy the bedding part?"

"Very much, thank you. When I get back to the city, I am going to pursue modeling. I want to be able to try for a schedule that fits better with yours. If I can work more from the city, maybe we won't be apart as much."

"If that is what you want to do, Brook. I am trying to make my schedule so that we are gone at the same time and home together. Or that we are in the same city at the same time. It doesn't have to be all on you to make this work."

"You seem to be doing all of the giving so far. I feel as though I don't contribute at all to the relationship."

"I don't want you to ever feel that way. What you bring to us is immeasurable. I am happy and I have not been in so long. I have you to thank for that."

"But you see, I am too, so we are even in that respect. I am asking what would be easier for you. Having a girlfriend who is a flight attendant or one who models?"

"How about one that stays with me, travels with me, carries my camera around. That would be the easiest for me."

"I need some independence, William. If I had plenty of money and offered you the same situation, would you want it?"

"Probably not. Not because I don't love and want to be with you, but because of my own identity."

"See, you are very reasonable. That is why I love you."

We want to have lunch on Fisherman's Wharf. We get back to the car and drive there. We actually pass by the girls. I yell to them but they don't hear me. It is funny to me that I am usually with them . . . how much my life has changed in a few weeks time.

Fisherman's Wharf is a sight to see. Large pots boil right on the sidewalks. You walk up to a vender and are served whatever they are cooking right there. You want a crab, they open the pot, grab one and hand it to you. Clam chowder or lobster bisque in a cup or even a bread bowl right there and you keep walking. It is always crowded, but at lunch it is all of humanity in the same place at the same time.

William and I push our way through the throngs of people. I have lobster bisque in a bread bowl and William has a soft shell crab. We find a spot on the grass and sit down. "Let's not leave here, William. We can become like the hippies of the sixties and sell flowers to the tourists. Make love in an abandoned building and eat other people's leftovers. We will be poor, but happy."

"As appealing as you make it sound, darling, I think I like how we live slightly better," he says as he kisses my cheek.

We walk to the spot where they turn the cable cars around to buy tickets to ride one. We have an hour wait, so William drives me to Lombard Street. We drive down the "crookedest street" in the world. Eight hairpin turns make up this part of the street. It's fun and we laugh all the way down. We make it back just in time for our cable car ride.

William hangs from a pole taking pictures as we ascend the hills of San Francisco. He scares the crap out of me, holding on by his elbow. He snaps pictures of me with the city and the bay in the background. "You should see yourself right now, Brook. You shine, glow and shimmer."

"Forget being a photographer, William, and write poetry!" I tease him.

"With you as my muse, I could be Dante." He laughs.

After our ride, we go back to the hotel to freshen up. William wants to go to Vessel, a nightclub. Hercules & Love Affair will be performing. I guess he is a fan. I make him promise that we won't stay out late. I want to run the Golden Gate Bridge with him in the morning.

William escorts me into the club and we are seated. It must be slightly early, as it is still relatively quiet. As I have said before, I am a people watcher, so I look around imagining who is paired up with whom. As I am looking, my eyes rest on the handsome man that I came in with. I smile and ask him, "A penny for your thoughts?"

"I was thinking that I am a lucky man to be here with clearly the most beautiful woman in the room. Now where is my penny?"

"I am going to the ladies room and when I come back, I will fish around for one," I answer him. I get up, kiss him and look for the bathroom. One of the servers points out where it is and

I walk upstairs. I complete my mission and open the door to leave. A man blocks my path. "Excuse me, please," I say.

"A woman like you should never have to be excused," he answers. I smile, waiting for him to move. He comes closer to me and lifts his hand to touch my cheek. "You are stunning. What is your name?" he continues.

"Please get out of my way *now*," I say as I move forward, hoping he will move back. He doesn't. Instead, he opens his arms to hold me. The music is now playing very loud and lights are flashing. This gives his face a terrifying glow. I push him in his chest and as loudly as I can, yell, "Get out of my way." He grabs a fist full of my hair in the back and positions his lips to kiss me. I try to turn away, but he has a death grip on my hair. I try to punch him but I can't get any leverage to swing.

Just when I think I won't be able to stop him, I hear, "I think the lady told you to get out of her way and leave her alone. Unless you want a bullet to ruin your evening, I would reconsider her request."

The brute releases my head and backs away. I can now see that William has a gun to the ogre's head. I look at him and slap his face. "Don't you ever put your hands on me or any other woman again without her permission."

"Look, lady, I don't want any trouble. I was just looking for a kiss. You are overreacting, mister." Now *he* is sweating.

Over his shoulder, I can see whom I assume is the security for the club running up the stairs. He gets to us and asks, "What is going on here? Do you have a permit for that weapon, sir? Put it away now."

"This man accosted me. He put his hands on me and tried to kiss me. My friend came to my rescue and stopped him from hurting me further." I yell at them.

"Do you want to press charges, miss?" he asks me.

"No, I want to be left alone."

He looks at William. "I want to see your permit." William gets his wallet out and provides him with the information he requests. When he is satisfied, he lets us go.

We walk downstairs and I turn to William and ask," Would you mind if we just left?"

He smiles at me and says, "Not at all, darling."

We walk out to the car and I stop to hold him. "Thank you for saving me. I couldn't get away from him. How did you know to come upstairs?"

"I saw him go up right after you. Guys don't take that long in the bathroom. I had a bad feeling when he didn't come right back down. I just wanted to check on you when I saw him and heard you yell."

"He cornered me and wouldn't let me go. He was going to kiss me." I shake my head at the thought. William holds me and bends down to kiss me.

"I am the only one to have that privilege. He knows that now."

"Yes, you made that quite clear."

William gets me back to the hotel and into our room in record time. "Why don't you take a bath and I will join you after I make a few calls," he suggests.

I nod my head and make my way into the bathroom. I run the water very hot and a few minutes after I get in William comes into the bathroom naked. I smile and shake my head, "You are so comfortable with your nakedness. I hope I can be so someday."

"It is just you and me here. I don't have any shame with you." He gets in behind me and snuggles me to him, continuing, "Are you okay now?"

"Better. The gun scared me some."

"I know and I am sorry. It was a fast decision and I didn't want to have to beat him to a pulp. If he had kissed you, I would have hit him."

Once in bed, William holds me all night, sometimes kissing my head or stroking my hair. It comforts me just to feel him.

CHAPTER 13

WITH THE NEW DAY, MY attitude adjusts and last night is forgotten completely. William and I are at the east entrance to the bridge at 5:00 AM, when it opens for pedestrians. I love to run when most of the world is sleeping. I have the sensation that I get to see the day before anyone else does. It empowers me somewhat. The views of the bay and the ships are unreal. It is windy, and a few times, it moves me sideways. William laughs and tells me it's because I am such a lightweight.

The bridge is 1.7 miles each way. When we get across the bridge to Marin County, we run for another mile and then turn back. I need my five miles or more and William, God bless him, indulges me.

Our run finished, we drive back to the hotel. We have an 11:00 flight, so we shower and have breakfast. One last spin around town in William's fancy ride and off to the airport.

I meet up with my cabin mates, tell them about our adventures and hear about theirs. The flight home is, thankfully, uneventful and we arrive four minutes early. Luke meets William and me and drives us home.

After I settle in for the evening, William shows me the pictures he took in San Francisco. "I want to get these printed because you will need them for your portfolio tomorrow."

"Why tomorrow?" I ask.

"A friend who works for the Ford agency set up a meeting for you tomorrow at 2:00. If you don't like them, I have a business acquaintance with ties to Wilhelmina. I can have something set up for Friday. If you are going to do this, you have to start to work before the spring season starts."

"All I have to do is speak and you start the ball rolling. I just hope it doesn't run over me in the process."

"That is why you have me, darling. I will make sure you stay ahead of the ball."

William holds me in bed as he usually does. His strong arms comfort. As his fingers work through my hair, he asks me, "How would you feel about taking pictures of the two of us naked in bed? I want artistic pieces, not pornographic. I have a vision of what I want. If we take them and you don't like them, I can delete the images."

"What do you want them for?"

"My study and in here. Just a couple."

"Okay. As long as they aren't graphic and I don't feel uncomfortable looking at them."

"If they come out anything like what is in my head, you won't even know that it is us in the picture."

I kiss him and say, "Make love to me, William, please. Slow and gentle."

"That would be my pleasure," he says.

On my run through the park in the morning, I see Link. "How are you?" I ask.

"Good. I don't see or hear you at all anymore, Brook. Have you been at the apartment?"

"Not much. I stay with William when I'm in town."

"Good to see that it's going well."

"How are you and Sandy doing?"

"Great. When she is here, we do the same as you. Honestly, I don't know why you two keep the apartment."

"We have a lease until next May. I guess we will need to discuss it before then. Tell Sandy hi for me."

"I will. Take care of yourself."

When I get back to William, he has the bedroom all set up to take the pictures. "Jump into the shower and be quick, darling. The light in here is perfect right now. I don't want to miss it," he says.

"I'll be fast."

I come out of the bathroom with a towel around me and William is walking around naked. I wonder if I will ever be as comfortable in my skin as he is in his. I notice he has changed the sheets to a light taupe set.

"Lay down, Brook, on your side facing away from the camera."

He covers my legs and most of my butt with the sheet. He continuously looks through the camera, adjusting me until he likes what he sees. Taking his remote he lays down in front of me and places his hand, fingers splayed, on my waist. He takes several shots and then gets up to look at them. "Perfect," he says, almost to himself.

He comes back over to me and places me on my back. He fixes my hair the way he wants it and then gets in with me.

"This one is going to look like we are making love, Brook, but you won't see anything."

He moves my legs around him adjusting the sheet so you can see some of his butt but none of my parts. His arm will block my breasts. He will be kissing my neck so the back of his head will block my face from view. He takes several shots and gets up to see them. "Wow. It is better than I thought, Brook. I am finished for now, darling. I'll meet you in the dining room after I print these. Go and have your breakfast."

When I finish dressing and deciding what to wear to the interview later, I go to the kitchen for some much-needed coffee. Angela is there with my coffee ready. "Good morning, Angela," I say.

"Good morning, Miss Kennedy. What would you like for breakfast?"

"Just coffee and some fruit please." I take my coffee and fruit and walk to the dining room. A few minutes later William comes in with his breakfast. He hands me the pictures. I start to go through them and he is right, as usual. They are artistic and beautiful. Clearly it looks like we are making love, yet you see nothing except the love between two people. There is one where his hand caresses my cheek and it is so sweet. I think that one is my personal favorite.

"I want this one. I can see the love in you and me."

"That one and this one are the best of the bunch," he says, showing me another. In this one, my head is back and he is kissing my neck. That particular one almost makes me sweat. You can imagine him doing all sorts of improper things to me. We were not having sex when we took the pictures. Even though I know that, my imagination says otherwise.

William and I are on our way to the interview with the Ford agency. I'm nervous, but the good thing is that I have a good-paying job already. If this happens, okay. If not, that's all right, too. We enter the building and make our way to the office. There are pictures of several well-known models on the walls but the one that grabs my attention is one of Channing Tatum, *Magic Mike*, himself. I practically drool right there. William stands behind me and says," Interested, Brook?"

"He is beautiful. Married, but beautiful still."

"Do I have competition for your affections?"

"Absolutely not. I don't date married men. I am just looking. No harm in that."

We are escorted into a conference room, and William introduces me to a woman sitting there. "Brook this is Carline Jeffery. Carline and I have worked on a few projects together. Carline, this is Brook Kennedy."

"I am so happy to meet you, Brook. William has told me a lot about you and I have seen your intake pictures. Did you bring a portfolio with you?"

"Thank you for meeting with me. I did bring the portfolio." I hand it to her.

Carline looks through the pictures carefully. She smiles at the few William took in San Francisco with him and me. "I see your influence, William. I don't know why you don't do fashion. You have an eye for it."

"You know why I don't do it, Carline. I did that for a whole year. The most torturous year of my life. Models can be bitches. Sunsets and beaches rarely protest."

"So true. Brook, I see a lot of potential here. I would like to send you for hair and make-up and set you up with a stylist. Then we will take some headshots. Do you understand what you are getting yourself into?"

"I think so, but perhaps you could enlighten me further."

"Modeling is a dog-eat-dog profession. The girls will smile and be sweet to you but at the first opportunity, stab you for a job. They will put something in your soda to make you puke. Something in your make-up to make your eyes swell. All while asking you to go to dinner with them."

"You make it sound so lovely. I can't wait."

"If you reach super model status, you will have to take care to avoid the drinking and drugs. Too much partying will show on your face first. Your face and body are your money. Take care of it or else you are gone."

"I am mostly interested in working here in New York. I want a job that has roots for me. I am flying four days a week now. I would like that to be much less."

"You can do that, be a local model. But to achieve the big money you would need to do Paris, Milan and London. Not every day, but you will travel some."

"I'm not against traveling, just not every week. I want a life and not out of a suitcase."

"Alright. I will set this up and get back to you with the particulars. William tells me you are a Thursday through Sunday girl."

"That's me. Unless *this* takes off."

She looks at me and says," Brook, this *will* take off. I don't offer makeover's to the general public. We invest in you and you make money for us. Cause and effect."

CHAPTER 14

LUKE DRIVES US BACK TO William's house. I stare out the window, thinking.

"What is wrong, Brook?" William asks.

"Nothing is wrong. I am afraid to change, I guess."

"Why is that? You know that you don't have to, don't you?"

"Yes. Once I do, though, there is no going back. That is what scares me."

"I am right here, Brook. I love you and I am never going anywhere. I support whatever decision you make."

William has work to do at the house. I wander, around thinking, making my head hurt. I pour myself a glass of wine and go to the roof garden. This really is a magical place. I relax on the chaise and call Sandy. She answers on the second ring." Hey, girlfriend."

"Hi, Sandy. It's so good to hear your voice."

"What's wrong? You sound weird."

I end up telling her everything that has happened in the last few weeks~ the pictures, San Francisco, and William. Lastly, I tell her about the modeling. "You should do it, Brook," she says. "I have always told you how beautiful you are. You would have a more flexible schedule than flying. That means more time for William. Do you want to marry him? Have children?"

"I love him. I would marry him if he asked. I definitely want children with him," I say, thinking that a few weeks ago I told him I didn't know him well enough yet. Funny how things can change so quickly.

"What are you waiting for? You have the invitation from the agency. Take it, Brook."

"How are you and Link doing?"

"I moved in with him, which is funny because it's next door! I guess we are both paying for a place neither of us uses. We should sublet to someone."

"When the lease runs out, I don't think I will renew it."

"I'm happy where I am, too."

We talk some more about family and work and then hang up. Next, I call Christina, Regina and Wendy, in that order, to get their input. They all agree that I should explore the modeling. It is a new adventure, I am told by one. My last call is to my brother. I haven't spoken to him since William took the pictures of me in the park. This conversation takes longer. After I catch him up, I tell him about the modeling. He tells me that if I want kids I can't be flying off for four days a week and expect everything to be fine while I am gone. By the time I finish my talk with him, my mind is made up. I am going to model and I feel good about the decision.

I pour another glass of wine, thankful that I brought the bottle with me to the roof. I let the wine work its magic on me while I listen to the muted sounds of the city. A short nap later, William is standing over me. "I didn't mean to wake you, darling."

"It's fine. I called everyone I know to get his or her opinion on the modeling thing. I have decided to do it."

"What pushed you over the edge?"

"I want children. I can't be flying four days a week and expect my children not to suffer for it. I don't want to be a part-time parent."

He lays down next to me to cuddle and says," How many children do you want, Brook?"

"Two or three, I guess. That is what I can afford to put through college, feed and keep clothes on them."

"And what if money weren't a problem?"

"Then it would be three or four."

We lie there, kissing and talking. I finally get up to make dinner for us. William stops me with one last kiss and says, "Tonight, I want to make love up here under the stars."

"William, there are two buildings taller than this one with a view of this roof. People will see what we are doing."

"They won't see us after dark, Brook. Just try it. If you aren't comfortable, we will go back downstairs."

"The things you talk me into, William. It is a good thing you don't use drugs or I would be hooked by now. I can't seem to be able to say no to you."

William has a Vulcan stove in his kitchen. Six burners and a grill in the center~a cook's dream. Angela keeps the fridge and cabinets well stocked. As I look through, I decide on Caesar salad with lemon-grilled chicken. Just as I am finishing, I call him to come down to eat.

"As soon as I opened the door, I could smell this, Brook. What are we having?"

"Chicken and salad. I am a model now so I can't eat anymore."

"Brook, you run. You are the most fit person I know. You work out more than I do."

We eat our dinner. It is light and scrumptious. William says, "That was so good. Thank you. I am going to take a shower. I'll be on the roof with wine when you finish."

I clean up and put everything away. I don't want Angela to have to pick up after us if I can help it. When I get into the bedroom, William has finished his shower and is nowhere to be seen. I take mine and put on my silky bathrobe. I cross the terrace to the stairs. He's right about the dark. The stairs are lit, and without that light, I wouldn't see them in the dark. I climb to the roof and follow the path to the chaise. I see William waiting for me. "Hi, Mr. Barry."

"Good evening, Miss. Kennedy. You look particularly lovely tonight."

"Thank you. I have a date with a sexy, handsome man this evening."

"Do you now? Let me know when he arrives and I will give him my spot on the chaise."

I laugh. "I am already looking at him. I don't know if he knows how much I love him, but I plan on showing him tonight."

"Wow, this gets better and better. So exactly how are you going to accomplish this?"

I open his robe and kiss his chest. He lays back to enjoy the feeling. My hand wanders down to feel him. I continue my explorations and kissing downward. William says, "Brook, we have discussed this. I want to pleasure you. I don't need what you are planning."

"That may be so, but this is *my* seduction. You are so giving, and this is *my* giving."

I move to take him. I hear him moaning and his breathing alters. He protests, but I know from this reaction that it pleases him. I continue to take him pressing, harder and harder. I feel him getting close. Suddenly he sits up and holds my shoulders. He looks at me and says, "No more, Brook. Thank you. That was wonderful but I am not coming in your mouth, not now not, ever."

He turns me over and enters me slowly. He whispers in my ear, "You were made for me, Brook. I take care of what is mine. You are not a toy or a plaything. You won't be treated like one." He circles his fingers against my powerhouse and says, "We are going to do this together, Brook. You come and your squeezing makes me come."

"I love you, William," I tell him with a kiss.

I feel the shudder start and I am lost in my moment of complete satisfaction. William presses deeply and joins me in his moment. As our collective breathing returns to normal, he says to me, "And that is how it is done."

"It would appear so. That was amazing." I look up at the stars. I think they twinkle just for us.

After we finish the bottle of wine, we return to our bedroom. I sleep in Williams's arms, knowing that he will always take care of me and I will take care of him.

I go for my run in the morning. I'm sure I have a shadow, but this one is good at hiding. I can't pick him or her out of the crowd. I find that several people stay on the same course as me. I feel great today so I do eight miles before heading back to the apartment. When I get there, William isn't home.

Angela tells me he went to the gym downstairs. I hate gyms and he loves them. I want to be in the fresh air and sunshine, not stuck inside.

I take a shower and get some coffee from Angela. Taking the coffee, I sit on the terrace to enjoy the morning sunshine. My phone rings. It's Carline. "Hi, Carline. How are you?" I say.

"Fine, Brook, and you?"

"Great on a beautiful day like today."

"I hope my news adds to your good day. I have set up appointments for you on Thursday and Friday. Hair and make-up Thursday. On Friday, you'll meet with our stylist. I'll e-mail you the times and locations."

"Thank you, Carline."

"One more thing, Brook. I assume you'll need to give your two week notice to the airline?"

"Yes, and I was planning to let them know when I go in on Sunday."

"Good. That puts us on a schedule to get you some exposure before the spring line comes out. You will have a break around Thanksgiving. I know William was planning a trip for you to meet his parents in a few weeks. You'll need to put that off until then."

"I understand. That won't be a problem. They don't celebrate Thanksgiving in England anyway."

"I didn't even think of that. You're right."

I hang up just as William finds me. He is fresh from a shower, with wet unruly hair. He bends over to kiss me. "You smell delicious, William. Maybe I will have *you* for breakfast," I say.

"I rather thought I was desert. Well, at least I was last night," he says with a grin and a wink.

"I was just talking to Carline. She set up the appointments for next week. She asked me to give my notice at the airline. Our trip has to be postponed until Thanksgiving. Is that a problem?"

"No, I didn't even tell them we were coming yet. Are you happy about all of this? Above all, I want you happy, Brook."

I get up and sit in his lap, "This is where I am the most happy, but as I cannot sit here all day, I am fine with being here as much as possible."

"I agree, this is a great place to be and I, too, wouldn't mind if you stayed. Can you leave the airline and not look back?"

"I will miss my cabin mates and the flight crews that I work with. But I can still see them. The flying, I won't miss. Being away from you was hard."

"We will have to do what we can to work together. I might be persuaded to do some fashion. I know Carline asks me weekly to do it. I might make an exception to work with you."

"That would be wonderful. See if you can set one up for, lets say, Hawaii."

"You naked on a black sand beach. Perfect!"

"I didn't say naked," I protest.

"I did," he answers.

CHAPTER 15

SUNDAY I GET TO THE airport early. I have my letter of resignation. As I pass through check-in I think about how I will only do this one more time at this airport. When I reach our gates, I see Nancy at the closest one. I wave to her to wait for me. Nancy is my immediate supervisor. She greets me with, "Here is one of my favorite people in the whole world. How are you, Brook?"

"I am really good, Nancy. I need to give you this." I hand her the resignation.

She reads it and says, "This is not good news for me, Brook. You won't be easily replaced."

"Thank you, that's nice to hear. I will certainly miss all of you."

"May I ask what you are going to do?"

"I have been offered a job modeling for the Ford agency."

"That is so exciting! I will be walking through the airport and I could see you on an advertisement. I will keep looking for you," she says hugging me.

I board the plane and see Bill and Steve doing their final systems check. I poke my head in the cockpit and say, "Hey, guys. I want to let you know I handed in my resignation this morning. I'll be here this week and next. I'm sure whoever takes over for me will buy into the jump houses."

"Wow, meet a billionaire and leave us. Who didn't see this coming?" Bill jokes with me.

"Good luck, Brook. I can't think of a better person to have a great life. I hope he treats you like the princess you are."

"I am not getting married. I have a new job."

"A job? Where?" asks Bill.

"The Ford modeling agency hired me to model for them. I start in two weeks."

"Wow, I am impressed. We always thought you were hot, Brook, but this is great," Steve says.

I walk away smiling. I get a similar reaction with my girls. *Sorry to see you go but have a wonderful life and don't forget to call.* I go through my usual routine with the passengers. We land in Chicago and go to our apartment. I run in the morning and get back to fly out.

We land in San Francisco. I am offered a shuttle to Seattle, and because I want to stay busy, I take it. I miss William so the more I stay working, the less time I have to think. Anyway, being here alone is nowhere near as much fun as with him.

I am off to Seattle and turn around to fly back. Sunday morning, I leave to come home. The passengers board and we taxi out to the runway. Everything goes smoothly until we are forty minutes or so from New York. Regina comes to get me in first class. She looks scared and says, "There is a passenger who is thirty-two weeks pregnant. She says she doesn't feel well. I think she is in labor."

"How far apart are the pains?" I ask.

"They are running together and she says she feels pressure."

"Ask the passengers in first class to move to coach. Where is she?"

"Christina is with her."

I walk back and find Mrs. Chisinau in active labor. I look at Christina and she nods to me that we definitely have a baby coming.

"Regina is clearing first class. Move her up there and lay her down." I grab our in-cabin sound system mic to announce, "We have a medical emergency. Is there a doctor or nurse aboard?" No one raises a hand, so I continue. "a paramedic or EMT?" Still no one. I walk up to first class. "Inform the captain and see if we can land sooner," I tell Regina.

"Get the first-aid kit and any clean towels," I tell Wendy.

I shift my attention to the mother-to-be saying, "Mrs. Chisinau, my name is Brook. Is this your first baby?"

"No, my second," she answers.

"Good because this is my first. At least one of us is a pro. Do you need to push?"

"Yes, I can feel his head."

"Wendy, I need the kit and that book now!"

We get her out of her pants, lay her back down, and cover her with a blanket. "You and I are going to make friends fast," I say. "What is your first name?"

"Jeanie."

"Okay Jeanie. I need to look and see if I can see the head," I look and there it is.

"The captain said he can't land any sooner. Philli, can't take him and everything else is further away," Regina informs me.

"Tell him it's too late anyway. Just keep it steady so I can stay on my feet."

Wendy arrives with everything I need except a doctor. "Read what it says about childbirth," I tell her.

"It says to keep your hand in front of the head to prevent him from delivering too fast and tearing. Firm, but gentle, pressure," Wendy says.

"When you feel a contraction, Jeanie, you need to push," I say.

I can see her scrunch up to push. My heart is beating like a jackhammer. I put on the gloves that are in the kit and press my hand against her. I can feel the baby moving against my hand.

"Watch for the cord to make sure it is not wrapped around the baby's neck," Wendy continues to read.

Jeanie is screaming in pain. Children in the back of the plane are crying. One fool is pressing the call button, as if we don't have enough to do right now.

"Keep up the good work, Jeanie. He has moved out more. The next push and his head will be out."

The shoulders are next, and I know that has to hurt. I am breathing deeply trying not to hyperventilate. Wendy continues to read the instructions to me. I have to help guide the shoulders out. Exactly how do I do that?

I speak to Jeanie, "How does this compare to your first? Is it going the same way?" She nods to me. Okay, I know we are fine for now.

"Push, Jeanie." I stick my finger around the baby's shoulder and he kind of pops out. One more big push and I have a baby boy in my hands. I clean him with paper towels as best as I can and then hand him to his mom in a blanket. The passengers applaud as soon as they hear him cry. Wendy lets Bill know that there was one more soul on board. Bill informs the tower. I went to pour myself a glass of wine. Screw company policy . . . . let them fire me.

I strap the baby against me as well as I can, in my jump seat for landing. Christina sits next to us with her arm around him. Wendy sits with Jeanie and straps her in.

As soon as we land, the emergency crew boards to help Jeanie and her baby off. I clean up, but I am still covered in blood and god knows what else. The passengers disembark, congratulating me as they exit. Bill and Steve come out of the cockpit. Bill says, "Well, Brook, you sure know how to go out with a bang."

"You think I planted her in the hopes she would deliver? I have never been so scared in my life."

"You sure didn't show it," Wendy says.

We walk up the skyway and I can see lights and a lot of people. When we get to the end, there are television cameras and a crowd. Nancy walks over to me and says, "You never cease to amaze me, Brook. Can you do an interview about what happened?"

"I would just like to go home and take a shower."

"You can do that, but they will find you. It's better to get it over with now," Nancy adds.

"Fine," I say.

I walk over to the cameras. The reporters ask their questions and I answer them. They take their photographs, and thankfully, within a few minutes, I can leave. I walk out to see William waiting for me. He takes one look at me and runs to my side. "What happened, Brook? My god are you alright? You are covered in blood."

"I'm fine. I delivered a baby while in flight."

He starts laughing. "My knight in shining armor saved the day for some poor woman. I can't believe you delivered a baby."

"Look at me. I am covered in baby puke. I want to go home and shower. And then I want a really big glass of wine and a back massage," I say with a smile "And then I want you to show me how to get a baby."

"We can practice, but for now no baby-getting."

"I will settle for practicing."

CHAPTER 16

IT IS STILL ON THE news Thursday morning. They replay the video of Jeanie and the baby getting off the plane. Then my interview. William continues to tease me. I hope it will all blow over in a day or two. I dress to get my run in before my appointment. I get down to the street and there is a mob of news people outside the door. I back up to the security desk and ask, "Have they been here all night?"

"I am afraid so, Miss Kennedy. Do you want me to call the police to get rid of them?"

"Don't bother. Everyone says if I talk to them, they will go away." I walk out into the pack of wolves. "I am going on my morning run. If you want to talk to me, you better keep up."

I smile as I jog to warm up. After I lose half of them, I hit my stride and the rest disappear. I have Josh singing "Brave" to me and I *feel* brave. I helped a woman bring her son into the world.

I run six miles and when I jog back, they are waiting for me. I stop to face them.

"No, I do not have any medical training."

"No, I did not know the mother previously." Why would that matter?.

"No, she is not going to name her son Brook." Are you kidding me?

"No, I am not going to get a reward."

"No, this does not make me want to become a doctor." This is the best one.

I finish with the inquisition and walk to the elevator. William meets me at the door of the apartment and says, "I just saw you on the news downstairs. Maybe this will satisfy their need to know and they will forget about you."

"I hope you're right. They ask stupid questions."

Taking extra care in my shower to shave and moisturize everything, it takes me longer to complete. My face and body are my paycheck now. Funny how things change. William told me to dress comfortably, so I go with jeans and a shirt. William kisses me and I meet Luke at the car. A few minutes later, Luke drops me off and tells me to call him when I am ready to be picked up.

I meet Carline and she takes me to the floor for my new hair and face. "Don't worry, but I'm sure they will cut your hair some. Shorter hair is more versatile for pictures," she tells me.

"I'm fine with that. One thing about hair is that it always grows back."

"Very true. They'll teach you about what make-up colors are best for you. I think you look great now but I am not the professional. Ask questions and learn as much as you can. In the beginning, you will do your own hair and make-up. Should you be on a major shoot, they will have people there for you."

"Thank you for all of your help."

"You are quite welcome. Have fun, and I will see you tomorrow for the style part of this show!"

For the next four hours, I am worked on like Eliza Doolittle, being turned into a wellborn lady. When the team finishes, my hair has been cut and lightened. The make-up brings out my green eyes so that they almost glow. I've been sitting still in a chair, so instead of calling Luke to pick me up, I decide to walk. I want to watch people's reaction to me. An unguarded response is exactly what I crave. I can see them walking towards me, and with all of the windows, I can see if they turn around to catch the backside. This isn't about vanity. It is research into my marketability. If I can't sell myself, this won't work. I sashay down the street, giving all I have into my walk.

By the time I walk to William's house, I know that I will be able to at least make a living doing this. Women as well as men turn to watch me walk away. I can't sell to women if they are threatened by me, but if they turn to look at me they must not be. I open the door and walk into the gallery. I can hear William on the phone, "What do you mean she isn't there. When did she leave?"

I walk into the living room. He looks at me and visibly relaxes. He says," Luke, she's here. She just walked in. Thank you Luke." He walks over to me, grabs me, taking me into his arms and says, "Where have you been? I have been worried sick."

"I walked home. I needed to prove something to myself. Why?"

"You didn't answer your phone. They told me you had left a while ago. No one knew where you were. I thought something had happened to you, Brook. I thought you had been kidnapped."

"I am so sorry, William. I didn't think about that. I didn't realize that you would even know I had left."

He is holding me so tightly, I feel his relief through his whole body. "If anything ever happened to you, Brook, it would kill me. If you change your plans, please let me know. I know that you are not used to checking in with anyone, but this is a different situation because of who I am."

"I understand that. I am so sorry I worried you, William. I will think before I do that again."

He continues to hold me, kissing my neck and face. He finally lets go and backs up to look at me. "Let me see the new Brook. Not that they could improve on you, as far as I am concerned. I like the hair. What do you think?"

"I love it. I will have to color it every few weeks, so that won't be fun. But I love the cut. What about the make-up? Do you like it?"

"*You look marvelous*," he says with a grin," but you always look splendid so there is no real improvement there. It is hard to make prodigious look better."

"You are not prejudiced at all about that, are you?"

"Not in the slightest." He laughs again. "Because you look so good, what should we do tonight?"

"Stay home. I have had enough excitement to last this week. I want a quiet evening home with you."

"That sounds delightful. We will order out and get a movie on the TV. Then we can cuddle and make out on the couch."

"You don't have to keep talking I'm in!" I continue, "I'm going to take a shower. I'll be right back."

"What do you want for dinner?" he asks.

"A salad with chicken or shrimp," I answer.

After I shower, I wear my pink satin and lace long nightgown and matching robe. I like how it floats around my legs when I walk. It makes me feel very sexy. I walk back into the bedroom and hanging over the bed is the print of William and me, huge and framed. It is incredible to see. There is a muted almost cloud-like feathering around the edges. You can see the very top of Williams butt before the sheet covers him. I am lost in the dream-like beauty of it. I stand there for a long time.

William comes in and wraps his arms around me, kissing my neck. He says, "Well, do you like it?"

"It is singularly the most beautiful work of art I have ever seen, William. How did you do the edges like that?"

"Magic. I have been hired to do your first shoot, my love. You will get to see the magic happen up close."

I turn to him and say, "My love, I get to see the magic regularly, up close and usually, it's personal."

He growls in my ear and says, "That may happen again, and soon."

We enter the living room just as the bell rings from security to let us know our dinner has arrived. William tells them to send them up. I am flipping through our movie choices when dinner is delivered. I decide on *The Words* because I am a big Bradley Cooper fan.

We eat our dinner and watch the movie. Both are very good. In William's arms, with my head on his shoulder, is the best way to spend an evening. William lays me down on the couch and kisses my breasts through my nightgown. He asks, "Should we make love here on the couch like a couple of teenagers?"

"When we have a lovely, huge bed in the other room with an exquisite print to gaze at? I don't think so."

He picks me up and carries me into the bedroom, depositing me on the bed. He stands in front of me and takes off his clothes, giving me the opportunity to fully appraise his face and form. Who needs foreplay with the show I get to see. I am ready, willing and able in seconds.

He stands me up to pull down the sheet and takes off my robe. He skims his hands down my arms and then grabs my nightgown to lift it over my head. He stands back, looking at me as if it is the first time. "Someday, some young man will ask me what the most striking thing I have ever seen is. I will tell him it is my Brook because that is the truth. The last thing that I will remember when I die is seeing you, like this. You stun me into silence."

We make love slowly and deeply and when I can take no more, I come loudly, grabbing the sheets and calling William's name. He follows me, emptying into me with a sated look on his face. He rests next to me, kissing my forehead. "Every time we do this, it feels better," he says.

"It is not possible for it to feel better than that did."

"We will see, won't we?" He smiles.

"I want to ask you what it was like growing up in your family," I ask.

"We always get into these deep discussions after sex. I was raised with wealth and privilege. Prince Charles is one of my godfathers. I played with Wills and Harry both at Kensington Palace and at our estate. I went to the best prep schools and university that money can buy. Have I bored you sufficiently for today?"

"I don't find it boring, it is quite interesting, really. It makes you who you are, William. The man I see is far from boring. In fact, I find him fascinating and incredibly sexy. He is kind, caring and he loves me. What more could I ask for?"

CHAPTER 17

MY STYLE APPOINTMENT IS NOT exactly what I thought it was going to be. I am coached on everything from undergarments to what hose to wear. I am cautioned to always look the part, even if I am grocery shopping. Unflattering pictures get as much press as beautiful ones. Maybe even more, so don't give them an opportunity to take one. After my color analysis and measurements are taken, we move on to what foods I can eat~protein, no carbs, no sugar and very little alcohol. They want to start a gym membership. I explain my preferred exercise and I am given a pass on the gym.

Not wanting a repeat of my last outing, I call Luke when I am finished. He comes to pick me up. From the look on his face, I can see that he is happy I finally understand the importance of my security. I ask Luke to drop me off at my apartment. I need to check on things and get my mail.

I am opening my mail when there is a knock at my door. I open it to find Link. "Hi, Brook. I heard the door close over here and I was just checking to see who came home," he says.

"It's me! Come in and catch me up on you and Sandy," I counter.

"She's great, we're great. Did she tell you she moved in with me?"

"She was more than happy to tell me, Link. I'm so happy for the both of you. We were talking about sub-letting the apartment."

"It's a nice apartment. You won't have a problem finding someone."

"Did Sandy tell you this week is my last rotation? I have a modeling job now."

"She told me. I think it's terrific. I'll buy whatever you're selling."

Link tells me some things about his work. I ask him to say hi to Sandy for me and he leaves. My phone rings. It's William. "Hi, darling," he says.

"Hi yourself. Where are you?" I ask.

"On my way to your apartment to get you. I can't let you spend too much time there. You might like it and leave me."

"I highly doubt that, William. I guess you haven't noticed that I *love* being with you. I'm finished here. I'll be right down."

When I get to the street, William is standing next to the car with his arms open for me. I gladly walk into them and kiss him. "What should we do with our evening, Brook?" he asks.

"I don't care. I'm happy right now."

"Perhaps I should take you to the gallery that just asked me to have a showing there."

"William, you have a show!" I say excitedly.

"They called this morning after you left. PX Photography Gallery. They're in Brooklyn. They want between twenty and thirty prints to show."

"I want to see it. Have you been there?"

"I have gone to a few shows there. They like to promote-up-and-coming talent. It will be a good step for me."

"I am so happy for you. You are so talented."

We get into the car and Luke drives us to the gallery. By the time we get there, it is closed but I get to see the location. We decide to have dinner at the River Café on Water Street. It is a charming restaurant with a magnificent view of the city. When they deliver our food, it looks like a work of art. Everything is so fresh and scrumptious. I devour all of it in a few short minutes . . .

"I was just lectured today on what to eat and what *not* to eat. I think I broke the rules," I say with a grin. "You won't tell on me, will you?"

"You will have to bribe me later. Right now I am enjoying watching you eat." He smiles.

On Sunday, I pack for my last flight with the crew. I love all of them so much. I kiss William good-bye and head for the airport. I am, as usual, the first one there. I start to ready the plane when the girls arrive with a bouquet of flowers. "They're gorgeous. Thank you," I say.

"We will miss you. You are the life of our party," Wendy says.

Once the passengers are on board, we take off for Chicago. Christina tells me that we are going shopping when we land. Our last shop therapy, as she puts it. We land and change in record time. Regina gets a cab and we are off to The Mag Mile. Michigan Avenue~460 stores, 275 restaurants and some 50 or so hotels. The most beautiful site in this girl's shopping experience. We have a few hours before everything closes, but you really need a few days to adequately shop it all.

In one boutique, I find a teddy that I think William will like. A while later, I find a blouse to take to England when we go. Regina finds a dress for a wedding. Christina buys a pair of shoes and Wendy finds two scarves. We are very happy with our prizes. We grab some "street meat" as Regina calls it, and head for the apartment.

I need a shower. When I finish, I call William to see how his day was. We talk for a few minutes and then I go to bed.

I am up early for my run. I spot my shadow and wave to him. I run seven miles today. I get back just in time to shower and get to the airport for check-in. Next stop, San Francisco. I have already accepted a shuttle to San Jose for tomorrow. I don't want to sit around for a day with nothing to do. Before I know it, I am on my way back to New York and William.

I say my good-byes to everyone. We all promise to stay in touch. I know I will see them again when I fly for shoots. I walk out into the sun and my very own photographer is waiting with a smile and flowers. I walk quickly to him to retrieve my kiss. I say, "My new life begins tomorrow. Where is the shoot?"

"It was my choice. I chose the river area of Tribeca. I want you to walk along the Hudson."

"Perfect. What is the weather for tomorrow?"

"Sunny and 85 degrees. You're going to be warm wearing raincoats. But I think the humidity will be low."

"I can bring music with me, right?" I ask.

"I have your iPod packed with the cameras."

"You think of everything. I am so lucky to have you."

"Luck has nothing to do with it. Divine intervention or destiny brought us together. One way or another, it's for life. You know that, right?" he says.

I look into his very serious eyes and say, "I love you and you love me. That is enough for me right now, William. I am not looking for anything more just yet."

I am off for a run first thing in the morning. When I return, I have a quick shower and breakfast. I wrestle with my hair to force it to my will and carefully apply my make-up. William wants a "fresh air" look. I meet him in his office for his approval.

"There you are, and you look splendid. The camera is going to love you today, Brook. Raincoat sales are going through the roof because every man will want his woman to look like you do in one."

"Very kind of you to say, Mr. Barry. The proof will be in the pictures, so to speak."

What can I say about standing around all day having your picture taken? It is fun to watch the people pass by. New Yorkers are very special people. They are so accustomed to seeing celebrities and world figures walking amongst them, that it is not a big deal to see one. Not that I am a celebrity, but they don't even stop to see what we are doing. The tourists, however, stop and watch for several minutes. I am sure they are trying to figure out if they know who we are.

I smile and pout. Walk and stand still. Turn and stare off into the distance. Profile, head up, head down, until my neck hurts. When William declares he has enough, I am so happy to hear those words. William walks over to me and says, "You did very well, Brook. It is beastly hot out here. Lets get you home and into a shower. I'll rub your feet for you."

Friday's shoot is for a nationwide chain's sale flyer. There are eight models on this one. Two children, two teenagers, me, another twenty-something man and then an older couple. We have two photographers who split their time between us. It's an inside shoot with several clothing changes each. It was a lot of standing around waiting for your turn. I need to bring something to read on the next one of these.

When William and Luke pick me up, I am exhausted. I ask William, "Is it alright with you, if we stay in tonight and do nothing?"

"It is fine with me to stay in, but I still want to do *something*."

I had forgotten I have that new teddy to show him. "Fine, we can play cards," I say with a smirk as I get into the car.

He swats my behind and says, "Strip poker, perhaps."

CHAPTER 18

WILLIAM'S SHOW IS THE THIRD week of October. He is busy getting ready for it, and I am modeling at least two days a week. I am very happy with my new job. I make more in the two days than I did in the four days with the airline. I am home every night with William. There is nothing more that I want.

The first week of October, I feel a cold starting. Within three days, I have a full-blown cough and runny nose. William makes me go to the doctor, and sure enough, I have a sinus infection. I am miserable and I can't work. Once I am on the antibiotic, I start to feel better.

I find William on the roof in the garden. It is a warm and beautiful Indian summer day. The leaves are changing. It's dusk~the most magical time of day for me. William is reading the paper when I lie down next to him on the chaise. "I'm feeling much better, William. I have one day left on the prescription. I am going to work tomorrow," I say.

"And exactly what are you trying, in your usual covert manner, to tell me, Brook?"

"You are going to make me say it, aren't you, William. Honestly, you are no gentleman." I get up to leave and he grabs my hand to pull me back down to him.

"I am a gentleman by birth, Brook. If you want to make love with me, you don't need to ask me. You don't need permission. Take what you want from me, Brook. I don't have to initiate every sexual encounter we have. I want you to want me as badly as I want you."

I kiss him and start to unbutton his shirt. I hear a low growl in his chest and he says, "There is my tiger. I want to see your stripes."

I am in his arms under the blanket, looking at the stars. William asks, "How was that, darling? Do you like being on top?"

"Yes. But I like skin on skin better."

"That's good. I like skin as well. I like that it is with you, Brook. I have looked the world over to find someone so that I can be as comfortable as I am with you. We better go inside. It is getting cold up here now that the sun has gone down. I don't want you sick again."

The evening of William's show, it rains. Thank heavens that it has little effect on the turnout. William looks so handsome in his suit. I am in a party dress. People wander through the gallery studying William's work. As he walks around, people stop him to ask questions.

In the far back of the gallery hangs the print of William and me in bed. The other favorite of mine hangs next to it. In that one, we are in profile with the sun between our lips. I find myself in front of them, taking in their exquisiteness.

"You like these pictures, yes?" a man asks me.

"Very much. Do you?" I reply.

"They are very good, but alas, not for sale. I would like *that* one for my bedroom and *that* for the library." He points to direct me to which one.

"They are lovely."

"Would I be able to ask you to pose for one like that with me?" He points to the nude.

"You should ask your wife, sir."

"My wife is not as beautiful as you are, miss, and that *is* you in the picture."

How could he possibly know that it's me? You can't see my face, or Williams for that matter. You can only see the top of his head and my jaw. "*You* want to know how I know that is you. Your jaw and neck, my lovely. There is no mistaking it. That *is* you. Now, politely answer my question, please."

"I'm sorry, but I would not pose with you for such an intimate picture. Who are you?"

"He is Count Dracula, Brook. Stay away from him. He will suck you dry." I turn to see William smiling at the man and me.

"William. I was just messing with your woman. She won't pose nude with me. And we both know that I am a much better lover than you are."

William closes the space between himself and this man. He grabs him in a bear hug and they slap each other on the backs. "Brook, this is my brother, Jonathan Barry," William says, shaking his head. "And Jonathan, this is Brook Kennedy."

"I am happy to meet you, Jonathan," I say shocked.

"And I am so pleased to meet you, Brook. My lovesick brother has told me all about you. However, he left out the part about you being so dazzling." He takes my hand and kisses it.

"Enough of that, little brother. Keep your paws to yourself."

"You didn't tell me your brother was going to be here."

"I didn't know until yesterday, so I thought he could surprise you."

"Will you be staying with us, Jonathan?" I ask.

"Well, not exactly with you. In the other apartment," he answers.

"What other apartment?"

"Brook, I know how uncomfortable you are with my wealth, so I haven't told you. I own the four apartments on our floor. Luke lives in one and Angela in the other. One is for friends or family to use when they visit."

I am stunned, again. He owns four multi-million dollar apartments. I ask, "Why do you tell me on a need-to-know-basis? Would you have ever told me?

"Like I said, you freak about the money thing. I don't want you to run. Therefore, I tell you things a little at a time to soften the blow. I don't *keep* it from you. I just don't go there until I need to."

"If you two are going to talk relationship shit, I am going to find a lovely to spend the evening with. Nice to meet you, Brook. I will see you in the morning for one of Angela's breakfasts."

"See you in the morning, Jonathan," I say.

"We will discuss this in bed tonight, William. That seems to be where I get the whole story with you. You better mingle with your guests. I'm going to get a glass of wine."

William sells several of his photos over the course of the evening. He also is commissioned by four people to provide portraits for them. A few local businesses ask him to do the pictures for their ads and menus. Overall, it is a very productive evening. The gallery wants to keep a few portraits to show and promises another viewing in the spring.

When we arrive home, we are both tired. Standing around talking is not something that I am used to doing. I decide to take a bubble bath to relieve my tired feet. A few minutes later William joins me. He embraces me against his chest and says, "Thank you for this evening. Your presence was a great comfort to me. You made me less nervous."

"You were nervous? You are always so self-assured. I didn't think you ever got nervous."

"You're wrong. I do. What do you think of Jonathan?"

"I like him. He did scare me in the beginning. I thought he was being inappropriate with me, asking me to pose nude with him. Now that I think of it, he was funny."

"He is funny all right. He is the comedian in my family. Emily is very serious and I am . . . . me!"

"Every time I think I have *you* figured out, I get a new piece to the William puzzle. Do you own any other piece of real estate in America?"

"No. Just the four apartments here. I have a flat in London. I will inherit the estate in Wessex. Before you ask, the estate has slightly over 2,000 acres of land, and the house has fifty-six rooms."

"Wow. I don't suppose your mom does the dusting?"

"No, no dusting. We have domestic help. Somewhere between forty-five and fifty, grounds keepers, housekeepers, stable hands, footmen, and the usual amount of help to maintain an estate that size."

"I guess so. You see, William, I don't even know what a footman would do much less have one. Does he take care of your feet? Cut your nails and such?"

William is laughing at me. He says, "No Brook. I am still able to cut my own nails. A footman has several duties~valet, butler, answering the door and seeing to the guests' welfare. He might help with serving food and moving heavy furniture for the maids to clean under. They are largely a status symbol. My family is very into what things look like. Old money does that to you."

"I am afraid to meet your family. I am not a refined lady like the women they are used to having visit them. I am a bloody American, and a poor one at that. What will they think of me, William? I am going to embarrass you."

He tightens his arms around me and says, "You could never embarrass me, Brook. You are lovely and charming. You'll have my parents eating out of your hands within minutes of meeting you."

"And if they don't think I am worthy of your affections, then what? Am I put on the next plane out of town?"

"I am bringing you there so that you can meet them and they can meet you. I don't have to have their approval. I would like it, but I don't need it. I need you."

"I think it might be easier if I stay on this side of the pond, I think you Brits call it. I want your visit with your family to be a nice one. I don't want you to have to explain my shortcomings."

"Oh, Brook, you don't have any," he says with a loud sigh.

I think I have made him mad. He gets abruptly out of the tub, grabs a towel, and wraps it around himself. Taking another one, he holds it open for me. I get up and step into it and he wraps it around me. He kisses me hard and says, "Brook, you give me peace and love. The two most valuable things that all of the money in the world can't buy. The two things that I have never had before. The two things that I won't live without ever again. If those are shortcomings, then I wish the entire world suffered from them."

CHAPTER 19

I GET BACK FROM MY run to find Jonathan in the dining room having breakfast. "Good morning, Jonathan. Did you sleep well?" I ask.

"Quite well, thank you, Brook. How was your night?"

"Very pleasant indeed."

"I see you have been for a run this morning. Did my dear brother go with you?"

"No, he didn't. He prefers the gym downstairs. Have you gone with him?"

"I have. It is a fairly decent gym. I prefer to run. I would love to run with you, if I may."

"I would like that. I run early every morning."

"Early works for me. What time exactly?"

"6:00 or so. I like to run in the park," I say.

"Good. I would love to run in the park. Tomorrow. What are your plans for the rest of today?"

"I don't know what William has for plans, but what would you like to do?"

"It has been five years since I have been in New York. I want to do the tourist thing. Would you like to come along?"

"I would love to. I have to check with William first before I commit to anything. Right now, I need a shower. I'll see you in a few minutes."

When I come back from my shower, William is back from the gym. "Good morning, darling." William comes to kiss me.

"Good morning. How was your workout?"

"Very good. How was your run?"

"Stimulating. Jonathan is going to come with me tomorrow."

"Really? I didn't know that you run, brother."

"I do when I have someone worth running after, brother. I started a couple of years ago. I haven't seen you in a while, remember?"

"True enough. Sorry. Mum reminds me all the time that I am not a good son. I will be home in a few weeks. That should pacify her for some time."

"Don't count on it. Neither of them wants you living here. They think you should live at the house and run the business."

"And what do *you* think Jonathan?" William asks.

"I think that you need to do whatever you need to do. I like running the company. You don't. I find it simple. It is everyone else who tries to complicate things. If I am happy and you are happy with our arrangement, then fuck everyone else." Jonathan raises his voice.

"Then we are in agreement. When you change your mind, we will discuss it. Until then, I'm good with this," William states.

Watching the brothers talking about their lives, I can see the familial similarities in them. Both are tall and handsome, with Jonathan having slightly darker hair. Both have athletic bodies and obviously work out. Both have killer smiles and striking eyes. And yet William is the one who commands my attention. I think it is the way he holds his body straight and unyielding. I can't help but to look at him alone. I find myself smiling at him. He looks quizzically at me and says, "What are you thinking about, Brook?"

"My thoughts are my own, William. Jonathan asked me what plans we had today. He wants to be a tourist in the big city. Did you make any plans for us?"

"No. Whatever you want to do is fine with me. I am going to shower."

By the time William returns, Jonathan and I have planned the day. William grabs a quick breakfast and we head out.

We start to walk downtown. William possessively holds his hand in the small of my back while we walk. Tucking me under his arm, he glides his hand around me, resting it on my hip. He kisses the top of my head as we walk. Jonathan wants to go to Times Square for his New York fix. He tells me he doesn't think he is in New York until he sees it. We stand there looking at the humanity that occupies the spot. I laugh as he does a spin around, eyeing everything.

"Now I know I am really here," he says with a huge grin. "Nothing like the atmosphere in this part of the city."

"It is special," I agree.

We continue to walk while Jonathan catches William up on all of the news from home. It seems that his mother hasn't been feeling well. They think she has diverticulitis. She will have to be careful about what she eats and hope that it calms down.

We grab a cab to take us to Little Italy for lunch. As we drive, I feel as though I am caught in a stereo system with the two British-accented men on either side, who continue to talk around me. We arrive at the restaurant and exit the cab. We are shown to a table and given menus. While I am looking over the offerings, Jonathan says," I should warn you that mum and dad are going to pressure you to make up your mind. They want an heir and you are not providing it quickly enough."

I watch William glare at his brother. Not wanting to be part of this very personal discussion between the two brothers, I excuse myself to use the restroom. I stay in there as long as possible without it appearing that I have fallen in. When I emerge, I can see the conversation hasn't gone well at all. William has a red face and Jonathan is obviously mad. I walk back to the table in time to hear William say, "She won't cooperate with me. Short of going to the Queen, I don't know what else to do."

I take my place at the table and say, "If you want to discuss something personal I can take a cab back home and leave you to it. I don't mind. It's not a problem."

"I don't want you to go. I have said all that I want to say on the subject," William answers me gruffly.

"Don't leave on my account please, Brook. I can be a complete boor at times. I am sure William can attest to that," Jonathan says.

I can only guess that I am not the kind of wife that Williams's family has envisioned for him. I don't blame them. I've told him the same thing, several times. I order a salad because quite frankly my appetite has vanished. When it comes, I pick at it, not really eating. William and Jonathan are noticeably quiet. Our lovely outing ruined, we head back by way of another cab to Williams house.

I make myself a cup of coffee and bring it into the living room to watch some TV. William joins me a while later with his own cup. He sits next to me and puts his arm around me. "I want to marry you, Brook. And I will ask you formally soon. I have some things that I have to settle first. I can't move forward until I do."

"I don't want to come between you and your family, William." I say with tears forming in the corners of my eyes. "We can't have peace if we don't have the love and support of our families."

"They do support us. You'll see that when you meet them. It's other things that I'm not at liberty to discuss with you just yet. Please don't be upset. I can't stand to see you cry over this."

Not wanting to upset him further, I drop my questions. He will talk to me about this when he feels ready to. It might be something uncomfortable or degrading and he can't share it yet. I understand this. There are things in my past I don't share either.

I make a turkey breast with sweet potatoes, carrots and baby peas for dinner. I find it fun to cook for the brothers. I call them to come and eat and they sit down to our feast with a splendid look on their faces. "I haven't had turkey in ages. This looks and smells bloody wonderful, Brook," Jonathan says.

"Brook is a fabulous cook," William states. "Why do you think I have to work out everyday. She is trying to fatten me up."

"I like to cook for you. There is nothing wrong with this dinner. No gravy, no butter or sour cream, just good, fresh food."

We have our dinner with a much nicer discussion between us than at lunch. We decide to get tickets for a show next weekend. Jonathan tells us that he will stay for two more weeks. Then we have two more weeks and we leave for England.

Jonathan says goodnight and leaves for his apartment. I want a relaxing bubble bath. I soak while I listen to Josh Groban's love songs. As I get out to dry off, I wonder where William is. Usually he comes in with me when I take a bath. I put on my teddy and a long silk robe and venture out to find him. I know he isn't on the roof because it is much colder tonight than it has been. I see the light on in his office and I stand in the doorway looking at him.

He looks up from his laptop and smiles at me. "You look lovely standing there. Come in and stand in front of me," he says, pushing his chair back. I walk over to him and take my place. He holds me by my hips and buries his head in my belly. Kissing me through my robe he says, "Why can't things be easy, Brook? Why can't I find what I want and simply have it? Why is it that happiness takes a backseat to duty?"

"That's a lot of *whys*, William. Things can't be easy because then we wouldn't appreciate them as much. You can't have everything you want for the same reason. I don't know much about duty, but my guess is it is the price you pay for having more than the average person. Your happiness comes with a price. Would you be happy if you drove a cab, waited tables or sold food on the street?"

"If we were together and married, I would be happy."

"Think about that, William. I see you eat at the best restaurants and you don't even look at the check. We stay at the finest hotels and you don't bat an eyelash at that bill either. You filled a closet with clothes for me before you even knew if I would wear them. Look at this apartment. How much you must have spent just for the art and statues in the gallery. A whole lifetime of earnings for some people. I am not saying you don't deserve it. I am saying that is the price you pay for the life you live."

"Do you think the cab driver would trade places with me if it meant he would never find happiness?"

"In a New York minute. You see *he* doesn't know what you know. He would only see this," I say, gesturing to the room. "He would not see this," I continue, pressing my hand to his heart. "You have to be happy with exactly what you have every minute of every day. It may not be what you want, but the alternative won't be either."

"Do you have any idea how smart you are? Do you know how much I need you? Please don't run away from me, ever."

"I'm not going anywhere. I have a closet full of clothes I haven't even started to wear yet!" I say with a chuckle.

William picks me up and sets me on his desk. He stands in front of me, pushes his laptop aside, takes off his shirt, folds it up and lays me down with my head resting on it. Opening my robe, he rips open the crotch of my teddy. He slides his hands up to cup my breasts and whispers, "Watch me." Taking one hand down from my breast, he moves his head to my curls. He begins to open me with the expertise he has shown me before. I arch my back from his desk as the first wave of pleasure begins. I lose every thought in my head, as he continues to pleasure me beyond comprehension. When I am wrung out, he enters me and begins to rub me. I am squeezing him as hard as I can because I know that he loves this. The sounds he makes send me over the edge again and he follows me into the abyss. When reason returns, he says," That is what I am talking about, Brook. Total happiness, with you."

"It is just about the sex, William?"

"No. It is the whole day. Your understanding, not pressuring for immediate answers. Dinner and then the best desk sex that has ever been had on any desk in the world."

CHAPTER 20

WILLIAM HAS A SHOOT IN upstate New York on Wednesday. He leaves very early in the morning and won't be back until Thursday. This leaves me to entertain Jonathan for the better part of two days. I make plans to meet him for a run first thing Wednesday.

I decide to run the Hudson River through Chelsea, the Village and Tribeca. We start out crossing the park through the sheep meadow. We run south on 8th Avenue to Columbus Circle, then we run to 57th Street and go west to 12th Avenue. Jonathan does well keeping up with me. I naturally don't give him the run of his life. I don't want to lose him in the city. We reach Canal Street and cross over to run back on Broadway. When reach Herald Square, Jonathan cramps up and can't go any further. I hail a cab and he hobbles into it. "I am so sorry, Jonathan. I never should have gone so far with you. I don't know your pace and I overdid it. Will you forgive me?" I ask.

"It is not your fault. I didn't want to wimp out, so I kept going long after I knew I was done. I have a hard head that way," he jokes.

"Like someone else I know," I say.

"Very much so, I am afraid. Very competitive bunch we Barrys are."

"Do tell. In all things, I'm afraid. He has to top his personal best all the time."

"You are talking about the eleven, aren't you?"

I blush to my feet and say, "How can you guess that?"

"Easily. I have been engaged in trying to top that for several years. I didn't have the benefit of his education, but I have done my own research. It is possible, I'm told."

In order to change the subject I say, "Can you walk into the building? I think if you get in the tub and run the jets, you will feel better."

"Don't worry about me. I will be fine."

I get him to the apartment and tell him to call me if he needs anything. I have a shoot in the morning. I have to be there at 9:00 so I won't run before.

This shoot is with children. When I get there, the studio is loud and busy with three girls and three boys under the age of six running around. I want to hug all of them, they are so cute. I want William's children so badly. I have the whole day to dream about that. Just before we get started, I call Jonathan to check on him. He tells me that he is still sore but feels better. He will take another jet bath and he feels that will help him further.

The shoot goes so well. Even these little children know how to pose and act in front of a camera. To watch them turn it on at the correct time and then turn back into children is so comical. I am tired, though, when I leave. I need some of the children's energy to get home.

I walk in the door and William is standing in the living room with a glass of wine for me. I walk into his arms and kiss him. "I missed you. How did your shoot go?" I ask him.

"Good. How was yours?" He asks.

"I had fun. We had six young children there. I was thinking of what our children might look like."

"Our children will be bloody fabulous! All twenty of them."

"Twenty may be a few too many, William. I was thinking more like four."

"Fine, I can live with four. I am thrilled that you want children. So many women don't."

"I want *your* children, not just any."

I finish my wine and leave to take a shower. I need to wash off the day's make-up and grime. When I come back, Jonathan is with William enjoying more wine.

"How are you feeling, Jonathan?" I inquire.

"Much better, Brook, thanks. The jet tubs that you have work wonders on fools' legs."

"I am the one who was the fool. I should know better than to push someone."

"Nonsense. I had fun prior to the pain. The wine is helpful to my recovery. Wine helps everything feel better!"

"I agree with that." I smile, "What would you gentlemen like to do for dinner?"

"I thought we might go to the Strip House for a steak," William suggests.

"Sounds good to me," I say.

We get ready and leave. The Strip House is on East 12th Street between Broadway and 5th Avenue. Luke gets us there in record time and we are seated. I want a New York strip with the goose fat potatoes. I want to be bad tonight. William orders a porterhouse with creamed spinach and Jonathan, a rib-eye with lobster bisque to start. Everything is so delicious, I want to lick my plate. The side dishes are large enough for the three of us to share. By the time we leave, I am uncomfortably full.

"I am going to walk back," I announce.

"I don't want you to walk. When we get home I will exercise you and you will feel better," William jokes.

"I don't want to hear this conversation. My wife is four thousand miles away and my hand is sore for it already. The next time I come to visit, she is coming with me."

"Is it just you two, or men in general, that are so lascivious?" I ask.

"I can't speak for every man, but I believe we are pretty much the same. Once you have had it, you want more," Jonathan offers.

We ride back to the apartment and Jonathan says goodnight when we get out of the elevator. William and I walk inside and I go right to the bedroom. From the doorway I turn to William and say," I am waiting for my exercise, my love."

With a big smile, William answers, "On my way."

Saturday night, we attend the theater to see *The Book of Mormon*. The story is about two missionaries who are sent to Uganda to convert the people to the Mormon faith. What they find there is a population with AIDS and debilitating poverty. It is raw and eye-opening. I feel changed after seeing it. We have no idea how good we have it in this country. Or at least I didn't.

Our last week with Jonathan consists of two shoots for me and one for William. I run every morning without Jonathan. We eat together every night. I have enjoyed his stories from childhood and the sibling rivalry that the two brothers share. Even though they tease each other relentlessly, you can see the love that they have for each other. When we take him to the airport Friday night, I am sorry to see him go. He hugs me and says, "I will see you in two weeks, Brook. Try to last until then, okay? If my brother doesn't treat you well, let me know and I will knock sense into him with pleasure."

"You have nothing to worry about. Your brother treats me very well. Almost too well. I can't wait to meet your family. I have enjoyed your visit with us and I hope you come back soon."

"We will see you in two weeks, brother. Do try to hold it together until then. I don't want any frantic calls in the middle of the night. Have a safe trip." William hugs him and slaps him on the back. Jonathan turns and boards the plane.

"Now that I have met your brother, tell me what your sister is like."

"She is very direct. You will know within three minutes of meeting her exactly what she thinks of you. If you don't measure up, that will be your last communication with her, ever. If she loves you, she will cut off her arm to protect you. I am lucky that she loves me because she has lost several arms on my behalf."

"She sounds wonderful. But will she love *me*?"

"I think she already does because she knows that I am arse over elbow about you. She wants me to be happy and she knows that you make me happy. The tough nut is my dad. He cares about the family as a whole, not it's parts. What is good for all is not necessarily good for me."

"He is a business man at heart. Your family is a business, isn't it?"

"Sadly so. We have public events that we are required to attend because of formality. Each of us has our charities that we champion. We have the shipyard and vessels that we own. There are other companies that we are partial owners of."

"That sounds like a lot of responsibility. That is why he is a tough nut, as you put it. He *has* to be in order to have this all work cohesively."

"He has helped to raise hurdles for me. I didn't stop it, but he and my mum gave it to me. Now I have to figure out how to remove the obstacle to my happiness and then I can move forward."

"Is there anything I can do to help? You see, *my* happiness is forever linked to yours."

"Just continue to love me and let me love you."

When we get home, there is a very large check in the mail for me from a shoot I did a few weeks ago. I take the check into William's study. I sit in the chair opposite him and say, "I received my check from the fashion shoot two weeks ago. I want to give you some of it for the upkeep on this place. I feel odd living here and not contributing to anything."

"I don't need, nor want, you to contribute to anything monetarily. You contribute in other ways, more than you will ever know. I want to take care of you, Brook. I need to. Please let me. Besides, you have your rent to pay and other bills until your lease is up."

"I will put it in the bank, but should you need it, please tell me."

He smiles at me and snickers. "I shall request the funds should I require them. I promise."

"Somehow I don't believe you, Mr. Barry. I don't think that I am getting the full truth from you."

"The truth isn't always what it is cracked up to be, Brook. Sometimes you are better off not knowing it."

CHAPTER 21

THE NEXT TWO WEEKS ARE a flurry of activity. I have four photo shoots and William has five. Thankfully, all of them are local, so we aren't traveling. We both have to pack and I have some shopping to do. I want to bring everyone a uniquely American gift. Not knowing most of them makes this a real chore. I buy things like Vermont maple syrup, Maine honey, Georgia peanuts, and California wine.

After I pack, unpack and pack again, I finally shut the suitcase and pull it to the front door of the apartment. Williams sees the disgust on my face at my indecision and says, "If you forget anything, we can buy it there. England *is* a civilized country. We wear clothes to cover our bodies. We even sell them to you crazy Americans."

He makes me laugh at myself. "I know that you Brits are civilized. At least *some* of you are. Last night I make love with a growling beast. He was all hands and lips and not at all civilized."

"I didn't hear any complaints last night when you were screaming 'William' at the top of your lungs. Very funny how daylight clears the fog of lust away so you can see plainly."

I walk over to him, wrap my arms around him and whisper, "But, alas, lust is so much more fun than civility. Don't you think?"

"Agreed. At least with you it is. Now, should we get this show on the road so that we don't miss the bloody plane?"

He kisses me and we are out the door. We ride to the airport in the rain. I hate to fly when it's raining. Once when I was attending, we slid off the runway in Italy in the rain. No one was hurt, but it sure scared the crap out of all of us. I pray it stops soon so the runway dries before takeoff. If not, William will have cuts on his hand from my nails digging into it.

When we do take off, thankfully, the rain has stopped. I curl up in my seat with my head on William's shoulder and fall asleep. I smile because this is my first cross-Atlantic flight where I have slept instead of watching everyone else sleep.

We wake up about forty-five minutes before we land. I use those few minutes to ask my stupid questions. "When I meet your family, do I curtsey to them?"

"No. You only curtsey to someone with an HRH in front of his or her name. You would curtsey the first time you see them that day. After that, you would just nod in their direction until the next day. My parents are Duke and Duchess, but not his or her royal highness."

"What should I call them? How do I address them to others?"

"When you meet them, they will tell you what to call them. When you ask a servant about them, you should say Mr. or Mrs. Barry or Duke and Duchess Barry."

"And when I ask for you?"

"Do you have clothes on or are you naked when you ask?"

"I would have clothes on."

"Killjoy. Ask for William or Viscount Barry, depending on the circumstance. Now relax, you are not going to the tower if you say the wrong thing. They will think that you are sweet to even be trying."

"I'm glad that you find all of this funny, William. When you meet my brother, you can wear jeans, a stained tee shirt and have an open beer in your hand and you will fit right in."

We finish our discussion just as we land. It takes a few minutes to taxi and secure the plane, then we walk out, find our bags and proceed into customs. I watch as William goes through. The agent looks at his passport and says, "Welcome home, sir. Did you have a pleasant stay in the US?" Then he nods his head to William.

"Yes, it was a very pleasant stay. But it is good to be home."

When the agent asks me what I am going to do here in the UK over the next two weeks, I am tempted to answer, "I am here to see if making love in an I-don't-remember-how-many-room-estate is different from doing it in a penthouse, but instead, I just answer, "Visiting friends and sightseeing."

When we get out and into the main concourse, a beautiful woman is waving and calling out Williams's name. I see his eyes light up. "Emily! You are even more beautiful than you were when I left. Emily, this is my Brook, Brook Kennedy. Brook, my sweet sister Lady Emily Thornton."

Emily closes in to hug me and says, "Please call me Emily. May I call you Brook?"

"Yes, please do. I am so happy to meet you. Thank you for meeting us here."

"The monsters are waiting in the car. When they heard I was picking you up, they insisted on coming. I hope that you don't mind."

"I bet I won't even know them. Have they grown up and turned into monsters so soon?" William jokes with his sister.

"I will leave it to you to judge for yourself."

We exit the terminal to a waiting limo. The door swings open and three squealing blonde mops fly out and run to William screaming, "Unil Bubs, we have missed you so much." They fling themselves into William's waiting, open arms, knocking him flat on the sidewalk.

I turn to Emily and say, "Triplets? Unil Bubs? What the hell?"

Emily returns, "They couldn't say William, so somehow it became Bubs. Jonathan is Jubs. They are definitely triplets, to my never-ending dismay."

When they finally calm down, William introduces me to them, "Lily, Leslie, and Lourine, this lady is Brook Kennedy, a very good friend of mine." The girls give me the once-over and, finding me deserving, two of them take my hands to lead me to the car.

There is a steady stream of conversation on the drive to the house. The three girls, whom I find out are a very grown-up seven years of age, fill in Unil Bubs on all of the local seven-year-old gossip. Who goes to whose party and who is not invited. The best and nicest teacher in school, and countless other important issues. William gives them his undivided attention, making the appropriate comments when asked for his opinion. I watch him with these children and imagine him with his own. William and I are invited to their "dolly and bear tea" on Tuesday and are asked if we wouldn't mind bringing the sweets, please. Mommy won't let them have any, I am told in complete confidence with a whisper in my ear.

I make the mistake of asking what time tea is. The shocked look on their faces is hysterical. They answer in unison, "Tea is at 4:00, like always." I apologize profusely, telling them that tea is different in America. They nod their heads at each other in agreement, that the Americans do things differently.

We pull on to a long, wide road that opens up to the sight of the house. From where I sit, I can't see over it, or find either end of it. As soon as we pull up several, people come out of the door and down the steps to greet us. William helps me out, with the girls in tow. I have three new girlfriends, especially if I show up with sweets on Tuesday.

William holds my hand and steps forward to introduce me. "Mum and Dad, this is Brook Kennedy. Brook, this is my mum Elizabeth, Duchess of Wessex and my dad, Warren Duke of Wessex."

"We are so happy that you are here, Brook. Welcome to our home and please call us Warren and Elizabeth," his mother says.

"Yes, quite so, Brook. Nothing stuffy here," his dad adds.

"Thank you so much for having me. It is such a pleasure to finally meet you. William speaks so often of you that I feel as if I know you."

William's parents hug and kiss him and we all walk into the house together.

William suggests that we go to our rooms and get settled and washed up before lunch. The footman carries our bags up to the east wing and puts mine in a room on the left and William's in the room on the right. I smirk at William and he gives me a stern look. I know he isn't going two weeks without sex. He can't go two days without it. This is going to be fun!

The footman leaves and William comes to my open door and fills the doorway with his body. He says, "So you think that it is funny that you have a room and I have a room?"

"Quite funny, actually. This must be English birth control. If you don't sleep together, you don't get pregnant."

"I have old-fashioned parents. They know that we live together and I am sure they guess that we fuck regularly, but in their house, we have the propriety of separate rooms. Respectability be damned, though, because I will sleep in here or you will sleep in there. Settle your things and freshen up. Come to *my* room when you are ready. We will have some lunch and then I will give you a tour of the Barry living history museum."

I unpack and take a shower. The water feels good on my sore shoulders from the flight. I get dressed and then venture into the hall to find William. I knock on his door and hear "Come in." I open the door to see William nude and lying on the bed.

I say, "What if it had been your mother or one of the girls paying you a visit?"

"They would have had a shock for sure. I would have told them it is your bad influence on me. I am only happy when I am inside you. They would understand."

"You want us to make love now?"

"That's the idea, Brook. It won't take long because I am ready to come now and we both know I can get you off very quickly. What do you say, my love?"

I remove my pants and panties on my way to his bed. He watches me and his erection grows as I move closer. I climb on the bed and crawl over to him. In one smooth motion, he climbs over me and positions me under him. He pushes himself inside me and starts to move. He's right. It only takes a few minutes for us to find our releases. He looks at me with a satisfied look on his face. "Afternoon delight, British style. Do you like?"

CHAPTER 22

AFTER LUNCH, MY TOUR BEGINS with the public rooms. There is a ballroom the size of a football field. It has four fireplaces that are large enough to walk into standing up. The logs are cut to a length of five feet and placed inside. The gallery mirrors the ballroom in size and shape and houses sculptures and paintings of family members long dead. One picture looks oddly familiar and hangs at the opposite end from where we came in. I walk to it, drawn just like the first time I saw it. Its sister hangs behind William's bed in New York.

"Does your family know this is you and me?" I ask.

"No one has actually said, but I have to guess they know. Jonathan certainly knows. He never has been able to keep a secret."

We walk through a well-stocked library with many first editions of Shakespeare, Bacon, Dickens and Austen. I swish my fingers lightly over them as if I am greeting my old friends. I hope I have some time to spend in here reading. I see the public dining room and the private, family dining room where we had our lunch. The kitchen and the men's and ladies' sitting rooms make up the majority of the first floor. All of the family and guest bedrooms are on the second floor, with the servants rooms on the third floor. The Barry's have ten live-in servants and several that come and go during the day.

"That takes care of most of the house. There is, in the basement, a wine cellar, the archives and the silver storage. Would you like to count the silver, Brook?"

"I think I will pass on that, William. The wine cellar sounds interesting, but looking at wine isn't half as much fun as tasting it."

"And neither of those options is as much fun as tasting you," he says looking at me hungrily.

"William, we just made love. What is wrong with you?"

"I am on holiday. When you have time off, you want to enjoy it. I told you I am happiest when I am buried inside you. That is just how it is, my love."

"I am feeling a little funny still. My head and stomach are fuzzy. Let me get used to the time, food and air change, please. I told you when I take this rotation for flying, I am a mess with the lag. It takes me a few days to adjust."

We have dinner with the family and I excuse myself early to go to bed. I am not much company anyway, sitting there and constantly yawning. I am sound asleep when I am woken by a dip on the other side of the mattress and the scent of aftershave, cologne and William. "Are you okay, darling?" he asks, holding me hand. "I am worried about you."

"I am fine, William. Nothing that a good night's sleep won't fix."

He puts an arm over me and pulls me into his warm, strong chest and says, "Sleep then."

When I wake in the morning, it is after 9:00. William is gone and his side of the bed is cold. I take a shower, not believing how long I have slept. I am the girl who is up by 5:30 every morning to run. Maybe that's what's wrong. I haven't run in three days. I need a run with some fresh air.

I find my way, by the smell of coffee to the dining room where I find William and Jonathan talking. "There she is," William says walking over to me. "We were going to come and get you in a few minutes. Jonathan and his wife, Eve, want to take us sightseeing today. Are you feeling up for it?"

With a huge grin I say, "Absolutely, but I need coffee first."

Half an hour later, I am ready to go. As the footman opens the front door for us, I see a black car driving up. William tells me it is Eve, Jonathan's wife. I have never seen this kind of car before. Jonathan explains, "It is a 1940 Bentley limo. One of six or so made that year. I had it fully restored."

"It's beautiful, Jonathan," I say as I climb in the back.

I smile at Eve as William says, "Eve, this is my girlfriend, Brook. Brook, this is Jonathan's wife, Eve."

"It is so nice to finally meet you, Brook. When Jonathan came home two weeks ago, I thought my marriage was over the way he went on and on about you. I can see now why his pecker was all bunched up."

The way she speaks has us all laughing hysterically. Jonathan shoots her a look and says, "Leave my pecker out of this, darling. Brook is dazzling, but she doesn't know it and that makes her beguiling."

I feel like I need an interpreter. I think Jonathan just said I wasn't stuck up, but I am not completely sure. It takes them forever to say four words.

We drive through the countryside with my car-mates pointing out important local sights. Jonathan wants to have lunch at his favorite pub in town, so we head there. "You must have their fish and chips, Brook, "Jonathan says. "They make them with a beer batter and serve them in newsprint, just the way it should be."

"Sounds good to me. I love fish, and I never have fries. My stylist will have a coronary if she finds out!"

"Fuck her. When you are on holiday, you have to live a little," Eve chimes in.

I think I love Eve.

The food arrives and it is fabulous. With the paper all oily, I know my arteries are hardening just at the sight of it. I dig in to the fries, and the fish is crunchy. However, within a few minutes, my stomach starts to roll, protesting the heavy oily mess I am giving it. I take a large drink of my beer, but that actually makes it worse. I excuse myself and make it to the bathroom just in time to heave it all into the toilet. I rinse my mouth and make it back to the table. I'm sure I am green by the way William looks at me with a frown. I smile at him and ask for an ice water with lemon. I don't eat any more fish and chips.

We finish our tour with a stop at a local shop that Eve loves. They sell pretty night things for ladies. With William and Jonathan hovering outside, Eve and I go in to look around. I find a beautiful short white satin nightshirt with pink lace and ribbons that I have to have. On the other side of the shop, I find little girl nightshirts. I ask Eve what size Emily's girls wear and buy them each one.

"You don't have to do that, Brook," she says.

"I want to. We are coming to tea on Tuesday and I want to bring them a present from their Unil Bub and me," I say laughing.

"The girls are the only people who would ever get away with saying that name. You should have seen him melt the first time they called him that. He was sitting on the floor with them when Lily tapped him on the shoulder and said,'"Unil Bub, can you tie my shoe peas?' I knew in that moment that I loved that man and I was glad he is my boys' Unil," she says with a smile.

Eve and I rescue our men from using rock-paper-scissors to settle an argument and we head home. I decide to take a nap before dinner. William wakes me with a kiss. "I am worried about you, Brook. This isn't like you at all. How do you feel?"

"I'm just so tired and my stomach is upset. I may have caught a bug on the plane. It happens all the time with the recycled air."

"That may be, but if you aren't better I am going to call the doctor and have you seen."

"So he can tell me I have a virus and that it will pass? I'm going for a run. I think I need to clear out my lungs."

"I will come with you. We can eat later."

I do feel better after the run. William and I have dinner alone and then we go to bed. William makes love to me inside his 700 year-old house, on a 200 year-old bed and I couldn't be happier.

Tuesday afternoon we are in the girls' nursery sitting on chairs too small for my butt. William has folded his 6' 3" frame onto a chair that is ten inches off the floor. His knees are around his ears and he has a huge grin on his face. We drink tea from plastic cups, with our pinkie extended of course. The girls serve the sweets that we brought, giving themselves the largest share. The bonnet that William has on is securely tied under his chin with a perfectly executed bow. Where is the camera when *I* need it?

We spend a few hours with the girls before Emily rescues us from bath time. I was afraid William and I were going to have some explaining to do if we got that far. We have dinner with Emily and her husband, Richard "please call me Dick." Not a chance in hell I am doing that! We kiss the girls goodnight and leave for our bed.

William holds me and says, "I am calling the doctor in the morning. I want you looked at even if it is a virus. I want to be sure. Because I feel so crappy, I agree to the doctor.

Thursday morning I find myself in the office of Dr. Martin. He is the Barry family doctor. I am called and proceed into his office. I sit down opposite his desk and he comes in. He extends his hand to me and says, "Hi, Brook. I am Dr. Martin. William tells me that you have been under the weather since you arrived here a few days ago."

"Yes. I don't feel like myself at all."

"What are your symptoms?"

"I am very tired. I feel nauseous. I vomited on Sunday but I chalked that up to eating greasy fish and chips. I mostly eat salad and grilled chicken, so that was an insult to my system on several levels."

"I see that. I want to run a few blood tests and look you over and then we will talk again. The nurse will help you into a room and draw the blood."

After I am looked over by the good doctor, I am waiting in his office for the results. He walks in looking at some papers and he sits down. "I think you will feel better soon. Some things take time. Morning sickness, for one."

"Morning sickness. Are you saying that I'm pregnant?"

"Yes. You are definitely pregnant. When was your last period?"

"I'm on birth control. I rarely even get a period and when I do, it is a day or two at the most. I don't remember when I had the last. This isn't possible."

"It is possible. Have you taken an antibiotic recently? They interfere with birth control and render it useless."

"I had a sinus infection the first week of October and I took something."

"That probably did it. That would make you six to seven weeks pregnant. Right about the time you begin to feel tired and nauseous. That would make your baby due the beginning of July."

"This just isn't possible."

"If you are sexually active, and knowing William like I do, I can guess you are, it is not only possible, but it is definite."

"I can't tell William. He is going to think I lied to him. That I am trying to trap him."

"If you think that, you don't know him very well. The one thing he wants more than *anything* is children. That is why he's . . . never mind."

"Can I stay here for a few minutes before I see him? I have to figure out what I am going to do."

"Of course. Please don't do anything until you have told him first. He *will* want this baby."

I sit there for a few minutes to allow this to sink in. I am not going to tell him until we get home. Now that I know why I feel like this, I can disguise my nausea. I venture out to William with a smile on my face. "Just as I thought~a virus. He said it would pass in a few days. Try not to eat too much greasy food."

"Good. I feel better knowing you are okay."

I ride back to the house with a smile on my face . . . I am going to have William's baby!

We spend the next few days visiting the historical sights around London. We go to the British Museum and the Victoria and Albert Museum. I envy the kind of relationship they had. She kept his room just as he left it until she died. She would go in and sit with his things and miss him.

At Madame Tussauds, I meet the Marvel super heroes and walk through a chamber of horrors, which makes me nauseous with the blood and body parts thrown everywhere. I am also introduced to the Royal Family.

William makes an appointment for us to view the Royal Family jewels ahead of the tourist crowd. I stand before the

Crown Jewels with the famous d Koh-i-Noor diamond in the center. It is one of the largest known diamonds in the world.

We join a tour that takes us to the White Tower which houses the amour worn by kings such as Henry VIII and his horse. Weapons and tools of torture are kept there as well even though there is not a torture chamber on the premises. The Tower was for the nobility, and they were not tortured, just decapitated. Lastly is the Chapel of St. John, which is lovely.

We drive by Big Ben and Kensington Palace. William tells me a story about him and Prince William running through several rooms and then coming face to face with the Queen. My William slid face down between her legs almost tripping her while Wills (Prince William) ran head first into her secretary, knocking him on his ass. With the grace of a queen, she cautioned the boys about running in the palace and continued on her way, smiling.

On Sunday, Williams's mother plans a large family dinner to introduce me to William's uncles and aunts and some cousins. After the dinner, William and I walk into the library where the younger of the guests are assembled. As we walk into the room, Williams's cousin and Emily are discussing the usefulness of a man's penis. "That is probably the most sophisticated knob joke I have ever heard," Jonathan says.

Emily starts, "It is just a tool used by men to convert virgins into what *they* consider a more useful way to spend their time."

"I have used mine to wean a lesbian from crack to a more productive member of British society," a cousin clarifies.

"I hug mine regularly, not wanting anything bad to happen to it," another adds.

"You hug yours regularly hoping you might obtain some free putty to use in your artwork, Lyle," Eve adds in.

"When one is a starving artist, one must be frugal with one's free putty."

I am in hysterics. British humor is highly recommended. Not wishing to pee in my pants, I excuse myself to use the restroom. When I come out, William's uncle is walking down the hall outside it. "You are lovely, my dear. I can see that William is over the moon with you. I am glad for that. He has been disappointed by his other affiliation. I hope that is rectified soon so he can move forward with you."

"Thank you. William is very special to me. I want him happy also. What affiliation disappointed him?"

"Why, Madeleine, of course," he says as he enters the bathroom and closes the door.

Who is Madeleine? Perhaps an old girlfriend? I walk back to the party with the discussion moving on to vaginas and what women use them to get. I look at William and smile. He is shaking his head at his family and their choice for after-dinner discussion. After a while, and because I can no longer keep my eyes open, I tell William I am going up to bed. Eve and Emily meet me at the door to ask if I would like to go to Harrods with them on Wednesday for a day of shopping. I tell them that I would love to and we make the plans.

I take a shower and crawl into bed. Sometime later, I feel William join me. He puts his arm around me and snuggles into me. We sleep.

CHAPTER 23

THE NEXT FEW MORNINGS I try to run. I do feel better if I get exercise and fresh air. Sitting around and eating all day is not my usual behavior. Wednesday morning I am at breakfast with William. "While you shop with the girls, I am going to go into the office with Jonathan and look some things over. I probably won't be back until very late. If you shop all day, you will be exhausted. If you are tired, don't wait up for me," he says, sweetly kissing my cheek.

"Okay." I kiss him good-bye and head back to my room to get ready for my day. A few minutes later, I come down to see Emily and Eve waiting for me.

"All set?" Emily asks.

"I'm ready."

As we drive to Harrods, I am filled in on the history. Harrods held several royal warrants for many years. After the whole business with Diana and Al-Fayed's son Dodi, he burnt the warrants in a spectacular fashion and filmed it. It is rumored that the Duke of Edinburgh, the Queen's husband, is banned from ever going in the store.

"But don't worry darling. William has an account there, so anything you want we will have him buy it for you," Emily states.

"I don't want William to buy me anything. If I see something I want, I will buy it myself."

"Don't be ridiculous, Brook. William is a billionaire and he wants to buy you things."

"This may come as a surprise to you, but I don't want William's money."

"Well for God's sake, if you don't want his money what *do* you want?" asks Eve.

"Just him. I don't like all of the stuff that comes with him. I can do nicely with my small apartment, cooking for William. I would be happy."

"He told us that and we thought he made it up. You would be with him with no money?" Emily asks.

"Absolutely. In fact, I might like it better. It would be quieter with just him and me."

We shop throughout the store. Eve and Emily have arms full of clothes taken out to the car for them. They shop for their children and those items go out. I find a belt that I like but when I figure out that this skinny little thing costs $350 US, I put it back.

"Don't you want the belt?" Eve asks me.

"Not at that price," I answer.

"William told us to make sure that you bought a few things at least. He isn't going to be happy when you come back with nothing."

"There are a few things that are going to upset William when he finds them out soon. This will pale in comparison to that. He will get over me not spending a ridiculous amount of money on a belt."

We find the food floor and stop for lunch. We have food courts in America. In Harrods, there are thirty-seven restaurants and even more gourmet shops~everything inside its walls. Whatever you can think of to eat, they have.

After some more shopping, I tell Emily that I have had enough for one day. We decide to drive back to the house. I am glad because I want a nap. We drop Eve off at her house and half of the trunk's cargo goes in with her. We make it to William's parents house and I help Emily organize the rest so it won't wrinkle. We are laughing as we enter the house. The footman announces to Emily, "Lady Madeleine is in the library awaiting your and Miss Kennedy's return."

I watch as Emily's face drains of color. I put my hand on her arm to steady her. "What's wrong Emily? Are you all right?" I ask concerned with her facial expression.

139

Emily turns to the footman and says, "Is anyone else home right now?"

"No, Lady Emily."

Emily looks at me and says, "No matter what she says to you, know that William loves you and wants to be with you. She hates him and wants nothing more than to ruin his happiness. Do you understand me?"

I nod my head as a feeling of absolute dread passes over me. Madeleine is the name that William's uncle referenced.

We walk to the library and I see a woman whose back is to me looking out the window. As we enter, she hears us and turns. She is tall with long brown hair pulled back on one side. She is beautiful and seems to glide when she walks over to us. "Emily, darling. I was beginning to think you would never get home," she says.

"And imagine my surprise to find out that you are here, Madeleine. To what do I owe this visit?"

"Why, I wanted to meet William's friend, of course. I heard a rumor that he brought his American . . . What should I call her? . . . *Lover* with him."

I watch her, wishing I was anywhere but where I am standing right now. She turns to me, appraising my appearance. I feel her eyes penetrate me.

"And *you* must be said lover," she spits out. "Where are your manners, Emily? Introduce us."

"Madeleine, this is Brook Kennedy, William's *girlfriend*. Brook, this is Lady Madeleine Barry, William's wife."

I can hear my heart pumping in my ears. I look at Emily and say, "William's *ex*-wife?"

"No, you bloody idiot! I am William's current and only wife. I see he didn't get around to notifying you that he *is* married. Pity, makes it very awkward to hear it from the wife," she said, clearly taking enjoyment in the telling.

"Brook, remember what I said," Emily says holding my hand.

I swallow hard and say, "Please excuse me. I am going to my room to lie down."

"It was a pleasure meeting you, Brook. I do hope you enjoy your visit with the Barry's."

I mount the stairs, almost unable to see because of the tears running down my cheeks. I can hear Emily raising her voice, telling Madeleine exactly what she thinks of her. I get to the room just in time to make it to the toilet to deposit my lunch.

After I brush my teeth, I decide I have to get out of here and go home. While I pack, I think.

He is married. That is what he meant by having to get out of something.

Do they have any children?

He can't marry me.

We committed adultery.

Everyone here knew he was married and no one said anything.

Jonathan knew, and the whole time he was with me said nothing.

Emily and Eve know and said nothing.

He is married.

I'm pregnant and he can't marry me.

I'm pregnant. I'm alone.

I call down to the footman. He answers the phone. "Hi, this is Miss Kennedy." I say. "Would you be so kind as to call a cab for me?"

"Miss Kennedy, Mr. Barry has left a car for your use."

"I don't want to use Mr. Barry's car. I would like a cab, please. And I would like to keep it between you and me, please."

"As you wish, Miss Kennedy. It should be here in half an hour."

"Thank you."

I finish packing. I write a hasty note thanking Mr. and Mrs. Barry for their hospitality. I write nothing for William. What could I say anyway? *Call me when you get a divorce?* On the other hand, *call me and we can make arrangements for you to visit your baby?* I throw up again. I grab my suitcase and head for the front door. I can see the cab waiting for me. I hand the footman the note for the Barry's and leave.

I don't remember the ride to the airport. I am in my misery and therefore not functioning properly. When I get through the sea of bodies at Heathrow Airport to find the check-in desk to change my ticket, I feel like I am going to heave again. I lean in to the clerk and say, "I am pregnant and I feel like I am going to throw up."

She hands me a couple of airsick bags and I smile gratefully. I'm amused because a complete stranger is the first person I've told that I'm pregnant. How sad is that? She knows before William. Before anyone.

The next flight for New York leaves in an hour. I sit in the waiting area trying not to think about the mess I find myself in. Trying to figure out what I should do. They call to board the plane. I find my seat and buckle up. I try to sleep as much as I can on the flight home. I watch the movie and read a few magazines. I see the ad with the children and me in one of them. That shoot seems like a lifetime ago. It was before I knew he was married, so it is in a different life. I was happy then, blissful in my ignorance.

We land and I find a cab to take me to William's house. There are a few things I need to pick up and I have to leave his keys. I ride in the elevator to his apartment and let myself in. Leaving my suitcase in the gallery, I walk to the bedroom. I pick up the picture of my brother and me, the one of my parents and one of William and me that I love.

My eyes settle on the one behind William's bed. I stare for a moment just as I did the first time I saw it. I hear a noise behind me and I turn to look. It's Angela. "Miss Kennedy, I thought I heard a noise."

"I'm sorry, Angela. I just stopped to pick up three pictures that I want."

"Mr. Barry called and asked that if I saw you to ask you to please wait here for him. He is flying back now and should be here in an hour or two."

"When he gets here please tell him I couldn't wait. I want to be alone. I'll call him when I can."

"I'll tell him but he sounded distraught."

"I'm sorry for that, but it was all his doing."

I pack the pictures in my suitcase. I put my keys on the table and leave.

I decide to walk home. I have been cooped up in stuffy estates and planes for a week and a half. I listen to my suitcase click over the seams in the sidewalk. Click, click, click as I walk. My heart synchronizes with the clicks. Then I start to click off the days I was so happy with William.

Click.-He met me for a drink at the airport.

Click.-Dinner in Miami.

Click.-Walking on the beach.

Click.-Making love the first time.

Click.-Taking pictures.

Click.-Chicago.

Click.-The opera.

Click.-Copacabana.

Click.-Telegraph hill.

I make it home before I max out on happy moments. I walk into my apartment, throw my suitcase in the bedroom, and fall on the bed. I pull the bedspread over me and try to sleep.

CHAPTER 24

I WAKE VERY EARLY HAVING slept most of the night. I feel slightly better, physically. Emotionally, I'm drowning in my sea of regret and misery. I check my phone and there are several messages, all from William. I don't have the will right now to listen to them. I begin to unpack when there is a knock at my door. I look through the peephole to see Link standing there. I open the door and stand back. "What are *you* doing home?" he asks.

"I live here."

"No you don't. You pay rent here but you live on 5th Avenue."

"Not anymore."

Link comes in and sits down. "You got coffee?"

"I don't know."

"I'll go get some. Be right back."

A few minutes later, he is back with coffee and cream. I think I love this man.

"All right," he says. "Spill. What happened?"

"Everything was great. Too good to be true, which is why it wasn't . . . . true, that is. I met his wife in England."

"Wow," he says with the look of disbelief in his eyes. "Wife as in married? Not ex?"

"That is exactly what I said. I found out something else while I was there, too."

"He has kids?"

"I know of one. The one he's going to have with me."

"You're preggers? How far? Does he know?"

"I'm due in July. I wanted to tell him when we got home and we were alone. That didn't happen, so he doesn't even know."

"Okay. What do you want to do?"

"I'm going to have the baby. I'm not going to tell him. I don't want him to just want the baby. I want him to want *me*. I want him not to be married. I wanted a future with him. I'll tell him eventually, but not now."

"He can support you. You won't have to work, Brook. You should think about telling him."

"I can support myself. I have a lot in savings. William wouldn't let me pay for anything. All my income went into the bank. I can work for a while and then I can live quietly until the baby comes. I'll call the agency this morning to tell them I'm back and to book me."

"Sandy and I are here for you, kid. I love babies. I'm not crazy about changing diapers but I can learn. Call me if you need me. Sandy will be back Sunday night and then you can tell her."

I call my agency. Carline wants me to come in so we can discuss what I want for assignments. I tell her I will stop in this afternoon. Then I sit down to listen to William's messages.

"Brook, I am so sorry that I didn't tell you about Madeleine. I married her, but she doesn't love me and never did. Please, Brook, talk to me."

"Angela said you would not stay to see me. I love you, Brook. I am in hell. Please talk to me."

"I have never even slept with her, Brook. She wouldn't before we got married and I chalked that up to wanting to be a virgin. On our wedding night, I just thought she was tired. By the next night I asked her if she was ever going to consummate our marriage and she said no. I left for the states three days later. I have asked her for a divorce countless times, as has my family, and hers and my lawyers. She wants to be a Duchess. I think she would kill my father to be one. Please call me, Brook."

"I am going back to England to have an audience with the Queen. If I can convince her to intercede on my behalf, I can get a divorce without Madeleine's permission. I want you to come with me, Brook. You can meet the Queen. When she sees how good you are, she will take pity on me and help get me out from Madeleine's clutches. I have to talk to you, Brook."

"My father got me an audience in January. I am going back for Christmas and I will see the Queen. Please come with me. I love you, Brook."

I walk to the agency. Carline meets me at the door. "I just had a conversation with William," she says, sadly. "He told me what happened. I didn't know that he was married. Not that it matters, but he's a mess. He was crying on the phone. I have never seen him cry about anything."

"How do you know he was crying?" I ask.

"He was sniffling and he put the phone down to blow his nose. He sounds awful, Brook."

"I am in hell, too. Can we go to your office? I have something to tell you in private." We walk to her office and I sit in the chair. I begin. "I need to work as much as I can between now and March. After that, no one will want me for a while."

"Will you go overseas? I have work in Italy and then Australia from May through June."

"I'll take the work in Italy. They won't want me in Australia."

"Why not?"

"I'm pregnant. I'm due in July. I will be huge in May."

"Does William know?"

"No, he doesn't and I don't want to tell him just yet. And I don't want you to tell him either."

"Interestingly enough, the work in Australia is for a company that is starting a fashion division in maternity wear."

"You are *kidding.*"

"No, I'm not kidding. They said to send a model, but a pregnant model would fit their need just as well."

"I could stay and have the baby there. Away from all of the drama here. Let them know that I want the job, if they want me."

"I'll tell them and I won't say anything to William. You *will* tell him about the baby, won't you?"

"Later, after he decides what he wants. If I tell him now it will sway his decision. I want him to want me for me, not because of the baby." I am near tears, so I get up and walk to the door. "Call me when you know?"

I walk outside and stand next to the building for a few minutes, breathing the crisp late-November air. I start to walk back to my apartment. I pass by several women walking with strollers. Funny, before I only saw a few, but now it's every other person. I keep walking and a car comes to a screeching halt at the curb next to me. The door flies open and William gets out. I turn away. He grabs my shoulders and says, "Brook, I have found you. Did you listen to my messages?"

"I did."

"You won't call me? Will you turn around and look at me?"

"I can't. You know how you control me. You own my heart. I can't look at you."

"I don't control you at all. You left me, remember. How do I control you?"

"You are making a scene, William."

"I don't give a fuck if I make a scene. I'll get on my knees and beg you to come home with me. Will that be enough of a scene to make you do it, Brook?"

"I love you, William. Not that saying that will change anything. You're married and she holds all the cards. I can't even say you lied to me because I never asked you if you were married.

I am going to Italy for a shoot after Christmas. I will be there until the end of April. After you talk to the Queen, you can find me there. I'm sorry, I can't do this."

I start to walk away, tears streaming down my cheeks. I make it back home and collapse on the couch. I can't take much more of the heartache. I will have a baby who is a nervous wreck because I am one. I make a cup of tea and watch a movie. At 8:00, I get up and go to bed.

The next two weeks pass by quickly. I work every day. The nausea passes but the fatigue remains. I run when I can and feel better for it. William sent me a letter the day before he was to leave for England. By the time I received it he had left. In it are all the same things he said in his messages, but it ends it with, "This is my last Christmas alone. Short of murdering her, I will be with you next Christmas."

I spend Christmas with Sandy and Link. They both keep telling me to tell William about the baby. I know that they are probably right. I know that he loves me. Now it has gone so far that I don't know how to tell him.

The second week of January I leave for Italy. By the time I land in Rome, I am exhausted. I check in to my hotel and sleep the whole day and most of the night. I wake early and go for a jog. I don't run full-out anymore. I have a small potbelly to think of.

I begin the shoot two days after my arrival. The mother of the photographer is at the shoot, too. She takes one look at me and asks him when "il bambino" is due. He laughs and says, "My mother thinks that you are pregnant with a baby boy. I am to tell her when your son is coming. I told her you are not pregnant, but she has second sight and tells me I am crazy."

"Please tell your mother for me that my baby is due in July. I don't know if it is a girl or a boy."

He looks at me with a frown. "You *are* pregnant. Why didn't you tell me? I would never have let you stay in a hotel if I had known that you were pregnant."

"I'm fine in the hotel. I like it there," I answer him.

"There is no cooking and restaurants are expensive. You will move today to my villa and live with my wife and me until the shoot is over. How could your husband let you do this?"

"I don't have a husband. I can't live with you. It wouldn't be right."

"What about the baby's father? I am moving you today, as soon as we finish here." He turns to his mother to tell her all that we have said, I guess. She keeps nodding to me and talks to him. When they finish their discussion he says, "You are having a boy. You can bet money on it. She is never wrong. You are living with us, no argument. Mama will have you fattened up within a week. I have four children so I don't offer you peace, just good food and safety."

And with that, I have a new place to live. The best thing about Italians is that they love to feed you. Angelo helps me with my bag and drives to his villa. When we arrive, his lovely wife and adorable children are lined up on the steps as if they were to be inspected. His wife walks down the stairs and takes my hand to greet me. She speaks to me in Italian, which I know very little of, but thankfully Angelo translates for me.

"This is my wife, Gratiana. My children Simona, Claudina, Salvatorio and Basilio."

I smile at their beautiful faces. "Hello. My name is Brook."

"My mother lives with us also. Her name is Natalia. I know the language will be a problem, but the children are learning English and can speak some."

I make my way into the house. Angelo points out rooms. He opens a door to a beautiful room and puts my bag on the bed. "This is your room," he says sweetly. "We eat at 7:30 downstairs in the dining room. The shower is two doors down on the right. Come down whenever you are comfortable."

I take his hand and say, "Thank you so much, Angelo." There are tears in my eyes.

He says, "No crying, only a happy baby."

CHAPTER 25

ANGELO AND I LEAVE EVERY morning for the day's shoot. Natalia or Gratiana stop by with lunch and he brings me back for dinner. I am treated like his sister. At night, I sit with his children and speak English with them. They are like sponges and pick up the language much faster than I learn Italian.

A week or so into my stay with Angelo's family he says, "Tell me about the baby's father. Why are you not with him?"

"He is married. He wasn't living with her. I didn't know about her."

"How did you find out?"

"I was at his family's house in England for a visit. I was shopping with his sister and his brother's wife. When we came back to his house, she was there. She told me that she was his wife."

"Why haven't they divorced?"

"I'm somewhat fuzzy about that. He wants one but she doesn't. He has a royal title and she wants to be a Duchess. She doesn't want *him*, just who he is, I guess."

"And what does Brook want?"

"I want a small house with a nice fenced-in backyard that my children can play in. A husband that loves me and a dog."

"And what does *he* want?"

"He tells me that he wants me. I believe him. I do think he wants me. I know that he will want the baby. His wife never wanted him and would not have children. He wants children."

"Why did you leave him?"

"When we first started to see each other, I didn't know who he was. He pretended to be American. He then told me who he was and I told him I didn't want any more lies. He promised to tell me everything. He left out the fact that he was married. I found out that I was pregnant a few days before I met his wife. I left without telling anyone and flew home."

"He knows nothing about the baby? Does he know where you are?"

"I told him I was going to Italy. He can find me. I'm not exactly hiding. The only people who know about the baby are my agent, two friends and you."

"What would he do if he knew?"

"He would come and get me."

"And this is bad?"

I burst into tears and say, "I don't know. He lied by omission, so now I'm lying. It doesn't make sense but that is what I'm doing. I was hurt so now I want to hurt him. I don't want to do this by myself but I don't want tell him. Do I make any sense to you?"

"You are pregnant. No woman makes sense when her hormones are crazy in her body. When my wife was pregnant, all I wanted to do was hold her. She was giving me my most precious gift~my children. She went from wanting me to hold her to screaming at me for getting her pregnant and then we did this three more times. Making love to her with her belly between us are some of the best memories I have. You are missing this. Someday you will be sorry for that. Believe me."

"You think I should tell him."

"I think you *need* to tell him. I think you will regret not telling him. I think he will hold this against you."

One Saturday, Angelo knocks on my door. I open it and he says, "We are going sightseeing today. Wear sneakers and come downstairs." When I get there, Salvatorio and Simona are waiting. The four of us get into the car and head into the city.

The first stop is the catacombs where the crucified Christians were buried. They were not allowed inside the city walls for burial. As we walk through, the children point out interesting markings and tell me the complete history. Next, we go to the Tivoli Gardens. Even though it is winter, it is still beautiful to see. Emperor Hadrian lived here and created his version of Eden. Angelo takes me to the Coliseum, which is simply magnificent. To imagine what took place here and to think of the people and animals that died horrible deaths makes my skin crawl. Lastly, we walk out to the Roman Forum, where the people of ancient Rome did their shopping.

On our way back to his house, Angelo tells me that next weekend we will get up very early to go to the Vatican. We have to be there before everyone wakes up and the crowds become too large.

Wednesday, a small package arrives for me. Carline sent it from the agency. After the shoot, I'm waiting for Angelo to pack up so I open it. Inside is a note.

> *Brook,*
>
> *Enclosed you will find a note from William, a check, and a CD. He calls me almost every day to check on you. All I have said is that you are fine and in Italy, as you instructed me to do. He begs me to tell you that he loves you. He is miserable without you. He is so very sorry for lying to you. He begs you to forgive him. If you want him to receive a message from you, please call me with it. I hope you are well.*
>
> *Carline*

The CD is Josh Groban. The cashier's check is made out to me for $50,000. I open the note and read.

> *Darling Brook,*
>
> *I haven't held you in four months. My arms ache with your absence. I had my audience with the Queen yesterday. She has agreed to intervene on my behalf so that I may obtain a divorce from Madeleine. She declared that my marriage was a sham and was never consummated. Therefore, I can apply for an annulment*

*if I want. I told her that I want whatever is faster. I told
her about you and my wish to marry. She will force
the issue with Madeleine.*

*I love you. I miss you. I found this CD in a music
store. The whole thing reminded me of you. I know he is
your favorite vocalist. The songs "You're Still You" and
"Home to Stay" are my songs to you. I hope you are well
and happy. Above al,l Brook, I want you to be happy.*

*All my love,
William*

Tears run down my chin. He doesn't mention the money, so
him. When I get to the house, I go to my room to lie down for a rest.
I put the CD in and listen to the songs. It's beautiful and relaxing.
The songs William picked are perfect. I fall asleep listening.

It is the middle of March and my assignment is nearing
completion. Angelo has two more weeks of work and then
he and his wife are going on a second honeymoon to Naples.
They ask me if I would stay and help Angelo's mom with the
children. I have nothing else to do, so I happily agree. The
children are loud but very well behaved.

Saturday morning at 6:00 Angelo wakes me up for our
Vatican adventure. This time we take Claudina and Basilio
with us. When we find the entrance, there are only twenty or so
people ahead of us. Angelo tells me we did well with our plan.
The doors open and we walk in through heavy security. We
are searched and metal-detected and finally enter the Sistine
Chapel. The words to describe it have not been invented yet. I
have goose bumps. Beauty, light, peace and tranquility all in
one place and here for us to enjoy.

We walk through Saint Peter's Square, admiring the statues
of the saints. We then walk to the Trevi Fountain to throw
our coins in and make a wish. Our last stop of the day is the
Spanish Steps. The children correct me with "Scalinata della
Trinita dei Monti." I climb the steps with the children, taking
them two at a time. The view is spectacular. The Trinita dei
Monti church at the top is breathtaking. We walk back down

the steps, passing by families who are sitting there watching the world go by. The steps are so wide and the children tell me there are 138 of them.

Again, when we get back to the house, I take a nap. The baby is taking my strength. I am told that is what boys do. Girls take the mothers good looks away. That is why Natalia thinks I am having a boy~because I am still pretty.

After giving some thought to Carline's note I call her. "Ford Models. Carline speaking," she says.

"Hi, Carline, it's Brook. How are you?"

"Brook, how good to hear from you. I'm fine. How are you?"

"I feel good. Tired, but good. I'm staying with Angelo and his family. He rescued me from the hotel when I told him I was pregnant."

"That's good. You shouldn't be alone all the time."

"I got the package you sent. Thank you for everything. I'm going to be here until the first week of April and then Australia. Tell William exactly where I am the beginning of the last week in March. Please tell him I will be on the Spanish Steps every day that it doesn't rain, in the early afternoon. If he wants to see me, that is where he will find me."

"I'll tell him, Brook. I know he will be there. Do you need anything?"

"No, thank you, Carline. I have found peace with this wonderful family."

The next two weeks fly by. Angelo has a tough time taking long shots of me because my little pot blew up overnight. I now have a beer gut. Angelo says it's his mother's and wife's cooking. Simona has her hand plastered to me every night, waiting to feel the baby move.

Angelo finishes with the assignment and we pack up for the last time. "I am sorry to see it end, Angelo. I have had a wonderful time with you," I tell him.

"This one is finished, but there will be others, no?"

"I don't know. I don't predict the future. Natalia does that. What does *she* say?"

"We will have to ask her," he says with a smile.

CHAPTER 26

ANGELO AND GRATIANA LEAVE FOR their vacation. Salvatorio takes over as the man of the house at the age of ten. I watched as his father told him it was his responsibility to take care of his siblings and grandma. He stood up straighter and told his father he would watch over all of us in his absence. I suspect he will sleep near the door with a shotgun for the duration of his father's absence.

The children are in school, so the days will be free. I help Natalia get the children off on Monday. We pick around the house and she leaves to do some shopping. I call Carline and say, "Hi again."

"Brook. How are you?"

"Fat, but good."

"You finally popped out?"

"You could say that. My even butt looks pregnant. I felt bad for Angelo. He had to tailor his shots around my baby parts."

"Angelo loves babies. I'm sure he didn't mind."

"He never complains. I wanted to know if you spoke with William yet."

"He called earlier this morning. I told him and he thanked me. He had to pick something up and then he was heading to Italy for you."

"He will be here Wednesday or Thursday then?"

"I would say so. I don't know what he had to pick up, do you?"

"I don't have any idea. I'll wait on the steps starting Wednesday. I'll call you later. Thanks for being my go-between."

Debbie Zello

I make several more calls that day, catching everyone up on my life. Sandy and Link are getting married. They think October, so I can be the maid of honor. Millie and Carol have both found new men. I don't tell them about the baby. William should know before anyone else does. We promise to get together when I come back home. Then I call Regina and leave a message. Christina isn't home either. I finally talk to Wendy. She tells me that Steve's wife is pregnant and due in September and Regina has a steady guy in her life. All of my friends seem to be happy. Knowing this makes me happy, too.

The children come home from school and the homework begins. I am okay with math because figures are the same in any language. The rest of their work is, let's face it, Italian to me! I help Salvatorio and Claudina with their English homework and Natalia conquers the rest. We have dinner and then we go out to the piazza for gelato. Once the children are in bed, I take a nice relaxing bubble bath.

I wake to a beautiful spring morning. It is going to be 65 degrees today. After breakfast, I walk the children to school. I want to do some shopping to find something for my hosts to say thank you. I find a shop that has Murano glass, also known as Venetian glass. I find a bowl with a matching platter that I think will look lovely in their dining room. I have it wrapped and leave the store satisfied with my purchases.

I find another shop that sells women's clothes. I want to find a nightgown and robe for Natalia. She wears a lot of blue. I come across the exact thing I am looking for and buy it. Now for the children. They have more toys than anyone needs. I pass by a jewelry store and see in the window necklaces with a cross on them. The family is very Catholic and I haven't seen crosses on the children, although all of the adults wear one. I go in and find two for the girls and two for the boys. It is a good thing that these are small because I am having a hard time carrying the heavy glass and the large box for Natalia. I get home and put everything in my closet.

The children come home, and once again, it is the chaos of homework. After dinner, we roast marshmallows on the porticato. I feel badly because I am not much company for

156

Natalia. She speaks very little English and my Italian is dreadful.

Wednesday, we get the children off to school. After we clean up, I pack some cheese, bread and a bottle of water and head out to the steps. I climb up near the top and sit. I watch people watching people. I engage in my pastime of making up the lives I would give them. I eat my lunch and leave in time to be home for the children. I don't see William. Thursday, Friday, and Saturday pass by with the same result. I sit for a few hours alone. I eat my lunch with strangers and walk home. It is going to rain tomorrow. Angelo and Gratiana are due home late in the afternoon.

Monday, with their parents home, I am free to sleep in, as I am not on get-to-school duty. I pack my lunch and leave for my post on the steps. I have become friendly with a little old man who is there every day with me. He nods and takes off his hat as I pass by. I say, "Buon pomeriggio. Come stai?"

"Buon pomeriggio. Bene, grazie. Come vanno le cose?" he asks me as usual.

"Bene, grazie. Arrivederci," I answer.

"A presto."

I take a seat and enjoy the sun. It is warm today so I take off my sweater and fold it in my lap. I lean against the side and fall asleep for a few minutes. I wake because a man has started to play the violin at the bottom of the stairs. The sound travels up and surrounds me like a hug. I don't recognize the melody, but I revel in its beauty. The afternoon passes and I leave to walk home. Angelo greets me at the door. "No luck today, Brook?" he asks.

"No. I am beginning to think he won't come. Maybe he has forgotten me. Or maybe he's tired of waiting for me to make up my mind."

"You don't believe that, do you?"

"I don't know. I miss him terribly. I want him to hold me."

Angelo walks over to me and takes me in his arms to comfort me. I begin to cry again. God, that pisses me off! I'm tired of crying. These damn hormones are driving me crazy. "Thank you. I'm okay. I'm going to take a bath."

I reach my room and start a bath. I have to start packing because my plane leaves Thursday night for Australia. William has three days to find me or I will be gone again.

Tuesday, I am back on my step waiting. This time, the man with the violin is joined by a man with a cello. Together they make beautiful music. Again, I go home without seeing William.

Wednesday, I don't see my old man friend at all. Angelo had offered to come with me and sit, but I gratefully declined. I see a couple with a little baby and I imagine that they met here on the steps and they come back every now and then to capture that feeling. Another couple catches my eye and I imagine that they are on a second honeymoon. They came here after they wed.

I am so warm in the sun that I drift off again. I am awakened by the deep baritone voice that I know so well. "Wake up, Sleeping Beauty." I open my eyes to see William's face and smile.

"I was beginning to think you were not going to find me," I say, sleepily.

"I am here now. I had to get some things in order. I have a lot to tell you."

"I have some things to tell you, too, William."

Continue on to William's story in Loving Brook.

Loving Brook

The Continuing Love Story of Brook and William

CHAPTER 1

WHEN I THINK BACK TO the first time I saw Brook, a warm and peaceful feeling comes over me. Watching her in her uniform talking to and helping my fellow passengers on that long flight to England. Her sweet creamy voice and the way she smelled floored me. Her outer beauty staggered me. However, her unassuming grace affected me like no other ever has. I was a pain always asking for something just to keep her coming back to talk to me.

The first time I touched her . . . felt like the sun shining on my face. All warm and comforting. Kissing her is akin to reaching the stars. Making love to her . . . heaven itself. She is all that I want and all that I need. She is the first woman I felt myself surrendering to. I was bewitched.

"As I understand the plan, you want to buy the two companies but dump the one division," I say to Jonathan.

"Yes. If we can buy under value, we will become the largest shipper in the UK. We will control the market, William, and we will set the prices."

"Okay. Make the offer and keep me informed on the negotiations. Now, if that is all we have to discuss, I would like to get back to the house. I left Brook in the hands of your wife and our sister. God only knows what debauchery has transpired."

"Surely you don't suspect that our women would lead Brook down the wrong path?"

"We are talking about Emily, Jonathan. The Queen of wickedness, for sure."

"True, but Brook wouldn't get involved with any of Emily's schemes."

"I hope not, but I want to get back to make sure."

I watch Jonathan clean up his desk. I dismiss the acquisition team and make my way out of the office to our waiting car. Once inside I call Brook to let her know that I am on my way back. Curiously, it goes right to voicemail. I don't leave a message. She will see that I called and call back.

As we drive, I use the time to read over the endless papers that Jonathan has given me to look at. Now, I remember why I hate the business world. Too much paper to deal with. Forty-five minutes later, we pull up to the house. I jump out, eager to see Brook and start our evening. I approach the door. It swings open with John, our footman, at his post as always. "Good evening, John."

"Good evening, Mr. Barry. I trust you had a good day."

"Very much so. Where is everyone, John?"

"The Lady Emily and your parents are in the library, sir."

"Thank you." I walk towards the library as Emily is coming out.

"William, I am so glad you are finally home." I can see by her face that something is wrong.

"What has happened, Emily?"

"We went shopping and when we came home Madeleine was waiting here. No one was home but Brook and me. I didn't know what to do. John had announced that she was waiting for us in the library. Before we went in, I told Brook to remember that you love her, regardless of anything Madeleine might say."

"What happened Emily? Get to it!"

"Madeleine introduced herself to Brook as your current and only wife. Brook looked ill excused herself and went upstairs."

"Where is she now?" I say panic stricken.

"That is just it, William. I had a retched quarrel with Madeleine and by the time she left well over a half an hour had gone by. I went to Brook's room to check on her and she was gone."

"What the hell do you mean gone?"

"She had packed her belongings and had John obtain a cab for her. She has left and I don't know where she went."

I run out to the door to talk to John. "John, do you know exactly where Miss Kennedy was going?"

"No, sir. She didn't say and I didn't ask. Is there a problem, sir?"

"Yes. Please call the cab company and determine where the cab brought her. Then have the car brought around, please."

"She did leave a note for your parents, sir. I gave it to your father upon his return home."

"Thank you, John. Make the calls, please." I run back to the library to see Brook's note. All it said was thank you for your hospitality and sorry to leave like this.

I jog to my room to grab my passport in case she went to the airport. When I get back downstairs, John confirms that is, indeed, where she went. I sprint to my waiting car and tell George to get me to the airport as fast as he can. I begin to make phone calls to get her flight information. She departs in thirty minutes. I won't make it there in time. I book myself on the next plane out, which is in two hours. I call Angela to ask her to keep Brook there until I can see her. She will do her best, but I know that Brook won't wait. If she were interested in an explanation, she would have waited here for one.

The wait for the flight and the flight itself are agony. I can see her face when Madeleine told her. The only woman I want meets the one woman who won't let me go. I have to make this right somehow.

As soon as we land, I call Angela. She tells me that Brook had been there. She took three pictures and left. Angela said she was staring at our picture over the bed for a long time. I wish I knew what she was thinking. I call her, and this time I leave a message. After a few minutes, I leave another and by the time I get home, another. By nightfall, I haven't heard from Brook.

My next call is to Madeleine. After a very unpleasant explanation on her part and a corresponding debasement on mine, I hang up.

At midnight, I call my father. "I need your help to arrange an audience with Her Majesty. I have to obtain a divorce from Madeleine one way or another. If she won't consent, then I will force her through embarrassment. Having to tell the Queen that she would not consummate our marriage will not be pleasant for her."

"Did you tell Madeleine that you were going to the Queen?" my father asks.

"Yes, I told her just before I called you. She said to do whatever I wanted, but she will not consent to a divorce."

"I will call and make the arrangements for you, son. It has been long enough. We all think highly of Brook. She will make you a good wife."

"I doubt that she will have me now. I think I have ruined that chance."

"She is hurt, no doubt of that. However, hurt heals and she does love you, which is evident. It was good to see you together."

"I would marry her today if I could."

"I will call you as soon as the arrangements are made. Will you be home for Christmas?"

"I'm not sure. I want to talk to Brook first. If she won't speak to me, I will probably come home soon."

I call Carline and she lets me know that Brook has been in touch with her. She is stopping by the agency today to discuss work. I don't want to appear like a stalker, but this is my best chance of catching her on the street and forcing a conversation with me. Luke and I find ourselves circling the streets adjacent to the agency, hoping to see Brook walking. Finally, in the late afternoon, I see her come out of the building. Luke crosses the road, pulls next to her and stops to let me out.

Brook sees me and turns away. I hurry to her and hold her shoulders. She recoils at my touch. I say broken, "Brook, I have found you. Have you listened to my messages?"

"I have," she says, coolly.

"You won't call me? Will you turn around and look at me?"

"I can't. You know how you control me. You own my heart. I can't look at you."

"I don't control you at all. You left me, remember? How do I control you?"

"You are making a scene, William."

"I don't give a fuck if I make a scene. I'll get on my knees and beg you to come home with me. Will that be enough of a scene to make you do it, Brook? Madeleine married me under false pretences. She didn't love me or want me. She wanted my title, money and the prestige that brings. I never consummated the marriage Brook. She refused me. She won't give me a divorce. I have to go to the queen to obtain one. My father is making the arrangements for me as we speak. Please forgive me Brook, for not telling you everything right from the beginning."

"I love you, William. I am going to Italy for a short time after Christmas. I will be there until the end of April. After you talk to the Queen, you can find me there. I am sorry."

I stand on the sidewalk and watch her walk away from me. I descend further into the hell of my own making.

CHAPTER 2

WHEN I CAN NO LONGER see her walking, I turn and walk back to the car. I get in and tell Luke, "Just take me home please, Luke."

"Yes, sir," he answers.

I find myself spending inordinate amounts of time in the bedroom, staring at the photograph of Brook and me. We were so happy together then. My phone rings and I answer, "Hello."

"William, darling, it's Emily."

"Hi, Emily. Is everyone all right?"

"Bloody well, William. How are you holding up?"

"Tolerable. I just saw Brook."

"Does she understand? What did she say?"

"Nothing really. She is going to Italy for a shoot after Christmas. She said that I could find her there after I speak to the Queen. Emily, when I saw her I jumped out of the car. She saw me and turned away. I caught up to her and held her shoulders and she fucking cringed. I touched her and she flinched like I was burning her. I have touched her everywhere and she has always welcomed my touch. What am I going to do?"

"You are going to talk to the Queen. You are going to tell her what a frigid bitch Madeleine is. You are going to tell her everything that has happened and then she is going to help you to get rid of Madeleine. Then you are going to find Brook and marry her and have several absolutely gorgeous children who love to run and take pictures."

"Thanks, Emily. I needed some perspective. I will be home next week and I am staying until I see the Queen and end this nightmare."

"Now that sounds more like my little brother the scrapper. You never gave up on a fight with anyone when we were growing up. I can't see you changing now. I know the Queen will side with you, William. Madeleine won't fulfill the basic duty to have children. End of contract."

"Thank you for calling, Emily. My love to all. I'll see you in a week."

"Good-bye, darling."

I stop by the agency the following Monday to see Carline. "Hi, Carline. How's it going?"

"Good, William. How are you doing?"

"Okay, I guess. I miss Brook every minute of every day, but that is my own doing."

"I guess so. What can I do for you?"

"The shoot that Brook is going on in Italy. With whom is she working?"

"William, I don't know if I should share Brook's information with you."

"I need to know that she will be safe there, that's all. If you have any reservations, I need to know."

"No reservations at all. She will be with Angelo. I think you know him from the South Africa shoot two years ago."

"Good. Yes, Angelo. He is a good man. He will take care with her. I am going back to the UK to get a divorce next week. I won't be back until I get it."

"What's the big deal, William? Here, you just file and everything moves along. Why is this such a process for you Brits?"

I decide to come clean with Carline and say, "It's because I am a member of the Royal Family. If my wife doesn't want to be divorced, I can't get one. I have to go to the Queen and plead my case for a forced divorce."

"You are a Royal? Who are you, William?"

"I am the Viscount Barry. Upon my father's death, I will be the Duke of Wessex. My wife would like to be a Duchess and that is the rub."

"She wants to be a Duchess but not a wife?"

"Right on the head, Carline. Too bad I didn't know that piece of information before I said 'I do,' because I wouldn't have said it."

"I'll tell you what, William. If I hear from Brook, I will let you know how she is. I can stay in touch with Angelo and check on her."

"Thank you. I would send security, but she is onto me and would be looking for them. I don't have the right anymore to protect her. I don't want to look like a stalker. I just want to keep her safe."

"I understand, William. I'll do what I can to help. Don't worry. Brook is very strong."

"Don't I know that. Have a good Christmas and I'll talk to you in the New Year."

"Bye, William."

I feel better that Carline will keep in touch with me. As I walk back to the apartment, I pass by Tiffany & Company. I walk past and turn back to go inside. I look at the engagement rings in the display when a clerk walks over to me and asks if he can be of service.

"Yes," I say. "I'd like to look at engagement rings, please."

"Yes, sir. May I ask your price range?"

"I don't have one. By that, I mean it is not about the price. I need the right ring, no matter the price."

"I see. Please follow me, sir."

I follow him to a private office area and sit in the offered chair. He excuses himself and tells me he will bring the stones and settings to me. I wait a few minutes and he returns with several boxes and eye loupes. "I warn you that I know very little about diamonds. I trust the reputation of this store that what you show me is the best that you have. I want a perfectly clear, flawless round stone of at least three carats set in platinum," I say. "I also want a matching wedding band with another two carats of diamonds. Then I want matching earrings and a necklace. The rings, I'd like ready for me within a week. The necklace and earrings can be sent to me in England."

He proceeds to show me several diamonds and settings. I pick what I think Brook would like, given my limited knowledge of her jewelry preferences. When the clerk figures out my bill, I think he has an orgasm at the thought of his commission check. I pay for my purchases and leave the store with his expressed thanks as he gleefully pumps my hand. I am glad that I can make someone happy.

Once home, I make a few calls to settle things, as I won't be back in the states for several months. I talk with Angela over coffee. "I am leaving sometime over the weekend, and I am not sure when I will be back. Close up the apartment and consider yourself on vacation. I will call you and give you notice of my return."

"Is there anything that I can do?" she asks, concern in her voice.

"Nothing. I have done this to myself and I am the only one who can undo it. If you need anything, call me. Otherwise, come and go as you please. Use what you like. I have left several signed checks on my desk. There is cash in the safe. All of the bills have been paid in advance for six months."

"Six months? You think that you will be gone that long, William?"

"I don't know. I am not coming back without her."

"Do you want me to close up here and come to England? I could do something there for you."

"That is very thoughtful, Angela, thank you. We have more than enough help there. Look at this as time off that you deserve for putting up with a bloke like me for four years."

"It has been my pleasure to work for you, William. All will be in order here and waiting for you when you return. Just call me once in a while to let me know how you are."

"I will. Now, will you speak to Luke and tell him of our conversation? I want the both of you to go and visit your families or travel somewhere. Don't just sit here waiting for me."

"I will speak to him."

I go about finishing the arrangements for my departure. I pack what I need and stop by Tiffany's to pick up Brook's rings. They are exactly what I wanted~rings fit for the beautiful woman that she is.

Luke drives me to the airport. I fly out to do battle with Madeleine for my freedom.

CHAPTER 3

"I TRUST YOU HAD A tolerable trip, sir?" George asks, knowing how quickly I've been turning about.

"Barely, George. Is the family home?"

"Yes, sir. Everyone is awaiting your arrival."

"Good. Let's not keep them waiting."

"Very well, sir. I have the car ahead of you."

We walk out to the waiting car, get in and drive off. It is a good hour to the house, minding traffic. I am tired when we get there. I walk in the door and remember that the last time I was here I made love to Brook that morning. A month ago already. The last time I made love to her. I pray that it is not the very last.

George takes my bag with Brook's rings in it up to my room. I walk to the library to see my parents. I open the door to see everyone engaged in a game of charades. "William, darling, come and save your mother from losing to Jonathan," my mother begs.

"If he were any kind of loving son, he would never abuse his mother so," I say, shooting a grimace towards my cherished brother.

"Quite right, brother. That is why you have always been the favorite," Jonathan replies.

"I am the favorite because of my good looks, charm and fabulous personality, dear brother."

"Lest we forget your unbounded humility," Emily adds, kissing my cheek.

"And my reason for coming home is to be with my loving family?"

"Your reason for coming home is to finally rid yourself of that parasite wife of yours," my father pipes in.

"And to that end, Father, do I have an appointment with the Queen?"

"Yes. The second week of January. It is the best I could do."

"That is fine. Where are my nieces and nephews? I want to see the most intelligent part of this family!"

"The girls are at a Christmas party with their friends and the boys are shopping with their mother," my mother tells me.

"I am going up to unpack and get settled. I will be down directly."

Once upstairs I have everything unpacked in record time. I walk across the hall, open Brook's door and step in. What I would not give to see her sitting on the bed waiting for me. I exit and close the door. I get back downstairs and hear the squeal of my nieces. "Unel Bubs, you came back!" Leslie yells.

"Yes, darling, I am here. Now come and give me a proper hug and kiss." I kneel down and accept her tight grip around me and her sloppy chocolate cookie kiss.

"Where are your sisters?" I ask.

"They are hiding. We have to find them. They were mean and wouldn't let me hide with them."

"We will fix them, Leslie. Tomorrow you and I will go out for a treat together without them. Would you like that?" I ask.

"Ever so much, Unel Bubs. Where will we go?"

"I will think on that and let you know."

Leslie and I start out to find her two sisters. We find Lily in the study behind a file cabinet. It takes us a while to find Lourine because I suspect she keeps moving. We catch up with her in the kitchen hiding behind Barbara, our cook.

"There you are, you little imp. I come to visit and you hide from me. It must be that you don't want the lovely things that I have brought for you from America. Fine, I will take them back when I leave and see if I can find three American girls who would like them."

"Please, Unel Bubs. We want them and we will be good."

I look at them with a fake frown on my face. "And you will be nice to Leslie and let her play in your games?"

"Oh yes, she can play."

I wink at Leslie. "Fine. You will find your presents on the table in the gallery." The three of them run off to find the dolls and clothes from American Girl that I brought for them. I can hear them squealing as I reenter the library.

"You spoil them too much, William," my mother admonishes me.

"Those girls and Jonathan's boys are all I have to amuse me."

"You will have your own soon, I feel it."

"I hope that you are right, Mum. First, I have to win the girl back. I think I would rather fight Goliath. I am nervous about talking with the Queen."

"Your father spoke to her secretary and gave an overview of your discussion. You just need to state your case and answer her questions. I don't see any problem. You deserve a proper wife in every sense of the word."

"You love me. The Queen only remembers me as the boy who slid between her legs whilst running after her grandson. I have an uphill climb just to be on an even foot with her."

"When she tells that story, William, she does so with a huge smile on her face. She was never angry about it. I think she loved the whole experience."

"With that in mind, should I slide under her when I see her this time?"

"I think you should stay on your feet. It is slightly different to have a thirty-two-year-old man slide under you than a ten-year-old boy."

"Quite so."

The girls come in with their mother. I am pulled down to sit on the floor with them and change the dolls' clothes. "You aren't doing it right, Unel Bubs," Lily says.

"You have to put her pants on first," Lourine adds.

"I will hold her and you dress her. I am a boy and we do things differently than girls."

A few minutes later, Jonathan's two boys join us. Maximilian is five and Hubert is three. "Unel Bubs, can you play . . . can you play crash the trucks with us?"

"What does crash the trucks entail, Max?"

"You and Hugh have trucks and I crash into them with my truck."

"That sounds dangerous, Max. Hugh is only three. I don't want him to get hurt."

"He won't get hurt. We play all the time."

So for the next half an hour, I play crash the trucks. My fingers are run over and crashed into, but the boys shriek with delight every time. Thankfully, dinner is called and I get my reprieve.

At dinner, my lovely companions are Lily and Max. Our conversation includes who at school is a bully and how hard it is to train Lily's new puppy. It seems he has taken a liking to Leslie's favorite blanket and has shredded it. According to Lily, the dog may not live if this behavior continues, especially if he decides he likes her blanket.

After dinner, Eve takes the boys home and Dick takes the girls to their house, leaving us to talk. "Have you heard from Brook at all?" Jonathan asks.

"Not a word. She left everything that I had bought for her at my house. All she took are the photographs of her family and one of us."

"That is a good sign. She wanted one of the two of you."

"Maybe."

"You will make your case, William, and the Queen will force the divorce. You will find Brook and she will forgive you and all will be well," Emily adds.

After a few more glasses of wine and an hour or two of discussion, I excuse myself for the evening. I climb the stairs to my room. My bed is a lonely place since Brook left it. I get in and try to fall asleep.

I spend the next week helping my mother ready the house for Christmas and helping Jonathan in the office. Neither occupation is my favorite. The ballroom is transformed into a winter wonderland. Every year on Boxing Day, my parents hold an open house of sorts. All of the townspeople are invited to come for a glass of wassail and sweets. It is a tradition hundreds of years old, and my mother loves it.

Jonathan has managed to purchase the two companies that he wanted, far below their market value. He does possess a terrific head for business. I profit daily from his expertise. I feel my days of living in America and taking pictures are coming quickly to an end. I will need to step up and help with the business to take some pressure away from him.

I send Brook a Christmas package with typical British items in it~a warm Irish wool scarf and hat, some English tea a few other small items. I enclose a note inquiring after her health. Nothing to delving just a little inquiry, although I doubt she will answer.

I have volunteered to take the girls shopping for presents for their parents. I don't know what I was thinking, but three days before Christmas I find myself driving them to the store. "Now girls, I only have two hands and three of you. How shall we do this?"

"Mommy holds Lily and Leslie's hands and I walk alone because I am the oldest," Lourine informs me.

"Fine. We stay together with no running off by yourselves. No hiding or any other games that you might have in mind."

"Okay, Unel Bubs," the three of them say.

Their mother gets a blouse, some scarves, and a hat. Their father gets a shirt, several ties and leather driving gloves. I get a stress headache and an urgent need for a glass of wine. We have everything wrapped and head to the car in one piece. When I drop them off at home, I have to come in for tea. Once again I am sitting in a too-small chair, with my lovely bonnet on, wishing Brook were here laughing at me.

CHAPTER 4

THE FESTIVITIES OF CHRISTMAS EVE start at 5:00, with my sister and her family arriving followed shortly by Jonathan's family. At 6:30 we gather around the table and eat. We start with our traditional parsnip and apple soup. Baked salmon with pistachio crust is next, then roasted leg of lamb. For dessert, we have mulled red wine jelly. It is really more like a pudding.

After our dinner, we sit by the fire near the tree and open some presents. We give out our gifts to each other. Santa's presents and our stockings are saved for Christmas day primarily because Santa hasn't come yet. The children unwrap their presents with gusto, paper flying and screams of delight. I participate in the festivities halfheartedly. When their parents announce that it is bedtime, I volunteer to read a story and tuck them in. I figure I can then go to my room and forgo any more conversation.

I enter the nursery to find my charges awaiting my arrival. All are dressed in their respective nightclothes, their favorite book in hand. I sit on the proffered pillow with the girls and boys rapt attention. I begin, "Twas the night before Christmas . . ."

I read Mark Twain's A Letter From Santa Clause.

Next is Rudolph the Red-Nosed Reindeer.

Finally, The Nutcracker and the Mouse King.

I look up to see Emily in the doorway, "It's been an hour children. No more stories. Unel Bubs has to get to bed so that Santa can come," she says. My charges scurry to their beds like rats from a sinking ship. All goes quiet and we kiss them goodnight. I close the door slightly and we walk down the hall.

"You are so good with them, William."

"No. They are good with me. I want some of my own to read to and kiss goodnight."

"You will."

"I'm tired. I'm going to my room. Please make my excuses to everyone."

"I'll see you in the morning. Goodnight."

I get to my room, shower and turn in. Holding my phone in my hand, I have all I can do not to call Brook. I scroll through my pictures, touching her face. I shut it off and begrudgingly close my eyes. I am woken early Christmas morning by a five-year-old knee to my stomach. I open my eyes to see Max sitting on me. "It's time to get up, Unel Bubs," he says. "We are all ready to open Santa's presents, but we need you to come down. Gram says we have to wait for you. Will you please hurry?"

"Give me a few minutes to wash up, Max, and I will be there directly."

Max leaves, giving me a chance to wake up fully. I manage to dress and take my place at the present-opening festivities. Eve, bless her, hands me a cup of coffee as Lily climbs into my lap so I can help her with a ribbon tied around her present. "This is hard to open, Unel Bubs."

"Yes, I can see that Lily. Let me cut it for you."

I cut the ribbon and she hops off my lap with her package. Max brings me three packages that Santa has left for me. I open them to find three Satya Paul silk ties and three Eton dress shirts. Santa has unquestionably great taste. The whole process takes almost two hours to complete and then we have breakfast.

Our dinner will consist of a chestnut soup, prawn Wellington, Christmas goose, ham, Brussels sprouts with bacon, sausage and herb stuffing, and roasted vegetables. The children love the crackers. Lourine pops mine for me and hands me my paper crown, my joke and gift. A Christmas pudding and cake for dessert.

After dinner, we listen to the Queen's traditional Christmas speech and at 6:00 we enjoy our Christmas tea around the fire.

Tea this year is mince pies, a delicious yule log and snowmen buns that are much like cupcakes for the children.

The children are put to bed and we enjoy our drinks and conversation. "A pessimist is just a well-informed optimist," Jonathan states.

"Quite so. And most men like smart women because opposites attract," Eve follows.

"You have heard the joke that on their wedding night a groom takes off his trousers and hands them to his wife and tells her to put them on. The wife says, 'I can't wear your trousers.' The husband says, 'Quite right, and don't forget that I am the one who wears them.' With that, the wife takes off her knickers, and tells him to put them on. He states, 'I can't get into your knickers.' She replies, 'And if you don't change your attitude, you never will!' Dick quips. My family erupts in laughter.

I look around the room at them enjoying each other's company. We are all laughing and happy. Emily continues, "Men are much like guns. You know that if you keep one around long enough you will have to shoot it."

"Yes, and women are much like tornadoes. They moan a lot when they come and take your house when they go," Jonathan comes back.

My father puts an end to the men-versus-women debate with his comment," And you can't live with them and don't want to live without them."

"Truer words were never spoken," I say.

"We have a most exciting day tomorrow and I will need all of you to help me so I am ending this evening with a goodnight and Happy Christmas," my mother says.

We all wish each other the same and go to our rooms.

Boxing Day is my mother's favorite, even more so than Christmas. The house is open to everyone who wishes to stop in for a glass of wassail, hot mulled apple cider, cookies, mince pie, brandy butter and yule log. The day starts with a fox hunt. My family doesn't use a live fox. Our dogs are trained on a stuffed one that the fox-master pulls through the woods on a rope . . .

At 2:00, the doors open for the townspeople and other visitor's. Usually by the end of the day, three to four hundred people have stopped by to wish good cheer.

I spot Dr. Martin across the ballroom and I walk to speak to him "Jeffery, how are you?" I ask.

"I am well, thank you, William. How is your lovely Brook feeling? Is she here? I would love to see her."

"No, Jeffery, Brook is in New York. We have not seen each other since shortly after she saw you."

"William, I am so sorry to hear that. May I ask what happened?"

"Madeleine was here and Brook didn't know about her. The conversation didn't go well and Brook left me. I have an audience with Her Majesty in a few weeks and I am going to ask for a forced divorce."

"Brook didn't tell you anything before she left?"

"Tell me what? Is she ill?"

"No, no, no. It is just some tests that I wanted to perform, nothing specific."

"She left while I was out. She said nothing to anyone. When I came back, she was just gone. I did speak to her very briefly in New York. I hurt her with my lie of omission. I have to make it right. Then I will find her and marry her."

"I wish you luck. The queen will see the right of it and grant you the divorce. Madeleine has not been a true wife to you. You should have more than a wife in name only."

"Thank you, Jeffery. It is good to have the support of friends and family."

As I talk with Jeffery, I see his eyes widen and he nods to me to look at the doorway. I turn to see Madeleine standing there appraising us. I turn back to him, and say, "And the bad penny never fails to show up."

"Maybe you can save the audience with the Queen if you can talk some sense into her today."

"I have spoken to her until I am blue from lack of oxygen. She doesn't care about my wishes, just her own."

"Nevertheless, one more try won't hurt," Jeffery councils.

I walk over to Madeleine and ask, "What do you want, Madeleine?"

"I am told it is not what I want but what you want. Isn't that why you're here. To try to be rid of me?"

"I have not hidden my desire for a divorce from you. You have known this since the third day of our marriage."

"We have been married almost four years, William. Why is it that you need this now?"

"I am moving forward. I have found someone with whom I want to spend my life. I will do this with or without your permission. You don't want me and yet you won't let me go."

"You took a vow for better or worse. Until death do us part, William," she states.

I move very close to her and say, "That can be arranged, Madeleine, should you so desire. Let me go. You can have the house and a generous settlement. Considering the three days that we resided in the same place, although not in the same bed, I'm being charitable. Don't misinterpret that for weakness."

"And then what do I do, William? I'm ruined never to have a title, a place in society."

"Sell the house and use the money to go somewhere and find some other unsuspecting man to sink your teeth into. I don't care what you do. If I go to the Queen, she will call you in for your side. Which leg will you stand on Madeleine? The 'I can't sleep with you because I don't love you' or the 'I can't sleep with you because I don't want you?' Either way, it won't wash with the Queen and you will be further embarrassed by it. Save yourself this and consent to the divorce." I walk away.

CHAPTER 5

THE HOLIDAYS OVER, JONATHAN AND I work on finalizing the paperwork on his acquisition of the two companies. My father's delight in having me at the office is apparent. I believe my days of doing what I want are nearing an end. If I am going to accept the money that my family association affords me, I need to be more responsible for the acquirement of said funds. I have relied on my brother's good nature and willingness to do the work for long enough.

I'm in a meeting with my father and brother when my father announces that he is retiring. "I have decided that with Williams's decision to resume his place, I am leaving. Your mother and I wish to do some extensive traveling and spend time together. Something that I have promised and have never delivered. I will finish out this year, giving William enough time to settle his affairs in the states. I will be in from time to time to observe the progress and check on my employees, but day-to-day operations are your responsibility alone."

"Thank you, Dad. I appreciate your faith in my abilities. Jonathan and I have very large shoes to fill. It should give you a good feeling that it takes two of us to even attempt to fill them," I pronounce.

"Quite right, William. I do not believe that I could do this alone. I am grateful that you are here to share the work," Jonathan adds.

"Good. Then we will finish this acquisition and get on with the building of this company to pass on to the next generation.

It is my wish, as it was my father's wish that we stay one of the largest employers in the UK."

The weeks pass by with me learning more about the operations of the shipyard every day. At night I formulate my plan of action with respect to my conversation with the Queen. I have been in her presence many times, but this is official and won't feel the same as a social meeting.

The day before I run through my argument with Jonathan in the office. "I think you have stated it well, William. I don't believe that the Queen would side with Madeleine and force you to stay married to a woman who won't have your children."

"I will know tomorrow. I will see it in her eyes."

As I am driven through the gates of Kensington Palace, my heart is in my throat. My future with Brook is riding on this one conversation. I am greeted by a representative of the Queen and shown through several rooms to an anteroom to her personal office. The door opens and a woman walks out and over to me. "Lord Barry, the Queen will see you now. She is right through that door." She points for me.

"Thank you very much," I say, hoping my nervousness doesn't show. I walk through the door to see my Queen sitting on a settee with her corgi next to her. I walk to her and present a polite bow. "Good morning your Majesty. You are looking well."

She offers her hand. I take it and kiss her fingers. She says, "William, I see you can walk as well as run. How divine. Please sit down"

"Yes, Your Majesty. I have learned a great deal in the last twenty years."

"I understand that you have a request of me, William. I am told that you have a marriage difficulty that you wish to discuss with me today."

"Yes, ma'am. As you are aware, the Lady Madeleine Barry and I were married almost four years past. She and I resided in the same house for three days past the wedding day. In that time, our marriage was not consummated. The Lady Barry refused the basic requirement of the marriage contract."

"I see, William. I have several deeply embarrassing questions to ask. Will you provide honest answers?"

"Yes, ma'am, that is why I am here. I want the honest truth to set me free from a loveless, childless marriage."

"Prior to your wedding, did you have physical knowledge of the Lady Barry?"

"No, ma'am. To my knowledge, she was a virgin bride. She refused my advances prior to the wedding and then continued the practice after."

"What did you make of her prior refusal?"

"In my foolishness I believed her when she said she wanted to be chaste before the wedding."

"What was her excuse on your wedding night?"

"Exhaustion, she said. She would not even welcome me into her chamber. She sent her lady to inform me."

"After that, what was the reasoning?"

"The day after, I went to her in the morning. She would not open her door to me. The day went by and I sent word through her lady that I would be with her directly after my shower that evening. I received a note when I exited my bathroom. It read that she was not able to entertain me that night or any other night. She had no desire to be a wife in flesh, only in name. Would I please honor her request? I left the next morning, stopping to speak with my parents and hers. It is my understanding that all of them gave her counsel on her duties, but she has still refused. Even if she consented now, I no longer have any feeling towards her."

She pats her dog's head and continues, "William, I take the institution of marriage very seriously. Three of my children have divorced, so I am aware of differences that cannot be overcome. Your situation supersedes all of the others. No one could expect you to live in a marriage such as this. Have you asked her for a divorce?"

"Many times. I secured a solicitor who presented her with papers, but she refused them. I have spoken to her face-to-face and she will not consent. I offered a generous settlement, but she refused that as well. You are my last resort, ma'am."

"I will need to speak with Madeleine before I give my judgment. So that you know, you would be due an annulment under this specific set of circumstances."

"That would take longer, ma'am. I wish to end this as soon as possible."

"After waiting four years, William, what is your hurry now?"

"I have met a wonderful woman. She is everything Madeleine is not. I wish to marry her as soon as I am free. I want to have children, ma'am."

"I see. I will request an audience as soon as possible. I doubt she will refuse my request."

I say with a smile, "No, ma'am." I stand and bow again. "Thank you for seeing me. Please give my well wishes to the King."

"I will, William. Good day."

I leave her with a lighter foot. I am not walking on air yet, but I feel as though this might end soon.

CHAPTER 6

AT DINNER THAT NIGHT, I relate my audience with Her Majesty. My father is a member of Her Majesty's Most Honorable Privy Council and as such, he will be in her company in two weeks. He is quite sure that she will mention to him the date of Madeleine's audience with her. Until then, all I can do is wait.

I call Carline regularly to see if she has any word from Brook. I want assurance that she is safe and well. Carline hasn't heard from Brook directly, but has received a call from Angelo. He told her that Brook has moved in with him and his family. He didn't want her to live at a hotel for an extended period of time. I know Angelo and I want to call him. I wonder if he would keep our conversation between him and me. That is my only concern. I relate this to Carline and she says to call him.

"Pronto?" Angelo answers his phone.

"Angelo, questo e William Barry."

"William, how are you? I'll bet it has been five years since we have seen each other."

"That is my fault, Angelo. I have been working in America. I haven't been traveling in Europe at all."

"Are you calling to tell me that you are going to visit? My mama will be so happy. You know how much she wants to fatten you up."

"Angelo, I am calling because I have a very important favor to ask of you."

"Anything, William, you know that."

"Don't be so quick to answer. I was told that Brook Kennedy is staying with you and your family while she is working on your shoot."

"Yes, she is here. She and my wife are out with the children right now. How do you know Brook?"

"Brook and I are involved with each other. I love her, but she left me."

"You are the married man who broke her heart? I did not know that you were married."

"It is a long and complicated story, Angelo. I am married, but I don't have a wife. I am in the process of obtaining a divorce but it is not an easy task."

"Brook told me that you are from the Royal Family, yes?"

"Yes. I am to be a Duke. My wife likes the title. She wants to keep that but not me."

"I see. I am sorry for your trouble. Brook is a wonderful woman. You are a lucky man, William. She loves you, you know this?"

"Yes, I know. What can I do for her without her knowing? Is there anything that she needs? Can I send you money or anything?"

"She is no trouble for us. The children love her. Gratiana thinks of her as a sister. My mama would sooner I move out than Brook. Fix your problem and come to her."

"Please don't tell her that we spoke. I don't want her to think I am checking on her, even though that is exactly what I am doing."

"She is very independent. She would be mad at me for talking to you. To save myself, I will stay quiet."

"May I call you again?"

"Yes. I will call you if anything happens and she needs you. Stay well, my friend. Ciao!"

"Thank you, my friend. Ciao."

I feel so much better after speaking to Angelo. I know Brook is in good hands. If Angelo's mama is feeding her, I also know that she is eating. When Brook is upset, she tends not to eat and she is thin enough.

I send a package to Carline to send on to Brook. I found a CD of Josh Groban's music that I know she will love. Some of the songs remind me of her. I also enclose a check for her and a note from me. I count the days until I can go to Italy and bring her home with me. I find myself opening the box that holds her engagement ring. I dream of the day when she will wear it.

Jonathan and I are closer than we have ever been. I enjoy working with him and I envy his business savoir faire. I am, in reality, learning from him. I actually take pleasure in going to the office with him every day. I miss the freedom of my former life, the outdoors and the beauty. However, I can do this more stable occupation.

At dinner my father announces, "I spoke with the Queen this morning. Madeleine has an audience with her tomorrow afternoon. The Queen told me that all will be settled soon. I am hopeful, son, but settled doesn't necessarily mean what we want. I want you prepared for the settlement to be either way."

"I have lived this way for almost four years, father. My only issue is Brook. Without the divorce, I won't have her. Without her, there is no me. I will not have children or a wife. Not much to look forward, to is there?"

"Don't give up on hope yet, William. If Madeleine tells the truth, and the Queen does tend to make that happen, your marriage will be over. However, if she can convince the Queen that it was you who deserted her, it might go a different way."

"I had to leave her like I did. I was hurt and angry. I was afraid I would force her to fulfill her duty to me and that would not have gone well. I was very sure that raping your wife would be frowned upon in our polite society."

"Society be damned! How can you marry someone about whom you profess your love to all who will listen and then shun his affections? How can you take a vow to welcome children into your life and then not allow the method by which they are conceived?" my father bellows.

"Therein lies the rub, Father. Professing and doing are two different things. We have questions and unfortunately Madeleine holds all of the answers and she isn't talking."

I wake the next morning and thankfully have a full day of meetings to get through. I won't have the time to stare at the clock wondering what is being said about my future. As I pack my briefcase for the ride home, my phone rings. I look and it is Carline. "Hello, Carline. Is Brook all right?"

"Yes, William, she's fine. I spoke to her and she told me to tell you that she will be waiting on the Spanish Steps in Rome every afternoon that it doesn't rain. She leaves in two weeks, William, so don't wait too long."

"I have to get something first, Carline. It won't do any good to see her without it. I will know in a day or two if I will have a future or not. Then I will go to Brook."

"I will let her know that I have spoken to you, William. I wish you both the best. I hope you end up together and happy."

"Thank you, Carline. From your mouth to God's ea, for it is out of my hands completely."

I ride home with Jonathan, discussing the day's events without mentioning the rather large elephant in the car with us. I feel him staring at me, sizing up my mood. I have never waited for a jury to decide my guilt or innocence but this is what it must feel like. To know that someone else holds your freedom is a terrifying sensation. I do not recommend it.

It is two days before a currier delivers to my door a letter with the Queen's seal on it. John brings the letter to me in the library. "Mr. Barry, this just arrived for you," John says.

"Thank you, John." I take the letter and see the Queen's seal. I hold it, knowing it is the end of the road for me.

"Open it, William. The suspense is killing me," my mother says.

With a deep breath, I break the seal and take the letter out of the envelope. I unfold it and read aloud.

The Honorable Viscount William Barry,

I am to inform you that after my discussion with both you and the Lady Madeleine Barry, I am of the opinion that the marriage between you is not a viable option. Your marriage was never consummated, and, therefore, the marriage contract was not fulfilled. It is thus determined by me that a divorce will be granted to you by the proper courts. This will take place without delay. The Lady Barry will maintain her household without any further funds from Viscount Barry. My wishes are final and irrevocable in fourteen days.

Most sincerely,
HRH Elisabeth II

"It is over, thank God. Madeleine must have told the truth. At least she did that," I say.

"William, I am so happy for you. Fourteen days and you will be free. That is the quickest divorce I have ever heard of. The Queen must have been very put out by what she heard," my mother responds.

"I am going to Brook in Rome and I am asking her to marry me. I have to check with my solicitor to be sure all is done and then I am leaving. I am afraid you will have to do without me again, Dad, for a few days."

"Go and get your girl, William. Everything else can wait."

It takes six days for my solicitor to obtain the proper paperwork dissolving my marriage, that I want to show Brook. As soon as I have it in my hand, I secure a flight to Rome. I race home to pack, remembering to have Brook's ring in my pocket. I feel like a teenager as George drives me to the airport. The millstone that has hung around my neck, drowning me, is replaced by a exuberance I haven't felt since I last saw Brook.

"Good luck, sir, and have a safe journey," George says.

"Thank you, George. I will call you to let you know of my return." I nod to him as I enter the terminal to catch the plane that will bring me to Brook and our new life together.

CHAPTER 7

BY THE TIME MY PLANE lands, I am too late to meet Brook on the steps. I know where to find her of course, but I do not wish to jeopardize Angelo's or Carline's relationship with Brook. I take a taxi to the St. Regis Rome Grand Hotel. As I enter the lobby, I am reminded of Brook challenging me on my lifestyle. I do like the best hotels and restaurants~she knows me well. I make my way to my suite, hoping that tomorrow night Brook will share it with me.

After a fitful night's sleep, I wake to a beautiful morning. My stomach in knots, I drink my coffee followed by two fingers of Laphroaig. Not enough to sedate me, just to help with my nerves. Finally, with her ring securely in my pocket and the divorce papers in my hand, I start my walk through the bustling streets of Rome.

As I near the steps, my heart is pounding. I am sweating as if I have run here. I stop to wipe my brow and try to quiet my nerves. My eyes lift to follow the steps up. I see her and my heart stops. There she sits, near the top on the left. She is leaning against the stones that form the stringers of the steps. She is sleeping and stunning to look at. I begin to climb the steps, never taking my eyes from her. As I reach her, my shadow casts over her yet she doesn't wake. I rest on one knee on the step below her and say, "Wake up, Sleeping Beauty." Remembering the ballet that I took her to see.

Her eyes slowly open. They focus on me, she smiles and says, "I was beginning to think you were not going to find me."

"I am here now. I had to get some things in order. I have a lot to tell you."

"I have some things to tell you, too."

"Do you want to talk here or would you rather my hotel or a restaurant?"

"I have to tell you right now before you say anything. I held you to a standard that I didn't hold myself to and I have to make it right first."

"I am listening, Brook."

"When I went to meet your family I wasn't feeling well. You took me to see Dr. Martin and he did some tests." She says looking ashen.

"I saw Jeffery at Christmas. He asked for you and said he wanted to do some further tests. I told him that you had left."

"He told me something that I was going to share with you when we got back home to the states. Then I saw Madeleine and I never told you. I did the very same thing that you did. I withheld something from you and I am sorry."

I watch as her eyes fill with tears. My heart lurches to a stop. "My god, Brook, are you ill?" I ask, afraid of her answer.

"No. I'm pregnant, William. I am going to have your baby," she says with a smile.

My universe tilts and then resumes spinning. "Did you just say that you are pregnant?" I parrot her.

"Yes, that is exactly what I said, William."

"Pregnant? You are going to have my baby? We are going to be parents?" I say with the widest grin I can muster.

"Yes, you heard me correctly," she says with a counter-grin.

"How? When?" I ask, thrilled by the news.

"It seems that certain antibiotics render birth control pills ineffective. When I had the sinus infection in early October, I took some. Dr. Martin said the information was probably on the papers that came with the prescription. However, like most people, I didn't read the instructions. We made love and I became pregnant. When I got to England, I started to feel the effects of morning sickness. I passed it off as jet lag. I am due to deliver in early July."

I move to hold her shoulders and I pull her to her feet. I wrap my arms around her and hug her to me. I can feel our baby between us. "I love you, Brook. I love the baby. Thank you for keeping it and for telling me."

"I would have never not kept the baby, William. That never even entered my mind. It was Angelo who helped me to see through my feelings to the truth of the situation. He and his family have been very good to me."

"I am glad that you had their support, Brook. I wish I had been here for you. I can't change the past but I am here now. I have my divorce, Brook. It is over. If you will have me, I want to marry you as soon as possible. I would have waited for a big wedding, one that you deserve. But in light of our developing baby, I think we should act soon. I don't want there to be a problem with legitimacy. Will you marry me, Brook?"

"I love you, too. I would love to marry you. As soon as we can."

When Brook speaks, the sky opens up to a vivid sun. I swear it shines down on just us and the light it puts in her eyes is the stuff love songs are written about. I take her hand and we descend the steps like two lovers lost in each other. We walk into the first café that we see. We are shown to a table. I sit next to her, not believing yet, that she has consented to be mine. I kiss Brook's forehead and she moves her face to kiss my lips. I almost expire right there. I have to restrain myself so that I do not to pull her onto my lap and devour her.

"Please forgive me, Brook. You said yes and I have something for you." I reach into my pocket and get the box. I open it and take out the ring. "I bought this in New York after I saw you the last time. I knew that I was going to do whatever I had to do to put it on your finger." I place the ring on her finger. She doesn't even look at it, so her. It is not about the ring for her~it is about the commitment. I place my hand on her little belly. She puts hers over mine.

"Pretty big, right?" she says.

"You have never looked more alluring than you do right now. You have never been more gorgeous. You are having my baby, Brook."

"William, I forgot. I am leaving for Australia tomorrow night for a shoot. I have signed a contract and I have to go."

"When does the shoot start?"

"May seventh, but I have fittings the week before. I was going early so I could sightsee. I have never been there."

"You have three options, Brook. Contracts were made to be broken. I can buy you out of this one. On the other hand, we can go to England, marry and go on our honeymoon to Australia so you can do the shoot. Lastly, you can leave on Thursday and I can follow you as soon as I am able."

"I think I like the second option. I don't want there to be a problem with our baby and his legitimacy. That scares me, William."

"You said his . . . is the baby a boy?"

"According to Angelo's mama, Natalia. She knew that I was pregnant before I was even showing. She said the baby is a boy and Angelo says she is never wrong."

"I know her and I believe it is a boy. I guess we will have a son, Brook."

"You know Natalia?"

"Yes. I have worked with Angelo before. Gratiana or Natalia would bring him lunch every day. Do they still?"

"Yes, they do. Their children are delightful and so loving. I can only hope that ours are the same. I have been helping them with their English and they are teaching me Italian."

"Really? What have you learned?"

"Sei bella and baciami."

"Interesting. You want to be kissed and you are beautiful. How about, sei l'amore della vita mia. Or, voglio stare con te per sempre."

"I don't know what that means."

"You are the love of my life. I want to be with you forever."

"That works for me as well."

"Will you stay with me tonight? I have a suite at the St. Regis. I want to hold you all night."

"I have to go back to Angelo's house and say good-bye. My things are packed. Will you come with me?"

"Definitely. I want to see them to thank them for taking such good care of you."

We eat some lunch and walk hand in hand to Angelo's villa. I stop periodically to hold her and kiss her. She feels so good in my arms. We get to Angelo's and I knock on the door. One of the children answers it.

"Simona, buon pomeriggio. Mi puoi aiutare?" I ask her.

"Si," Simona answers.

"E tua padre a casa?"

"Lui sara con voi presto."

A few minutes later, Angelo comes to the door. "William, how are you?"

"Very well, Angelo. Brook and I are here to say thank you and good-bye. It was wonderful of you and your family to take such good care of her. Thank you, my friend."

"Come in, please. Mama will be so happy to see you." We walk in and Natalia comes over to us. She hugs me and I kiss her cheeks.

We sit and have a conversation that includes me as the father of Brook's baby and the fact that we are getting married. Angelo and his family wish us all the happiness in the world. We collect Brook's belongings. They want us to stay for dinner, but as I explain to Angelo, I haven't seen Brook in five months and I want to be alone with her. He winks at me with a knowing smile. Brook presents her gifts to all of them and we take our leave.

Walking to my hotel with my Brook makes me one happy man.

CHAPTER 8

BROOK AND I ORDER ROOM service when we make it back to the hotel. We stumble into the suite in each other's arms, kissing. My mind is so full of plans and visions of what our lives will be. I love this woman and I will protect her until I die.

"I still have to tell you what happened after you left, Brook. Come and sit on the couch with me." We walk over and sit. I continue, "When I returned home that day, Emily was so distraught over what had transpired. She blames herself for not thinking quickly enough to stop the whole thing from happening, to protect you and me from Madeleine's malice."

"None of it is Emily's fault. I don't blame her for anything. Go on, William."

"Madeleine grew up with Emily, Jonathan and me. She lived at the next estate from us. She is an only child and spent every day of the summers at our house. She is closest in age to me, so I guess we became closer than the others did. I went to university and we lost touch somewhat. When I finished, she was there again, every day. I was a randy guy when I came back, as you might guess after what I have told you all ready."

"Yes, I can guess you developed quite an appetite for sex in college. Something I have benefited from, thank you," she says with a knowing smile.

"She wouldn't sleep with me . . . nothing, not even oral. She said she wanted to be a virgin and I guess I respected that so I didn't push it. With our parents' repeated prodding, I asked her to marry me and she accepted. The wedding was huge and attended by everyone, including the King and Queen. Graced with their presence, we were really married.

It was a long and difficult day, so when she didn't receive me to her room that night, I just thought she was exhausted. Because she was a virgin, I knew it would take time so I just went to bed. The next day, though, she would not welcome me again. The morning of the third day, I went to her to consummate our marriage, period, no excuses. She informed me then that we would never consummate it. She would not have children and was only interested in a platonic relationship with me."

"It is not so much that I necessitate an heir, but I wanted children of my own. Let's face it, part of the reason to live with someone is to be able to have sex regularly. I knew I could not live without it. Your hand can only do so much~it is the foreplay that drives you wild. I require that physical touching. I left immediately after the discussion. I went first to my parents and then to hers. I made arrangements for her household finances and went to America to start a new life away from here."

"Why, especially after our discussion about not having secrets, didn't you tell me about her?" Brook said, looking hurt, again.

"Looking back, I should have. At the time, I thought you would run and I couldn't lose you. You were buried in my heart by then, Brook. As it turned out, I lost you because I didn't tell you."

"What happened after I left? I know you followed me, but after that?"

"I went back and my father obtained an audience with the Queen for me. The only way out of a royal marriage that is contested is through her. She has a way to make people do her bidding. She is a little thing, but very persuasive."

"I can imagine. Maybe it's the crown?"

"No, it's the eye! She casts an eye at you and you tremble. When I was young, I was playing with Wills at the palace. Running through rooms, I stumbled and slid right between her legs. I thought I was going to the tower with the look that she gave me. My mum told me much later that she was very amused by the whole thing."

"So you went to see her and . . . ?"

"I told her everything. She told me that she had to hear Madeleine's side and she would let me know of her decision as soon as possible. A few weeks later she had the meeting and I received this letter a few days after that." I hand her the papers to read.

"So Madeleine told the truth? Or did the Queen just believe you?"

"I don't actually know. I don't in truth care. I am free of her one way or the other. Free to marry the woman I love who just happens to be carrying my baby. My mum will lose her mind when she finds out. She is all about the grandchildren."

"What are these papers?"

"Those are from my solicitor confirming that next Friday I am duly divorced. I am giving her the house that she lives in but no money after that. She has no claim to title or any other thing of mine, ever."

"Can she appeal or is this finally it?"

"No appeal. She signed the papers, as did I, gladly. I am yours, Brook, body and soul. I am thinking that next Saturday is a fine day to get married. What say you, Brook?"

"I say that next Saturday would be a fine day to marry the man that I love more than anything."

"I will call my parents to start the process. Do you want anyone to come from the States?"

"It doesn't give anyone much time to make plans, William. I don't know."

"I will charter a plane for anyone that you want to be here. It won't be a problem. Make your calls and I will make mine. I'll charter the plane to leave New York on Wednesday night and return on Monday. They can stay at the estate."

"I'll call tomorrow. I am tired. I think I will take a shower. Want to join me?"

"I wish I could but if I see you naked I doubt I will be able to stop myself."

"Stop yourself from what?"

"Taking you, of course. I want you. I am on fire here." I say, honestly.

"William, what do you think? You're not going to touch me? The baby isn't due for another three and a half months. Then I need time to recover. You think we aren't going to make love for five more months?"

"I don't want to hurt you or the baby. I don't think we can."

"I was pregnant in October and November and we made love regularly. You didn't worry then."

"I didn't know that you were pregnant, darling. Now I do."

"If you don't make love to me then I am not going to marry you. How do you like that? You won't hurt me or the baby. We just have to be inventive with my belly. You won't mind that, will you?"

"Inventive, you say. Are you sure there is no problem?"

"None whatsoever. It is done every day, all over the world."

"I'll meet you in the shower. I have to call my parents first so that they will stop worrying."

I reach my sister and give her the good news. Emily will convey our conversation to everyone. I told her to make the arrangements for a wedding. Just family on my part, as I have all ready inconvenienced everyone once before. We will marry in our chapel on the estate and have a dinner in the ballroom. I don't tell her about the baby. I want Brook to see their faces.

I enter the bedroom and I can hear the water running. I take my clothes off and enter the bathroom. Slipping into the shower behind Brook, I have to breathe deeply to slow my heart. The sight of her is more than I can describe. She glows and her smile is so inviting. I wrap her in my arms and say, "I thought I loved you before, but what I am feeling now, is so much more than love. The words have not been invented yet, Brook. Forgive me for not being a poet or a songwriter. All I can do is to give you everything I am and all that I have and hope that is enough."

"You are more than enough, William. You are my everything, my love and life and the father of my child. You are all that I want or need . . . my future. I have to draw from your strength, William, because I don't have an abundance of it. I have learned from this that together we can succeed, but apart I am lost. I will never leave you again."

My heart skips with her admission. She will never leave me . . . I thank God for that. I kiss her and pull her to me. I feel the baby moving inside her. "I don't know if I can do this, Brook. I can feel the baby moving. I can't wrap my head around it."

"How do you think I feel? I am kicked from the inside. I have had some time to get used to it and you will, too. In the meantime, just concentrate on you and me. Look at my eyes and not my belly. Make love to me, William."

I turn her to face the wall of the shower. Pulling her hips back slightly, I feel her breasts. I let the sensation of the water cascading down her back surround me as I enter her from behind. I hold her with one arm as I find her powerhouse that lights up my world. I hear her cry out in pleasure as she sinks against me. I follow her and hold her as she shudders through her release. She regains her footing in a few minutes and I ask," Brook, are you okay?"

"Perfect," she responds, turning to look at me.

"And the baby?"

"Couldn't be happier. Aren't all children happy when their parents love each other?"

"I can't argue with that logic. I guess we can do this."

CHAPTER 9

I HOLD BROOK ALL NIGHT. I listen to her even breathing with my hand resting on her belly until I finally fall asleep. I wake in the morning to Brook kissing me. Is there anyone in the entire world as blissful as I am right now? Not possible. "Good morning, darling," I say. "What a brilliant way to be woken up. Should we head for home and tell my family about the baby? Or do you want to stay here and make love all day?"

"We could go home and make love all day there. As much as I love it here, I am ready to begin our life together. We have a wedding to put together, after all. I have to find a dress of some kind and other details that I can't even think of right now."

"Why can't you think of them?"

"Because of what you are doing to me right now," she says smiling.

"What am I doing to you, Brook?" I ask with my own smile, raising my head from her breast to look at her.

"If I am not mistaken, William, you call it building my desire. Or something like that. It's a British thing, I think."

"I see. So only the Brits take their time to make the experience memorable? That is unfortunate. Not for you, though. After next Saturday, Brook, your body belongs to me and I intend to enjoy every inch of it. My body belongs to you and I want you to take every advantage of it that you can."

"Then we have a bargain. I will love you and you will love me . . . bliss."

Debbie Zello

I move her to top me. "I guess we will see how strong those leg muscles are, my darling. Take me and do your best to drive me wild," I say teasing her.

A few minutes later, she has me trembling with my release. I tell her, "Ti amo piu di quanto amo la vita."

"What does that mean, William?"

"I love you more than I love life."

"That's lovely, thank you."

We shower and dress. I call to make our flight arrangements. Lastly, I call home to give our flight information to the family. George will pick us up at the airport. I watch Brook as she packs. My eyes drinking her in, having missed the sight of her for so long. She asks me, "What are you staring at, silly?"

"You came back to me. You're having my baby, Brook. I'm staring at a damn miracle."

"You better start packing or you'll miss the plane home," she says, ever the responsible one.

We pass through our gate holding hands. Taking a seat waiting for our flight to be called, I turn to Brook and ask, "How many of your friends will come for the wedding?"

"Sandy and Link. Wendy, Regina and Christina from work. Millie and Carol. My brother and Laura. Will Angela and Luke make the trip?"

"I'm sure they would. You want them there?"

"I think that would be lovely. Will we ever live in the States again?"

"I have taken over some of the responsibility of the business from Jonathan. My father wants to retire and travel. I don't know how much I could do from America. Would it distress you to live in the UK?"

"It's not just your business, William. You have a title and with that comes responsibility. I think I could live anywhere as long as you are there. We can visit regularly."

"Speaking of title, the Queen's birthday celebration is in two weeks. It will be your first public appearance after our wedding. You will need something spectacular to wear. You will be introduced to Her Majesty as my wife."

"That is a little scary, William."

"I know, Brook. It is the first of many occasions that you will be expected to attend. As you said, with my title comes responsibility. That goes for you, too. You need to either support a charity or establish one. You will attend public events in my stead. It's a lot to ask, but it is expected. Can you do this, Brook?"

"It comes with you, William. It's part of the package. I have a baby on the way, William. What becomes of him?"

"The baby will have a nanny or governess or both, depending on what you want. I had a nanny. Both Emily and Jonathan have nannies for their children. It is expected that you will have help with our children."

"I always thought I would raise my children."

"You will, Brook. Just with help because you will have responsibilities and duties to perform. Much like a working mother. Can you do this?"

"What choice do I have? I can't leave him alone or take him with me, it seems. How do I pick a nanny?"

"With a service and with both Emily and Eve's help. They have been through this and will gladly give their advice."

I can see her apprehension. I am asking her to put her baby into a stranger's hands. It's normal and accepted in my circle, but foreign to Brook. I have to continue to be aware of my wealth overpowering her. One hurdle at a time. Brook being comfortable leaving her baby is first.

George greets us at the airport saying, "Welcome home, Mr. Barry and Miss Kennedy. I hope that you had a pleasant trip."

"We did, George, thank you. How is the family?"

"Everyone is waiting for you and Miss Kennedy to arrive. Sir, there are photographers outside. I'm not sure if it is for you or if someone else is arriving today."

"It won't matter. When they see us, they will take the pictures anyway. Brook, darling, you go with George and I will take a taxi home."

"No, William. We go together or not at all. Let them take their pictures. They can say what they want. You and I know what the truth is. I'm not afraid of them."

"When someone is after you, Brook, paranoia is just good thinking. They want a story. Some dirt to entertain the masses. You have done nothing wrong, but you will be vilified along with me."

"We do this together, William. A united front is easier to defend than if I go one way and you go the other. I'm going to put my arm through yours, showing my ring. We are going to smile and look every bit the couple in love that we are."

"You are one brave woman, Brook. I'm in awe of you. Let's go get them!"

We walk out and the cameras spring to life. Everyone wants that perfect shot. Questions fly at us, but we continue to walk to our car. George opens the door for us and I put Brook inside. I turn to the photographers and say, "Thank you for this warm homecoming welcome for my fiancée and me. Any further questions you have will be handled through my office." I hand my card to the closest man. I sit next to Brook and she kisses me.

"See, that wasn't so bad," she says.

John informs us that the family is in the library in anticipation of our arrival. Brook and I walk arm-in-arm through the door. Our smiling faces are met by equally large smiles on my family's faces. My mom bolts over to us, hugging Brook. "I am so glad you're here, darling. We couldn't be happier about the wedding. You look lovely. You're glowing."

"She is glowing because she has a secret to tell you, Mother."

"A secret! I love secrets. Do tell."

"In July, William and I are going to have a baby," Brook announces.

"Bloody hell! Congratulations!" Jonathan shouts.

"Well done, son!" my father declares, walking over to shake my hand.

"Another baby. I couldn't be happier," my mother affirms.

"The girls will insist on babysitting. To hell with that, I want to baby-sit!" Emily states.

We sit down and Brook recounts all that she has done in Italy. Everyone inquires as to how she has felt. We move on to wedding plans. My mum and Emily have been busy securing a caterer, decorator, florist and minister to actually marry us. They hand-delivered invitations to our aunts and uncles, a few cousins and friends. All is set for Saturday, April 6th at 2:00.

"I need a dress for the wedding and, William tells me, the Queen's birthday. I don't know where to go or who to see. Can you help me, Emily?" Brook asks.

"You know how much I hate to shop. I will make an exception for you, Brook, darling. I will pick you up in the morning and we will go see Sarah Burton of Alexander McQueen Designs. Alexander passed away a few years ago and Sarah was named creative director. I loved his sharp angles and he was a bit of a bad boy. She has done well for herself. She designed Catherine Middleton's wedding dress as well as her sisters."

"A bad boy?"

"He was known to write obscenities inside the Prince of Wales's suits. Just the kind of balls that you want in a designer. He will make you something smashing," Emily says.

"I guess I put myself in your hands. I'll see you in the morning. I am rather tired. I think I will go to bed. Goodnight everyone."

I walk over to Brook and say, "I'll be up shortly, darling. I want to talk to the family for a few minutes. If you are asleep, I won't wake you."

"It's okay to wake me. I want to know that you are there," she says. I watch her walk to the stairs. Then I turn back to my family.

"You didn't know about the baby, did you?" Emily asks me.

"No. Jeffery Martin told her. She wanted to surprise me once we returned to New York. Madeleine changed that plan. Brook was so upset that she kept it to herself. Angelo helped her to change her mind about telling me."

"What was she going to do?"

"Have the baby alone, in Australia. Tell me after. She tells me that she isn't a strong person and yet she was going to do this without help. I am so glad that I will be here for her."

"You are going to be a great father, William. The best. Is the baby a boy or a girl?"

Debbie Zello

"Brook doesn't want to know. Angelo's mom says it is a boy. I'm told she is never wrong. I don't care. I just want him and his mother with me."

I say my goodnights and climb the stairs. I open the bedroom door and Brook is sleeping. I crawl in bed with her and snuggle up to her, wrapping my arm around her. She holds my hand against her belly and we sleep.

CHAPTER 10

WITH SO MUCH TO DO before the wedding, we get up early. Brook is off with Emily to find her dress and I am off to the office to finish some work. Jonathan has handled the acquisition of the other company and we are on track with all of our overseas operations. I walk in to his office to talk about Australia.

"Brook signed a contract to do some modeling for a maternity wear designer in Australia. She has to be there on May first. The contract runs for five to six weeks depending on their ability to shoot outside."

"That cuts it close to her due date doesn't it?" Jonathan asks.

"Three to four weeks. Very close for me. I want to by out the contract but she won't go back on her word. I am going with her. I can work from there and we can teleconference if need be."

"Almost everything can be done from there. I will handle what can't be done from here. Don't worry, go with your wife."

"At some point I will make all of this up to you Jonathan. You have been very patient letting me find myself."

"If Eve had turned out to be like Madeleine, I would have run too. Brook is going to be a great wife and mother. I'm happy for you William."

I leave the office to go home and work on my vows. I have some things that I want to say to Brook. I don't want the standard vows. Ours isn't a standard love. I am in my home office when Brook gets back from her shopping. She finds me and says, "There you are. John said that you were home but I couldn't find you."

"We have a few more rooms here than we are use to. Chances are I would be here or the library or our bedroom. I don't wander much further than that. Unless I smell something, and then I might check in with Barbara in the kitchen. Come and sit on my lap."

"The last time I went to your office William, you laid me across your desk and made love to me."

"Would you enjoy a repeat performance? I can lock the door."

"Too many people here William. I wouldn't be comfortable knowing they might hear us."

"Brook, we are always going to have people around us. To run a house this large we have to have the help. There will be times when someone might hear us. So what? So they know that we make love and enjoy it. They do it too."

"I'm sure but I can't hear them."

"I understand the difference. I don't know how to help you with that. But I will tell you right now that I'm not going to stop making love with you just because someone might hear us. What if we play music loudly? How did you make out with your shopping?"

"I will have a dress for our wedding and the Queens birthday. He wants to do some for after the baby is born. I don't know what I might need so I told him to wait on that."

"Order whatever you want Brook. There will be social engagements that you need to attend. Be prepared for them."

"What are you working on in here?"

"My comedy routine for the next gathering of my friends. I thought I might educate them on the proper way to excuse yourself to use the loo."

"You must tell me. I have to know."

"A sixth grade teacher asked her class that question. The first boy said he would just say he had to go. The second boy said he would say he wanted to be excused. The third boy said he would say that he had to shake hands with a good friend that he hoped to introduce her to after dinner."

"Which boy was right?"

"She didn't complain to me after dinner in fact she was quite happy to meet my friend."

"William you are incorrigible. I hope you don't teach our children things like that."

"That and more my love. You will have to be the good parent. Go and pamper yourself and let me finish my work. I will find you when I am done and maybe we will scandalize the help."

She shakes her head at me as she walks out. I want to work on my vows without her knowing. There are things that I want to say to her, promise her.

I enter our room and I can hear her singing in the bathroom. I open the door to see her in the tub with her earbuds in surrounded by bubbles. I walk in and start to undress. Watching me when I drop my pants she says, "Oh my!" I love that I can do that to her.

"Who are you listening to?" I ask as if I don't know already. I sink into the tub behind her.

"Josh Groban. Have you heard his song 'Below The Line'?"

"Not yet."

"It's about being kind to those who have less than us because it might be us someday. We have to love one another and help each other. I think I have found what I want to do. I'm going to start a charity that helps people who are just above the line. Trying to hang on so that they don't go below. There is little help for those people. Often we want them to wait until they are desperate before we help. I want to keep them from going that far."

"I think you are cut out for this Duchess gig after all Brook. I'm proud of you and what you will accomplish. I will call John Pope. He helped me to start my foundation. He is very good at marketing and organization."

I feel the baby move. I ask," How is he today?"

"We had better stop saying he because she might take offence. The baby is fine today."

"We could put a stop to the he/she if you wanted to find out for certain."

"I know. There are so few real surprises now. I thought it would be fun to wait to find out. If you want to know, I will do it."

"I can wait too." I move her hair aside and kiss her neck. "I have something that I want you to wear tomorrow."

We get out of the tub and dry off. I walk to my dresser and take out the box containing the necklace and earrings that I purchased. I hand the box to Brook saying, "I purchased this along with your ring. It's your wedding present darling."

Brook opens the box and brings her hand to her mouth looking at the items inside. "I have never seen anything so beautiful William. It's too much."

I see worry in her eyes. I say, "What's wrong?"

"What if I lose them? I'm afraid to wear them."

"They are insured darling. They are not family heirlooms; if you lose it, we replace it. Wear them please."

"Thank you. I will treasure them always." She kisses me with love.

The morning of our wedding, I am a wreck. My solicitor is bringing the final divorce papers over. Until I actually see them, I won't be comfortable. Brook is readying herself in her room and I am pacing in the library. John knocks and walks in saying," Mr. Andrews sir."

"Thank you John. Come in Walter, please."

"Wonderful morning William. A happy day for you and Brook."

"Now that you are here. Please tell me that you have the papers."

"Right here William. It's over for you. Signed, sealed and now delivered."

"So this is what it feels like!" I say as I look over the papers. I see Madeleine's signature and mine. The approval and seal of the court. I continue, "Four years. Wasted. Well, it's over. In one hour, I will do it all over again. This time I have the right one."

"I believe that you do William. Brook seems to be perfect for you. I wish you all the best."

I take the papers in to my office to put them in a safe place. Jonathan and Rob Kennedy walk in.

"We have been looking for you William. I saw Walter Andrews come in," Jonathan says.

"He brought the papers. It's all done. How are you Rob? Did you sleep well?"

"Very well thank you. Your estate is amazing William. I got lost finding my room last night. I must have taken a wrong turn or something."

"That happens. It's great when your five and playing hide-n-seek. Have you seen Brook yet?"

"Yes. She looks lovely. Happy. I have you to thank for that. She is a good person William. She will be a terrific mother and wife. I trust you will be a good husband to her and father to your children."

"I love her, Rob. I have hurt her but I'm making up for that. As for the baby . . . I'm over the moon at the thought of being a father. I can't wait to hold him or her. I'm in trouble with Brook for calling the baby a him all of the time."

"Knowing Brook, you'll be in trouble quite often over your marriage. Best you become use to that now. My advice to any man contemplating marriage is "yes, honey" becoming second nature to you."

"I look forward to it. Making up with Brook is unparalleled. Worth being in trouble in the first place. I guess we should go out and mingle with the guests. There are some people I need to introduce you to."

In the library, I find some cousins, aunts and Unels. I introduce Rob. I see Brooks's friends talking in the hall and I wave to them. After a few minutes of talking John announces that we should make our way to the chapel. I walk with Jonathan, who is serving as my best man, to the chapel door.

"I wish you all of the happiness that you deserve William. Brook is wonderful," Jonathan states. I smile and nod.

When everyone is seated, Jonathan and I walk in to take our places on the front. A violin begins to play as my three nieces walk in holding their flowers. Emily is followed by the most striking sight in the kingdom, my Brook. She is wearing an off-white dress covered in lace. Her hair I pulled back with flowers twined through it. My mouth goes dry. Her smile blocks out the sun. I can only hope that my face portrays the heart full of love that I have for this woman.

She walks to me and I hold my hand out to her. She gives me her hand. I bring it to my lips and kiss her fingers. I wrap my arm over hers and cradle her hand with mine. We face the minister and he begins. When he finishes with our standard vows he turns to Brook and says," William has asked to speak directly to you Brook. Go on William."

I look in Brook's eyes and say," I haven't always been careful with your heart Brook. I promise that will never happen again. I didn't believe that I could feel this way about another person. You came into my life and showed me how to love, and taught me what it takes to be a good man. I am the one who is honored to have you as my wife. I promise to love you, cherish you and protect you. I will always be here for you. I will be the best husband that I can be. YOU . . . ARE . . . MY . . . LIFE!"

Silent tears fall down my beautiful wife's cheeks. I wipe them with my thumbs. Brook says," Thank you, William. I love you so much."

We turn to face our families and friends and the minister pronounces, "I am so pleased to introduce you to Mr. and Mrs. William and Brook Barry, from today forward until death, husband and wife."

A loud cheer rises from all in attendance. I kiss my wife and touch her belly. I can feel my baby moving. I hope he is as blissful as I am.

CHAPTER 11

"CONGRATULATIONS, WILLIAM AND BROOK. IF everyone would raise their glasses, I would like to say a few words about my much older, and frankly less handsome, brother, and his stunning new wife. When I met Brook, I tried to persuade her to forget about William. She wouldn't come to her senses and now we are here at their wedding.

"It is my sincere hope that you continue to be as contented and idyllic as you are now, eternally. I can't think of any two people better suited for each other. I look forward to the arrival of my niece or nephew and the remaining brood that will no doubt follow. To Brook and William!"

I take my wife in my arms to dance with her. I feel like I have had to share her all day. I know her friends and brother are here and she wants to spend time with them. Nevertheless, I am jealous of not having her complete attention.

"Are you happy, my love?" I ask her.

"So happy, William. How about you? Are you sorry yet?"

"Never! You haven't sat down much. Are you tired? I don't want you to overtax yourself."

"I am fine. I don't want to miss anything. This is my one and only wedding."

"You better believe it! Unless your next husband steps over my dead body."

"William, don't even say something like that. Take it back, now."

"Sorry, luv. I'm not going anywhere. At least not without you."

I dance with my mother, Emily, and Eve in rapid succession. Lily, who has danced with Brook already, wants to dance with me. I pick her up and twirl her around the floor. I hope I have a girl with Brook. Lots of girls. I get around to dancing with Sandy. She says, "Brook looks very happy, William. So help me if you ever hurt her again, your balls are mine. Got it?"

"The thought of you with my balls will haunt me nightly. I will endeavor to not let that happen. Rest assured."

Sufficiently chastised by Sandy, I move on to dance with Millie and Carol. I receive almost the same threat of losing my balls in a most unpleasant fashion. I marvel at how the threat of ball loss trips off the tongues of these sweet ladies so easily. By the time Wendy, Regina and Christina take their shots at me, I feel the need to wear some sort of protection. I anticipate a strike at any moment. I have never encountered a fiercer set of friends. I am glad that my wife has them.

With most of the guests retired for the evening, Brook and I climb the stairs. We walk to our room and I take her in my arms, carrying her across the threshold. I kiss her as I set her down. "Hi, Mrs. Barry. How are you feeling?"

"Happy. Tired, but so happy, Mr. Barry. And you?"

"I feel very happily married. I feel elated. Drunk with pleasure."

"I get the picture!" Brook says, laughing. She removes my jacket, vest and tie. While she unbuttons my shirt, I remove my cuff links. When my shirt hits the floor, I turn her around to unzip her dress. I slide it from her shoulders and it pools at her feet. I pick her up and set her on the end of the bed. I kneel before her to remove her shoes and stockings. Standing, she grabs my belt, removes it and unzips my pants. She slides them down. I toe off my shoes and remove my socks.

"So this is what you do on a wedding night," I joke.

"And every night thereafter. Until death us do part."

"Every night sounds good to me. Twice on weekends?"

I remove her bra and lay her down on the bed. Removing her panties, I move between her legs and say, "I want you to remember this night for the rest of your life, Brook. I intend to give you pleasure until you ask me to stop. Remember your gardenias?"

"Yes."

"Good." I lower my head and begin to satisfy my wife. Around her fourth orgasm she says, "Gardenias. I am cramping a little, William. You have to stop."

"Are you okay? Is the baby okay? God, I didn't mean to hurt you."

"I'm fine, don't worry. Come here and just make love to me."

"Are you sure?"

"Yes. Slow and gentle. I want you."

I watch her reaction as I enter her. I keep my eyes on her to scrutinize any discomfort. When I relax to give in to the feeling of her, it isn't long before I explode through my release. I lie next to her, cuddling with her. "I'm a lucky man. I have a wife I love who loves me. All that I am and everything that I have is yours, darling."

"All I have ever wanted is right here." She places her hand over my heart.

We accompany our guests to the airport to see them off. Promises of a visit after the baby is born are made. Brook and I ride back to the house. I encourage her to take a nap. I can see that she is still very tired. The closer it gets to the Australia trip, the more I wonder about the logic of going.

I insist on Brook resting the entire week after the wedding. The most stressful thing I encourage her to do is have a manicure; pedicure and prenatal massage at our local salon.

When she arrives home, she looks so much better. "I think you need to visit the salon once or twice a week, Brook. I want to pamper you. I hate the thought of you working in Australia. Please let me fix this."

"No, William. I gave my word. This may be my last shoot. I have a feeling I won't be able to continue modeling after the baby. I have duties."

"Emily said you have interviews on Friday for a nanny. I don't want you to exhaust yourself, so go easy."

"I promise to be good. Emily and Eve went through much of the pre-interview stuff for me. I think there are only five candidates left."

"The Queen's party is Saturday night. We don't have to go if you're not up to it."

"William, she helped us with Madeleine. We have to thank her."

"She helped me Brook. You don't owe her anything. I warn you, though. Madeleine could be there. I don't think she will go, but she can."

"That is fine. She won't bother me. I doubt that my presence will bother her."

I arrive home early on Friday to assist my female family members in choosing the nanny for our baby. Two candidates catch all of our attention. We agree that the choice is between Allison Daynard, a twenty-year-old, perky redhead with an associate's degree in early childhood development, and Martha Pennington, a thirty-year-old disciplinarian with ten years experience. I am at a loss to decide. I almost wish we were having twins because I would hire both of them. One to have fun with and one to keep them on the straight and narrow.

As I finish dressing in my party finery for my Queen, I glance at my wife of one week. Her dress is light blue with small flowers embroidered on the top. Her little belly is slightly in view. I am amazed that she has only gained eight pounds. She glides over the floor to me. I open my arms to take her in. "You shouldn't look this lovely, Brook. All of the ladies-in-waiting will be jealous of you."

"Unless I am mistaken, Mr. Barry, I am a lady waiting, too! I am counting the days until I see our baby."

"That you are. I stand corrected." I hold her in my protective arms and kiss the top of her head.

"We should get going. We don't want to be late. I think your parents have left already."

"I'm ready." I hold out my arm for her to take. She places her small hand and arm through mine. As we walk through the hall to the stairs, I say, "I have sent for Luke. I want him to accompany us to Australia. I think I will have him stay here for the baby."

"Why, William? Do you know something?"

"No, Brook. I'm being proactive. Luke is in my service and not being utilized in America when we are in England. I don't need him to look after an empty apartment."

"You're sure that there isn't a threat that you are aware of?"

"I promised you, Brook. No more secrets, ever. The best way to protect you is if you know there is a problem. I don't have any information that we are in any danger."

"Do you still carry a gun?"

"Yes. John has one and so does George. Anyone who drives any of the family carries a gun, Brook. Jonathan and Emily's family are protected, as are my parents. It is part of the bargain."

"John the footman? He seems so docile."

I chuckle. "I'm going to tell him you said that," I say. "John, my love, is a former trained sniper in her Majesty's army. He looks all gentlemanly for a reason. No one would suspect he is deadly accurate with a weapon."

As we pass by John on our way to the waiting car Brook stops and says, "I just learned something about you, John."

"Yes, ma'am," John replies.

"Thank you for your service to your country and to us. I feel better knowing that you are here."

"Thank you, ma'am. It's my pleasure to serve this family."

The receiving line to greet the Royal Family is long and moves slowly. No one would have the audacity to ditch the line and enter through a different door instead of greeting the Queen. Therefore, here we stand.

"Who is our nanny-to-be, Brook?" I ask.

"I'm leaning toward Allison. She's fun and sweet. I want our children to have a happy childhood. There is plenty of time to behave when you're grown. You are little for such a short time."

"Whatever you want is fine with me. You'll be with her much more than I will. I want you happy with the choice."

We continue to chat until we find ourselves steps away from her Majesty. "Hello, William. So good to see you again," the Queen says.

"Thank you, ma'am. Allow me to introduce to you my wife, Lady Brook Barry. Lady Barry, this is Her Royal Highness The Queen."

"A pleasure to meet you, my dear. William has told me of you. I can see why he is so smitten. Much happiness to you both on your marriage."

"Thank you, ma'am. Happy birthday to you," Brook says.

We move on and I say, "Well done, Brook. Your knees can stop shaking now."

"How did you know that my knees were shaking?"

"A good guess. Arrived at through years of experience with royal interactions."

"You are royal, my husband."

"As are you, wife. In fact, I am thirty-third in line for the crown. Be careful . . . someday you could be Queen."

Brook throws her head back laughing and says, "God help the commonwealth if I become Queen."

CHAPTER 12

BROOK AND I HAVE A wonderful time at the Queen's birthday. We dance and talk, enjoying each other's company. I introduce Brook to many of my friends and business associates. In the future, she will be socializing with them and their wives. After dancing with my uncle, Brook mouths to me that she is going to the ladies room. I nod and smile as I watch her walk away. I continue my conversation with my cousin as my uncle joins us saying, "You are one jammy dodger, William. Brook is bloody brilliant."

"Don't I know it, Uncle. I can't believe she has taken me on."

I keep an eye on the door, wondering what is taking Brook so long when I see Madeleine walk out. As I walk quickly to the door, Brook exits looking shaken. I get to her side and say, "Are you all right?"

"Madeleine was in there. She congratulated me loudly on our speedy marriage, saying the ink wasn't even dry on the divorce papers. Then she said she understood the hurry, not wanting our child to be a bastard. Lastly, she said that polite society will still consider him a bastard because you were married to her when he was conceived."

"I'm going to fucking wring her bloody neck."

"No, William. We are going home. I want to lie down and I want you to hold me. I want you to kiss me as you do and make me forget to even breathe."

I make our excuses to leave. Saying good-bye to the Queen, I escort Brook to our car. "You look very tired, darling. I think you need a back rub tonight."

"That would be lovely, William."

I get her home and undressed. I sit next to her and rub her back. She asks, "Will the baby be a bastard, William? How important is that distinction?"

"We are married, Brook, and I am the baby's father. Legally, the baby will not be a bastard. What people think is unfortunately out of my control. What venom Madeleine spreads is also out of my control. However, I am also free to spread the truth about her. She needs to be mindful of that. I intend to remind her of the fact."

"I wish you were just William the photographer sometimes. We could have had a baby without being married and no one would have called him that name."

"I am painfully aware of the differences. Several facts remain, Brook. I am desperately in love with you. I am blissfully happy. Overcome with joy because of the baby. And for the first time, looking forward to the future."

"I'm glad that we leave Wednesday for Australia. I need to get out of here for a few weeks. Maybe she will run out of steam while we are gone."

I hold her and she falls asleep. She has had enough upset. The rest of this pregnancy will be happy if I have to cry blue murder.

When we are in the air on our way to Sydney, I tell Brook about where we are staying.

"It's called the Skyhouse~the top three floors of 129 Harrington Street in Sydney. The forty-third floor is living room, dining and kitchen. Forty-four is the bedrooms and the forty-fifth is a roof spa and garden. I might be able to talk you into making love on a roof again. I'm getting hard just thinking about it."

"Calm down, sailor. Who said I was doing anything with you? I'm a married woman and not interested in any shenanigans."

Leaning in so no one else can hear, I say, "It is my intention, Mrs. Barry, to have full use of every amenity that the Skyhouse has to offer, including but not limited to, shagging in every room. I'm on my honeymoon . . . remember?"

"I'm not quite sure of what exactly you are on, but I confess it sounds like fun. What if we don't go back, William? Would there be a problem with me having the baby there?"

I turn her chin to look at me and say, "Wherever you want to have the baby is fine with me~England, Australia, Italy, even America. You tell me and I will get you there. You aren't attached to any of the doctors that you have seen."

"I'm attached to you. I want you there and someone to catch the baby. If we don't have the baby in England, it won't matter to you?"

"Not in the slightest. I want you comfortable, Brook. Nothing else matters."

I see her visibly relax. I think I lifted the weight from her. It never occurred to me that she was uncomfortable delivering in England. Thoughtless on my part.

We land and Luke retrieves our luggage while Brook and I arrange for our car. The car is brought around and Luke is in heaven. I found a 1966 fully-restored Bentley for us. Luke says, "Well done, sir."

"Thank you, Luke. Do you think that you can handle her?"

"I think so, sir. I will give it my all."

I open the door for my wife and get in behind her. She looks tired from the flight. I was going to have Luke take us around to see the city, but now I think I will just take her home for a nap.

The Skyhouse is all that it was promised to be. Spacious, modern and views from every corner. The master bedroom occupies one whole side of the second floor. The other four bedrooms are on the other side and Luke takes one of them. If Brook decides to have the baby here, I will send for Allison and she will take another bedroom. The third floor is amazing with the largest hot tub I have ever seen. I wish Brook could use it, but hot tubs are not good for expectant mothers.

Once I have Brook in bed for her nap, I call down to finalize the arrangements for the house cleaners and cook. When I am satisfied that we have the proper help, I go to check on Brook. She is sleeping soundly and I marvel from the door. There is no one lovelier than my wife, in the entire world.

Brook wakes up from her nap and I have Luke show us the sights. We stop at Mrs. Macquaries Point to watch the sun set over the Opera House and bridge. I hold my wife in front of me and kiss her neck. "That feels good, William."

"I'm glad. It takes so little to make you happy, Brook. I'm a lucky man."

"Wait until I'm in labor and screaming at you for getting me pregnant. Then we'll see how easily pleased I am."

"You can yell at me all you want. I'll take any abuse you throw at me. With what you are giving me, no price is too high to pay."

We dine at a small bistro near the water and I take Brook home. Brook and I shower together under a waterfall. I wash her long beautiful hair and soap up her body, paying extra attention to her little belly.

"You are really into the baby thing, William. Many men aren't as interested."

"You and this baby are all that I have wanted for a long time, Brook. The fact that I get both of you at the same time just makes it better for me. You have changed my entire life and I could not be happier."

We get in bed and I fold my body around her, giving her my strength. She snuggles against me and sleeps.

I feel Brook stirring against me. I breathe deeply and sigh. With my eyes still closed, I feel a tentative hand close on my erection. Brook begins to stroke me. I growl in her ear, "What exactly are your intentions this morning, Mrs. Barry?"

"I was told my husband was on his honeymoon. I thought maybe we could act like honeymooners this morning."

"I wouldn't want to waste a perfectly good woody, so what will it be, my love?"

"Surprise me," she says, turning over on to her back. I lift up her nightgown to take her nipple into my mouth. She moans her pleasure. Kissing down her body, I tell her belly, "Sorry, baby. Mummy has needs this morning. You are about to get a daddy wake-up call."

Brook giggles and says, "You are very bad, telling your baby that."

I proceed to pleasure my wife until she is gasping for air. Turning her on her side, I lift her leg over my hip and slowly enter her from behind. I stroke her with my fingers until both of us are sweaty with our fulfillment.

"You did wake him up, poor thing. It is very good that we don't remember what happens before we are born."

"What happens in utero stays in utero," I quip.

I get up and into the shower. While I dress, Brook takes hers. We walk downstairs together to meet our cook and housekeepers. Luke has gone over the details with the staff. Brook and I enter the kitchen and sit at the counter.

"Good morning, Mr. and Mrs. Barry. My name is Constance and I will be cooking for you while you are in Australia. Mr. Luke has given me a list of the foods that you prefer and what you don't like. If you want anything other than that, please tell me. Will we be entertaining while you are here?"

"We don't know anyone here right now. My wife is expecting, but will be working a few hours a day for six weeks or so. We might have a dinner party or two with her associates."

"This is the house for entertaining, sir. No one would ever refuse your invitation. Margaret and Joy are the housekeepers and they double at parties as servers. I also have other chefs that work to prepare. We just need a day or two notice."

I look at Brook and smile. "It could be fun, don't you think?" I ask.

"All we need is friends. That sounds like a song. I am going to scope out the photographer and the designer today. I want to see where the shoot is. Get the lay of the land, so to speak. Are you coming with me?"

"Do you honestly think that I would let you go by yourself? Remember me . . . overprotective crazy man that hired people to run with you?"

"I have been trying to place your face for a week now. I do remember you!"

We laugh and get funny looks from Constance. We eat our breakfast and I call Luke to give him our itinerary for the day. He will program the GPS so we don't lose our way around Sydney.

Our first stop is Edward Nelson Design Studio. Brook and I go in and ask to speak with him. A tall, dark-haired woman comes out and says, "Hi, I'm Edward Nelson. How may I help you?"

"You are Edward?" Brook asks. "I thought you were a he."

"Everyone does. I am the fifth daughter. My father wanted a junior. I'm the last so, I'm Edward."

"I'm Brook Kennedy Barry and this is my husband, William Barry. I'm the model for your new maternity line."

"Brook, it is a pleasure to meet you. William too. This is going to be fantastic. I was so happy to hear that you are expecting. I didn't want to have to pad the clothes. It never looks right."

"When do you want to start the fittings? I'm ready when you are."

"Tomorrow is Anzac Day, we will be closed. Let's start on Monday, say 9:00."

"That works for me. What is Anzac Day?"

"It is the day that we honor all of the brave men and woman who have served our country."

"I see. It's like our Veterans Day in America."

"Yes, very similar. William, your sister and my sister were at university together. I am familiar with your family."

"Bridget Nelson is your sister?"

"Yes. I am so glad that you remember her."

"She spent several weekends with my family. How is she?"

"Happily married and living in France."

"We are on our honeymoon of sorts. I will be hanging around from time to time. I worry with the baby and all."

"My sister called you the billionaire playboy when she was in school. I guess you had quite a rep."

"I didn't know him then. Somehow that analogy doesn't really surprise me. I think he has calmed down somewhat," Brook says with a smirk.

"Somewhat! I thought I was behaving very well," I say, dejected.

CHAPTER 13

LUKE DRIVES BROOK AND ME to the studio of Cole Stevenson. We walk into an art gallery in the center of Sydney. I ask a passing salesperson for him. I am slightly nervous because if Edward is a woman, Cole could be too. Australia is very progressive. A tall, white-haired man walks towards us.

"I'm told you are looking for me," he says.

"I'm William Barry and this is my wife, Brook."

"Very pleased to meet you."

"I'm the model for Edward Nelson Designs. We have a shoot next week," Brook says.

"Hello, Brook. I'm glad you stopped by. I can give you the once-over."

"The once-over? I'm not sure what you mean."

"I can size you up. Check your coloring. I like it when I can meet the people I'm working with before the shoot."

Brook and Mr. Stevenson discuss the shoot while I wander off to view the photographs in the gallery. He is good. I like his work. While I'm looking, my phone rings, "Hello."

"William, it's Emily. How are you and Brook doing?"

"Good, Emily. How are you and my girls?"

"They miss their unil and aunt. So do I."

"Come and visit. Our apartment is big enough, and we would love to see you."

"The girls are in school, William. How is Brook feeling?"

"She is amazing. We are at the photographer's studio right now. They are going over the shoot for next week. I am so happy, Emily, I'm almost afraid to say it."

"Don't be, William. You should be happy. Everyone sends their love. Rub Brook's belly for me."

"I will. Love to everyone. Bye."

I feel Brook's hands on my back. "Are you ready to go?" she asks.

"As soon as you are, my love. Are you hungry or tired?" I ask.

"No. Let's drive around and see the sights."

We drive to Bondi Beach. We park and I help Brook out of the car. We walk the beach with my arm around my wife. "Have you thought of a name for the baby yet?" I ask.

"If it is a girl, I was thinking Willa Brook. If it's a boy, do you want a William?"

"I was thinking Warren after my father. Warren William George Henry. What do you think?"

"Henry after the VIII? Will he chop off his wife's heads?"

"My grandfather was Henry and my mum's was George."

"I love it. I hope he looks like you with this," she says as she feels my chest and stomach.

"I can't give him that. Unfortunately, it takes work to have all this."

We continue walking the beach and talking about the baby. The sun dances across her face and hair. The breeze blows a tendril across her lips. I pick it off and kiss her. "I think I am going to keep you pregnant, Brook. You shine from within."

"Thank you. I'm not sure that I want to stay pregnant. I miss running. I need the freedom it gives me."

"It won't be long and you'll be running again. Pushing a pram in front of you!"

"I was thinking Allison could entertain the baby while I run. I don't think pushing a pram is a safe thing to do."

"Quite so, my love. Allison will be invaluable to us. I plan on sleeping with my wife and not sleeping."

We walk back to the car and continue our drive along the coast, looking out at the Tasman Sea. I can see Brook tiring so I have Luke turn back to take her home. She rests her head on my shoulder as we drive. I walk her into the house and sit her on the couch. Kneeling in front of her, I remove her shoes and rub her feet. Resting her head on the back, she moans as I massage her. She says, "You are so good to me, William."

"The gift that you are giving me is so precious, Brook. You are the one who is good to me. Nothing that I do can compare."

"I love you, William. Carrying your baby is the best thing that I have ever done. I am helping to give life. I'm constantly amazed by that thought."

She leans forward holding my face she kisses me.

While Brook is at her fittings over the next three days, I am in contact with a local tour company, arranging for some sight-seeing. Australia is a fascinating country. I want Brook to see and hear a kookaburra. I want her to have an experience in the outback. The Blue Mountains are on my list.

I manage to get tickets to see Bryn Terfel at the Opera House for his one performance in Australia. I have heard him sing before in England. I'm sure that Brook will love his bass-baritone voice.

I'm getting some sun on the roof when Brook gets home. I watch her walk to me from the stairs with a smile on her face. "You look comfortable on your chaise. Have you been dreaming?" she asks.

"I was just waiting for you to get here. Sit with me." I move over to make room for her. "You smell like the ocean," I continue. "Were you at the beach?"

"I went with Cole and Eddie to block shots and check out some locations. I think we are going to the cove and Bondi for a few shots."

"How do you feel, darling? You look tired."

"I'm a little tired, not bad. I try to rest in between things. I sleep in the car. I'll be fine. Cole is very conscious of the baby. I'm sure he won't overwork me."

"Good because I don't want to have to remind him to go easy. I will if I see you not able to keep up. You and the baby come before any pictures."

Brook snuggles into me and I kiss her temple. "Constance has made us a delicious dinner and then we are going to the opera. Do you feel up to it?"

"I want to go. We can always leave early."

"Yes we can. Anytime. Why don't you go shower or take a bath. Relax before dinner."

"A bath sounds lovely. Find me when dinner is ready."

I watch her walk back to the stairs, thinking just how lucky I am.

The Opera House is amazing. The architecture is ultra modern. The acoustics are simply exceptional. The concert is exactly what I had expected~ phenomenal. Next weekend we will tour the Blue Mountains if Brook isn't too tired.

Brook's first week of shooting goes well. I am grateful to Cole for the breaks he gives Brook. I think he is as in tune to her needs as I am. He also puts her on a three-day week. She works Monday, Tuesday and Thursday.

Wednesday morning I'm on a conference call with Jonathan as Brook walks in to the study. "Hold on, Jonathan,. Brook just walked in." I turn to Brook and ask, "You need me, darling?"

"I hate to bother you, but will you be long?"

"Just a few more minutes. Are you okay?"

"Fine. I'll be on the roof when you finish."

I turn back to resume the discussion with Jonathan. A half an hour later I find Brook on the chaise, soaking up the sun. "Do you have room for me?" I ask.

"Always. I wanted to know if you would take pictures of my belly. You know, naked."

"I would love to. Do you want to do it now? How about up here in the sun."

"It's a little chilly and windy for me without clothes. I think it's only sixty-five today."

"Okay, where?"

"Maybe in the bedroom. We can move the chaise over by the window."

"That will be lovely. I'll get it all set up and come back to get you. I want you to lie here and rest. It will probably take an hour or so."

I had Luke to help me move the chaise and set up the tripods and cameras. The afternoon sun is just coming around when I finish the set-up. The light is perfect. I return to the roof for Brook. As I reach the top of the stairs, she smiles and stops my heart from beating. I should have brought a camera with me to capture the moment. I walk to her and say, "I'm all set. I need to get you naked. I have a surprise for you."

"I like surprises. Animal, vegetable or mineral?"

"I think animal. I want to pose with you, holding you and the baby."

"I love that idea."

The first photograph I take is of Brook and me standing, facing each other. Her hand on my chest and my arm around her, covering her breasts. The look on our faces shows the love that is between us. Next, I am behind her with my arm covering her and a hand on her belly. After that, it's all Brook. I place her on the chaise with a sheet across her hips. I could never tire of looking at her but she finally tells me she has had enough, so I stop.

After being with a naked Brook for over an hour, I pick her up and walk to our bed. I know my days of making love with her are numbered, so I take it slow. Feeling every inch of her body, and bring us to a height that rolled through us for what seemed like forever.

CHAPTER 14

BROOK AND I LEAVE FOR our tour of the Blue Mountains. Our guide picks us up at 8:30 Friday morning. Brook looks radiant as usual. It has grown cooler here, as fall has begun. Brook wears one of Eddie's designs. I have a feeling we will have a closet full before the shoot is over. She and Eddie have grown quite close over the last week or so. They have very much the same personality and temperament. I open the car door for Brook and help her in. Coming around to the other side, our guide gets out and says, "Mr. Barry, my name is Hud and it my pleasure to show my Australia to you and your lovely wife for the next two days."

"It's a pleasure to meet you, Hud. Please call us William and Brook. Hud is a different name. How did you come by it?"

"My given name is Hudson. I shortened it to Hud." I get in and Hud continues our conversation. "I understand that you want to see koalas, roos and kookaburras. The best place to guarantee that is the wildlife park. You might see them in the wild, but I know you will see them in the park."

"We put ourselves in your hands, Hud."

"We will be spending a lot of time in this car, so if you are too hot or cold, please let me know. Also, any stop you would like to make, just ask. How long have you been here?"

"A week or so. My wife is modeling for one of your designers."

"I see that you are expecting, ma'am. When is your baby due?"

"In early July. I feel huge already," Brook answers him.

"My wife is expecting as well. She only has a week or two to go. This is our first and I can't wait to hold her. Are you having a boy or a girl?"

"We don't know for sure. I suspect it's a boy. How is your wife feeling?"

"Better because the weather turned cooler. She swelled up over the summer with the heat. She gained almost fifty pounds and that didn't help. How about you?"

"I've only gained around eleven pounds. I follow a strict regimen. It hasn't been easy, but I have loved every minute of the pregnancy."

We ride out of Sydney with Hud giving us a complete history of the surrounding land. It is clear that being a tour guide in Australia is far more than a job to him. His knowledge and passion for his country is admirable. An hour and a half later we are at the entrance of the park. Hud wants to stay with the car, but Brook and I insist that he accompany us everywhere.

When Brook spots the koala bears, I think she actually bounces with excitement. They have a section where you can hold one and I find myself in line with my six-year-old wife. The pleasure I get from her reaction makes my day, and I can't help but grin.

Our next find are the kangaroos. I draw the line here. I know of their propensity to kick, and I am not going to let Brook anywhere near them. We watch the other tourists get into the pen, taking their safety into their own hands. Lastly, the kookaburra sings to us. I use that term loosely. It sounds like laughing rather than singing. It has a harsh, high pitch to it and a few minutes is all that you need to get the full effect. We grab a sandwich at the concession stand and get back to the car as a light rain begins to fall.

Driving further into the Blue Mountains, we head to Wentworth Falls. We are at the bottom, looking up to one of the most beautiful sights that I have ever seen. The water cascades over the rocks and lands on a section of terraced rocks. It spills over the rocks in smaller torrents, creating a majestic and peaceful sound. I take countless pictures of Brook with the rocks behind her.

Hud brings us next to the skyway where we board a tram to transport us over the Jamison Valley. From here, we get a spectacular view of the surrounding mountains. We see Mt Solitary, the Three Sisters and amazing cliffs of sandstone. I have visions of plummeting to the valley below, but I keep my over protectiveness to myself. The look on Brook's face quiets me. With more pictures taken, I can see that Brook is tiring. We don't spend much time looking out before I suggest we return to the car.

We find a cozy hotel to spend the night in. For the first time in my life, I am not comfortably ensconced in the penthouse suite of a five-star hotel. I think Brook is smirking at me, although she says nothing about it. I open the door to our room and I am appalled at it's size. "I think your closet is larger than this room, William," Brook says. "How are we ever going to stay here? We might even touch each other as we pass to the bathroom."

"Your teasing will not go unpunished, Brook. I know that my preferences are somewhat unreasonable to you. You must admit that this room is overly small."

"William, this room is average for a regular hotel. I have stayed in hundreds of room all across the world similar in size to this. You live in a different realm than most people."

"Thankfully, I have you to remind me of this on a regular basis. You keep me grounded, Brook. When I fully take over my duties, I will have you to help me deal with regular people outside of my ivory tower."

Brook showers while I listen to the news. We have dinner in the restaurant connected to the hotel. As soon as we finish, I sweep Brook back to our room and into bed. She protests that she is not that tired but is asleep within minutes. I revel in the fact that I am the man who has the pleasure of sleeping next to this earthbound angel.

Hud is piloting us into the outback. He explains to us that saying "outback" in Australia is funny. Almost all of Australia is considered outback. Outback means, to them, relatively unpopulated areas. Since most of the country has a small population, except for few large cities such as Sydney and Melbourne, a vast percentage is outback. Hud points out rock formations that we pass by and tells us the history and culture of the aboriginal people who live here. It is all very rugged, wild and unspoiled by man.

In the early afternoon Hud takes us back to civilization via a different route, allowing us to see more of his country. Brook rests her head on my lap and sleeps most of the drive back to the apartment. It is almost 9:00 when we arrive home. I wake Brook and thank Hud for a most enjoyable two days. I place a hefty tip in his hand and wish him and his wife a happy and safe delivery. He does the same to Brook and me.

Brook and I sleep late, recovering from our Australian adventure. When I come out of the shower, Brook is awake and smiling. "Thank you again for the trip through the country. I loved every minute."

"You're welcome, darling. I wanted to see the country with you. I want you to rest today. I have some work to do, so I will be in the study most of the day. If you need me, come and find me."

I make my way to the study to wade through a small mountain of paperwork that Jonathan has sent. Along with the e-mails and other various correspondence, it is four hours before I get up to stretch for a few minutes. I find Brook sleeping with a book on her chest, lying in the sun by a window. I walk into the kitchen to find Constance making our lunch. "Hello, Constance. How are you today?" I ask.

"Very well, sir. How are you today?" she says.

"I feel great. Has Brook told you about our tour of your beautiful country?"

"Yes, she did. I know she had a wonderful time. I have been to the Falls many times, and each time it takes my breath away."

"Quite so, I'm afraid. The beauty of nature far surpasses anything else. That's why I chose to photograph it for so long. Now I am a business man and not a dreamer."

"You should never give up dreaming, sir. That is the best part of life. I know the responsibilities of marriage and children ground us, but our dreams can lift us. We can be, do and go anywhere in them."

"I married my dream, Constance. Brook is my be, do, and go anywhere. With her, everything is possible."

"That's the way you should feel. I see the love between you. You will have a good marriage, sir. Now, how about some lunch? Is Mrs. Barry ready to eat?"

"She is sleeping right now. I will eat here and bring Brook a tray after. I want her to rest as much as possible."

I eat my lunch as Constance makes a tray for Brook. As soon as I finish, I bring it to her and wake her saying, "Sleeping Beauty, wake up. I have lunch for you." She stretches like a cat and opens her striking eyes.

"I was dreaming about you and the baby."

"Is that so? What about us?"

"You were holding the baby and talking baby talk. It was so perfect, William."

"I am well versed in baby talk, Brook. After all, I am an unil to five of the little creatures. I missed most of Jonathan's boys, but Emily's girls and I spent a great deal of time together before I left for the States."

"I'm famished. What's for lunch?"

"I have Constance's vegetable soup and a turkey sandwich. How does that sound?"

"Delicious." While Brook eats, I say, "I was thinking about having a small dinner party next weekend. We could invite Eddie and Cole and maybe Hud. You and his wife could talk babies."

"That would be lovely. I'll go over it with Constance. If the weather holds out and we can continue on the same schedule, I'll be done with everything here in about three weeks."

"That's splendid. I want you off your feet and resting for that last month. Are we staying here?"

"I've actually been thinking about that. If I stay here, I will be flying back to England with a new baby. I think I would like to go back and have the baby there. It just makes more sense to me. It's a long flight with a new baby."

"I agree, but it has to be your decision. My mother will be over the moon if you are there when the baby is born. She loves to smell new babies. I'm told it is the best smell in the world."

CHAPTER 15

EVERYONE ACCEPTS OUR INVITATION TO the dinner party. I laugh because Constance's words come back to me. Brook has gone over all of the details with her. Constance has brought in another chef to help with the prep. Margaret and Joy will help serve. The menu sounds delectable:

Scallops with white wine and herbs
Spicy hasselback potatoes
Wombok salad
Roasted baby carrots with /thyme
Strawberry and cream bread pudding

Hors d'oeuvres and cocktails are at 7:00 with dinner at 8:00.

I walk in to the bedroom just as Brook is finishing her hair. I stand behind her, moving her long curls to the side and kissing her neck. "You smell divine, darling. New cologne?"

"You always ask that. It's called soap. I use it regularly."

"Then it is a scent called Brook. I'm captivated. Our guests should be here in a few minutes. I just checked the kitchen and Constance has everything under control. The table is set and the house looks superb. You're quite a hostess. I'm a lucky man."

"I think we are both very lucky. Maybe blessed is a better word. We almost lost it all, William."

I turn her around to face me and say, "Once again you cut through all of the bullshit to the heart of it all. My stupidity and your hard head . . . what a pair." I kiss her forehead and walk back into the bedroom. "I'll go down and wait to greet everyone. You take your time, darling."

I meet Joy on the stairs. She says, "I was just coming to find you, Mr. Barry. Two of your guests have arrived. They are waiting in the living room for you and Mrs. Barry."

"Thank you, Joy," I say as I reach the bottom. Walking to the living room, I see Cole and his wife, Samina, looking out the window at the stunning view. Cole turns and says, "So this is what money can buy? I just apologized to my wife for not having it. My jealousy overflows, mate."

"It shouldn't. I have contributed little to my wealth. I spend old money. I have benefited from having frugal ancestors. I'm told several of them roll over daily with some of my antics." Thankfully, they laugh. I continue, "Please don't mention money in front of Brook. It is a sore spot with her. She is embarrassed and offended by it."

"How is Brook today?" Cole asks.

"I'm very good, Cole. Fat and happy is the saying, I think." Brook walks over to kiss Cole and Samina.

"You should have seen me when I was pregnant if you think that you are fat, Brook," Samina declares. "You'll have your figure back in no time with how small you are. You carry well, my dear."

Eddie and her husband, Josiah, arrive, followed shortly after by Hud and his wife, Katie. After everyone stares out at the view, I give a tour of the apartment. The drinks and hors d' oeuvres are ready when we reenter the living room.

"Brook mentioned that you are a landscape photographer, William. I know you worked out of New York. Have you worked here at all?" Cole asks.

"No, unfortunately. Your country fascinates me but I have never been here before. I have mostly done work for large tourist sites and hotel chains. They want professional photos taken for pamphlets and such."

"So no people?"

"I have a large portfolio of Brook but she is the only human subject I can tolerate working with. I had a few unfortunate incidents with testy models and discontinued the practice of using them."

"I would love to see what you have done of Brook."

Smiling, I say, "You will have to ask her. They are primarily nudes. Tasteful, but nudes nonetheless."

All eyes shoot to Brook. She blushes, shaking her head at me. "William just took naked baby pictures of us. You can't see anything but my baby belly and our arms."

"Our arms?" Eddie says.

"Yes. William is naked in them too. I'm not the only exhibitionist in the family. I have a willing accomplice."

"I wanted to do that too, but Hud wouldn't let me," Katie says.

"It's not too late. If you want, I would love to do that for you, Katie. Brook will be at a shoot on Monday. Why don't you and Hud come over," I offer.

"I'm not getting naked with you," Hud says, his macho showing, "so you can just forget about that."

"No one said you had to be naked. Brook and I did a few when we first got together. They were so striking because look at what I had to work with," I say as I kiss Brook's temple. "Doing the baby pictures was just a natural progression for us. Let me do this for you, Hud. It's all digital anyway. You see something that bothers you, we delete it."

Brook gets up and walks to the study. When she comes back, she hands the pictures of us to Katie and Hud. "What time on Monday, William?" Katie asks looking at the pictures.

"So you want to do this? Any time, I will be here all day."

"I'll call before we come if that's all right."

I nod my head. The pictures are passed around with everyone commenting on how good they are. "I think you should continue with photography, William. You have a good eye and technique," Cole offers.

"Thank you, but my obligations have changed and I need to change with them. My father and brother have run the family business while I was the quintessential playboy in America. I lived for four years doing exactly what I wanted to do. The money I made paid for my housekeeper and driver slash bodyguard and nothing else. I have to make up for that by helping my brother so that my father can retire and enjoy life. I won't stop taking pictures. I have a baby on the way, after all."

"And a strikingly beautiful wife to boot," Cole adds.

Brook blossoms into a full blush as she mouths to me stop. I smile at her. I know she is uncomfortable with all of the "beautiful Brook" talk. I move on to a different subject. "I know you have a maternity line, Eddie. What other designs are you interested in?"

"I have a women's line and I want to get into men's and then children's eventually."

"Very ambitious. From what I have seen of Brook's wardrobe, you have talent. I wish you luck."

"Thank you. It's a very competitive field," Eddie answers.

Constance informs us that our dinner is ready. Brook and I show everyone into the dining room. We eat with the conversation flowing easily between us. Josiah asks," What does your family do, William?"

"We have a shipping fleet and some smaller companies."

"Barry Shipping?"

"Yes, that's right."

"No wonder your brother needs your help. Isn't that the largest shipper in the UK?"

"I'm afraid so, yes."

"If you're Barry Shipping, that means you're a duke or something, right?"

"Right again. I'm not a duke until my father passes the title to me. Until then, I'm technically a viscount."

"So, you are royalty? A member of the Queen's family. My wife is designing clothes that a duchess is modeling." Josiah's eyes fly to Brook.

She smiles at him and says, "Do you have a problem with that?"

"Not a problem, really. Just a question. Why are you modeling when your husband is a billionaire viscount?"

"That is a long story. I signed the contract to model before William and I got married. I wouldn't go back on my word and break the contract, so here I am."

"I have met principled people before, but this is beyond what anyone else would under the same circumstances, Brook. How long have you been married?" Cole asks.

"A month now. I didn't tell William about the baby for five months. We had some things to work out."

"I was still married. Brook didn't know. I had never lived with my wife and never obtained a divorce from her. I needed the Queen's permission for a contested divorce."

"And we think the Royals have an easy life without difficulties. Good to know that you are as screwed up as we are!" Samina quips.

"You have no idea," I answer.

We have our dessert and coffee back in the living room, the view of the lights of Sydney surrounding us. Our guests go to the windows repeatedly to look at the city below us. "I would never leave this apartment if I lived here. This view is magnificent," Eddie says.

"Can you imagine the roof garden in the summer on a star-lit night . . . perfect!" Cole adds.

"You are welcome to spend next weekend here. If Brook feels up to it, I'm taking her to Melbourne for the weekend. You'll have the place all to yourselves."

CHAPTER 16

I HAVE CHARTERED A PRIVATE yacht to take Brook and me to Melbourne. The ocean is cold but the view is breathtaking. Brook snuggles into me, covered by a thick blanket. "Thank you for this, William. It's so beautiful and peaceful."

"Anything for you, darling. You know that."

It takes us all day to get there, but at 4:30, we arrive at Port Phillip. Because it was restful for Brook, she still feels like doing something so we walk around Center Place. We walk in and out of the shops. Brook finds some things for the baby. We watch the street artists. Brook finds a café that she wants to try for dinner.

The restaurant boasts a fresh catch menu, so every day is different. The offerings are posted on a chalkboard. Today the catch is luderick with turmeric and dill, deep-fried black spinefoot and poached threadfin salmon. Brook and I look at each other. I raise my shoulders in my your-guess-is-as-good-as-mine gesture and say, "I'm going with the salmon."

"Me too. I have no idea what luderick is and I don't do deep-fried."

We order two salmon dinners. It is the best that I have ever had. I'm not sure what they poached it in but the taste is exceptional. We give our compliments to the chef and take a cab back to the yacht.

Our captain has our berth toasty warm for Brook. We undress and get in bed, snuggling up to each other. I am happy to hold my wife without expecting anything further. I know that sex has become uncomfortable for her in the last few days.

She has said nothing but I feel her wincing with discomfort. I have not become celibate by any stretch, I'll simply take care of my needs singularly.

I wake in the morning to a steaming cup of coffee and a smiling face. "You look like you slept well, darling. You are a good wife. You come to me with coffee," I say, stretching and stifling a yawn.

"Today is just your lucky day, husband. The captain had coffee perking and I grabbed us a cup." She walks to the door.

"Don't leave, Brook. Sit and talk to me. We are always going in different directions. This little boat trip affords us the perfect opportunity to talk."

"What do you want to talk about?"

"I want to know why you ran after Madeleine talked to you. Why you didn't wait for me to explain. Why you wouldn't talk to me in New York. Why you kept running. Why you didn't love me enough to trust me." When I say the last sentence, Brook looks as if I have struck her. I immediately regret saying it.

"I had just found out that I was pregnant. I was in the throws of morning sickness and complete exhaustion. I was so happy about the baby." She begins to cry but continues. "I wanted to wait to tell you until we got back home but I couldn't wait. I was going to tell you that day as soon as you got home. She said I was an idiot. I can still hear her say it. She said that she was your current and only wife. 'I see he didn't get around to notifying you that he is married. Pity, makes it very awkward to hear it from the wife.' That's exactly what she said. I ran more at first to get away from her than you. Once I got to New York, I wanted to hurt you like I was hurt. She is right. I was an idiot."

I grab her, hold her tight and say, "NO, NO, NO, Brook! None of this was your doing. It was my fault entirely for not being honest with you. I just wish you had stayed to hear the explanation. Now that you know what happened between us, would you have stayed with me?"

"I was so messed up that day. I don't know the answer to that. I know now that I love you enough to trust you with the baby's life and mine."

"Then that is enough for me, Brook. We are done with the past. I can forget about it now. Are we good?"

"I'm good with putting everything behind us. I am so grateful that she let you go so that I could have you."

Our talk makes my heart lighter.

We take a taxi to the National Gallery of Australia. The exhibits are the ballet and fashion. So appropriate for my Brook. We walk through the fashion area with Brook pointing out to me different aspects of design. I feign interest and smile at the suitable times. We move on to a room that has a remarkable stained-glass ceiling. The sun is out and the colors that cascade around the room are breathtaking. Brook and I are mesmerized for several minutes. The last exhibit of the ballet spans the Australian Ballet Company from its inception to the present. I find this more interesting.

We have tickets to tonight's performance of Legally Blond the musical at the Princess Theatre. We take another cab to the theater area and find a restaurant for dinner. I talk Brook into having a glass of wine. "One glass is not going to hurt the baby. At this point, the development is done and he is just maturing and putting on weight. He might even like to have a nice sleep."

"Okay, one glass. Thank you for this trip, William. I know you are as interested in fashion and the ballet as I am in hunting or fishing. I love you to distraction."

"What's wrong, Brook. You look upset."

"I think I'm getting a little nervous about the delivery. The closer it gets, the more I think about it."

"Okay. What is your concern?"

"That everything will go all right. That the baby will be healthy. I'm sure they're normal worries."

"Of course they are, darling. Every mother wants the best for their children. Not to be sick or hurt. I'm here, Brook. I'll be right next to you the whole time. You couldn't keep me away."

Her smile reassures me that she is pacified with my answer. The last thing I want is for her to be worried about her delivery. Especially when there is nothing either one of us can do about it.

I watch Brook enjoy her wine and dinner. We both ordered chicken. Our waiter suggested it, as he knows the farm that it comes from. Brook says, "I think it is the first free range chicken that I have eaten. I don't want to insult him, but it tastes the same to me. Perhaps my palette isn't as developed as his." I pay our check and we walk the few blocks to the theater.

It is slightly windy tonight and as we walk, Brook's hair whips around her face. I have my arm around her shoulders and she snuggles into me. "Are you cold, darling?" I ask. "Do you want my coat?"

"No. I'm enjoying your arm around me. I like the feeling of possession."

"I don't want to possess you. I just want to have you with me and to know you're mine."

The theater performance is well done. Brook and I enjoy the singing, dancing and jokes. We take a cab back to our boat and turn in for the night.

Sometime around three in the morning, I hear the engines start. We need to get off early to make it back before dark. As the captain turns the boat around, it reminds me of the movie Overboard. I have to hold on to Brook to stop her from slipping out of bed. I wrap my arms around her and pull her close. Falling back to sleep, I inhale her scent and I am at peace.

By the time we wake up, we are a third of the way back. The captain informs me that we should be back around four in the afternoon. We have our breakfast in the tiny galley. I bundle Brook up to take her on deck for some sea air. I have instructed the captain that I don't want to sail too far off the coast. I don't know these waters and in case of emergency I want us close to shore. I also know that Brook likes to be able to see land.

I hold my wife between my legs as we look out at the blue-green ocean. Her hair tickles my neck. "Who are we going to have as godparents for this little one?" I ask.

"I haven't even thought about that."

"I would like to ask Jonathan and Rob to be godfathers."

"We need two? I only have one, my Unel Ron."

"It's customary to have two or more. They are our only brothers. The problem is godmothers. Emily and Eve will most likely want to be. But you have Rob's wife and girlfriends."

"I love Emily and Eve. Could we have them and Laura?"

"This is our baby. Until he is old enough to make his own decisions, we get to choose. We will ask the three of them."

"That was easy. What's next?"

"We have hired Allison as our nanny. I think I would like a governess to actually teach him. Allison will be busy with our other children and I don't want to send him to school right away."

"Why not? The girls go to a regular school."

"The girls' last name is not Barry. Jonathan's boys are not going to regular school. They will hire a governess this year."

"How worried is Jonathan?"

"We don't have any specific threat, Brook. With the economy as it is, there are some people who might think that kidnapping a wealthy child, is a way to make a quick buck. I don't ever want it to be our child. I can prevent this if they aren't put in the way of these people."

"Because I have no expertise in this, whatever you think is best is what we will do. I hate the thought of sheltering them so, but the thought of losing them is a nightmare I can't face."

"I am sorry that we have to live like this, Brook. We always find that for every good person there is a bad one. I can't allow the bad ones to hurt you."

I feel a shiver run through her. I don't know if she is cold or frightened, so I hug her closer.

After lunch, I have Brook lie down for a nap while I plug away on my laptop. Jonathan has sent me a project to work on. All very dry, but I will do my best. As the time passes, the captain informs me that we are a half an hour from Sydney. I wake Brook so she can wash up and gather her things. I kiss her forehead and say, "It's time to wake up, darling. We need to get our things together."

She grabs my shirt and pulls me to her for a kiss. I rest my head on hers and she says, "I can't wait to make love facing you. I miss you."

"Me too, more than you will ever know. A few more weeks, my love. Have patience, it will come. When it does, we are not coming out of the bedroom all day."

"What about the baby?"

"He can bond with his grandparents, aunts and uncles."

CHAPTER 17

BROOK FINALLY FINISHES THE SHOOT with Cole and Eddie. Everyone is pleased with the outcome. I marvel at how quickly Brook takes people into her heart. Both Cole and Eddie invite us to come and stay with them any time we want.

On June 14, we board a plane for the twenty-three hour flight to London. I am very glad that Brook changed her mind about having the baby in Australia. This long of a flight with a new baby would have been a nightmare. The first leg of the flight is fourteen hours to Abu Dhabi in the United Arab Emirates. We have a two-hour layover there to stretch our legs. The last flight is seven hours to London. There is an eleven-hour time difference. Needless to say, we will spend the whole day sleeping when we get home.

I have some paperwork to catch up on and multiple e-mails to answer. Brook has her romance novel and Josh Groban's music to listen to. I hope she can sleep. Part of the way through our first leg, I have Brook turn in her seat and put her feet in my lap. I massage her legs, as I don't want her to have a problem sitting for this length of time. When we land, we go for a walk around the area near our gate. We board the plane at the last possible moment.

"How are you doing, darling?"

"I'm okay. I'm glad that we had an extended time in Australia. If we had only gone for a week or two it would not have been enough time to recover from this flight."

"You have the added discomfort of a pair of feet in your belly."

"I think he is sleeping most of the time. Getting ready to keep us up all night, no doubt."

"I told you, Allison will soon be our best friend."

"Do you think the baby will be confused as to exactly who his mother is? I worry that if he spends so much time with Allison he'll forget me."

"You are going to be home most of the time, darling. Allison is there to assist you. The baby already knows your voice. He has been listening to you for nine months. He knows who you are."

We finally land in London. After we go through customs, I see George waiting for us. He helps Luke with our bags and we are once again sitting for the drive home. As we approach the house, I see my parents waiting for us on the steps. George must have called them as we got near. I open the door to exit the car and say, "Hi, mum. You look younger every day."

"You say the loveliest things, William. Come and give me a kiss."

"With pleasure. Dad, how are you?"

"Good, son. Brook, darling, how are you feeling?" he says, kissing Brook.

"I'm good. A little tired but well."

"You look beautiful, Brook," my mother says.

"Thank you. Are Emily and the girls here?"

"No, darling. They are going to give you a day or two to recover before they descend on you. The girls can't wait to see your baby bump."

"She doesn't have much of one. When you were carrying William, you were as big as an elephant," my father teases.

"Yes, but look at what I was carrying," she says pointing to me.

"Good for you that I wasn't this size. Let's get inside. We can talk in the library."

We all walk in and proceed to the library. My mum says, "Allison has been here for a week. She oversaw the painting of the nursery and placement of the furniture that you ordered. If anything isn't to your liking it can all be changed."

"I'm sure it's fine. I went over all of the details with her before I left. Now it's just waiting to fill the crib."

"That's the worst part, darling. The waiting and wanting it to be over with," my mum says.

"We are pretty tired. I think we will go up and take a nap before dinner," I say, standing to take Brook's hand. I walk her up to our bedroom, stopping to look in the nursery. Brook tears up when she sees it.

"It is so beautiful, William. Just what I wanted for the baby. Thank you for indulging me."

"You're welcome, darling. I want you to be happy. If this does, it then it is a small thing."

After our nap, we unpack and go down to meet my parents for dinner. As I suspected, Jonathan, Eve and the boys are here along with Emily, Dick and the girls. Poor Brook is inundated with questions and people feeling her belly. Leslie is plastered to her and won't let go. Lily follows her around like a lost puppy. I sit in the high-back chair in the library and watch the proceedings with a smile on my face. To see Brook as the center of attention with my family warms me because she is the center of my entire universe.

"Antie Brook, Mummy said I could help her if she baby-sits for your baby. When can we do that?" Lily inquires.

"The baby has to get here first, Lily. Right now the baby is happy right where he is," Brook says, patting her belly.

"When is he going to come out?"

"I don't know, darling. We have to wait and see. It won't be a long time. Just a few more weeks."

"A few more weeks? It has been forever already," Lily says, dejected.

Brook giggles and walks over to me, sitting on my lap. She whispers in my ear, "And she isn't the one who is pregnant. She has only known about the baby since April."

Brook and I recount all of our adventures in Australia. The girls regard us with rapt attention when we talk about the koala bears and kangaroos. They make us promise to take them there when they get older. Frankly, that is a promise I don't mind keeping.

Brook and I excuse ourselves to go upstairs. We are both still suffering from jet lag. I need to go into the office tomorrow for a while to get some things done. I fold my wife in my arms and sleep.

I dress as quietly as I can because I don't want to wake Brook up. On the ride to the office Luke says, "Mrs. Barry asked me last night if I was sure that I could get you to the hospital in time. She is concerned that if you are at the office with traffic, you won't make it. I assured her that both George and I have worked out every scenario and we have the routes down to thirty-two minutes. If she is home, we can get her there in twenty-three minutes."

"She is worried about everything. First baby syndrome, I'm told. It would be a blessing for her if I didn't make it in time. That would mean she went fast. I don't think she realizes it could be hours."

"Yes, sir."

"I think that I am going to have you drive Mrs. Barry and I will have George drive me. She knows you better, Luke, and I think she trusts you more. I want her to be as comfortable as possible."

"As you wish, sir. It will be my pleasure to make her feel safe."

"Thank you, Luke."

When I arrive back home at the end of the day I find Brook in the nursery looking at baby things. She looks up and says, "Welcome home, William. How was your first day back?"

"Like I never left. What did you do today?"

"I was daydreaming about the baby being in the crib. I guess I'm like Lily~I want the baby now."

"I confess, the waiting is killing me too. I want to hold him and you."

We walk down to find my parents in the library, reading. My mum smiles as we walk in and says, "I was just thinking about you, Brook. Eve, Emily and I are having a small baby shower for you this Sunday afternoon. It will be just the family and a few very close friends."

"You didn't have to do that. It's very kind of you but I feel funny asking for presents when I have so much already."

"It isn't necessarily about the presents, Brook. It's more about the bonding process. The family doesn't know you very well. This gives all of us a chance to know you better. And besides, I can eat cake and justify it. Please don't take that away."

Brook readies herself for the shower and I decide to go to Jonathan's house while the women fuss over Brook. I don't want to get involved in the hen gathering.

Jonathan and I play pool until I feel enough time has passed and it is safe to go home. When I get there, Emily meets me at the door, looking the same way she did when she told me about Madeleine's conversation with Brook.

"What happened now, Emily?"

"A package arrived yesterday for Brook. Mum thought it was a baby present so she put it in the ballroom for today. Brook opened it in front of everyone. It was from Madeleine. In it were onesies and printed on them were phrases such as, Who is my daddy? and My daddy is a cheater. There are six of them, William."

"She vilifies me, yet it is she who didn't want to fulfill her obligations. Where is Brook now?"

"Resting in your room. She was very upset. Everyone comforted her. We told her that Madeleine's opinion does not matter to any of us. We love her, William."

"I know that. I'll go to her."

I walk up the stairs to the bedroom, seething with anger. I stop outside the door to calm myself. Opening the door with a deep breath, I see Brook lying on the bed. She turns to me as I walk in. I lie down next to her and hug her to me saying, "I'm sorry, darling. You keep paying for my mistakes. I would sell my soul to go back four years and not marry her."

"Do you believe that the baby is yours? Do you have any doubt?"

"I know that the baby is mine, no doubt. Don't let her make you feel this way. Technically, I did cheat on her. I can't deny that, but I never would have if she had been a wife to me."

"I hope she finds someone because then she will have something else to occupy her time. Then maybe she will leave us alone."

CHAPTER 18

I HAVE MADE AN APPOINTMENT for Brook and me with John Pope in order to establish the foundation that Brook wants to support. On our way there, Brook doesn't seem to be her usual, happy self. I ask her, "Are you feeling all right? Did you sleep well last night?"

"I haven't been sleeping that well for a week or so. I can't get comfortable and I have to go to the bathroom so often. I just get to sleep and I have to get up."

"I'm sorry, sweetheart. I wish I could help. I feel like a eunuch, unable to perform."

"All evidence to the contrary, my love. I'm visual proof of your ability to perform."

"I think you know what I mean, darling. I want to take some of the burden away from you, but I can't."

We arrive at John's office. At the reception desk I say, "Mr. and Mrs. Barry to see John Pope, please."

"You may go right in, Mr. Barry. Mr. Pope is expecting you."

Brook and I walk into his office. He stands to greet us. "William, how long has it been?"

"A few years, John. I want to introduce you to my wife, Brook. Brook, this is John Pope."

"Very nice to meet you, Brook," he says, shaking Brook's hand.

"A pleasure, Mr. Pope. William tells me that you can help me set up a charity."

"Please call me John. I set up foundations every day. What do you hope to accomplish with yours?"

"I want to help the people who don't qualify for the assistance that the extremely poor receive. They are just above the line, so to speak. They can't get the same help yet they still need it. The children who can't get free lunches at school because their parents make as little as one hundred dollars above the limit. They can't feed their children on one hundred dollars a year."

"How are you going to funnel the money and to whom?"

"That is what I need help with. In the US, we have the Red Cross, the Salvation Army, even the St. Vincent de Paul society. I don't know what exists here."

"I will do some investigating and come up with a list of organizations that might be trusted to help. I'm guessing you want your name on the charity?"

"No thank you. It should be called . . . Just Above the Line, or something analogous to that."

"You don't have to decide that right now. I will start the paperwork and get things established. It will take a few months to roll out. It looks to me that you will be busy for the next few months anyway. I think an October launch with a large fundraiser would be a good idea. Does that fit your time frame?"

"That would be a good time to start. The baby will still be portable and I can drag him around to meetings."

"You have Allison, darling. Leave the baby with her or bring her with you," I remind her.

"I know. I still want to do things myself, like all of the other mothers around the world."

I smile at her and her independence. I will have to let her make the decisions about Allison's role with the baby. We finish our discussion with John and stand to leave. John says, "Good luck with the delivery, Brook. Keep me informed with any ideas that you have."

"Thank you, John," Brook says.

"We will talk soon, John. I think you still owe me a round of handball if I am not mistaken," I add.

"I was hoping you had forgotten about that. My ego can't take another crushing blow like the last!"

"Maybe I'll go easy on you."

"Since when has that ever happened?" he says, laughing.

We get to the car and I tell Luke to take us home. Brook looks tired and I want her to rest. Ten minutes into our ride, Brook looks at me and says," William, I think my water just broke."

"Do you want to go home or to the hospital?"

"Home to change and call the doctor. He may not want me this early."

"I'm calling him now," I say, taking out my phone and dialing. I describe the events to the receptionist and wait. Finally, she comes back and says to go home for a while until Brook is uncomfortable. She says it could take some time.

Once home, Brook goes up to shower and change. I find my parents to tell them that the baby is on the way. "Where is Brook now?" my mum asks.

"She is taking a shower. Her water broke in the car. She is going to rest and wait upstairs."

"If she needs anything, come and get me. Otherwise, I will be right here waiting. I hope she has an easy time, William."

"Me too, more than anything. She is tired already. She hasn't been sleeping well.

"She will sleep better knowing she has a beautiful baby sleeping beside her tonight. All of the pain and sleeping trouble goes away the exact minute you see the baby. All part of the miracle of birth."

"I'm going up to lie down with her. If we need anything, I'll send for you. Thank you, Mum."

When I open the door to our bedroom, Brook is on the bed. I lie down beside her and put my arm around her. "How are you doing, darling? Is there anything I can do for you?"

"I feel okay. My back hurts mostly. At least I'm not wet anymore. I didn't like that feeling. No wonder babies cry."

"Let me rub your back for you."

We lie there while I rub her back, talking about the future. After a few hours Brook tells me that she is very uncomfortable and wants to go to the hospital. I call her doctor to inform him that we are on our way. Carefully, Brook and I descend the stairs, stopping once for a contraction. At the bottom, my parents hug her and me and we are soon in the car. We make our way to the hospital with Luke driving. I see him smiling in the mirror, although he says nothing.

We arrive at the hospital. I check Brook in as the delivery team helps her into her room. She undresses and is examined and then I can go in and sit with her. "Is there anything I can get or do for you, darling," I ask.

"Not right now. They said Dr. Reynard would be in soon to see me. I feel better just being here."

The doctor comes in and explains to us all of Brook's options for pain relief. Brook wants to try to have a natural childbirth. I try to talk her out of that but I lose the argument.

I watch as Brook breathes through the contractions. As they come closer together and gain strength, I see Brook's resolve weaken. After several hours, I finally convince her that an epidural will at least give her time to rest. I call in the nurse. She examines Brook to find that she is now too far along for the epidural. She has no choice now. Brook grabs my hand and squeezes it through every contraction. I rub her back and speak in a hushed tone, encouraging her through each one. I give her a piece of crushed ice and cool her with a washcloth.

The nurse comes in to check her again and informs us that it is time for her to start pushing. Several people come in and start to shout different instructions at Brook.

"Push here."

"Tuck your chin."

"Grab your legs."

I can see Brook fatiguing with every command. I know that I have had enough so I stand up and shout, "Okay, that is enough! From now on, I am the only one to talk to my wife. Everyone else is to be silent."

I kick off my shoes and climb in behind Brook. She leans back into me and I feel her relax. I wrap my arms around her and place my hands on the top of her belly. I whisper in her ear, "We are going to do this together, darling, just you and me. I want you to take a deep breath when I say to and let it out.

Then take another one and hold it and we are going to push our baby out together."

The nurse nods to me that a contraction has begun. I say, "Now breathe, Brook. Let it out and breathe in, hold it . . . push Brook . . . keep pushing, darling . . . that's it . . . your doing wonderful, darling . . . let it out and take another . . . hold it, Brook, and push . . . harder, Brook . . . keep going . . . one more time, sweetheart . . . hold it and push . . . that's it . . . he's moving, Brook . . . breathe, darling, and rest."

I run my hands down her belly softly. I tell her, "Match my breathing, Brook. You can feel me breathing. Follow me."

The nurse nods again and I say, "Ready, darling? Let's do it again. Breathe in and out . . . in again and hold it . . . push, Brook . . . that's it. You're doing great . . . I can see him, Brook . . . don't stop . . . breathe out and in . . . hold it and push again, Brook . . . push, push, push, darling . . . one more, Brook . . . stop, darling, and breathe."

I massage Brook's shoulders, telling her how well she is doing. The doctor says with the next push his head should be out and then to stop pushing so he can clear the nose and mouth. The nurse nods again and I begin, "Okay, sweetheart, breathe in and out . . . in and hold it and push . . . bear down, Brook, and get him out . . . push, Brook . . . that's it, darling. You're almost there . . . stop, Brook. His head is out. Look at him, Brook. That's our baby!"

"I want to push, William. It hurts. I want to get him out," Brook yells.

"I know, darling. Just a minute so the doctor can help him breathe."

"All right, Brook, let's get him delivered," the doctor tells her.

"Breathe in and out, darling . . . in again and push . . . push, Brook . . . keep going . . . harder, Brook . . . that's it . . . one more," I say. Then the sweetest sound in the entire world. Our baby cries.

Doctor Reynard places our son on Brook's belly. He is covered in muck and blood and I have never in my life seen something so beautiful. Brook and I are crying. "Thank you, darling, for this most precious gift," I say as I kiss her forehead.

"I would like to say anytime, just not right now," she laughs.

I cut the cord and they take my son to clean him up. I climb out from behind Brook so that they can complete the delivery process. I call my parents so that they can hear Warren cry. My mum quickly joins him in crying. My stoic father congratulates us. I know how happy he is that we are naming the baby after him.

I gaze over at my wife holding our son and I smile because at this moment, I'm at peace with the world.

CHAPTER 19

REN WAKES BROOK AND ME around 1:30 in the morning on our first night watch. I get up from the cot that has been brought in for me to take him out of his bassinette. He is so wet, I feel badly for the little man. I get him changed and bring him to Brook for his feeding. She slides her nightgown down and Ren latches onto her breast. I smile and say, "Just like his old man. So eager for some . . ."

"William! Please don't turn this into something sexual. I'm trying to be a good mom here. I want him to nurse for a while, but if you are going to make crude comments I won't be able to."

"Please forgive me, darling. I'm jealous of my own son. I want what he has. I'll wait patiently for the next six weeks to pass but then I'm keeping mummy up all night instead of him."

"He hasn't kept us up all night. He slept four hours. I think that is very good."

"Did you see how my father lit up when he saw Ren? He melts like butter when you put a baby in his arms."

"Your mom and sister melted, too. I hope Emily has more children. She is so good with them."

"When they come out three at a time, it puts a damper on the thought of having more. She is afraid of having another multiple. It took her over a year and then she had surgery to get her body back. I'm told eighteen pounds of baby does things to you."

"I'm sure. Thank god we just had one."

I sit on the end of the bed to watch Ren eat. His little cheeks move in and out. He makes little noises of contentment. Brook lifts him to pat a burp out. I ask, "Can I do that? You feed and I'll burp."

"Use this cloth because you won't like it if he spits down your back."

I pat and rub until I get the desired response. I pat some more until he cries, hungry for more. I give him back to Brook saying, "Spoiled already."

"You can't spoil a baby. All they want is to be fed, changed and loved."

Once we get Ren back to sleep, I rub Brook's back and she gets back to sleep. I lie on my cot watching my little family and thinking about how lucky I am.

My parents, the house staff, my sister and her family, and my brother and his family are all assembled around the front of the house to welcome home my wife and son. Brook's face lights up when she sees the love of my family. "I can't believe they're all here, William."

"It's a very special day, darling. Welcoming home a new Barry."

We can see the girls almost dancing with anticipation of seeing the new baby. Jonathan's boys seam slightly less enthusiastic. I'm told, though, that they are happy it's a boy because now they are tied with three each.

Brook and I get out of the car. I remove Ren's car seat and carry him towards the crowd. Leslie beats her sisters to his side and says, "He is so little Unil Bubs. It's going to take forever until we can play with him."

"Unfortunately, Leslie, not forever. In a year or so he will be running after you," I answer her smiling.

"Let me have my nephew. All of you hens have held him. It's my turn," my brother says, laughing.

I hand Jonathan the carrier and we all head inside. In the library, Jonathan sets Ren on a table, and quickly divests him of his straps and has him in his arms. I watch the capable father holding my son, kissing his head and whispering to him. My heart is so full. Clearly, it doesn't get any better than this.

"Can I trust you to watch my son while I take his mother upstairs and get her settled?" I ask.

"I think I know what I'm doing brother. But if he shizz his kecks, one of the ladies will get him."

I walk Brook up to our bedroom. Helping her undress and get into bed I say, "I want you to rest, darling. We will take care of the baby. When he is ready to eat, I'll bring him up to you."

"Okay. I'm tired and there are so many people down there. I don't feel up to doing a lot of talking."

"You just had a baby~no one expects you to." I kiss her and close the door as I leave. I get back downstairs just as the champagne is being passed out. I take a glass as my father says, "Raise your glass to the newest member of our great family. To the new Viscount Warren William Robert George Barry, the future Duke of Wessex."

"Here, here," the family responds in unison.

"And to his mother, the Lady Brook. To her health and happiness with gratitude for this most precious gift," my mum pronounces.

"To the Lady Brook," all reply.

Ren is passed around to everyone. Even Max and Hugh want to hold him. He starts to fuss and I check him to find that he is soaked again. I begin to climb the stairs to take him to Brook. In the nursery, I change Ren's diaper. As soon as I have him cleaned up, I take him in to Brook.

"I have a hungry boy here. He is all changed and ready for dinner."

Brook smiles and says," Good because I'm ready to see him. Has he been a good boy?"

"Very good. He has entertained the whole family. Now it's our time with him."

Brook nurses him while I hold his hand, examining his little fingers. I say to Brook, "He really is amazing. Look at his little hands and feet~so perfect. We are very fortunate, darling. So many aren't."

"We are blessed, William. We are way above the line. I want now, more than before, to throw myself into the foundation. Seeing this little one makes me want to save as many as I can. Losing even one is inexcusable."

Time passes very quickly. We hold Ren's baptism in August with Emily, Laura and Eve as his godmothers and Jonathan and Rob as godfathers. Brook is simply stunning in a blue dress by her now-favorite designer Sarah Burton.

There are two more days to go until the six weeks are over. I have told Brook exactly what she has coming to her so she won't be surprised. What she doesn't know is that it will happen in Ireland. I'm taking her for a long weekend on our real honeymoon. The first one didn't count in my view. Unless I can make love to my wife face to face, it's not making love.

Allison and Ren will accompany us, as I know Brook will be more comfortable being able to nurse him. Ren will be in Allison's suite, giving Brook and me the ability to reconnect.

I walk into our bedroom and see Brook looking out the window. I approach her, staring at the back of her nightgown. It is open to the top of her bum. I sweep my hand down her back and under the gown saying, "I don't think I can wait, Brook. Not with you dressed like this. Isn't five weeks and five days a long enough recovery?"

"I don't know. Should I call Dr. Reynard and ask him?"

"I'll call him and explain man-to-man. Wait here. I'll be right back."

"William, don't you dare! I have to see him on Friday. I won't be able to look him in the eye."

"Brook, I think the good doctor knows what we do. I'm even willing to bet he does the same, regularly."

"I know that, too. Allison is out in the yard with Ren getting some fresh air. We have a half an hour before she comes back if you want to do something."

"Something?" I ask, knowing exactly what I want to do. I hold her in my arms kissing down her neck. I look into her eyes and say, "You feel so good in my arms, Mrs. Barry. Your lips taste so sweet." I pick her up, walk to our bed, and lay her down. I strip off my shirt, socks and pants. Climbing in next to her I whisper, "I'm going to do something . . . right now."

I didn't last half as long as I wanted to. Three months of no sex, six weeks plus the last part of her pregnancy, preceded by one month of backwards pregnancy sex, has left me with the less-than-envious lack of control~I usually have. At least the dam has been breached and the floodwaters can continue to run. I almost expect to hear a choir of angels sing at the beginning of my orgasm.

"I hope I didn't hurt you, darling. I fear I was somewhat overcome in the moment."

"You didn't hurt me, William. I was just as eager as you."

We lie together for a few minutes, enjoying the feel of each other. I finally get up and dressed. Putting on my shoes I say, "I'm going to see Ren. Find us when you're ready."

I find Ren and Allison in the nursery. Allison is changing him when I walk in, "How is my son today, Allison?"

"Right as the rain, sir. He has been a very good boy today, Mr. Barry. We just came in from our walk. He loves to see the leaves fall."

"He doesn't know what's coming. I like to see the leaves fall too until I think about the cold winter winds that follow."

"Agreed. I'm not much of a winter lover either. I much prefer summer warm to winter cold."

"I am surprising Mrs. Barry with a trip to Ireland this weekend. We will fly out on Friday night and return on Monday afternoon. I want you and Ren to accompany us. You will have your own suite with Ren, next door to ours. Luke will also accompany us. He will spend most of his time with you and Ren. He is there for and Ren's protection, and yours."

"Why do we need protection?"

"Ren would be quite a prize to a kidnapper Allison. You might be hurt in the taking. Luke is an armed, well trained bodyguard. I would not be opposed to you having some training as well, should you so desire."

"Bodyguard training or self-defense?"

"Luke's main focus should something happen, is to protect Ren. I carry a gun and I have taken self-defense classes. I will send you for whatever training you'd like."

I can see that she is thinking about it. After a few seconds she says, "I think I want to start with self-defense and then do bodyguard training. If someone wants to hurt Ren, they will have to go through me first."

"I appreciate your loyalty, Allison. I don't expect you to get hurt protecting our son. He is my responsibility. I will speak with Luke to see what we can set up for you. In the meantime, will you pack Ren for the weekend, please?"

"Of course. We will be ready."

"Thank you." I pick Ren up and hold him against my shoulder, "Now, we are going to find our mummy, aren't we Ren?" I walk out of the nursery and into our bedroom. Walking to the bed, I place Ren in the middle and climb in next to him. I begin to massage his little legs, straightening them. I move up his body to his arms. He smiles at me and gurgles, the whole time. Brook comes in from the bathroom saying, "I thought I heard the little man in here. Has he been a good boy for his daddy?"

"A very good boy indeed. He has grown so much, Brook. He is very strong. It must be the mother's milk that he gets~powerful stuff to be sure."

CHAPTER 20

REN SITS SECURELY IN HIS car seat between Brook and me in the first-class section of the plane. Luke and Allison are behind us. It is a short flight~only one and one-half hours. Ren is sleeping and Brook is listening to Josh Groban. I have papers to read over. Ren draws a crowd of admiring attendants.

"How old is he?" one asks.

"Just six weeks," Brook answers her.

"What is his name?" asks another.

"Warren, but we call him Ren."

"He is so handsome. Is he a good baby?'

"He is our first, so I don't have a big comparison. He is a good boy for us."

"You should have many more when they come out as cute as him."

"Thank you. We think he is pretty special."

We land and find our luggage and car. Luke drives us to The Merchant Hotel on Skipper Street. There are three suites waiting for us. The hotel is a Victorian in the historical district. We are shown to our suite by a very exuberant bellhop. He tells us, "The spa will send someone right to your room for a massage, sir. And the best of the best come to our nightclub. Authors, politicians, celebrities . . . you name them and they will be there tomorrow night."

"Thank you for the information. How do I set up spa appointments for the ladies?"

"I would be glad to do that for you, Mr. Barry. When do you want them and what services are you looking for?"

"I think tomorrow afternoon for Mrs. Barry and Miss Daynard. I think a massage, manicure and pedicure. If you could set that up, I would be grateful."

"Consider it done, sir. I will stop back with the times. Have a good evening."

I tip him and he leaves us to our evening. Brook is holding Ren to the window and showing him the lights of Dublin. I walk over to her and hold her shoulders saying, "What does our son think of his first trip out of country?"

"I think he is going to make an excellent traveler. I am going to nurse him and then we can go to dinner. I told Allison that she can do as she wants until 8:00 and then we can go out."

"Good. I have spa appointments for you and Allison tomorrow afternoon. I think Ren and I will go for a walk and get some air while you ladies have some fun."

"That is very thoughtful, William. What will we do tomorrow night?"

"I think we might go dancing. Our bellhop tells me the nightclub here is exceptional."

"You will take me dancing, ply me with alcohol and then take advantage of me, Mr. Barry, won't you?"

"I was rather hoping that you would take full advantage of me."

She turns to Ren and says, "Did you hear your father, Ren? It sounds to me that your daddy needs some attention."

"Damn right he does."

We have our dinner in the hotel restaurant. I hold Brook's hand as much as possible. She looks lovely in an ocean-blue dress and matching five-inch heels. I stutter through dinner, picturing those heels around me. As soon as we finish our coffee, I whisk Brook back to our room. Opening the door, I step back so that she can walk in first. The room is lit with candles and flowers decorate every available surface. The smell is intoxicating. Brook swings around to hug me and says, "I can't believe you did all of this, William. It's beautiful. Thank you."

"All for you, my love."

Debbie Zello

Chilling is a bottle of 1988 Krug Brut, my personal favorite. A platter of strawberries, plain and chocolate-covered next to it. On the bed is a light pink teddy with matching oh-so-small panties that I picked out in person. Brook walks over to pick up the items. "Are these for me or you?" she asks.

"I would attempt to put them on my, darling, but I fear they would look much better on you, at least for a short time."

Brook walks into the bathroom with said articles in her hand. I hear the shower start and I almost go in to join her. I stop because I want tonight to be more than a quick encounter. I want to worship her for what she has given me.

As she comes out of the bathroom, I go in. "I'll only be a minute." I say. I hurriedly take a shower and put on my lounging pants.

Brook must be watching TV because I think I can hear voices. Thank god, I don't exit the bathroom with an anticipatory tent in my silks because sitting on the couch is Allison. Brook sits in the chair with Ren nursing. I quickly find a tee shirt to put on. "What happened?" I ask.

"I'm so sorry, Mr. Barry. Ren was crying and he wouldn't take the bottle. He had worked himself up to a sweat and I finally called Mrs. Barry. She said to bring him over."

I look at Brook wearing the oversized white terry robe provided by the hotel, knowing the pink loveliness under it and say, "Do you want him to stay with us?"

"Could we, please? I don't want him to be upset," she says with a look of relief on her face.

"Of course, darling," I say. Tomorrow, Ren and I are going to have a father-son talk. I have some explaining to do about mummy and me. "Allison, please get some of his things together. I will help with his bassinette. We will be right back, darling."

Allison and I walk to her suite. She apologizes the whole time. I finally say, "Allison, we are not mad. He is a baby and, as such, unpredictable at best. You did the right thing in calling. We want you to come to us with anything, any problem."

"Thank you, Mr. Barry. He is such a sweetheart of a baby. I didn't know what was wrong when he wouldn't take the bottle."

266

"I think sometimes they just want their mums. Nannies and governesses raised me, but sometimes I just wanted my parents. It's natural, Allison. It's not you."

We retrieve Ren's things and bid Allison good night. Brook and I lie on our sides with Ren between us. I have one of his little hands and Brook holds the other. "His fingers are so small and delicate. His toes look like little balls of dough on the end of his foot. How did we get so blessed, Brook?"

"I don't know. Thank you for not being mad at Allison. She was so worried that you would fire her for not being able to quiet him."

"Am I that much of an ogre? I never thought of myself as unreasonable. I'm disappointed, yes. My son has terrible timing and I'm going to have a man-to-man with him tomorrow."

"Really! I can't wait for the report on this conversation. Your first father-son conference. What fun!"

I get up and put my now-quiet son in his bed. Coming back to Brook, I lay her on her back and rise over her. "Do you have any idea just how precious you are to me? Can you guess what you do to me? What having you with me means to me?" I ask her.

"You're going to make me cry, William. Don't you know that I feel the exact same way about you? You are my reason for living, the best part of my day and my dreams at night."

I kiss her, starting the fire inside me. I wanted to worship her tonight, but once again I give in to the desire to just devour her. As I enter her, I ask the question that I should have asked three days ago. "Are you on the pill or something?"

"No. We want more children, don't we? This is how we get them, William."

"So soon? You don't want to wait a while?" Cold water showering my libido. I come to a screeching halt in my progress. "I thought we would take some time for us before we started again. A year or so maybe. You want another now?"

"I may not get pregnant right away. I'm nursing and sometimes that is a natural birth control."

"With our track record, I can't rely on an old wives' tale. Are you sure about this? I can use condoms although I don't relish that option."

"I'm sure. I want more children. I want your children, William. If they are born close, I hope they will remain close."

Resigned to do her wishes, I resume making love to my wife. As I watch her pleasure rising, I increase my pace until both of us pass over the cliff of our desires. I flip over, still joined to her so that she can rest on my chest and say, "If we are going to continue our family, I had better learn to like breast milk."

Brook swats me.

CHAPTER 21

REN WAKES US AT 5:00 AM., soaked and hungry. While Brook tends to him, I call to have coffee brought up to us. I sit on the couch and watch Brook mothering our son. She moves as if she has done this all her life. I marvel at how easily she has taken on her roll as his mother.

"You should go back to sleep, William. You are not used to being up this early."

"I'll be fine. Maybe I can catch a nap with Ren later."

Brook and Allison leave for their spa appointments as Luke and I take Ren for a stroll through a nearby park. Women who want to get a look at Ren stop us frequently. Luke says after one such encounter, "I think I might take Ren alone the next time. He seems to be a chick magnet, if you don't mind my saying, sir."

"I don't mind at all, Luke. In fact, I had a similar thought. Are you looking for a chick, Luke?"

"I might like to find someone to be with. It wouldn't interfere with my loyalty to you."

"Luke, I don't expect you to be celibate. You should have a life, a family . . . I was even thinking that you and Allison would make a handsome couple."

"No offense meant, but she is not my type. She is lovely but I like some meat on the bone, sir. Allison is too skinny for my taste."

"I take no offense Luke. I won't tell her either. I'll be on the watch for Marilyn Monroe or Sofia Loren."

"Now you're talking, sir. If you see them, send them my way."

We continue our walk. We near a pub. I turn to Luke and say, "I think the time has come for Ren's introduction to the finer aspects of being a man. I need a beer. You in?"

"Is this a covert operation or is Mrs. Barry in on the introduction?"

"I believe this falls under the-less-said-the-better title. I doubt that Mrs. Barry would be happy about this aspect of his education."

"Very well, sir. My lips are sealed after the beer passes through them."

"Good. Well done, Luke."

We enter the bar and take a seat. I order two pints of Guinness. When the distinctive brown concoction arrives, Luke and I toast the ladies. Ren starts to fuss, so I reach over to take him out of his pram. He is, once again, soaked. I get him changed and get his bottle out. Luke walks it to the barmaid to see if it can be warmed for him. A few minutes later she comes back with it, saying, "The little man is hungry, isn't he?"

"Always," I answer.

"I can give him his bottle if you would like, sir."

"Thank you for the offer," I say. "But I don't have much time with him and I enjoy feeding him." I hope she is not offended, but there is no chance of a stranger holding my son.

We finish our beer and order two more. Ren plays quietly with his feet as Luke and I converse about nothing in particular.

My eyes are on Luke when I see his posture change. His eyes are on the door of the pub. I still when I see him move his hand to where I know his gun rests. He shifts to the end of his seat as his foot moves the pram to within reach of both himself and me. The hair on the back of my neck is at full attention. My breaths are shallow, matching his in speed and depth. He looks at me directly and then to the door of the men's loo. No words pass between us as I rise from the chair and grab the handle of the pram. Without looking back, I move Ren to the door and push him through. No one will go through that door unless they go through me first. Turning to face the direction that Luke faces, I bend to pull the gun from my ankle holster and move it to my pocket.

Luke is standing with his right hand still inside his jacket. I draw the line from him to his target~a man at the end of the bar. The target turns to face Luke. He has a curious smile on his face. He says, "Luke, is that you?"

Luke nods his head but doesn't relax his hold on his gun. I watch the two of them, not knowing if it is going to be fight or flight. The target says, "Are you on duty?"

Again, Luke nods his head, not moving his eyes off him.

"Okay then," he says, moving his hands to open his jacket to reveal his gun. He removes it with two fingers of his left hand and lays it on the counter, pushing it away from his reach.

Luke motions to me to get Ren. As I pass by the barmaid, I press into her hand some money. I pick Ren up, leaving the pram behind. Standing near Luke, he says, "Back door, sir."

I turn and walk to the rear of the pub to find the back entrance. Luke is right behind me with his eyes forward to where we just left. Once outside, I hail a passing cab and we get in. "Where to sirs?" the driver says.

"Just drive," Luke answers.

Luke is still looking behind us when I finally find my voice and say, "What the fuck was that, Luke?"

"His name is John Seratt. He used to guard, but I was told that he contracts out now. Hired killer. I wasn't taking a chance that my information was wrong."

"I appreciate that. Now, what to do about the pram? I don't want Brook to know what transpired here, but I left the pram at the pub."

Luke looks at the cab driver and says, "Do you know where there is a baby store? We need a pram."

"Yes, sir. I will take you there."

Once inside the store, I stand in front of a display of at least twenty different prams. I look at Luke. "Which is the one we had this morning?" I ask.

"I'm not sure. I think it was blue. That narrows it down to six."

"Luke, you are usually very observant. I was counting on you to know which one it is."

"Sorry, sir. Put a face or a gun next to it and I'm your man. Baby stuff is out of my parameter of knowledge."

"Which is worse, coming back without the pram or with the wrong one?"

"I think I have changed my mind about finding someone and settling down. I can't take the stress."

"This is no time to wimp out on me. I have to make a decision for Christ's sake." I think for a moment. "I'm just going to buy one. If it is the wrong one, then I will have to tell her the truth about what happened. You know this means I might never get laid again?"

"Yes, sir. I'm definitely not getting married. I made up my mind right now."

I do the "eeny, meeny, miny, mo, this one has got to go" form of decision-making and pick a pram. Once it is assembled, I place Ren in it and we leave. While we are walking back to the hotel, I tell Luke, "If this goes badly, Luke, I'm throwing you under the Brook bus. I can't have a second sexless marriage."

"Understood, sir. I'll take the fall. She already doesn't have sex with me. It won't be a sacrifice."

And to think I had my brother as my best man. Clearly, Luke has my back.

I wheel Ren into our room to see that Brook is not here yet. With Ren sleeping, I lay down to take a nap with him.

I am awakened by someone kissing my neck and whispering in my ear, "I have found my two favorite men sleeping. Lucky me!"

Without opening my eyes, I grab her around the waist and lift her over me. Pushing her into the mattress, I hover over her to kiss her. I growl, "You smell so good, taste so good, feel so good. I think I'll keep you."

"Good, because I can't see how you would get rid of me. Did you have fun with Luke and Ren?"

"It was a very interesting day. How about you and Allison? Have you had enough pampering for one day?"

"Quite enough. I feel like jelly, all wobbly."

"I like jelly. I might have some right now," I say as I move to cup her breast. I start to unbutton her blouse as Ren begins to stir. Brook looks at me, smiling, and says, "I thought you were having a talk with him."

"I didn't get around to that, obviously. I get the impression that Ren wants to be an only child."

Brook giggles. "I can take him to Allison," she says.

"No. I can wait until tonight, but so help me, he better cooperate with us. My patience can only go so far."

"I pumped at the spa this afternoon. He will be good because he will have me. Allison is going to wear my shirt and we hope to fool him."

"Tell her not to turn on the lights. The milk and shirt are a great idea, but he knows who you are, my love."

I come out of the bathroom to see Brook at the window. Muted lights illuminate the room enough for me to see a very short black leather skirt, thigh-high black boots, and a semi-see-through black lace top on the mother of my son! I clear my throat and say, "Excuse me, miss. I'm looking for my wife. Have you seen her?"

"Very funny. You took long enough. I'm starving and I want to dance."

"Fine. Change and we will leave."

"Why would I change? I think I look great! We are going clubbing right?"

"I am. You are going to change. I can't take you with that outfit on. Some caveman who thinks he has the right will try something. If I remember correctly, we have been down this road before, Brook."

"I'm with you, my knight in shining armor. No one will come near me with the animosity radiating off of you."

"My acrimony can only do so much. If you insist on going like that, maybe I should have Luke come with us," I say, remembering this afternoon's event.

"I want Luke to stay with Ren. I won't even go unless I know he has Luke and Allison."

"I can see that I am once again thwarted in my efforts with you, madam. If anyone comes within two feet of you, there is going to be a problem."

Throughout dinner, I spot other men and their appreciative glances at my wife. To know that I am having dinner with clearly the most beautiful woman in the room is unnerving. To think that every other man would gladly step over my dead body to take my place is demoralizing. If I can get her back to our room tonight without killing someone, it will be a damned miracle.

We have no problem getting past the line and into the club. I don't even have to open my wallet. One look at Brook and the bouncer almost creamed himself. I felt bad for him as I brusquely walked past with my arm securely around her hips. I wanted to tell him that she delivered a baby without drugs six weeks ago. Then I thought, TMI~let him have his illusion. My wife is more of a gladiator than he is.

We are shown to a special side section of the club with posh white leather seating. I'm sure they think Brook is an actress that they can't place the name of. Anyway, to make a long story short, after we are given several rounds of drinks and munchies, I am dancing with my famous wife when I am tapped on the shoulder. Ready to punch out the first of what I think will be many admirers, I turn to see Cole Stevenson. "My god, Cole. What are you doing here?"

"Good to see you, William, Brook darling. I'm here to see some family. My cousin is the manager of this club."

"Small world. We are on a holiday, celebrating. Our son is six weeks old!"

"Say no more, my friend. I can guess what the celebration is."

I look at Brook, who has turned a beautiful shade of pink. Cole pinches her cheek and says, "Don't worry, Brook. I won't tell anyone."

"Thank you, Cole. I am appreciative of your discretion."

"Where is this baby boy that I have heard so much about?"

"With his nanny up in their suite. His mother wouldn't come without him. Frankly, neither would I. He is amazing, Cole."

"He comes from good stock with both of his parents. Please kiss him for us. Samina will be so sorry that she missed seeing you."

A new song starts. I step aside to give Cole Brook's hand so he can dance with her. Fine, one man I can trust to return my wife to me. I take the opportunity to visit the loo.

By the time I get back, Cole is returning my wife to her seat. Brook kisses him good-bye, promising to call and visit soon. Brook and I dance a few more times until she says she has had enough. We walk arm-in-arm back to our room. Once again, I try for the worshiping-Brook evening, and this time I succeed. Mine is the name that she calls out as each orgasm runs through her. My seed, that spills into her and my child that will grow within her. And I am thankful for that.

CHAPTER 22

UPON OUR RETURN, BROOK THROWS herself into her charity work with the same enthusiasm she shows all of her loves. Ren cooperates with his mother by sleeping through the night and accepting Allison's role in his care. Brook weans him down to the morning and bedtime. She doesn't say, so but I think the two feedings are more for her benefit than his.

The first fundraiser is a 5K and 10K road race through the countryside. The first weekend, I find myself in my running shorts beside my wife. It takes her about four hundred meters to smoke my jacksie. I smile as she leaves me with a wave over her shoulder. Allison has Ren waiting at the finish line. Once I reach the line, I spot Brook, who looks as fresh as a daisy while I am ready for traction.

The next event is a masquerade ball at the estate that takes place on Halloween night. My mother is in a tizzy all week because everything has to be perfect. Brook takes care of the decorations, refreshments, and entertainment. I find out that morning that I am to be Mark Antony to Brook's Cleopatra. I don my attire for the evening and walk into the bedroom to face Brook. "Am I to wear something under this skirt or is this a ploy to find a secluded spot for some private entertainment?" I say, moving my skirt aside to show my state of wanton undress.

Brook, with a knowing smirk on her face, says, "I'm not sure what, if anything, they did wear under their skirts. I happen to like private entertainment." She walks over to me and runs her hands down my chest.

"Careful, Cleo. You may not want to start something we can't finish. I could easily be talked out of an appearance in favor of being buried inside you all night."

"Just how well that might go over, considering we are the hosts of the affair, is beyond me, darling. We can play all day tomorrow. Tonight belongs to my kids."

I find a pair of boxers that are short enough not to show below my skirt. Brook helps me wrap the ties of the sandals around my calf. When I am presentable, I take my wife in my arms and kiss her. "Poor Cleopatra never looked this gorgeous," I say. Brook is wearing a long gown that resembles spun gold. It is wrapped around her like a second skin. She has on a black collar-length wig with a serpent crown and her makeup is spot-on.

With my sword firmly at my side, Brook and I go to say goodnight to Ren. Allison smiles when we walk in and says, "Wow, you look smashing! Please make sure that your pictures are taken. I'm making a scrapbook for Ren."

"That is a great idea, Allison. Thank you for thinking of it," Brook says.

I hold Ren and give him a kiss. "Goodnight, Ren. Be a good boy for Miss Allison. If you need us, we'll be right downstairs."

"I'm sure we will be just fine, sir. Have a good time. I hope you raise a lot of money."

"Thank you, Allison."

Brook kisses Ren next and hands him back to Allison. We put on our masks and make our way to the stairs. When we get to the ballroom, several people have already arrived. We split up so that we can thank everyone for coming. I find my parents with Prime Minister David Cameron and his wife, Samantha. I shake his hand and say, "Thank you so much for coming, sir. My wife, Brook, and I are honored."

"Not at all, William. We are happy to attend for such a worthy cause."

While we make small talk, I spot Brook talking to Dr. Jeffery Martin. Jeffery is dressed as Peter Pan. He is quite dashing in his green tights and tunic. I ask to be excused so I can join in

Brook's fun. As I get close to them, I say, "Tell me please Brook, who has better legs, Jeffery or me?"

"I'm not a leg girl, William. You know that. I go more for the backside. So if you two would turn around, I can give my honest opinion."

"That is not fair, William. I believe Brook has had her hands on your backside so you will have the advantage of prior knowledge."

"Fine, we will call it a draw. I have always been a fan of equality."

Brook takes the stage to start the auction. I am so proud of how relaxed she appears in front of several hundred of England's upper crust. She begins, "Good evening. I am Brook Barry. Welcome to what I hope will be an annual event for the benefit of Above The Line. When I married William earlier this year, he encouraged me to find something that I could sink my American teeth into. I was listening to a song by Josh Groban and thought about the families that need help but don't qualify for it. In many cases, just a couple hundred dollars keeps a family from slipping below the poverty line. If we can stop that from happening, save the children from their family collapsing, we have to do it. The many families that we are currently helping appreciate your continuing support."

"One of the things this charity assists with is helping parent's to further their education so that they can find better-paying jobs. One mother wanted to work from home as a medical transcriber but lacked the computer to do it. She now has one and her weekly paycheck feeds and clothes her three children. They are staying above the line because of people like you."

"When you place your bids on the items we have tonight, please remember those who have so much less than any of us do. Think of just how far above the line you are. Thank you so much."

As she exits the stage, Jeffery leans to me and says, "When you have your union negotiations, you better hope Brook is on your side. If she goes over to them, you're fucked."

"Don't I know it!"

With the bidding about to begin, Brook and I take our seats. It takes slightly over an hour to auction off all of the items that Brook has managed to wiggle out of people. The auctioneer tallies everything up and finds Brook to give her the final count. Brook takes the stage again. "May I have your attention please," she says and waits for everyone to quiet." I have the final tally for tonight's ball and auction. Our children and their parents will benefit from the f186,000 that you have so generously contributed this evening. Thank you again for coming."

I watch Brook make her way back to where I am sitting. She is stopped at every row to talk to someone. She is so graceful and elegant, and gliding past her guests. I watch her with a smug look on my face for sure. I don't deserve her, but thankfully she hasn't realized that yet.

When we have seen the last guest to the door, I hold my wife and kiss her. She wraps her arms around my waist and says, "Well, Mark, I'm tired. What do you say we see if Alexander Helios is sleeping and go to bed ourselves?"

"I'll check on Ren, you go in and ready yourself for bed."

I enter the nursery and approach Ren's crib. He is sound asleep, his tiny thumb securely in his mouth. I sweep his hair across his forehead and whisper, "Your mum won't like the thumb sucking, little man." I place a kiss on his cheek and he sucks harder. Smiling, I walk to our room. I find Brook in the bathroom washing her face. She sees my smile and asks, "What is so funny?"

"Your son. I found him sucking his thumb. I told him you won't like it and he just continued to suck it. Defying us already!"

"I know, right? I saw him this morning and told him he was going to ruin his teeth when he gets them. He paid no attention to me except to smile around the thumb."

I get into bed and Brook follows me a few minutes later. She snuggles next to me, resting her head on my chest. I stroke her hair as she says, "I love you, William."

"I know. I'm a fortunate man. I adore you, darling, every minute of every day." And with that, we both fall blissfully asleep.

Brook's last fundraiser for the year is a concert the first week of December. The concert is at Union Chapel in London. It is a working church, well known for it's work for the homeless and those in crisis. The concertgoers sit in the pews. Brook loves the whole idea of it. Three local bands have donated their talents, as Brook can be very persuasive. What Brook doesn't know is that through a friend of a friend, I have contacted Josh Groban. I have been in contact with his agent and have been promised that he will attend to sing a song or two if he can work it into his schedule. Unfortunately, I won't know if he can make it until he actually shows. If he does, I will earn extra husband points. If not, at least I tried.

The afternoon of the concert, I still haven't heard one way or the other about my surprise for Brook. We leave for the concert, kissing Ren goodnight.

"Be a good boy for Miss Allison, Ren. I don't want any bad reports," Brook says, passing him to me.

"Quite so, little man. Any trouble and you will have me to answer to. I love you. Sleep tight."

Brook and I are going to stay overnight at my bachelor apartment in the city. It is the first time that we have left him for a whole night. My parents are home and there is a house full of people, but Brook is very nervous that something will happen. I'm sure she will be up at dawn ready to get back to him.

Luke drops us off at the door of the Chapel and he continues on to the apartment to drop off our bags and check it for cleanliness and order. He will come back for the concert. Brook busies herself with the final details as I sit and watch the proceedings. The concert is sold out, with several rows saved for some of the people that the Chapel serves. Brook felt that they should be here, as do I.

The first band takes the stage, and six songs later, the second group sets up their instruments. There is a ten-minute intermission in between each for the removal and set-up. It is during the set up for the last band that I'm told by the stage manager that Josh has indeed come. He has graciously consented to sing two songs at the end of the evening. Because we are in a church, he will sing "Jesu, Joy of Man's Desiring" and of course "Below the Line", which led to Brook's idea for her charity.

Brook comes back to her seat and looks at me, Cheshire Cat grin on my face. She asks, "What are you grinning about?"

"I think the whole evening is going so well. I'm happy for you."

The last band takes the stage, and four songs later, they finish. Brook starts to walk toward the stage to say goodnight when I stop her. "I think they are going to do an encore, darling. Give them a few minutes.

The stage crew wheels out a piano to center stage and the lights dim. The MC for the evening approaches the mic and announces, "We have a special surprise for all of you tonight. All of you know that this is a concert to benefit the charity that Mrs. Barry founded to help families near crisis. What you may not know is that a song co-written and sung by a very popular American vocalist inspired her. Mr. Josh Groban is that artist, and much to our delight, he is here tonight to sing it for her."

Brook turns to me and says, "You did this."

I smile and nod, thinking, big husband points. Josh comes out to a whopping round of applause.

He stands in front of Brook and says, "This is for you."

My eyes are on Brook throughout the entire performance. I hope that Josh doesn't fall in love with her because I might actually lose my wife by the end of the song. Maybe this wasn't such a good idea after all.

You can hear a pin drop as he sings his final song. I have to give it to him . . . he is riveting. I can see why Brook is so enamored with his voice. He finishes to a standing ovation. He walks to the steps to take Brook's hand and bring her onstage with him. She walks into his arms and hugs him gently. She takes the mic and says, "I don't know how to thank you for being here, all of you, for coming and donating to these families. My heart is so full right now, I fear it might burst. I hope you have a blessed Christmas and the most happy, healthy New Year possible. Thank you and goodnight."

CHAPTER 23

BROOK HAS THE OPPORTUNITY TO speak with her music idol, Josh, for a few minutes before he has to leave to fly to his next concert. It's a good thing that I'm not terribly jealous because I feel if he asked, she would go. To thank him for his appearance I make a large donation to his charity, Find Your Light Foundation.

Once everything is in order, Brook and I get in the car to leave. She moves over to me and climbs in my lap for the ride. Wrapping my arms around her, I say, "I don't think you are very safe riding like this, my love."

"I'm not safe in your arms?"

"Actually, I do fear for the safety of your body right now, but I meant that you should be in your seatbelt."

"What is going to happen to my body?"

"I believe that you know exactly what I am capable of, my love. No doubt you can feel what I am thinking right now," I growl, knowing she can feel my desire at her hip.

"Shhh, Luke can hear us."

"Luke is busy driving, watching out for us. He doesn't pay any attention to what is being said. Isn't that right, Luke?" I say louder.

"Sorry, sir, I didn't hear what you asked," Luke says.

"Never mind, Luke. Thank you."

"Luke, I think my husband is very hot," Brook says with a grin.

"Would you like the air conditioner turned up, sir?" Luke asks.

"That won't be necessary, Luke, thank you. Mrs. Barry was making an observation," I counter.

Brook starts to remove my tie. Then she starts to unbutton my shirt. I counsel her, "Don't go too far, darling. If you want a public display of affection, I'll go there with you, but remember this is London. The paparazzi are everywhere and dying to get the right picture to sell to the tabloids. A picture of us in flagrante delicto would bring a high price."

"I can't keep my hands to myself right now. How much further to your apartment?"

"The flat is in Belgravia. It's an old area, with a very Mary Poppins feel to it. I believe you will like it. We are almost there. I think you can wait."

"I have never been very good at waiting but I'll try. I don't want Ren to be embarrassed by his parents' behavior."

I laugh and say, "No, he will have his own to worry about, no doubt. God knows my parents were afraid to open the paper on several occasions with Jonathan, Emily and me. Actually, Emily was the only one who did make it into the papers."

"Emily, really? What did the very proper Emily do?"

"While at university, she and several friends went to Rome for a holiday. On a dare, she and two others stripped down to their bras and knickers and jumped into a fountain. Needless to say, the Romans frowned on their fountain being used as a pool and they were promptly arrested. My parents nearly had a heart attack. Jonathan and I were angels compared to Emily."

Luke pulls up in front of the flat and we get out. I open the door, holding my breath as I have Brook walk in first. I say, "Remember, this was my bachelor flat. This is where I partied and shagged. I wasn't planning on raising a family here."

"Clearly," Brook says, walking up to the stripper pole in the living room. I watch her as she appraises my choice of decor. A large, fully-stocked walnut bar with ten stools occupies the entire wall to her right. There are four couches in a square in the middle of the room. "No television?" she asks.

"I have a room for that down the hall."

She follows me through an arch to the hall. I continue, "TV is on the left, two guest rooms on the right, loo on the left and master in front."

She continues to walk to the master. She swings open the door and we step in. In front of us is my custom-made king-and-a-half bed. She looks at me with raised eyebrows, "A bed for only two?"

"Not really."

"How many, William?"

"There have been five on a few occasions."

"Five. Four women and you?"

"Three women, one man and me."

"You have been with a man and three women at the same time?"

"I wasn't with the man. I have never had sex with a man. He and I had sex with the three women at the same time in the same bed."

Gone is the playful Brook from the ride over. I now question my decision to bring her here. She walks over to the closet and I say, "You may not want to open that, Brook. This was my fuck pad. I know you don't understand that. I have told you about my experiences, Brook. Ask me what you would like, and I will answer you honestly."

She opens the door and walks in. I watch her as she passes the toys, chains, cuffs, boxes of condoms, gels, clamps and so much more. She gets to the end and turns to face me. "You used this stuff? Is this what you like?"

"I have used all of this at one time or another. I liked it when I did it. The women liked it, too. I have never forced anyone, raped anyone. I didn't make anyone do anything they didn't want to do."

"Why haven't you mentioned this to me?"

I walk to her and take her in my arms. "I don't need any of this," I say. It is just here. I haven't been in the flat for over four years. I have everything I want with you."

"I must be very boring to you. My skills are limited to the basics. The first time I ever made love outside was with you. I had only been in a bed before that."

"Boring? No way. You are the first woman that I have ever had unprotected sex with. The first time we made love just us, skin on skin, I thought I would lose my mind. Every time since then has been beyond words. You take me to a place I have never been before and I don't want to ever leave."

"You tied women up to have sex?"

"I have."

"Have you ever been tied up?"

"No."

"Do you still think about doing that?"

"Never."

"I don't think I could do that. I wouldn't be comfortable with it."

"It is not an issue, Brook. I would never even ask for that from you." She places her hand on my cheek. I say, "I'll call Luke and have the car brought around. I'm going to take you to a hotel. This is not the place for you, my love."

"No. It's late and I'm tired. I understand that you had a colorful life before I came into it. I just worry that you might tire of me over time."

I lift her chin to look in my eyes and say, "There is a snowball's chance in fucking hell that will ever happen, darling."

I walk Brook out of the bedroom and into one of the guest rooms saying, "We are going to sleep in here tonight. There are too many ghosts in the other room. Tomorrow I will have the flat emptied of all the rubbish that I collected in my youth."

"Why do you keep the flat?"

"It is in a very good neighborhood. Jonathan and my father have stayed here in bad weather if they couldn't get home safely. Someday Ren will want his own place and this will be his."

Brook changes while I strip and get into bed. What started out as a wonderful evening has turned into a hot mess quickly. Brook comes to bed and rests her head on my shoulder. She turns my face to her and kisses me. She looks at me and says, "William, will you make love to me?"

"After all that, you still want to make love?"

"I don't think that you have ever made love here, have you?"

"I didn't love any of the women who have been here until you. So, no, I have never made love here."

"Good, then this will be the first time."

Thank god for first times!

Walking into the library the next day, I find my father in the study. I sit down in the extra chair to talk to him. "I want you and mum to book your world tour to start after Christmas. It is time that you did something together away from here. Jonathan and I can handle the business."

"Funny that you should mention this. Your mother and I were talking about where we want to go just the other day. After hearing you and Brook speak about Australia, we thought we would start there. We could do Africa and South America in January, February and March, then move to America for April, May and June."

"Good, make the arrangements. I want you back for Ren's first birthday and then I am going to take Ren and Brook to the states in August. Brook won't been home for a year and Ren needs to meet his American family."

"I'll put your mother on it today. Thank you, son, for stepping up. I didn't want to pressure you into a decision, but I am very happy you made it."

"Me too. But it wasn't me, it's Brook. She is my stabilizer."

CHAPTER 24

WALKING IN THE DOOR FROM a very long day with union negotiations, I ask John, "Is Mrs. Barry home?"

"Yes, sir, she is in the nursery with Master Warren."

"Very good. Thank you, John."

"You're welcome, sir."

I climb the stairs and walk to the nursery. I lean against the doorjamb and watch Brook play on the carpet with our son. She looks up to see me and says, "Look, Ren, Daddy's home. Watch what he can do, William." She flips Ren onto his stomach. He lifts himself up and rolls over. Brook claps and Ren giggles.

"I know he isn't quite ready for Cirque du Soleil, but I think he is amazing," she says proudly.

"He is amazing, darling, just like his mother." I kneel down next to Brook and blow raspberries on Ren's soft stomach while he giggles. "That is the nicest sound I have ever heard."

"How did your day go, William? Are the negotiations difficult?"

"Not really. It's going over everything line by line that is tiring. I swear it has one thousand pages. I know it is not that many but it feels like it is. What did you and Ren do today?"

"I went for a run this morning while Ren ate and had a nice bath. We played, and after lunch, I took him for a walk. He likes cats."

"Cats? Why cats?"

"I think the dogs scare him. Hounds are so rambunctious and big. We found a couple of cats in the barn. I picked one up to show Ren and he squealed and kicked his legs. He likes cats."

"What did he think of the horses?"

"We didn't get to close to the horses. We are still working on small game."

"I'm going to change and get comfortable," I say, chuckling as I leave the room.

"I'll come with you," she says, putting Ren in his crib with a toy. "Allison, Ren is in his crib and I'm going to my room."

"Okay, Mrs. Barry. I'm right here," Allison responds from her adjacent room.

I get to our room and throw my jacket on the chaise. I toe off my shoes as I watch Brook walk in close and lock the door. I lift my eyebrow and say, "Why, Mrs. Barry exactly what are your intentions?"

She saunters over to me and starts to pull out my tie. "I thought you might like an appetizer before dinner."

"With Allison right across the hall? What if she hears us?"

"I'll keep quite."

"Not if I have anything to do with it, you won't. What happened to the woman I married who was so afraid of the help knowing that we fool around?"

"She figured out that they probably guessed that we do, so why try to hide the facts?"

My shirt hits the floor and my pants follow. I lift her dress over her head and carry her to our bed. She sheds her bra and panties and then pushes me to my back. She says, "This is for you, my love." She takes me into her mouth.

"You didn't tell the truth, Brook, when you said you had no skills. I am sorry, but I beg to differ."

We're late to dinner. When my mother asks why we were late, I tell her honestly that we were trying to produce her another grandchild. My father almost drops his wine laughing at my mother's horrified reaction to the truth. I doubt that she will ever ask again.

When my mum regains her power of speech, she recounts to us their travel plans. "We will start out in Australia and New

Zealand," she says. "We have a three-week photographic safari in Africa scheduled. Our next stop will be South America. I want to take tango lessons in Brazil."

My father gives her a sideways glance and says, "Tango lessons? Whom do you plan on having as a dance partner, darling?"

"You, dearest. At our Boxing Day party next year we can have a demonstration for our guests."

"I don't think that is wise, darling. You are aware, are you not, that I possess at least two left feet? I don't plan on being the center of attention when the world discovers that fact."

"Anything can be learned with the right mindset. Will and devotion are all you need. You have plenty of both, my love."

"Flattery will not help your crusade, darling. I will willingly watch you while you devote yourself to your tango lessons."

Defeated, my mother moves on. "Then we move on to America. I know we will end up in New York and stay at your apartment. We don't really know what else we want to see. We have been to LA, Miami, Houston and Chicago. If you and Brook wouldn't mind writing down a few of the places you think we should see, that will help us with our plans."

"Any interest in the tallest thermometer, largest ball of rubber bands, or the collection of paper clips?" I ask.

"You don't mean that, do you?"

"All available for your viewing pleasure," I assure her.

"I think we will just stick with the run-of-the-mill tourist destinations, thank you."

"Pity, the thermometer really is something to see. We'll work on a list for you. When do you actually leave?"

"January 4th, and we return on June 22nd, in plenty of time for Ren's big day."

"Good, because we can't have a proper celebration unless you are here," Brook says.

"Why, Brook, darling, you are starting to sound positively British," my father states.

"She is British by injection, so it takes time before it completely takes over," I joke. "And I plan on injecting her regularly."

"Then I should expect another grandchild to be on his way by the time that we get back home."

"God willing," I say.

A few weeks pass. One morning after making love with my wife, she asks me, "Could we have a Thanksgiving dinner? I want to keep some of my American holidays for Ren."

"It so happens that we have a holiday called Stir-up Sunday that is near your Thanksgiving. The tradition is to make a Christmas pudding. Everyone in the family takes a turn to stir the pudding and make a wish. We can combine the two if you would like."

"That would be great. Just like Ren, a little of both of us."

We have our Thanksgiving Sunday on December 1st along with stirring our Christmas pudding. Brook explains the whole idea of her feast to Emily's girls and Jonathan's boys.

"The Indians came to dinner at your house, Auntie Brook? Was Unil Bubs there?" Leslie asks.

"The Indians were at the first Thanksgiving. There have been over two hundred celebrated since then. Last Thanksgiving we were here with you, remember?"

"I prefer not to remember that time in my life," I say.

"I agree. Not my favorite memories," Brook snuggles next to me on the couch.

"Mummy said you are going to have more babies. When you do, can we have Ren?" Lily inquires.

"You can tell your mummy to get you a new baby. I'm afraid Ren is staying with us," I answer.

Ren entertains everyone with his new trick. The girls follow after him as he rolls from one side of the room to the other. I know that he will be crawling soon and then running. I kiss Brook's cheek. What a difference a year makes.

Christmas Eve is a happy one. Ren plays baby Jesus in the family pageant. Through the drawing of straws, Lourine is Mary and Joseph is played by Max. Lily, Leslie and Hugh fill in as angels and the wise men, changing quickly behind the curtain. All goes well until Hugh says that he has a gift of

Frankenstein, and we all lose our composure in a fit of laughter. The children are aghast that we would laugh at such a pivotal moment in their play, which then makes it even funnier. We all struggle to control ourselves as the children continue despite our interruption. We finally reach a most delightful conclusion with a standing ovation by all.

Ren sleeps through the whole affair as a good baby Jesus should. He is given the MVP award for his participation. The children open their presents from us and their grandparents. With the announcement that Santa is on his way they all scurry to their beds. We stay up for a few minutes more and then Brook and I say goodnight to everyone.

I move to hover over her, wanting to give her the present that she has had many times before but still greets with the same degree of enthusiasm as the first time she received it. I tell her as I enter her, "I love you now and forever."

"I know you do, William. And I love you now and forever."

Christmas morning with five screaming children at 5:00 AM is more than anyone can take. Their parents won't let them open Santa's presents until everyone is up and in the room. They send Max in to jump on us and wake us up. I look at Brook and say, "Someone better have coffee waiting or this is Max's last Christmas morning."

"It's Christmas, William. Don't you remember when you were little?"

"That was a long time ago. Most of it is a sex, drugs, alcohol and rock'n'roll blur."

"I don't believe for one minute that you did any of that when you were seven. I'm talking about believing in Santa."

"I remember~old guy in a red suit. Father Time."

"You are hopeless. Hurry up and come with me and don't be such a Scrooge."

The children are in a Santa-induced frenzy by the time we join them. Wrapping paper flies past my head. Brook is on the floor in the midst of the fray, alternately helping Hugh and Lily cut the ribbons on their packages. Next year, Ren will be on her lap, no doubt squealing with delight as his cousins are doing now.

CHAPTER 25

BROOK AND I SEE MY parents off. They promise to keep in touch as they travel the world. I would like to take Brook on the African safari someday.

Ren is fascinated by watching the airplanes take off and land. Every time we move away from the windows, he cries. We must have a pilot or world traveler on our hands. He takes after Brook with her love of flight.

We arrive home just in time for our little man to take a nap. He rubs his eyes as I kiss his head and lay him in his crib. I know I'm bragging here, but he is a beautiful boy with his sandy brown hair and deep, clear green eyes. He has his mother's nose and sexy lips. He will break hearts all over England in a few years.

Brook is in the kitchen going over the menus for the coming week with Barbara. I take the baby monitor and go to the study to answer e-mails. One is from Angelo. He and Gratiana will be in England in February for two days and want to see us, especially Ren. I answer that we will be here and they must stay with us if they can. They were so good to Brook. I would like to return the favor.

I look up and see my wife at the study door. She asks, "Will you be long?"

"What did you have in mind?"

"I thought we might go for a run. Barbara and John said they would watch Ren until either we or Allison get back."

"I could use the air. Will you get my trainers for me, please?"

"I'll be right back."

Brook comes in and I change my shoes. I remind her that she came to the dance with me and she has to leave with me. "What does that mean?" she asks.

"Don't take off and leave me behind."

"I'm sorry. I find my zone and I don't think."

"I don't mind being slightly behind because the view is fantastic. Just don't smoke me with your five-minute miles."

The air is crisp and fresh. Brook and I cover about six kilometers before we turn to head back. My legs are burn on the last three. I am spent. Brook looks like she could do it all over with out a problem.

We get back to the house to find Ren on the floor of the kitchen with a wooden spoon, banging on an arrangement of pots that Barbara has set up in front of him. Drum-playing pilot, could be! I leave him with Barbara to get in a tub and soak my muscles. Brook comes in and turns on the jets. "Thank you, darling. I have to get back to the gym and soon. My young wife is hard to keep up with."

"I'm only seven years younger than you. You make it sound like twenty. Besides, you get plenty of exercise in other ways."

"Why, Brook, to what are you referring?"

"Don't be coy, William. It really doesn't suit you. You know exactly to what I refer."

Brook takes a quick shower and then rescues Barbara from Ren to bring him to his nursery to play. When I finish my bath, I find her reading a book to him in the rocker. Ren seems to be more interested in how the pages taste than what they say. Brook has such patience with him. He is very wise to have chosen her to be his mother.

"Do you need me, darling?" I ask.

"No, we are just reading. You have work to do. We'll be down later."

Our next function is a sweetheart's dance fundraiser for my charity. I champion the cause of art and photography for children. Many times, those programs are the last to be funded. If the children have a love of art, I want them to have the same opportunities that I had to pursue it.

The ball is to be held in the Edinburgh Suite at the Thistle Marble Arch hotel. We are expecting almost five hundred people to attend. This serves as the major fundraising event for us. The rest of our donations come from endowments for the arts and private donations.

Brook is once again stunning in a silver, beaded gown. Every eye in the room is trained on the door as we make our entrance. We walk to the center of the room and the orchestra begins to play the Tennessee Waltz, which is Brook's favorite. I smile at her and say, "Everyone here is wondering what this music is. I have no doubt they don't even know where Tennessee is."

"You don't give them much credit, William. I am sure they know that Tennessee is in the US. I love the words to the song. 'Can I have this dance for the rest of my life? Will you be my partner every night? When we're together, it feels so right. Can I have this dance for the rest of my life?'"

"Well, can I?"

"Absolutely. I love you."

At the end of the month Angelo and Gratiana phone to let us know that they won't be coming after all. Natalia isn't feeling well and they don't want to leave her alone with the children. I tell them that we might get there in the fall. March passes, and finally in April, we start to feel the warmth of spring.

Easter Sunday morning, I am kissing Brook's breasts. Moving down, I dip my tongue in her belly button. She giggles. I kiss across her abdomen, moving down to the promised land when she giggles again.

"What is so funny? You're not doing much for my ego, wife."

"I have something to tell you. That's why I'm giggling."

I look up from my ministrations to see her smile. I say, "Okay. What?"

"I'm pregnant. You are going to be a daddy again."

I crawl back up to her face and say, "You're sure? Thank you, darling. That is the best Easter present I have ever received."

"I think I'm due in the middle of December. Maybe we will have a Christmas baby."

We hug and kiss and I make sweet, gentle love to her.

Jonathan, Emily, and their families have come for Easter dinner. We make our announcement to them about the new baby. Emily grins and says, "When are you due, Brook?"

"In December."

"That is two of us, then. Dick and I are expecting as well."

"In December? What fun! Do the girls know yet?"

"No way! They will make me crazy. We won't tell them for a few more months. They don't understand that it takes time. They will want the baby now."

"What are your odds that it will be more than one?"

"Around 50-50. When we had the girls, we were told about multiples on Dick's side. Lourine and Leslie are identical. That could happen again very easily."

"I think I would love to have twins, but three is one too many!"

Brook has some trouble with morning sickness. I feel so badly for her, and yet she bears it with a smile on her face. The woman exudes happiness and light all around her. By the end of June, all of this sickness has passed just in time for my parents to come home.

We all go to the airport to greet them. As I look around, there are six children and six adults yet somehow I feel outnumbered by the rug rats. How are we ever going to do two more at one of these functions?

Jonathan spots Mum and Dad and the girls run to hug them. Ren claps his hands in his pram. Hugh decides to climb in with Ren while Max suddenly has to go to the loo and I mean NOW! Eve takes Max while we all walk to my parents. After everyone gets a hug and kiss, we are on our way back to the house so that we can hear all about their adventures.

"I think even you, William, will be astounded with the pictures we took in Africa," my father says.

"We brought each of the boys an African war mask and the girls a headpiece," my mother says.

Debbie Zello

"The next show-and-tell day they will have a story to share," Emily states.

"Please, Emily, those three must always have a story to tell. They are your children, are they not?" Jonathan throws in.

I see Brook roll her eyes as she realizes that the Barry family wars are about to start. I decide to defuse the situation before blood is shed. "Where did you go in the States?"

"We went to LA and San Francisco. We saw the Grand Canyon. Then we flew to Niagara Falls and then drove to New York City. That was a very long drive~I don't want to do that again."

"Did Angela take good care of you?" I ask.

"She is so wonderful, William. She did everything for us. I have questions, though, about your choice of art, William."

"Which piece?"

"The one your bed."

I watch as Brook turns a beautiful shade of pink. I say, "And what is wrong with that particular piece?"

"It is more of my daughter-in-law than I ever thought I would see. Also, it is quite suggestive in its form."

"First of all, you can't see any more of Brook than if she were wearing a bikini. Secondly, it's in the bedroom~not for the general public to view."

"The first time I saw it was at the gallery, with many of the public viewing it," my very helpful brother points out.

"Damn, I forgot about that."

"William had my permission to show the picture. I knew that I loved him then and I thought the love came through in the image. If you love someone, there is nothing unseemly about a portrait like that. It shows the beauty in our relationship," my wife says, defending me. Leave it to her to shut my family up.

CHAPTER 26

REN'S BIRTHDAY MIGHT BECOME A state holiday next year, if the next one is anything like the first. Brook invites every child from the village to a garden party. There are clowns, jugglers, magicians, puppet masters, pony rides, face painters, hair braiders, non-permanent tattoo artists, bounce houses, cotton-candy makers, and caramel apples. You name it and we have it. After watching some parents walking around with their children, I doubt if anyone in town will talk to us for a few weeks with the sugar high the children are exhibiting. Oh well, so much for public relations.

Ren is speaking in full sentences now~pity it is in a different language from what we speak. A few words come through perfectly clear~mummy and daddy. But the clearest is NO! "Do you want to eat now, Ren?" NO! "It's bedtime, Ren." NO! "Do you want to solve the world's problems now, Ren?" NO! I'm thinking drum playing pilot politician is where he is headed.

By the end of July we have our travel plans to go back to America with Ren. We will leave on August third and stay for three weeks. That will give Brook enough time to see everyone. I worry about her being five months pregnant with another long trip, but she says everything will be fine.

My parents see us off at the airport. Our entire carry-on bag is taken up with Ren paraphernalia. How can someone so little have so many bits and pieces? I had Angela purchase a crib, highchair and stroller for us. Next time we visit, we will need two of everything. My study has been turned into a nursery.

Ren makes a good traveler. He plays and takes a nap. By the time we land, he is ready to run and Brook is ready for bed. We told Allison to rest on the flight because we knew we would need her to take him after. Angela meets us at the airport with the limo. Luke is stunned that she could drive it. My Angela is a woman of many talents and I appreciate every one of them.

As soon as we leave the airport proper, I remember why I love the city so much. It is a living thing. It breathes, moves and has it's own light. Every car here has a horn and it becomes an extension of its driver's voice. Cut me off and instead of me thinking you're an idiot, I can honk my horn to tell you that. Picture one hundred thousand people doing this at the same time and you have New York City. I drink it in and smile.

Angela informs me that we have a new door attendant on the day shift. Sonyaht started a few months ago. Your first line of security is at your door, so I will make his acquaintance immediately. We arrive at the apartment and manage all of our luggage. By the looks of things, we plan to stay forever not just three weeks. Brook, Ren, Allison, Luke and I go down to meet Sonyaht. Luke stays to talk to him about our security dos and don'ts.

I make Brook take a nap and she lies down with Ren. Soon both of them are sleeping soundly. I make a few phone calls to inform my family of our safe arrival and then pour a glass of wine and go to the roof garden. I see that Angela has Ren proofed the area. She moved everything that you can climb on away from the safety fence that surrounds it. The hot tub now has a lock. The koi pond has a perforated Plexiglas lid. Ren will love that! He can sit on the water and watch the fish. The woman is amazing, creative and indispensable to me.

Around my third glass of wine, Brook joins me in the garden. She lies down next to me on the chaise.

"Sleep well? You look less tired, my love."

"That's how I know this one is a girl. I'm not as tired as I was with Ren. Am I uglier? I remember what Natalia said~a boy makes you tired and a girl takes your beauty."

"I'm sorry to tell you, darling, but if it's a girl she will be ugly like me because you have never looked more beautiful than you do right now."

"Even with my big belly?"

"Especially with your big belly. That is my baby in there. Please do not make disparaging remarks about my offspring," I say, frowning at her.

"Yes, sir. My apologies."

"So, what are our plans, darling? I know that you have made plans with everyone."

"I have invited everyone for dinner on Saturday night. Angela has made all of the arrangements with a caterer. She wants to keep Ren with her on a few nights. She said she wanted to get to know him. Isn't that sweet?"

"Angela is a treasure in every way. Ren may not want to come back with us!"

"I know. Anyway, after that I don't have any firm plans. Is there anything you want to do?"

"I want to take Ren for walks in the park. I have to show him the place that I first knew I had to keep his mum in my life. I know he is little, but we have to take him to FAO. Schwarz. I guess we could see what's on Broadway if you would like to go to a show."

"That sounds like fun. Date night with my favorite date."

We hear Ren talking on the monitor. Brook moves to get up, but I stop her and say, "I'll get him. I want him to see this. We'll be right back."

Standing in the doorway of my former study, I watch Ren talking to his SpongeBob. He has him in one arm as he points at object in the room with the other. He spots me and yells, "DADA!" What a wonderful sound.

"Your mummy is waiting for us in the garden, Ren. Do you want to see the fish? I have a feeling that you need your nappy changed."

I clean him up and carry him to the roof. He spots his mum on the chaise and wiggles out of my arms to run to her. He throws himself at the chaise, and Brook leans over to help him up.

"How did my little man sleep? Do you feel better, Ren? Daddy wants to show you the fishies."

Ren looks at me and holds his arms out for me to pick him up. I take him over to the fishpond and set him down on the top. He lies down face first to watch the fish swim by. I squat down next to him and run my fingers through his hair. He is talking to the fish. "Babble, babble, babble, fissie, babble."

I turn to Brook and say, "I should have brought my camera up with me. He is so damned cute talking to the fish."

"Call Angela and ask her to bring it to us."

I call Angela and ask her if she, Luke, or Allison can bring my camera up. She tells me she will be right up. She wants to see Ren with the fish. A few minutes later, I am snapping picture after picture of Ren, Angela and Brook.

The next morning, Brook and I, with Luke in tow, take Ren for a walk in the park. He is fascinated by the pigeons. We are spotted by a few photographers who take our picture. Brook throws a blanket over Ren so he is not visible in the shot. So much for our low profile in the States. My wife has become the celebrity with her modeling and charity work. The funny thing is that today she is wearing one of Eddy's designs and she makes sure to tell them that.

We walk to Schwarz to watch Ren's amazed-but-frightened look at the toy soldier who opens the door for us. He wants out of his stroller the minute we get inside. Luke folds it so he can carry it more comfortably. Brook and I each take a hand and Ren shows us through the store. Several purchases later, Ren is back securely in his stroller and I'm now the pack mule.

Our friends arrive Saturday around 5:00 so they can spend some time with Ren before he goes to bed. Carline from the agency, Sandy, Link, Wendy, Regina, Christina, Millie and boyfriend, Carol and boyfriend and finally, Bill and Steve, the pilots from Brook's flights. Jay and Ted, who are fellow photographers, might stop by after dinner. They had previous plans for the evening. After cocktails and our visit with Ren, Allison takes him to Angela's apartment to put him to bed. Brook was worried the noise of the party might keep him up. A cranky, tired Ren is not a pleasant sight.

The evening progresses as we catch up on all of the gossip at the airline. Carol can't seem to keep her hands off of John and I almost expect them to disappear for a quickie at any moment. I remember those days fondly.

"If you are ever interested in working again, Brook, I have photographers who want to work with you. I guess the word has gotten out thanks to Angelo and Cole that you are a dream to work with," Carline says.

"I doubt it, but thank you. I loved working with them, too. They took very good care of me," Brook answers.

"Do you miss flying?" asks Wendy.

"I miss seeing all of you. I miss a few of my regulars. The flying, however, not so much because I'm still flying just not for work. Ren, William and my charity keep me busy. Now with the new baby, I won't have much free time."

"Do you promise to be back for the wedding?" asks Sandy.

"The baby will be six months old by then. I'm sure we will be able to come for a week or two. I don't want to miss seeing you and Link get married."

"Good because I want you to stand up with me. It's not going to be a large wedding. Maybe fifty or so people, but I want you there."

Around midnight, Brook and I get into bed. "I had a wonderful evening. How about you?" she asks.

"It was really nice to see everyone and catch up. We should make sure that we come back at least once or twice a year to visit. I love this city and didn't realize how much I missed it until we came back."

CHAPTER 27

REN HAS DECIDED TO LEAVE us and have Angela adopt him. This probably has to do with the ready jar of cookies she uses to bribe for kisses. I'm almost tempted to smooch her myself. With her and Allison around, Brook and I can do as we please.

I'm having lunch with Brook when the phone rings. I say, "Hello."

"Dada, Dada," a familiar little voice says. "Mr. Barry, Ren wanted to call you and Mrs. Barry. Somehow, he thinks you are in the phone," Allison states.

"No problem, Allison. We are almost finished with lunch and we will be heading back. Do you need anything?"

"No, sir."

I can still hear Ren calling Brook and me. I hang up and tell Brook, "Your son has a phone fetish."

"I hate the phone so who does he get that from?"

"I haven't a clue. Maybe Emily~she has one glued to her most of the time."

As soon as we get off the lift, Ren runs to Brook yelling," Mama, Mama."

"Hi, little man. Have you been a good boy this morning?" Brook asks him.

Brook gets an open-mouth sloppy kiss from Ren. He holds his little arms out for me to take him.

"Come here, Ren, and give me a kiss," I say. He does.

Then he wants down, running somewhere. The child is perpetual motion to the extreme. I watch as Allison runs after him, grateful it's not me.

After Ren's nap, Allison brings him to the roof where Brook and I are relaxing in the afternoon sun. Brook is reading a novel and I have the Wall Street Journal to skim through. Ren is once again on top of the koi pond, this time sticking his fingers in the holes to "tickle" the fish.

"Are you and Mrs. Barry going out tonight?" Allison asks.

"No, we're in this evening. Would you like to go out?"

"I thought I might look around."

"Go, enjoy yourself. If you're not sure where to go, I can give you some suggestions. If you would like to see a play, I can get the tickets for you. You should ask Angela or Luke if they want to go with you."

"I will. Thank you."

We watch her leave, presumably to ask Angela or Luke if they want to go out. Brook says, "Allison is so good with Ren. She loves him and he loves her. I told her that she has a position with us for as long as she wants."

I reach over to rub Brook's belly and say, "If we keep this up, it will be a long employment."

"I want more children. Don't you?"

"Tons more. Until you say enough. I especially enjoy making them."

"Somehow I knew you were going to say that."

"You know me so well, darling."

I get up to join Ren at the pond. He is talking to the fish as they swim. I ask him, "Ren, what do the fishies do?"

He opens his mouth to imitate the fish breathing. Brook and I laugh. I smooth his hair and say, "That's right, Ren. Silly fish."

I obtain tickets to see Once on Saturday night. I have heard a few things about the production and one thing in particular that will surprise Brook. Luke drives us to the theater. "I think we will go to a late supper after the show, Luke. We'll walk or take a cab. I want you to stay with Ren, please," I tell him.

"Very good, Mr. Barry. I hope you have a pleasant evening."

"Thank you. If you have need of us, I will have my phone on."

I take Brook's hand to walk into the theater. We are shown to our box seats. Brook looks lovely in a black dinner dress with a silver shawl over her shoulders. I smile as several men pass an appreciative glance at my wife. One out-and-out stares at her. He catches my stare back at him and glances away.

The musical gets under way and I sit back, waiting for a particular moment to watch Brook's reaction. The play is very good and the actors are doing a wonderful job entertaining us. Finally, the music starts for the song that I have been very patiently waiting for. I watch Brook's face slowly turn to recognition. "Falling Slowly" is one of the songs on Josh Groban's CD. Apparently, he loves the song, too. When the song is finished, Brook turns to me and says, "Did you know that song was in the play?"

"Yes, I did. That's why I chose it. Are you pleased?"

"You are very thoughtful. Only you would find something like this for me. I adore you, William."

"Hearing that makes the entire performance even better, darling."

Leaving the theater, we walk to a nearby bistro for a late dinner. I hold Brook's hand as I drink my wine. I ask her, "What are we going to name this baby?"

"I still like Willa Brook if it's a girl. I thought Robert William if it's a boy, after my brother and you."

"Just two names for a boy? You're going to break with tradition? The entire Barry family plot might overturn."

"I know Ren had to have the four names. Do all of the boys need that?"

"Usually. But it's our baby, Brook, and if you only want two then that is what he will have."

"I'll think about it. I don't want to upset all of the dead relatives. It's bad enough that you married an American."

"It's the best decision that I have ever made. And all of the dead relatives know that."

"Do you have any particular plans for this week? I know we leave a week from Monday."

"I have to get over to the gallery to pick up the photos left from the showing. I am out of the photography business. I don't want them to have to store them any longer."

"I'm having lunch with Carline on Friday. She wants to show me a new studio that they just refurbished. I think she wants to entice me to do more work."

"Brook, if you want to continue to model, I'm not opposed to it. I want you happy. If you need to work to have that, then please do. I'm not locking you up in a musty old estate, surrounded by staff and continually pregnant."

"Well, that is good to know. I don't know if I want to or not. I already feel like I leave Ren too much. I'll think about it."

We finish our meal and I have the maitre d' call a cab for us. As Brook and I ride back home she says, "Thank you for yet another wonderful night, William. I had a fantastic time."

"My pleasure, darling. So did I."

Over the next few days, Brook and I take Ren for walks in the park, back to see the tin soldier at FAO Schwarz, and to a dinosaur exhibit at the Museum of Natural History. At night, Brook rests in my arms and we make love.

Friday morning at breakfast as Ren throws his French toast at me, I say, "Ren, you are in a foul mood today. I think you should go back to bed for a nap."

"I think he knows that he is going to be trapped on a plane again in a few days," Brook says.

"I'm going to be trapped on one too, but I'm not throwing my breakfast around."

"You're not one. And you're hungry. Ren doesn't eat enough to keep a small bird alive."

"Are you concerned?"

"I was but the doctor said he won't starve himself. They go through phases. He said when he is a teenager, he will eat us out of house and home."

"He will. I did, and so did Jonathan."

"I miss everyone. The next time we come we should bring the family with us."

"We can ask. My father won't come if Jonathan and I are gone. Someone has to run things at home."

"I'm sorry. I forgot. You're right."

"Are you having lunch with Carline today?"

"Yes. I spoke with her yesterday. I told her I would be there around 11:00. Are you going to the gallery?"

"Yes. Luke and I are going probably around the same time as you are. I have a few errands I want to finish and I'll be home for supper."

When Brook and I are ready to leave, Allison brings Ren to us. She tell him, "Say good-bye to Mummy and Daddy, Ren. Say 'Have a nice day, Mummy and Daddy.'"

"Bye, Ren. Be a good boy for Miss Allison. Give Mommy a kiss. I love you"

Brook passes Ren to me. I hug him, give him a kiss and say, "We will be back after your nap, little man. Be a good boy. I love you." I pass him back to Allison saying, "If you need us Allison, just call. I can be back within a half hour, traffic permitting. Angela is here, too, if you need anything."

"We will be fine."

"I would prefer that you not go out, as Luke is coming with me."

"Of course. We will find something to do. I will take good care of Ren, sir. You don't have to worry."

CHAPTER 28

"WILLIAM, IT IS SO GOOD to see you. What have you been doing?" Russ, the owner of the gallery, asks me.

"It's good to see you, Russ. I have been very busy. I have a wife and a son and another on the way. I have taken over some of the responsibilities of the family business. I live in the UK now. How is business here?"

"Slow, I'm afraid. I keep hoping it will pick up, but it hasn't. If you don't mind me asking, what is your family business?"

"Mostly shipping. We haven't been hit that hard. I feel badly for people like you, Russ."

"I'll survive somehow. It's bound to turn around."

"I stopped by to pick up the remaining photos from the showing. I think you will be glad to have them taken off your hands. You have been kind enough to store them for a long time."

"It's quite all right William. I have them in the back. Follow me."

We walk through the gallery to the back storage. Against one wall are the six framed photos that I left. Luke and I pick them up and walk back through to the car. Luke places them in the trunk and covers them with a blanket. I walk back in to say good-bye. "Russ, thank you again. If I ever decide to photograph again, I will call you."

"Do you have time to go to lunch? I was just about to close and grab a bite. I would love the company."

"As it is, my wife is at lunch with a friend. I would love to go."

Luke drives us to a pub that Russ's cousin owns. We walk in and sit in a booth. I ask Luke to join us. He is much more of a friend to me than an employee.

I recount to Russ what has been going on in my life. I tell him about Brook and my wedding. Our honeymoon in Australia and the beauty that we saw. Living at the estate. Brook's charity and meeting her idol Josh Groban. Russ relates his family's events including a new grandchild. Before I can even finish my story over two hours have passed.

"I'm sorry to end our discussion, but I still have a few stops to make and I told Brook I would be home for supper. If you are ever in England, Russ, I do hope you will contact us. It would be no trouble at all for you to stay with us."

"Thank you so much for the offer, William. I might just do that."

Luke drives Russ back to the gallery and we drive off. My next stop is a camera shop on the Lower West Side. I had dropped one of my cameras off there for repairs over a year ago and I need to pick it up. I go in, pay my bill and storage fees, get my camera and leave.

My last stop is at my solicitor's office. I need to sign the power of attorney for him to act in my stead. With my home in England now, if I have business here, I need someone who will handle it. I can't be flying back and forth with Brook and the children. And I don't want to come alone.

I am discussing my holdings with Curtis Lieberman, my attorney, when my phone rings. I say, "Excuse me for a minute, Curtis. It's my wife." I answer Brook's call.

"William, is Ren with you?"

"No. I haven't been home since we left this morning. Isn't he there with Allison?"

"I came home a few minutes ago. He isn't in his room or in the apartment or on the roof. Angela is checking Luke's apartment and hers."

"Is his stroller missing?"

"Yes."

"Maybe she took him for a walk in the park."

"Without telling Angela or leaving a note?"

"All right, calm down. I will leave right now and come home. I'll be there in less than half an hour." I hang up and call the front door. "Hello. This is William Barry in the penthouse."

"Yes, Mr. Barry, sir. What can I do for you?"

"My son and his nanny . . . have you seen them today?"

"Yes, sir. Miss Allison took him for a walk this morning."

"They haven't returned?"

"No, sir."

"What time did they leave?"

"About ten minutes after Miss Angela. I would say around 9:45."

"Can you pull your security tapes, please? I am on my way and my security will need to see them. I need what you have in the street also."

"I don't have the authority to do that. I'm sorry. Is there a problem?"

"My son is missing. There is a big problem. Whoever you have to contact that has the authority to pull the tapes, you need to call now!" I hang up.

"Curtis, I will be in touch."

"If there is anything I can do to help, William, please call me. Good luck. I'm sure your son is fine."

I run to the street and get in the car. I apprise Luke of my conversation with Brook and Sonyaht. I call Angela. "Angela, what is happening?"

"I checked all three apartments and nothing is disturbed. Allison and Ren are not in your apartment. Ren's stroller is gone."

"When did you leave? How long were you gone?"

"I left right after you. I went to get groceries and pick up dry-cleaning. I was gone about two hours."

"Then what?"

"Ren's door was shut so I thought he was napping. I didn't look for Allison. I did some housework. I was starting dinner when Mrs. Barry came home."

"I'm calling the police, Angela. I hope that I will be there before they arrive. If not, don't leave Brook's side for any reason. Do you understand?"

"Yes, sir. This is all my fault."

"No, Angela. I told Allison not to go out. It is most definitely not your fault."

I place the call to the 19th precinct. "This is William Barry. I am calling to report a missing child."

"Yes, Mr. Barry. How long has the child been missing?"

"His nanny took him out around 9:45 this morning and has not returned with him."

"Is this unusual?"

"Very. We are here on vacation. She doesn't know the area except for a small section of Central Park. We are from England."

"I will send a detective over to talk to you. What is the address?"

"800 5th Avenue. Penthouse."

"I know the building, sir. I'll send over the best we have."

"You may need to notify the FBI, my son is a Royal."

"Yes, sir, I understand. I will discuss this with the captain and go from there. We will be there as soon as we can."

"My wife is pregnant and home alone. I do not want her questioned at all until I get there. Please start with the door attendant and the security tapes."

"Yes, sir. Understood."

I hang up and call Brook, "Darling, are you all right?"

"My son is missing. No, I'm not all right."

"I called the police. I'm sure it won't be necessary, but I called just in case. Allison is very responsible. I'm sure there is a logical explanation for her absence. She lost track of time or ran into someone she knows. There could be many different scenarios."

"Are you far away, William? I need you. When will you be home?"

"A few more minutes. Luke is breaking several laws to get me there as quickly as possible. I will stay on the phone with you until I walk in the door."

"I want my son, William. I'm so scared. Where could he be?"

"I'm almost there, Brook. Don't be scared. I'll take care of everything. We will find him," I say, sounding more confident than I feel.

"What if someone hurt Allison and took Ren? He could be halfway around the world by now," she says, crying.

"Or he could be in an ice cream parlor with Allison and a friend having a cone. Or in the park petting a dog or watching the pigeons fly," I say, using my voice of reason.

"He should be here with me reading Curious George. Having his dinner and getting ready for bed."

"Yes, darling. I'm pulling up to the door now. I'll be with you in a few minutes."

Luke pulls up in front of the building. He and I jump out. The police are talking with Sonyaht. I run in. "I am William Barry. Do you have the tapes?"

"Yes, we are looking at them now. I am Detective Charles Brennan and this is my partner, Detective Chuck Mac Murray."

I extend my hand to shake theirs and say, "What do the tapes show?"

"Exactly what you said. Your nanny and son left at 9:45, immediately after you and your housekeeper. But instead of her turning towards the entrance to the park, she went the opposite way. She headed downtown. Do you have any idea where she would have been going?"

"As far as I know, this is the first time she has been to the US. I don't believe she knows anyone here. I have no idea where she was going."

"I want to talk to your housekeeper and your wife," Brennan says.

"They are in the apartment. Please follow me."

CHAPTER 29

I SIT WITH BROOK ON the couch with my arm around her and her head on my shoulder. Detective Brennan asks, "What happened when you came home, Mrs. Barry?"

"I went to Ren's room. The door was closed. I thought that was odd because it was so late in the afternoon. He never naps that late. He wasn't in the room. I began to look in the other bedrooms and then I went to the roof. I didn't start to be concerned until I didn't find him there. I went to the kitchen to speak with Angela. When she didn't know their whereabouts, I called William."

"Due to the amount of time that has passed, I believe we have a missing child here," Brennan says. I look to Angela and nod to the kitchen and then to Brook.

Angela says, "Mrs. Barry, would you please help me in the kitchen. I think we should make some coffee and snacks. I could use the help."

"Yes, of course," Brook answers.

I wait until they are out of the room and then I continue, "My wife is five months pregnant. For the time being, I don't want anything discussed in front of her that is of a negative nature. I have to think of her and the baby. If you have any questions or observations or anything, please discuss it with me in private."

"I'm sorry, Mr. Barry. I understand your concern. That was thoughtless of me. We need space to set up a command center. We will tap your phones and monitor calls. If a ransom demand is made, it usually comes within thirty-six hours."

"Luke will show you to the empty apartment next door. You can use it as your offices."

"We need pictures of your son and his nanny if you have them."

"Yes. I'll get them. I have to call my family in England. What kind of ransom will I be looking at?"

"I'm sorry to sound clinical, but how much are you worth?"

"Nothing without my son. My family's wealth is over a billion. Much of that is in land and equipment. We own a shipping company. I can lay my hands on several million in liquid assets. More will require loans against assets."

"Make your calls and get the information. Until you are contacted by the kidnapper, you won't have a figure to work with. The FBI should be here shortly. They are more versed in negotiations than we are. I am very sorry, Mr. Barry. I have a two-year-old son and I can't imagine what you are going through."

"Thank you. Just find him, please."

I walk into the bedroom to call Jonathan. He answers on the fourth ring. "Hello? Who the fuck is calling at four o'clock in the morning?"

"It's William. Jonathan, Ren is missing and we presume he has been kidnapped."

"What?"

"Ren is missing. Allison took him out this morning and never returned with him."

I can hear rustling of sheets and I assume Jonathan gets up. He says, "William, what can we do to help?"

I can hear Eve asking him what is wrong in the background. I say, "I need to know how much money we have in reserves. If a ransom demand is made, I need to know how much cash we have and how much we can borrow or liquidate in a hurry."

"Ten million won't be a problem. Up to twenty is doable. After that, we will need to borrow against assets. I'm going to fly out as soon as I can, William."

"No, Jonathan. I need you there to help with securing the money. There is nothing that you can do here. You need to tell the family. This will hit the papers soon," I say finally feeling the weight of the situation and silently tearing up.

"I'll send Emily and Dick. The girls can stay here with us. You need family with you and Brook. I'll keep Mum and Dad here helping with the children."

"Okay. Brook can lean on Emily." I start to break down completely. "What will we do if they hurt him, Jonathan?" I say wiping tears and swallowing hard. "What if Brook loses the baby?"

"Don't talk like that, William. They will find him and Brook will have the baby. I'm going to hang up so I can start to make arrangements. I'll call back as soon as I speak to Emily and our accountants. I have to wake everyone up, so give me a couple of hours. If you need me, call, please."

"I will. Thank you, Jonathan."

"I know that you would do the same for me. No thanks required. Take care."

I walk back to the living room and two men walk up to me. One says, "Mr. Barry, I'm Agent Walsh and this is Agent Gallagher. We are with the FBI and assigned to your case. The detectives have been bringing us up to speed on what they know about your son. I have some additional questions."

"Yes, of course. Please sit down."

"Exactly what is missing from your apartment besides your son and his nanny?"

"My housekeeper said his stroller. I'm afraid I don't know what else."

"I need to know. I want a list."

"I'll ask Angela to get that together for you."

"How did you hire your nanny?"

"Through an agency in England. Both my sister and sister-in-law hired theirs through the same agency. They were comfortable with them, so we used them too."

"I need that information as well. We will send someone to talk with them. Have you ever met or spoken with anyone that your nanny is friends with or dating?"

"No. She never went out or dated anyone that I know of. She seemed to be a homebody, happy to be with Ren and us.

She didn't even have a cell phone until I got it for her. As far as I know, our numbers were the only ones in it."

"Have you called her?"

"Repeatedly. It goes right to voicemail."

Brook and Angela walk in with coffee and snacks. I ask, "Angela, would you please make a list of what is missing from Ren's and Allison's things?"

"Absolutely, Mr. Barry."

Brook walks over to the windows and looks out. She says, "It's getting dark. If she was going to bring him back, she would have been here by now. He is really gone." The tears run down her cheeks. I walk to her and hold her. I speak close to her ear, "You have to eat something and you have to rest." My hand moves to her belly and I rub it. "This baby needs you, too."

A few hours pass. The police have set up their taps and listening devices. Luke has supplied them with pictures and descriptions. Angela compiled the list of missing items that included clothes for both Ren and Allison. She found the cell in a drawer. With that, it is concluded that Allison did indeed take Ren herself.

At midnight, I finally convince Brook to lie down and try to rest. Jonathan calls back to let me know that Emily and Dick are on a private jet on their way here. Three investigators from Scotland Yard are on the plane with them. They will assist in the American investigation. My mother and father are distraught. The accountants are working on the numbers and I will know soon what I have to work with. Still no call for ransom.

Brook joins us in the living room around 4:00 AM. I watch her walk in~her shoulders are slumped and she has a worn look on her face. I go to her and hold her hand to walk her to the couch. I say, "Brook, darling, I know how difficult it is, but I wish you would rest."

"I have tried, William. It's almost morning and we haven't heard anything from her. Why won't she call? Why is it taking so long for her to contact us?"

"I don't have the answer. Mr. Brennan says it is a waiting game."

"Have they found out where she went?"

"We are going to get an update soon. I'm going to have Angela make something for you to eat."

"I can't eat. I tried to and I just brought it back up. It helps if you just hold me."

"That I can do."

At 9:00 AM, Mr. Walsh comes in to brief us on what they have discovered. Luke has left for the airport to pick up the investigators, Emily and Dick. I keep my arm around Brook as he begins to speak. "We have been able to follow her and your son with sidewalk cameras from your door until she flagged a cab. She boarded a bus to Philadelphia at 11:30, arriving at 1:53. From there she took another cab to a local car dealer. She bought a 2005 Chevrolet Malibu, paying cash. She was given temporary plates and paid a premium to carry the dealership's insurance. From there, we have no idea so far in what direction she went."

"Why Philly?" I ask.

"We believe it was the next bus to leave the city. She would have waited another forty-five minutes for the next bus. If she has a plan on where she wants to go, now she has a car."

"The local police have the car and plates to look for?" Brook asks.

"Yes, ma'am. Everyone in a thousand-mile radius has the information. It is on the news and the AMBER ALERT has been activated. Everyone that can be is looking for your son."

"Should we do a news conference to ask for her to return him safely to us?" Brook asks.

"That's up to you, Mrs. Barry. The more exposure you have, the better your chances that someone will see them and report it. But I must tell you that there is a risk that if it gets too hot, she might rid herself of your son."

"What do you mean rid herself?"

"She could leave him somewhere or, worst-case scenario, kill him."

CHAPTER 30

EMILY, DICK AND THE AGENTS arrive. Emily throws her arms around Brook and me. Dick grabs Brook to hug her and says, "How are you holding up, kid?"

"As well as can be expected," she answers.

"What can we do for you?" Emily asks.

"Just having you here helps," Brook says.

The agents introduce themselves to me as Emily takes Brook outside to get some air.

"I'm Geoffrey Hulbert and this is Naomi Somers. Ryan Japes is talking to the FBI agents outside. We have several people running down leads on Allison. We have gone over her papers at the agency. Someone is on the way to speak with her last employer. We are going to find your son, sir."

"It's not for lack of trying," I say. "My wife and I appreciate all of the efforts that everyone has made to find our son."

"Who recommended Allison to your family, Mr. Barry?" Miss Somers asks.

"She came directly from the nanny agency. My sister and sister-in-law both hired their nannies from the same agency. We were comfortable with the decision. The agency assured us that a complete background check had been done. We had references and I know my wife called them."

"And her questions were answered. The problem is, did she know exactly what questions to ask?"

"I don't know what you mean?"

"I'm sure she asked if Allison liked children and was good with them. Did she ask why they no longer employed her?"

"Yes. They said she left to be closer to London."

"Why did she need to be closer?"

"I don't know. I didn't ask that."

Agent Walsh walks in the door and comes over to me. He says, "They found the car at a rest stop on the New Jersey Turnpike. The rest area has been searched and they are not there. We are looking at the surveillance tapes to try to determine why she went there and to make sure she still had your son with her. We should know in a few minutes."

"Thank you."

Brook and Emily walk in from outside. Emily comes over to me, kisses my cheek and says, "I convinced Brook to have some fruit and cottage cheese. After we eat, I'm going to lie down with her to try to have her get some rest. She said you have a press conference at 4:00 this afternoon."

"Yes. It's right downstairs, outside the main door to the building. I didn't want to go to a studio. Brook didn't want them in the apartment. She said they would keep asking questions and would never leave. This way, we can walk away when we have had enough."

"Good idea. Wake us up at 3:00 so Brook has a chance to freshen up before she has to go out there."

Dick sits next to me on the couch and asks, "What is the plan?"

"So far it is waiting to see if she contacts us. They are chasing down leads, asking questions. I have never wanted to hurt someone in my whole life. I can make an exception with Allison. I would like nothing more than to wring her neck for what she has put Brook through. Thank you for coming. Brook looks better because Emily is here."

"I could not have stopped Emily from coming if I wanted to. She was packed before Jonathan called back with the flight information. If you need help with the wringing of Allison's neck, I'm sure Emily will be available."

"She is one hell of a big sister."

At 4:00, Brook and I walk through the doors to the waiting media. We have prepared a speech and then we will take a few questions. I begin. "Yesterday morning, our one-year-old son was taken from us by the woman we trusted with his care. Allison Daynard has been Ren's nanny since he was born. My wife and I need our son to be returned to us. He is our child and loved not only by us, but also by our extended family and friends."

"I know that everything is being done by the authorities to bring about his safe return. We also need the public's help to find him. If you see him or Miss Daynard, please call 911 and report it. Please help us to bring our son home. Thank you."

After I answer several questions rehashing what I have already said, Brook and I walk back inside. I ask, "Are you all right, darling?"

"As good as I can be under the circumstances, I guess. How are you doing?"

"About the same. I am so glad that Emily and Dick are here. I'm drawing from their strength."

"Me too. Emily understands me. I'm tired, I think I will lie down for another nap. The baby has been so quiet today. I think she understands that something is wrong."

"I have a call in to have you seen by a doctor. I want you to be checked."

"Okay. If Allison sees the news, do you think she will call us?"

"I hope so," I say, but the truth is that I doubt it. Someone will have to turn her in for us to find Ren. I don't think she intends to give him back.

At 9:00 Sunday morning, I get another update from Agents Walsh and Gallagher. "Allison's former employer told the investigator about a conversation she had two days before Allison submitted her resignation. Allison asked if they thought they were going to have more children. The woman thought Allison was worried about her job security. We think she was going to take their son. When the woman said she couldn't have any more because of a medical condition, Allison left to find a family that was going to have more."

"I don't understand the significance of that."

"She wouldn't take your only child, but if you were having more she would take your first."

"Why? Why not have her own?"

"We are checking on that. Maybe she can't have her own. Or didn't want to for some unknown reason. We are not dealing with someone who connects all of the dots here."

"She has done pretty well so far. She hasn't been caught. Don't make the mistake of underestimating her, Agent Walsh. She fooled us for fourteen months."

"The next thing is the surveillance at the rest area. It is very grainy. We can't make out much and she walks off to a part of the parking lot where there is a gap in the footage. She doesn't come back into the frame. So, she either had another car there or someone picked her up."

"Where does that leave us? Do you have any guess as to where she might be headed?"

"No, sir. We can't find any connection to her in the US. As far as we can tell, she is a British citizen without American ties. If she knows anyone here, she did a very good job of hiding him or her. No calls or mail, no internet communication~it's bizarre. I have never seen anyone without a friend or family anywhere. It's like she just appeared out of nowhere."

I am in constant contact with both my parents and Jonathan. They all want to fly over. I finally tell them that if we haven't heard anything in a week, I am bringing Brook back to them. The stress of having all of the detectives in and out of the apartment with the updates is wearing her out.

I am facing the inspectors from the Yard while they give me their latest report on Allison. Miss Somers says, "We found a doctor who treated her for the flu two years ago. On the medical form she filled out, she listed an accident when she was seven. She also wrote that she was unable to bear children."

The sound that comes from behind me is both primal and gut-wrenching. I turn to watch as the horror of what was just said fills Brook's eyes. She says, "She can't have children. She intends to . . . keep . . . Ren . . . forever."

I watch as her eyes roll up. I catch her just before she hits the floor.

The story of Brook and William continues in Raising Ren

Excerpt from Raising Ren

CHAPTER 1

I REMEMBER THE DAY MY life changed. I was seven, riding in the car with my parents and twin sister, Allison. We were laughing and tossing a ball between us. My father was driving when the truck hit us head-on. I remember wondering what all of the noise could be, so loud and dirt flying over me. In slow motion, I saw my father fold under the dashboard, the truck moving over the place where he once sat. There was the heat on my legs as the water, oil, and gas poured out over me. Then, the fire.

It was far away, but moving slowly toward me. My sister and I, strapped securely in our car seats, screamed for our parents to help us. Big, strong hands grabbed my belt and, with a knife, cut me out. Pulled through the broken window, I was placed on the ground several feet from our car. The blue man ran to my sister, repeated the same motion and got her out. Carrying her over to my side, he said, "You girls stay here. I'm going to try to help your parents."

Allison had blood, cuts, and gouges all over her from the glass. I looked down my body and I saw a lot of blood on my pants. I could see it seeping lower towards my feet. I wanted to scream, but nothing would come out. I felt so strange, and then I went to sleep.

Two days later, I woke up in the hospital. Allison was in the next bed, all wrapped up in bandages, her arm in a cast. I hurt everywhere, but mostly in my belly. A nurse came in and told us that Allison and I would be fine once we got some rest. My aunt was coming from England to help us. I went back to sleep.

Aunt Charlotte was sitting on Allison's bed when I woke up again. She is my mom's sister. I had seen her only twice before, once when I was three and she came here for a visit, and then last year when my pop-pop died and we went to England. She had a nice smile and she smelled good.

"Don't cry, Allison. Your mummy and daddy will always be looking out for you and Amy," I heard her say.

"But I will never see them again," Allison replied.

"Not being able to see them doesn't mean they are not there."

"What's wrong with Amy? All she does is sleep," Allison asked.

"Amy wasn't as lucky as you. You broke your arm, but Amy broke something on her insides. She had to have an operation to get better."

I tried to sit up, but it hurt more so I just said, "I'm awake, but I don't feel good."

"You'll feel better in a few days, darling. You need time to recuperate," my aunt said. "In the meantime, you'll stay here. Then we will go to your house for a few days and figure out what we are going to do."

By the time Allison and I got out of the hospital, the funerals for my mom and dad had already taken place. Between my aunt and a few neighbors, my parents' closets had been cleaned out and much of the furniture in the house was gone. All that was left was our beds, a couch, and the kitchen table. We didn't own the house so I guess it had to be done, but it was damn depressing to come home to nothing. My parents were gone and all of our stuff with them. A child psychologist would make a whole lot of crap about that later.

I'm in bed but not asleep, when I hear my aunt's voice. "Amy might need another surgery. I don't want to take her away from her doctor, so I'm leaving her here with a close neighbor.

I'll bring Allison with me and then come back for Amy later."
I don't remember which thought made me more afraid, more
surgery or being left alone. Either way I was screwed. More
fodder for the shrinks.

To make a long story short, a week later I stood outside
of my neighbor Mrs. North's house while my sister and aunt
waved goodbye to me with huge smiles on their faces. It will be
thirteen years before I see Allison's face again. In the interim,
I will have very little to smile about.

Mrs. North was nice to me for the five months that I lived
with her. I went to the doctors and it was decided that they
had done all that they could for me. I wouldn't be having any
more surgeries. The one thing I was left with, besides a scar
worthy of any Frankenstein movie, was the fact that I would
not be having any children of my own. A large piece of the
trucks grill had perforated my abdomen and I lost an ovary
because of it. The damage extended to my uterus. I would have
scar tissue that would make it improbable, if not impossible, to
carry ever a child.

When I was well enough, I went back to school. I came in
one day to hear Mrs. North's end of a conversation with my
aunt. "I know that you paid for the funeral. Yes, you told me
they didn't have any insurance. Many people can't afford life
insurance. I know you are not made of money, but neither am
I. She isn't my responsibility. I told you I would keep her for
a little while so that you could straighten out your finances.
The time has come for you to take her. I'll give you another
week, but if you don't come and get her or send a plane ticket,
I'm going to call child protective services. She will end up in
foster care."

I turned around and went back outside to sit on the steps.
That conversation would be a few more sessions with the
shrink. "Why do you have such low esteem, Miss Daynard?"

"I have no idea, Doctor Asshole. I know it wasn't my
fucked-up childhood."

I digress. Sure enough, a week later I was all packed up
and on my way to a foster house. Mrs. "You can call me Sally"
Cresnow, was also a nice woman. She fed me mac and cheese

two times a day, seven days a week, for nine months. Breakfast was Cap'n Crunch cereal and water, no milk. You see, my milk ration was used to make my mac and cheese. Waste Not, Want Not, was on the sign over the kitchen sink.

I had a bed in a room that I'm sure was a walk-in closet at one point. I had clean sheets the day I arrived and they were probably washed only on the day I left. No need to waste water cleaning them in between. I needed the water for my cereal. We always followed the waste not, want not rule. At least when it came to me.

Mrs. Cresnow didn't hit me, though. The same cannot be said about Mrs. Naylor. I spent twenty-two months, eighteen days, and seven hours with Mrs. Naylor. After the first few weeks, I realized how fitting her name was. Nail-her was just what she did to me on a regular basis. I have to admit, she was good at it. Rarely did the marks show, and, if they did, they were in spots that a child might have a black-and-blue spot anyway. Knees, elbows, shins, hips~all easily explained should anyone take the time to ask. She had nothing to worry about because no one ever did.

I always looked dirty. Greasy hair, worn-out and unwashed clothes, sunken eyes from malnutrition. The best and only meal I got every day was from the lunch ladies at school. I often wished they were foster parents.

I hated weekends. Every other kid in school loved them. Weekends to me were two days of unrelenting pain and hunger. I know what you are thinking . . . why didn't I tell someone? I was ten years old. My aunt told me that my parents were watching over me. I figured if they were watching and did nothing to stop this, who was I going to tell? Ask anyone who was abused why they didn't tell. I had never been invited to anyone's house. I thought everyone beat and starved children.

Mrs. Naylor needed the check that the state paid her for taking such good care of me. She told me that if I ever did or said anything to disrupt that check, she would find me and kill me. I believed her. After all, she could beat me and no one cared. Killing me would not be that hard.

I was summoned to the office one day after lunch. Two police officers were there when I walked in. The principal told me they wanted to talk to me. The tall blond one said, "Amy, we have to take you to a different house today. Mrs. Naylor won't be able to take care of you anymore."

"Why?" I asked.

"She was arrested this morning. She's in jail."

"Did she kill someone for not getting her check?"

"No, she didn't kill anyone. She did something else."

"Did she hit someone or something like that?"

The brown-haired officer knelt down next to me and said, "Did she hit you, Amy?"

"I'm not supposed to tell you. I could get into a lot of trouble."

"You are never going to see Mrs. Naylor again. She was caught buying drugs from an undercover officer. She can never be a foster parent again. You can tell me anything that you want to."

"You're sure? Because she'll kill me if I tell."

The officer turned to the principal and said, "We are going to need an office, please."

He took my hand to walk me into an empty office. It was the first time in three years that I felt cared for. I know it was his job, but I still liked the feeling. He sat me in a chair and moved the other chair so that our knees touched. He held my hands and said, "It's okay now to tell me and Officer Brown everything that you want to tell. No one is going to hurt you."

I spilled my ten-year-old guts. I told them everything, all of it. I pulled my shirt up to show them the bruises~old, faded ones and brightly-colored fresh ones. They saw my ribs that were so close to the surface, you could easily count them. He pulled me off the chair and onto his lap. He wrapped his arms around me and held me while I cried. He called her an animal and said it was a good thing she was already in jail because if he had to find her, he would not be responsible for what happened to her before he got her to jail. Much later, I figured out that he meant he would have killed her. That made me happy.

He was right. I never saw Mrs. Naylor again. Next, I was sent to a group home because of "housing problems." That meant that they didn't have a foster parent for me. The group home had seven other residents, ranging in age from fourteen to twenty-six. I was ten and a girl, two very bad things to be.

More to come in Amy and Allison's tale. Thank you so much for reading.